THE DREAMER

CAROLINE LEE

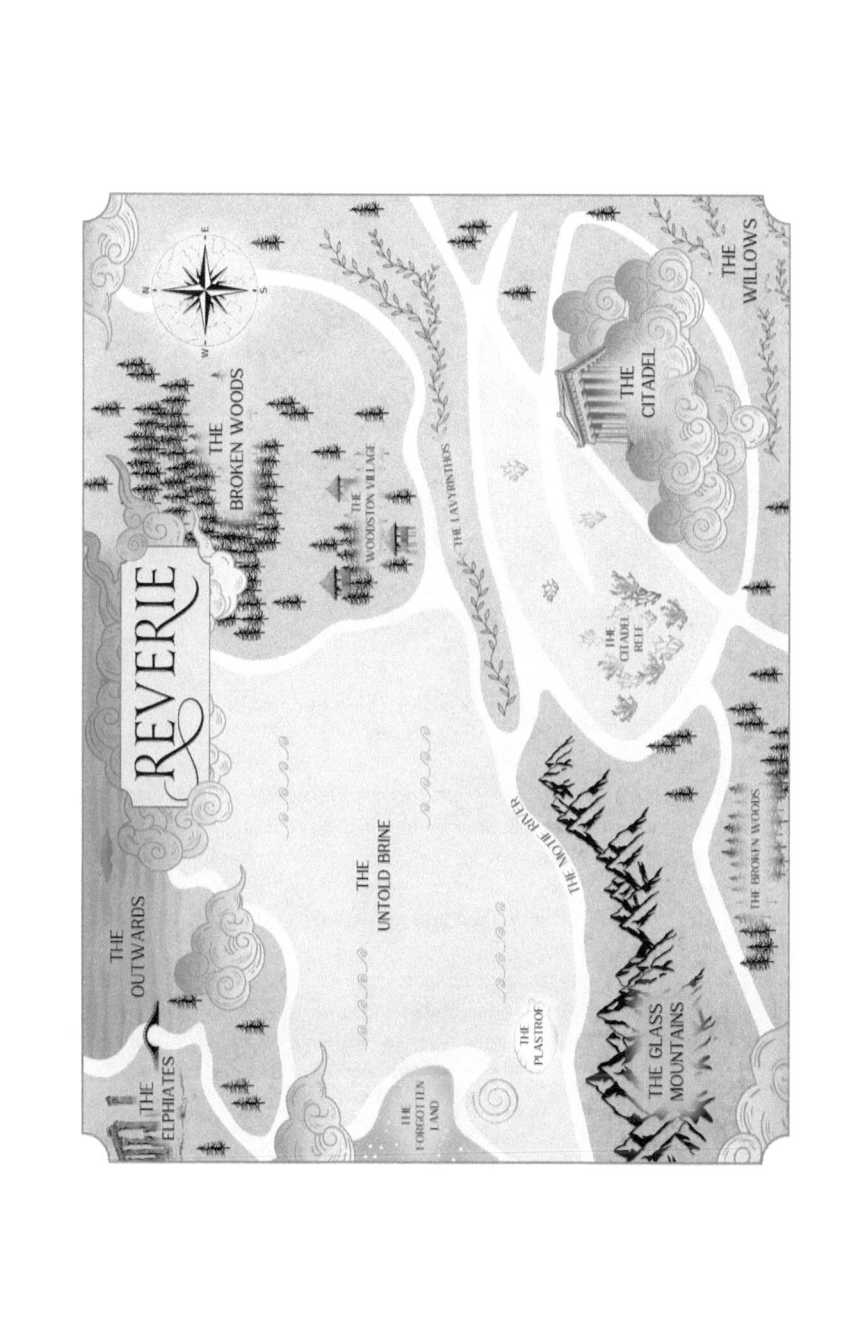

For those whose imaginations were too big to keep inside your head—
Ignore the noise and write on.
And for those who dare...dream on.

PRONUNCIATION GUIDE

The Main Characters:

Piper Knell – *PIE-per Nel* (*Nel* rhymes with *shell*)
Colik – *CAH-lick*
Lulu – *LOO-loo*
Blaze – *BLAYZ*
Steele – *STEEL*
Himyla – *HIM-luh* (*luh* rhymes with *huh*)
Patryk – *PAT-rick*
Morry Ovid – *MOR-ee O-vid* (*vid* rhymes with *bid*)
Penelope – *peh-NEL-oh-pee*
Ailin – *AL-lin* (pronounced like *Allen*)
Deeno – *DEE-no* (Nickname for Dermont)
Ciara – *KEE-R-uh*
Aisling – *A-leen*
Cyril – *SIGH-rill*
Eda – *EE-dah*
Oneiroi – oh-NYE-roy – The Gods of Dreams

The Gods, Celestial Beings and Constellations:

Morpheus – *MOR-fee-us* – God of Dreams
Phobetor – *FOH-beh-tor* – God of Nightmares; called Phobetor among the mortals
Phantasos – *FAN-ta-sos* – God of Illusions; Shapeshifter of dreams
Icelus – *EYE-seh-lus* – Dream God of Prophetic Dreams; called Icelus among the gods
Nyx – *NIKS* – Primordial goddess of Night; Mother of the Oneiroi
Hecate – *HEH-kah-tee* – Goddess of the Moon, Magic, and Thresholds between Realms
Astraea – *uh-STRAY-uh* – Maiden or Keeper of the Stars
Hera – *HEH-rah* – Queen of Olympus
Zeus – *ZOOS* – King of the Olympians
Apollo – *ah- PAH-lo* – God of Light and Prophecy
Pan – *PAN* – God of the Wild
Pollux – *PAH-luks* – "Immortal Twin"
Castor – *KAS-tor* – "Mortal Twin"
Orion – *oh-RYE-on* – "The Hunter"

PROLOGUE
THE GATE OF HORN

The black-winged God of Dreams swept through the sleeping minds of humans, racing his brothers toward the shadowed mouth of Erebus.

Morpheus spiraled down the stairway of ash and shadow, slipping through one Gate of Ivory. Then another, each one leading to a human's stage of REM sleep. Tall and lean, with skin like onyx cloaked in starlight, his form shifted with every descent.

Only ivory.

He knew the rules: One gate for false illusions and one gate for truth. Because the truth would be a dangerous game.

The God of Dreams wore robes the color of deep indigo sleep, the fabric shimmering faintly, and stitched with constellations that pulsed in rhythm of dreaming hearts. Around his shoulders hung a mantle of midnight feathers, plucked from the wings of forgotten dreams, and at his wrist, a brace of gold beat.

The god who formed human dreams moved like a lullaby, both haunting and holy, looping himself into the fragile gates of humans' sleeping minds. He witnessed black dreams of flying, falling, teeth and shadows, his purpose being to sweep away human nightmares.

"Humans dreaming of wings to fly and excessive heights to fall," he muttered to himself as he exited another false dream. "They have no idea what they gave up."

It had been ages since humans had truly touched the Dreamworld, when they danced with gods beneath constellation skies, wearing dreams like crowns. Now, they only *dreamed* to be like gods, never to know that the gods continued to control human dreams.

"Ha!" he scoffed at the irony of it all. It both amused and saddened him.

Yet even under Zeus's command, he and his Oneiroi brothers found ways to play their quiet games as they fulfilled their divine duty.

Rid a child of a nightmare here.

Slip in a whisper there.

They were true thieves in the night, their mischief well-earned after ages spent weaving false dreams across the mortal world. He knew that without gods, humanity had no fate, though sometimes he wondered: *and without humans, what meaning did the gods have?*

He paused, glancing over his shoulder as a chill crossed his wings.

Icelus. He could feel one of his Oneiroi brothers, clever and near.

Morpheus rounded one last spiraling step, dust and starlight floating around him, when another gate appeared to his right. This one was made of horn—a gate of truth.

A shiver ran through him as he stopped in front of it. A forgotten shape pulled at the edges of his remembrance, as he had not passed through a Gate of Horn since the Silver Age.

"*Kérdos mélas oneiros*," came a whisper behind him.

Icelus passed him like mist, his form half bat and half angel. Translucent wings stretched wide behind him—one feathered in pale gray, the other veined of smoke. His body was wiry and shifting, his limbs too long, his face only half-formed. His eyes were watchful, chaotic, and unbothered.

He dipped his head, unapologetic, then vanished back into the shadows before Morpheus could curse at him.

"Cheater," Morpheus grumbled.

As the God of Nightmares and Beasts, Icelus bent any rule to win. He didn't care that turning into a shadowed monster was not part of the rules. He delighted in slipping between forms, in clawing into a sleeper's mind with a smile half-divine and half-devourer, dragging fear up from the subconscious. He was beautiful only when he wanted to be, though that was rare.

Morpheus dismissed his brother and turned his attention back to the horned gate.

Why did it appear?

The gate shimmered like a dying star on the verge of collapse. Its glow dimmed, the boundary between dream and nightmare unraveling. And just before it vanished entirely, the *true* God of Dreams stepped through.

Immediately, the air changed. It was thicker and heavier, not like inside a black dream, but *inside a dark memory*. No nightmare bled through. No shadow stretched. No lie took shape.

An unnatural shiver ran down his spine. And then he saw her.

A young girl stood on a ledge beside a rose window with faded white trim. She stared into a blinding white emptiness while behind her, dust swirled on a staircase. She stood at the glass like a soul waiting to be released.

Morpheus flew to her and followed her gaze, only to see blinding nothingness. It was an untouched canvas with no illusion or memory. No truth either.

Which type of dream was this?

He knew he should have left right then, but something

stopped him. He now noticed the shimmering red string latching from her wrist, tying her loosely to the Gate of Horn itself.

This dream—*this girl*—should not exist.

His wings fluttered back instinctively, his eyes widening at the realization that this was a dream he had touched long ago. He wasn't sure how he recognized *her* among all the ages of dreams, but he had been in this girl's dream before.

He'd passed through the Gate of Ivory then, but he remembered it well—

The dream wore a human shape. Her face was still wet with tears as she slipped into REM sleep, silver trails cooling on her cheeks as the black dream took hold. Smoke curled through the air, and a woman's scream ripped through the dark. The dream had pulsed around her, thick with heat, choking ash rising from a place in her waking world that was unidentifiable.

Morpheus couldn't stop the fire since it was from her waking world, but he could stop the black dream unfolding in her sleep.

To do this, the God of Dreams shaped a lie. He created cool fingers to brush away her tears, a calmness woven into each stroke. He had reached for the blaze, having gathered its fury into his palm, curling the flame into both dust and silence. Before the illusion held, her eyes had snapped open—

Something tugged at Morpheus as his own memory caught up to him. In that dream, she had awakened before he could help her...

He turned back to the window, and though it was still white, behind it something else pulsed. Something that frightened even a god.

It was the Fray.

He cursed inwardly for letting himself be distracted and foolish enough to enter a Gate of Horn at all. No god was to ever touch a true dream again, let alone tie one to the Fray.

It all clicked. He must have tied this girl's dream to the Fray itself, no longer forged with gods' mercy or human will, but iron law.

What if he were to untie it?

An internal battle stirred within him. There were laws and oaths and there was what was forbidden and what had once been right.

Once, gods could touch dreams.

Once, they could shape a human fate.

Once, they could create Dreamers.

He looked at the girl again. She was still so young and utterly unaware of what she could become.

Out of mercy that was irrational even for a god, Morpheus intentionally disobeyed for the first time in many ages.

He extended his hand and gently tapped the rose window, just loud enough to startle her. Hoping to undo what he thought he had done before, a thin crack webbed across the glass with warning. Children feared sudden sounds, so even in the Gate of Horn, it should be enough to wake her. To jolt her free from the black dream's grip and cut her tie to any gate of horn *or* ivory once and for all.

That should do, he told himself.

Without looking back, Morpheus slipped out of the Gate of Horn, his wings trembling, dismayed by what he had *nearly* caused... what he had just ended to fix it.

Back in Erebus—the land of dreams, where stars clung to a sky that never fully darkened and rivers flowed in spiral patterns through mist—shadows thickened as Morpheus landed, his wings still unsteady.

Phantasos leaned lazily against a column he conjured from vapor, arms folded. "You lose," the weaver of illusions said with a half-grin.

"I was distracted," Morpheus muttered, brushing dream dust from his shoulder. Where he carried the burden of prophecy and Icelus thrived on terror, his other brother observed. Phantasos favored dreams wrapped in metaphor rather than meaning, a stage of symbols, where every human face was masked.

The air around him shifted subtly, reshaping itself into fragments of the nightmares he had just lifted from sleeping minds: a lion with a child's eyes, a ship stitched from whispers, a staircase spiraling into nothing.

"Stayed within the ivory?" Phantasos asked, one brow raised. Compared to the others, this brother was the most measured, composed, and maddeningly calm. His features were fine and unreadable. A marble statue half-finished. Smoke curled around his form like a second robe, always shifting, never quite revealing what lay beneath.

Morpheus hesitated. "Where's Phobetor?" he asked, ignoring his brother's question.

"Why call me by my mortal name? Don't tell me you didn't notice?" came Icelus' voice, smooth and cold, echoing from behind. He stepped forward, wings folded like shadowed-edged blades, his eyes glinting with the chill precision of a dream turned weapon. "The human saw me."

His gaze pierced Morpheus, who shifted uncomfortably, jaw tight.

Phantasos's eyes sharpened. "What human?"

Icelus ignored him, staring upward into the void where stars should have been. "Fascinating, isn't it? That humans dream all this and still never realize they could control it." A pause, something darker threading beneath the idle tone. "That they *long* for it. Age after age. They close their eyes and reach for something they cannot name, something just beyond the edge of sleep. And they never ask what it costs them to keep reaching."

"What human?" Phantasos repeated, this time firm.

Morpheus stilled.

Icelus' wing twitched, but still, he didn't answer. "Now we're just gatekeepers. By Zeus's law. No more shaping, no more truth, only falsity." His tone was flat, a judge reciting someone else's sentence.

Phantasos stepped forward, eyes narrowing. "Do not forget the Reverie Laws."

The Gods of Dreams knew the story well: long ago, during the Silver Age—when gods allowed humans to walk openly among dreams—the R-Laws hadn't existed. But when mankind abused the gods' gifts, Zeus locked the Dreamworld behind gates of ivory and horn, confusing both gods and mortals as to which gate would grant humans immortal dreams. From then on…

"No gods are to interfere in human dreaming," Phantasos finished, voicing the thought in Morpheus' mind. "No dreams are to be tied, but to rid them of fatal nightmares. The Fatales enforce the Reverie laws now…and they do not forgive. Like the Fates."

Icelus sneered but said nothing.

"Humans are not what they once were," Phantasos pressed, ignoring his brothers' looks of ignorance. "No longer children of gold or silver. Yet…a few were granted second chances. Fallen Angels turned into stars to guard the Dreamer's belt. Silent protectors of the Dreamworld."

"The gods wrote exile into human bones," Morpheus said softly, though his words tasted of ash. He couldn't stop thinking of the girl or the Gate of Horn. Of what he had seen pulsing with her: a red strand that should have never existed, born of a god's guilt. *His* guilt. Of the world she had stumbled into without knowing the price of the door she'd walked through. *Her* dreams had led her there. That much had always been true. What he hadn't anticipated—what no law had prepared him for—was that she would long for it. Not just dream it. *Long* for it, the way only something born of two worlds could.

"You can't exile a dream," Icelus murmured, voice silk and thorns. "It always finds a way back." His eyes cut to Morpheus. "Especially when it was never fully mortal to begin with."

Phantasos caught the look. "What did you do, Morpheus?"

Morpheus didn't speak at first, but his wings curled slightly, defensively. Beneath his skin, his essence trembled. He no longer could hide it. He knew that Icelus knew…but how?

"If Zeus discovered what…if the Fatales came—" He forced his thoughts into order. "She was only a child. She was not meant to be tied," he said at last. His voice thinned, frayed with something between deeper guilt and defiance.

"Pity is a stubborn thing," Icelus said, "and some dust… some dust deserves to remember." His gaze slid sideways to Morpheus. "Especially the dust that carries both mortal longing and something far older underneath it."

Phantasos's gaze sharpened. "Remember what, exactly?"

Morpheus said nothing, but the silence answered for him.

Icelus' smile curled lazily. "You forget the old verse, brother: when the dust remembers, even the gods will tremble."

Morpheus' feathers tightened behind him. "Two phrases of different meaning, *brother*."

"Are they?" Icelus tilted his head. "A girl who longs for a world she was never supposed to find. A world that longs for her in return. Mortal enough to dream it. Divine enough to survive it." His wings spread slightly, each word landing like a stone dropped into still water. "That is not a coincidence. That is a design. And someone in this room knows whose."

The silence that followed was not empty. It was the kind that rearranged things.

"Old verses are just stories," Phantasos said finally, though his voice had lost its flatness. "And stories are all humans have left."

"Not this one," Icelus replied.

Phantasos gave a short, uneasy laugh. "Humans now are blinder than ever. They don't even believe in gods, let alone Dreamers. We are hardly nursery rhymes...if not just forgotten myths."

"Except us," Icelus said, stepping closer. "And the Dreamers already there..." His eyes shifted to his brother, who shaped human dreams with message and prophetical promises. "And the one coming. The one that will be neither fully human nor fully ours." His voice dropped, something between warning and reverence. "The cost of her longing is already being counted. The question is whether she understands what she is paying with."

"*Yes*... There is the one I—" Morpheus stopped mid-sentence at the sound of a soft, melodic chord ringing through the air:

Apollo's lyre. It meant Zeus was calling.

They fell silent, sharing a look too aged to name, then unfurled their wings. With a simultaneous but weary breath, the three Oneiroi brothers rose toward the heavens.

THE SCRIPT OF
THE ONEIROI

Fragment from the Book of Reverie Laws, translated from Dreamtongue:

R-*Law 1: A Dreamer must choose another Dreamer over a human.*
R-*Law 3: Dust must not pass freely between the waking and the dream.*
R-*Law 5: At the Constellation Ball, each Royald shall share the final dance with the one they are bound to.*

Below the Reverie Laws, in ink older than sleep itself:

O-*Law 0: Dust of the Silver shall no longer live free.*

CHAPTER ONE
THE OLLOPA TRAIN

I t began like every dream one loses to morning light. Until it turned on her…

I was climbing a spiral staircase made of glass or ice, I couldn't tell which, each step echoing without sound. The air was white, not cloud white, not snow white, but a white so pure it erased the edges of everything, even me.

Up and up, I went, my hand trailing along a railing that I couldn't physically feel, until the stairs ended at a single, rose-shaped window. The glass glowed and I pressed my palm against it, expecting cold, but it was warmer than my own skin.

Something moved beyond it, so I leaned closer, eager to see out. The glass softened under my palm, the carved rose frame bleeding into living petals. They trembled once, then fell away, scattering into the air like crimson dust.

I stepped forward, and the whiteness melted into moonlight, cool and heavy, spilling over fig leaves. The air was warmer now but still, silvering the roses until their petals looked carved from bone. The garden was empty. No caretaker. No children.

I stood in the center path, barefoot, the air warm but unmoving. The old stone fountain rose before me, its usual angel gone, and in its place loomed a lion of marble, taller than I was, its mane flaring around its face like the burst of a sun. Its eyes glowed a deep grey, alive with something sentient, and yet fearful, waiting for me to save it. From what though?

A rasp cut through the silence.

From behind the lion, a figure emerged, hooded and faceless. A nightmare given flesh, its long, needlelike sword gleamed with a red string coiled around its wrist, slicing at the lion's mane. Each lock fell heavy to the cobblestones, and with every cut, the color in the lion's eyes dimmed, yet never died.

My chest tightened, and a strange pull tugged at me, a curiosity that urged me closer, toward something wholly unknown. In the ripple of water pooling at the fountain's base, three more shapes appeared before me.

One radiated light so bright it burned the edges of his form, crowned in sunlight, silent and unreadable. Beside him, a woman was cloaked in shadows that shimmered of peacock feathers, her lips curling in a smile that promised nothing safe. Behind them, a third figure hid in the depths of darkness, her eyes twin distant stars piercing.

I opened my mouth to speak, but my throat locked.

The faceless figure paused, marble dust dripping from its sword. Slowly—horribly—it turned to me.

And it was no longer faceless. It wore my face.

My breath snagged.

Was this a shadow in my dream… or had it already tipped into a nightmare?

Dreams could twist, could blur, could lie, but nightmares claimed you. And yet, something about the air, the stillness, and the way the lion watched me like I was its last hope, made the question knot in my throat.

Before I could decide, before I could even breathe, my own stolen voice slid through the dark:

"You wish I was a shadow in your dream," it rasped, tilting its

head. "Know that nightmares are far worse. Shadows mimic darkness…
nightmares stir it. They wake the black dust inside a shadow, and they
close the eye that chooses between dream or terror."

Its smile sharpened—

"And I am the one you wish you'd never dreamed."

Piper jerked upright, clutching the sides of the narrow, metal-framed bed. Her heart pounded against her ribs, loud in the still silence of Olympus House. She blinked hard, breath ragged, her eyes shooting to the cracked clock on the wall.

3:33 A.M.

She stared at it, bewildered. Only three minutes had gone by.

There was no way.

Within seconds of waking, the dream began to blur. Only the feeling remained, imprinting on her mind like a tattoo she hadn't chosen.

She rubbed her eyes, half-expecting to see stars floating across the ceiling, but there was just the bitter cold of Olympus House.

She shivered, pulling her blanket tighter, the frost from the poorly sealed window creeping in as usual. The radiators hadn't worked since October, comfort wasn't something orphanage homes worried about, especially not for someone who had *aged out* of one but had stayed. Tonight was one of those nights.

Piper's thoughts drifted back to the dream. There had been something to remember. She was sure of it. *A window, maybe? Shapes in the dark?* It all slipped away the harder she tried to hold onto it. It erased as quickly as it came.

She scrunched her eyes shut, trying to find a strand within

her memories that might lead her to what she'd forgotten, but the dream had already sealed itself shut behind her. Like it didn't want to be remembered. Like someone else had closed it off for her.

Maybe it was just a trick of her mind. Leftover pieces from yesterday, or the day before, stitched together to fill the silence of sleep. That's what her caretaker, Penelope, always said, anyway: *Dreams are just another place to feel. And nothing more.* This didn't feel like *nothing*.

Groaning at her own restless thoughts, Piper flopped back against the thin pillow and pulled the blanket over her chin.

She took a deep breath, willing her mind to quiet. It didn't. In fact, the more she tried to calm it, the more it scattered. Her thoughts raced. Her feelings tangled up. The dream clung to her like a bruise she hadn't earned.

Minutes blurred as she tossed and turned, until finally, exhaustion won.

Her body stilled and her eyelids stopped fluttering, the last thought in her mind before the dark took her again being:

Oh, but to live in a dream.

Piper couldn't wake up, not completely anyway. Her consciousness was alert, but her body didn't seem to want to follow. Curled in a fetal position on a hard surface, she was trapped in some paralysis.

Wake up! she screamed, but her voice was mute. Panic hit as something rumbled beneath her, vibrating up through her bones.

Was she moving?

Then, an echo, soft but unfamiliar, whispered in spurts in her mind:

"Desire... Knowing... Will..." They came as a command from an invisible entity, with a wave of colors following soon after: *A deep red. A spiraling yellow. A flash of pulsing blue.*

A few simple words and colors, but it was enough to spark something inside her.

So, with every ounce of strength, Piper willed herself to move.

Move, body, move!

It was slow at first, but there was a hesitant flick of the fingers, then the twitching of her feet. Her limbs shook and the grip of the paralysis began to loosen.

Let me go... NOW!

Piper's body jerked. The vibration intensified, and an aggressive bump lifted her off the ground, miraculously freeing her. Her eyes snapped open, and her body sprawled out in a star-like position. Catching her breath, she found herself staring up at the roof of a machine forged from golden metal etched with symbols so intricate they looked to be drawn by the hands of a god.

Suns, lyres, arrows, and shooting stars wove their way across the ceiling, each engraving glowing faintly with the pulsing motion of the train itself.

She blinked, trying to make sense of her surroundings, though nothing of this made sense. She was certainly not in Dublin anymore.

"A train?" Piper muttered, the words dry and small in the vast air as she pushed herself up, realizing that the floor beneath her wasn't solid in the usual sense. It shimmered with a glass-like clarity, a translucent material that allowed her to peer down into a rushing blur of clouds and color.

Some world she could not name passed beneath her like a living painting in motion. She tried to track the train's movement, but her eyes couldn't keep up—treetops like green brushstrokes, a silver ribbon that might've been a river, and a blob of blue resembling a body of water. It was as if she had been lifted from her waking world and placed inside a dream spun from the very fabric of constellations she did not know.

Maybe she had.

Piper pushed the rest of her body upright using a seat beside her, placing her hand onto the plush velvet. It was red and deep like the roses in her caretaker, Penelope's, garden. A soft heat bloomed in her palm. It was sunlight captured in cloth spreading through her fingers and into her chest, warming her insides in a way that Olympus House, or the shadows of her sleepless nights, never could.

Figures draped in flowing silver robes, still and silent, sat in pairs in the seats. They wore silk masks across their mouths, leaving their eyes and upper part of their noses visible. The silver hoods covering their faces cast subtle shadows over their features. They appeared statuesque, unaffected by the train's movement or vibrations.

She waved a hand before one of them, yet their catlike eyes remained still, unblinking.

"I wonder who would win a staring contest... Them or the guards at the Tower of London." She laughed under her breath.

As if her voice was a trigger, the train shifted, putting her off balance.

Taking a few forward steps to steady herself while careful to not accidentally fall into one of the robed figures, something touched her foot. Glancing down, she saw a small, brown leather-bound book.

She hadn't fallen asleep with a book.

It looked more like a journal than a novel, with a red velvet string hanging out that matched the color of the train seats. Etched on the cover was the title: *Book of Godspells.*

"Godspells?" She had never heard that word before, but as she went to pick it up, the train jolted again. Struggling to regain her balance, she scanned the rows for an empty seat, spotting one near the door at the far end of the train cart.

Leaving the book where it was, she moved toward the open seat when something else caught her eye. Through the narrow window of the door in front of her, she saw cart after cart stretched beyond, each one echoing the last, like reflections caught in a twisted mirror.

The windows themselves were tall and arched, in the shape of a teardrop, tapering gracefully at the top. Looking closer, the exterior of the train was gilded in shimmering gold, polished to perfection, catching and reflecting every ray of a reddish light that gleamed from the world beyond.

The wheels of the chariot were massive, the shafts resembling blazing rays, spinning so fast that they blurred into rings of light as the train raced across the sky.

Is this what it's like to ride a lightning bolt? Or a shooting star?

Captivated by the flash and gravity of the strange train's sleek outer coat, there was a harder jerk that caused Piper to lose her balance again, this time falling directly *into* the door.

Having expected the door to stop her fall, instead it gave way, and she crashed into open air. Air roared around her like a scream, the ground already gone.

Piper's breath caught in her throat, and for a split second, she was weightless. Then a hand—firm, warm, and impossibly steady—closed around her waist, as if waiting for her fall. In one swift motion, Piper was yanked away from the door. It slammed shut behind her, sealing away the fall like it hadn't just nearly swallowed her whole.

The hand let go of her and she hit the floor hard, knees jarring, breath torn and heart hammering. Trying to catch her breath, she finally looked up—

He stood there, watching her, pale hair glinting silver-white beneath the train light, his coat dark blue—almost black—and elegant, embroidered with ink-dark lace that drank in the air around him. His face was calm and unreadable.

His eyes—one an icy blue, the other, a storm cloud grey—didn't just look at her. They *searched*. Like he was tracing the outline of something lost, something he shouldn't be able to see. Piper froze under that gaze, heart unsteady, and breath caught somewhere between awe and warning. He was what she'd call beautiful, but not safe. He looked like the older boys in the books she devoured, the ones who weren't just dangerous on the page, but in all the ways that made the book good and bad.

To all the gods, right now, he stood too close. He was a secret meant to be found. The danger in his gaze flowed through his every movement, quiet yet captivating.

"Thanks," Piper said, her voice dry. "For the whole saving-my-life thing." The air buzzed faintly between them.

She forced herself upright, her cheeks burning admittedly not from the fall.

He nodded once. "No problem." There was no smirk, no charm, just a certainty as if he already knew how this would go.

She narrowed her eyes, sensing cockiness in his tone. "Were you just waiting for me to fall?"

He tilted his head, lazy and deliberate. "Would you prefer I had?"

"You don't even know me."

"Didn't need to," he countered. "You were about to become dream dust. That tends to skip the small talk."

Dream dust?

The phrase chilled her, but he was already moving, one boot hooked on a nearby seat like he belonged here, on this train, in this dream. Maybe in her head.

"So, what? You *haunt* this train for fun?" she asked, folding her arms.

He glanced over, a small smile curling at his lips. "Only if it is important."

Something uninvited fluttered in her chest.

"Who are you?" she asked as confidently as she could.

He gave a sly smile. "No one you need to worry about."

"You're not from my world," she said, her quick tone matching the beating of her chest. *He couldn't be,* she added in her mind. He was too regal-looking to be any boy she had ever met in her waking world.

"Neither are you." His gaze caught hers and held it. There was no cruelty behind it, just a plain and sharp truth. "You shouldn't be here," he added, quieter.

"Then why did you save me?"

He looked away, but she noticed something flicker in his eyes. "Because once a human steps on the Ollopa train," he said, "they have a hard time letting go."

"The *what* train?"

"O-L-L-O-P-A train," he spelled it out, as if she were a child.

Piper's body heat instantly rose.

What arrogance!

She couldn't wrap her head around this boy, though he wasn't a boy at all. He looked older than her, but there was something doubled in him, like he moved with two reflections instead of one. As if her dream had shaped him in the same mirror-crafted way that only belonged in myths. Captivating. Disarming. A fleeting vision designed to challenge her every sleeping—or dreaming—moment.

It was only a dream. It had to be, right?

"So, Dreamer, what's your name?" he asked, his eyes watching her every move.

"Dreamer?" Piper questioned, her thoughts diverting from his looks to his words.

"Well, you're human, and if you're on the Ollopa train, that means you're dreaming," he said, as though it were the most obvious thing in the world. Piper said nothing, but her eyes gravitated to his grey eye, which was deep and mysterious.

"Are you going to tell me your name?" he pressed, his eyes still locked on hers.

"Piper," she answered slowly. "My name is Piper."

He nodded, his eyes tracing her features, memorizing her. His blue and grey eyes were like a riddle she couldn't figure out.

"Why are you looking at me like that?" Piper asked, feeling vulnerable under his gaze.

"I am not looking at you like anything specific," Colik replied quickly, his glance moving away from her. "Do you have a last name? All humans have last names."

"Why do you want to know my last name? How about you? What is your name?" Piper asked, her curiosity challenging his. She felt like a child on a playground trying to figure out if a boy liked her or not.

"Colik," he answered with a shrug. "Before you ask, I do not have a last name. I am not a human." His name sounded strange to her.

Not a human?

Her eyes bore the question, but if he caught it, he wasn't ready to answer it.

"Knell," she finally whispered, shaking her head.

"Excuse me?" Colik leaned in slightly, looking at her inquisitively.

"My last name is Knell," she said louder. Colik nodded again as if thinking deeply about something. After a long silence, he asked, "So, tell me, Piper Knell, what are you running from?" He leaned in closer, his sharp features catching the light of the train's aesthetics.

Damn, he was hot.

"I am not running..." she started, trying to keep her thoughts straight. Her voice was sharper than she intended.

Colik let out a short laugh, a sound that resonated with a mixture of amusement and forced understanding. He was still leaning in, no longer against the seat next to him, but a subtle step away. There was an electric tension in the air.

Was that the train?

His laughter was disarming, cutting through the weight of the moment and inviting a reluctant smile from her lips. "Oh, but you are," he replied, his tone teasing. "You may not be *sprinting*, but you're definitely running from something. Perhaps even from yourself."

The last part sounded more like a question than a statement.

His words stripped something bare in her chest. She wanted to argue, to refute his statement, but deep down, she knew he could be right. *Too* right.

She looked around in hopes of shaking off the tension rising in her body.

Why didn't he look like the others?

"So, I am right?" He pressed, watching her carefully like how a hawk watches its prey. She didn't like him staring like that. He had one hell of a poker face, where Piper, on the other hand, did not.

"Why would you think I am running from anything?" she challenged again, straying away from his sudden accusation.

"Well, this train is to protect human dreams of those who run. A chariot the Greek god Apollo forged for this world."

He looked like he could be the Greek god Apollo, she thought, the words coming to her mind unapologetically. She bit her lip to keep from accidentally saying the words out loud.

"Apollo is known for his chariot of the gods to protect mortal refugees," he explained.

"You act like Apollo is a real god."

"What makes you think he is not?" Colik gave a grin, one that made knots form in Piper's stomach.

"But you said I am dreaming, so none of this is real. The train, Greek gods, you..." She was unsure how this was all going on in her head while she was sleeping. This dream was the most real one she's had in her un-purposeful twenty years of life.

When was she going to wake up?

"Just because it's a dream doesn't mean it isn't real, some-where," Colik shared, then moved to the seat that she had intended on sitting down at before she became distracted. He looked back at her and patted the empty cushion next to him, implying for her to follow. Each seat came in pairs.

Reluctantly, she sat down next to him, and her heart instantly skipped a beat. Or two. *Was the dream doing this to her? Or him?* She was embarrassing herself.

Piper blinked, trying to correct herself, or at least distract her body's reactions. "What did you mean you aren't human? What then, does that make you?"

His tone dropped, rich with warning. "In this moment, I am walking with the Routs."

How cryptic.

"The Routs?"

What the f—

"The Dreamers of chase. Not all dreams seek rest, Piper Knell." He pointed to the silver hooded figures surrounding them. "Some hunt."

"Hunt what?"

"You—humans."

Her breath caught. "Why humans?" Her heart raced faster and not in a good way. *Yeah*, she was ready to go home now.

He studied her for a long, unreadable moment, then, "Because you shouldn't exist here."

The words hit her like ice cracking through her veins.

Colik turned his body to face her completely, his fingers flexing, as if refraining from touching her.

"You're carrying it," he murmured. "Dust. *Human dust*, and too much of it at that."

Before she could react, his fingers gave in and grazed her wrist. It was barely a touch, but it unraveled something inside of her that she couldn't explain even if she wanted to. She felt the heat. The pressure. How light it was against her skin. She was being unstitched from the inside out, like strands of herself were rising from her skin, tugging at her memory, maybe even her sense of self.

She gasped and yanked her arm away. "What did you just do?"

Colik exhaled slowly, unfazed by her reaction. "You feel like a star still being written," he said calmly. "Like the beginning of a god's apology."

Her vision blurred at the edges, her knees shaking uncharacteristically. Thankfully she was sitting down.

"I feel—light-headed," she whispered, putting her hands on her knees to stop the shaking.

He nodded slowly. "You should. Dreamers feed on dust and you're full of it."

"Is that supposed to be a compliment?" He was making her head spin, and her words all jumbled.

"I haven't decided."

Her eyes searched his. Something was off. "Did you take something from me?"

"No," he said. "I touched what was already coming loose." He took his hand off her completely.

"That doesn't make it better."

"No," he admitted. "Though it is true."

She looked down at her wrist. It was still warm and tingling, something having passed between them. Unseen but real. And the worst part? For whatever crazy reason, she wanted it to happen again.

Suddenly, she noticed something by her foot again. She saw what it was and gasped. The *Book of Godspells*. It was back. Or had it never left?

She looked around but *no*, it moved, because she had seen it over—

"What is that?" Colik asked cautiously, his eyes flickering to the book, confusion darkening his face. He glanced around as if expecting danger to surface.

"What the—" she bent to pick it up this time, surprised by its warmth and brightness. Her fingers tingled where they touched the cover, its edges curling like it had traveled through time.

"It appeared by me when I first arrived, before you caught me. And now it is over here…" Her voice trembled with confusion, but Colik's eyes widened with each word.

"Open it," he demanded.

She hesitated at first, then obeyed. The pages were blank. Page after page, there was still nothing.

"I don't see anything," she said, voice tight.

Colik sprang to his feet so fast the seat shook. "Don't lie to me."

"I'm not. Look!" She turned the book toward him.

His expression shifted from surprise to alarm. He stared at the empty pages like they might strike back.

"No writing."

Colik's gaze lingered on her, or perhaps on the faint ember-like glow leaking from the book's spine.

"That book was written in *godspells*," he finally said quietly. "It should never be blank."

"Then why is it?"

"Because it's waiting."

"For what?"

"Well, I would have thought *you*." His words landed like a stone between them, and he rubbed the heel of his palm over his blue eye. He suddenly looked paler. "Clearly that is false."

Piper's pulse thundered as she looked back at the cart door she'd almost fallen through, then to the ground she had woken up at on the other side.

"What does that mean?"

Instead of answering her, he turned sharply toward the back of the cart. "Follow me," he said urgently. Something in his voice knotted her chest. "Leave the book. It is no use to you."

For the second time, she left the book and followed.

At the far door, his palm pressed the frame. The surface rippled, peeling back to an impossible sky of shifting color.

"I think it's time for you to go," Colik said, matter-of-factly. "If you want to leave," he said without looking at her, "you'll have to jump."

Her heart stopped cold. "Jump? Are you serious?" That was not how she'd imagined waking up.

He nodded once. "That's the deal. Always the deal."

"I'm not trying to die."

"No. You're trying to wake up." His eyes flicked to hers. "That's what falling is, isn't it?"

Piper swallowed hard, feeling an odd pull away from the door despite wanting to escape.

Would I remember this when I wake up?

"Why does it feel like this dream is trying to keep me?"

Colik's gaze sharpened as if she'd finally asked the right question. "Because something inside you wants to stay."

"You are here for?" she asked.

"I'm here to make sure you choose." He stepped aside, gesturing to the open door.

Despite the strange elements of this dream world, no friction slowed them. "I can't make that choice for you."

Her eyes darted to the shifting hues outside, then back to him. "So, I jump," she said. "Or what?"

He watched her casually. "Or I can push you."

Her eyes snapped to his. "Wouldn't that be cheating?"

"Cheating what? The dream? Death?" His mouth tilted in a lopsided way that made her throat tighten, but he didn't answer.

"If you push me, it's your choice, not mine."

"Not if you give me permission." He stepped closer, close enough for the heat of him to press against her back. His voice dropped to a low murmur. "You'd have to count down, of course. I'm not doing all the work."

She took a shaky breath. "How do I know I can trust you?"

"You don't."

The coldness of his answer twisted her stomach.

He tilted his head, studying her like a puzzle he didn't want to solve too quickly. "Three choices: jump, let me push you, or stay."

"Stay? Forever?"

His expression softened. "The Ollopa train doesn't stop for humans. You'd be a ghost in someone else's dream— protected, maybe, but always alone."

"I'd wake up eventually."

"No," he said softly. "You wouldn't."

She couldn't find words to argue that.

His gaze sharpened, losing its teasing edge, piercing like he'd seen something in her he wasn't ready to let go.

"You're not meant to stay," he said quietly. "You must know that you won't remember any of this."

Her breath caught. She didn't mind waking up, but forgetting this? Forgetting *him*?

Something inside her fought the urge to hold onto the memory, even if he was just some dreamy boy in her dreams. She smirked at the thought.

"Why not?" she asked, though the answer already settled in her bones.

Colik hesitated before exhaling, as if the truth weighed on his chest. "Because you're human and humans naturally forget. Your world rewrites what it can't explain."

"What if I want to remember it?"

His jaw twitched sharply. "Then I'm sorry."

That word landed heavier than it should have, as if he wished she could remember too. There was no trace of amusement left.

"You're not a dreamer, Piper. Just a human who dreamed

a little too far. So no, this place won't stay with you, no matter how real it feels right now."

"Past their REM?" she echoed, the words catching in her throat. "So, I could come back here?"

He didn't answer, but a slow nod toward the open air beyond the door was enough.

"You need to decide."

Piper stared at the terrifying unknown, then back at him. Her stomach twisted painfully. She was ready to wake up. This time.

"Fine," she said, steadier than she felt. "Push me."

Colik stepped behind her, slow and deliberate. His presence was impossibly warm against her back, the tension humming off him like a live wire. He held himself still.

"Will you trust me?" he murmured, low and dangerously close.

"Fine," she repeated.

Colik raised an eyebrow but said nothing.

Piper closed her eyes, feeling his shape behind her. His fingertips brushed her lower back, barely there, but it burned like a brand. Every inch of her came alive with awareness—the weight of his silence, the stillness between them, and the way her heartbeat was in sync with the pulse of the train.

"Count for me," he said softly, but solemn.

She swallowed hard. "Three... two... one—" She stopped herself. "One more thing."

Colik stilled. She didn't need to look back to know he was waiting.

"If those who come on this train are running, then what are *you* running from?"

For a moment, he said nothing, then leaned closer, if that was even possible. The curve of his smile brushed her hair.

"We all have something we'd rather not face. Even Dreamers."

His answer didn't scare her, but the honesty in his voice did. It was the first thing he'd said that felt real.

She nodded once and whispered, so quiet she wasn't sure he heard, "Thank you."

There was a long pause before Colik spoke, barely above a whisper. "If you know what's best for you, you won't try to come back."

Piper wanted to tell him she wasn't afraid, but that wasn't true. She was afraid of forgetting, of waking up and losing the memory of how close this felt to being real. Of how close she'd come to feeling truly alive.

Colik's fingers lifted from her spine.

CHAPTER TWO
THE OLYMPUS HOUSE

"Piper! Wake up!" There was a loud bang on her door.

Piper's eyes fluttered open, the sharp morning light dragging her away from the dream. She sighed, the weight of this reality settling over her. She'd been dreaming, but now, as the familiar cold walls of Olympus House came into focus, a deep longing filled her chest.

"It's Christmas tree day!" The high-pitched squeals echoed down the hall. She groaned. It did nothing.

"Why do I even bother?" she muttered.

She stared at the cracks in the ceiling she had memorized too many times to count. Twelve, exactly. Her fingers traced the worn mattress, feeling where years of use had frayed the fabric thin.

Her gaze drifted to the frost covered treetops beyond the window. Her life was no Cinderella story, not even the rags-to-riches kind. She lived in rags, too, but without any magic to change her fate.

Magic…

The dream. The memory hit her all at once. The Ollopa train. Colik. The book. Colik telling her she would not remember it.

She remembered everything, but how?

"Piper! Hurry up, or we'll start without you!"

She tossed off the blanket and reached for the sweater on the dresser. It was a washed-out grey, thinning from years of wear. She'd bought it herself with chore money Penelope had given her. It was the first thing she'd ever owned, and it still fit six years later. That was the orphan life.

The sleeves swallowed her hands. The silver flecks near the hem had faded to nothing, but to Piper they were scattered stars hidden in cloth.

Sometimes, when the house was quiet, she still caught herself at the upstairs window, the one that overlooked the street. As a child she'd watched for her father there. Sixteen years of that had drained the hope out of her, leaving only the habit. Now she stood there measuring the distance between Olympus House and the rest of the world. Counting cars. Wondering what it would feel like to just go.

It wasn't the cold that made her chest ache. It was knowing she wasn't waiting to be claimed anymore. She was waiting to leave.

Until she found a way out, this place would keep her like it kept all the others: fed, sheltered, but quietly stuck.

A forced smile tugged at her lips as she turned toward the stairs.

Today was Christmas tree day.

Olympus House was dreary most days, but Christmas tree day was different. The cold hallways smelled of pine instead of mildew, and the children forgot their troubles long enough to fill the rooms with noise.

In the common room, chaos reigned. Dusty boxes of old decorations scattered the floor. Children wrestled with tangled lights, argued over garlands, and generally ignored all instructions.

"Piper!" Ciara ran to her, breathless, cracked glitter star in hand. "Help us with the ladder!"

"Not until the tree is decorated."

Ciara fake-pouted and twirled away.

Piper knelt to untangle a string of lights, half-listening to the noise around her. Ciara's twin, Deeno, caught her eye across the room and grinned. It was crooked and mischievous and so familiar it ached. He had the same quality Morry had always had, that particular brand of cheerful scheming that made trouble look like an invitation.

Last Christmas, Morry had appeared at the door with a bag of chocolate coins and the absolute conviction that Olympus House didn't need a chimney to have magic. He and Deeno had passed them out like co-conspirators, solemn and ceremonial, until Penelope caught them and the whole thing collapsed into laughter. The children had talked about it for weeks.

He would have been in the thick of it today. Climbing the ladder before anyone asked him to, tugging her into the mess by the wrist, laughing until Penelope called both their names. Without him the room felt full of the wrong kind of noise—loud enough, but none of it meant for her. She moved through it like a ghost haunting a life she hadn't quite managed to live in yet.

Piper leaned against the wall, ready to watch instead of participating, when the doorbell rang. No one else heard it through the laughter and jingle of bells, but Piper did.

She peeked around the corner in time to see Penelope crack the front door open. A woman stood on the step, tall, well-dressed, with a coat cinched at the waist, her arms wrapped around a cardboard box.

It wasn't the box that stopped her cold.

Tucked against the woman's side was a book. Old, leather-bound and with edges that curled like smoke.

Piper's stomach dropped. It looked exactly like the book from her dream. The *Book of Godspells*.

How could that be possible?

A shiver crawled down her spine. Dreams and the waking world weren't supposed to cross like this. Were they?

Penelope stepped onto the porch and pulled the door mostly closed. Through the crack, Piper watched her take the box, fingers lingering. A whiff of warmth drifted in—bread, maybe muffins.

"You didn't have to do this," Penelope said softly.

"I did," the woman replied. "I know what it's like."

Piper recognized the type. She was most likely one of the mothers—hers not among them—the kind who left their children because they couldn't keep them. Not yet anyway.

That was the quiet truth of Olympus House. It was not officially an orphanage. Most children had parents somewhere, born into situations too tangled for the world to make room for. It was a halfway place for children who were loved but not yet able to be claimed.

Some parents came back but most didn't.

Piper's throat tightened. She'd stopped waiting for her father years ago, but the ache was still there—a hollow space where love should have been, alongside the silent absence of a mother she'd never meet. He'd left her alone in a hospital and never returned. That was how she'd ended up here.

She was twenty now, far past when the others moved on, but with nowhere to go. Penelope had kept her on as an extra set of hands—phones, paperwork, deliveries, appointments. It was steady work that kept her clothed and fed, but it wasn't a future.

She wanted a purpose. A place of her own choosing. Instead, she was stuck in an in-between, living among children waiting for their old lives while she didn't know how to start a new one. She didn't want to *just be*. She wanted to belong somewhere outside these walls, to burn down the quiet lie that this was enough.

She stepped away before the woman noticed her. As she retreated toward the common room, a faint shimmer caught her eye. A red string, soft as the bookmark in the *Book of Godspells*, lay by her foot. She reached for it, but before her fingers could close around it, it flew away on an invisible breeze.

Penelope's heels echoed behind her moments later, followed by her usual clap.

"Everyone! Outside to the rose garden!"

The children scrambled. Piper followed slowly.

The garden was small but stubbornly alive, roses flaring red, white, and pink against the grey December sky. Penelope moved among the bushes with shears, her hands finding each stem with the ease of long practice.

"We may not have fancy ornaments," she said, "but that doesn't mean our tree can't be beautiful. Each of you will pick one rose."

The children cheered.

"Why roses?" asked Aisling, fourteen, still teetering between belief and understanding. "Why not just make ornaments?"

"Ornaments break," Penelope said. "Roses bloom even when the season says they shouldn't. Like all of you."

Deeno held up a rose like a sword. "So, this rose is the orphan of decorations?"

"You are something else, Deeno," Piper said.

He grinned. "You pick one, you never know what you'll get. Could be cute and pink." He shrugged. "Or could stab you in the thumb."

Penelope crouched beside him, plucking a soft pink blossom. "Not orphan. Just a child waiting to be taken back home."

Deeno smirked, hiding it the way orphan children learn to. Make it a joke and keep the rest underneath.

"Yeah, well," he said, "tell that to the ones missing petals. Those guys have seen things."

Piper laughed despite herself.

One by one the children drifted back inside, their voices trailing away down the corridor until the garden held only the sound of wind and shears. Piper stayed without deciding to. Something kept her feet on the frost-bitten path, watching Penelope move to the far edge of the garden where the roses grew darkest and closest to the stone wall.

Penelope didn't look back. She selected a single red rose with the quiet authority of someone who had done this ten thousand times, tilted the stem, and cut it clean.

Then she pressed her fingers against the petals. Not examining them. Not brushing away frost. *Pressing.* Her gloved palm flat against the bloom, deliberate and still, the way you press your hand against a wound.

Piper's breath caught.

The color left the rose the way heat leaves a room, all at once, from the inside out. The red drained to the edges and then beyond them, replaced by a black so deep it shimmered, as though the petals hadn't simply darkened but had been filled with something that had its own faint, internal light. Midnight breathed into silk. The shimmer pulsed once. Twice.

Piper's hand flew to her mouth.

Penelope did not flinch. Did not look down. Did not change her expression by a single degree. She simply set the rose on the stone wall with the same unhurried care she used for everything, brushed her gloved hands together once, and turned toward the house.

Piper's eyes snapped back to the rose.

Red. Perfectly, completely red. Frost-kissed petals, ordinary winter light, no shimmer, no darkness, nothing. As though the last ten seconds had not happened at all.

She looked at Penelope's back. At the normal set of her shoulders, the normal rhythm of her walk, the normal way she held the shears at her side.

Then at the rose again.

Red.

You're tired, she told herself. *The light is flat out here. Rose petals look strange when they're cold, when the frost catches them from the wrong angle, when you've been staring too long at something without blinking.* There were a dozen reasonable explanations, and she arranged them in a neat row in her mind, and not one of them touched the hum that had started low in her chest the moment Penelope's palm had flattened against the bloom.

Not one of them explained why she still felt it.

She followed Penelope inside without a second glance back. Or told herself she didn't glance back.

She glanced back.

The rose sat on the stone wall, red as blood, perfectly still in the windless air.

The hum in her chest didn't stop until she was back in the house.

The bare pine of their Christmas tree was already filling with thorns and petals. Penelope held the ladder steady while Ciara placed the glittering star on top. It wobbled but held. The children gasped with delight.

From the corner, Piper smiled. For a moment she forgot the leaking ceilings, the peeling paint, the quiet truth that no one was coming for her. For a moment it felt like the Christmases she had read about in books.

"Who is ready for breakfast?" Penelope called.

The food hall was the biggest reminder of where they came from. Peeling paint, sagging ceiling, dim lights on rusted chains. Mismatched tables scarred from years of use. Benches that squeaked. Windows too grimy to let in proper light.

Piper sat at the far end, in the same spot for the past sixteen years. It was far enough for the illusion of peace. She was too old for the bedtime stories, too old for borrowed cardigans, too old for the small hands that tugged at her elbows like she was a permanent fixture.

Permanence was an illusion. Kids came and went. Some reclaimed, some fostered, some simply gone. For those who faded out of the system, they just stayed. Piper being one of them. All she had were these four walls and the endless role she'd never auditioned for: the big sister. A role she'd outgrown years ago but everyone still expected her to play.

"You talk in your sleep," Deeno announced, climbing onto the bench across from her.

"Stop creeping past my door."

"I'm a sleepwalker! Whoooo—"

"You mean a nosy condition," she muttered.

Ciara dropped down beside him. "He talks in his sleep too. Last night he said: *beware the silver apple.*"

Piper's eyebrow rose.

Deeno went red. "Stop! I told you not to tell—ll!"

"You drooled too," Ciara cackled.

"Tell us another one of your dream stories, Piper," Aisling said, sliding in next to them as if she had been ease dropping.

Piper sighed. "Then you leave me alone."

All three nodded, but she swore Deeno had his fingers crossed behind his back.

"I was in a big shiny forest," she began. "There was a river made of silver that flowed like melted stars."

"Fancy," Ciara whispered.

"Aren't stars yellow?" Deeno asked seriously.

"*Just listen.*"

"Across the river was a girl. Young. Silver—her skin, her hair, everything. Like she was made of molten metal."

"A robot," Deeno said.

"Or fairy," Ciara said.

Piper shook her head carefully, trying to define it herself.

"Neither. She was human-ish. But I couldn't see her face. It's always blurry." Piper paused. "She says my name. Over and over. Every time I try to answer, she drifts further away."

"Moon ghost," Deeno declared. "Hovering over your bed. Asking for blood." He threw up his hands. The girls laughed.

"She's not a ghost," Piper said. "She feels real."

"Maybe she is a silver child," Aisling offered quietly.

Piper blinked. She hadn't connected the two somehow. "Yeah, something like that." The phrase sat strangely on her tongue, familiar in a way she couldn't place.

She finished her dream story, adding made up scenes for added entertainment when the twins eventually left, whispering theories down the hall. Aisling slipped away after them leaving Piper to sit alone with the echo of her own words.

A Silver Child.

Outside, the sky was dull, the clouds drifted like an eerie fog. She thought of the silver girl. Her glowing body, her hidden face, her child's voice calling across that strange river.

It didn't feel like just a dream anymore.

Why was she calling her name?

Piper's fingers tightened around her spoon as the question repeated in her mind. She didn't know what that place was, only that it couldn't possibly be worse than staying here.

CHAPTER THREE
THE BLIND BOY

Piper slipped out of Olympus House the moment she could. She'd cleared the breakfast table, sorted a few bills, and made sure the children were fed and tucked into their holiday festivities—the small duties that filled her mornings like clockwork.

She had no destination in mind, only the need to move, to keep her body in motion so her thoughts wouldn't calcify into the same tired loop. Dublin in winter carried its own kind of weight: cold, damp, and unyielding, with sudden bursts of icy rain that rattled the cobblestones before vanishing as quickly as they came. The air smelled faintly of metal and old stone.

She pulled her coat tighter, blending with the stream of people who moved briskly past with collars up, hoods drawn. In the way Dubliners did, some met her gaze briefly with the kind of wry, weather-worn smile that said: *It can be miserable, but it's ours.*

Christmas lights were strung overhead, tossing soft color into the grey: red bleeding into green, green into blue, all of it edged with the silver glint of wet wire. Somewhere nearby, the smell of roasted chestnuts made her stomach twist with hunger. She didn't stop.

She drifted past Morry's old school, locked up for the holidays, its playground a silent grid of puddles. A royal blue scarf hung looped over the stone gate, its fringe twitching in the wind. Piper wondered, not for the first time, what it would be like to have belonged there—to have been part of the laughter, the crush of students, the inside jokes that carried past graduation. Her own education had been quieter. The kind you could fold away into a single room.

The city carried her forward. She studied passing faces the way some people read headlines: quick, curious, wondering about the stories tucked behind them. Did they feel at home in their lives, or were they, like her, restless for something just out of reach?

It wasn't until she stopped that she noticed where she had ended up. The steps of the Dublin Library and Archive rose before her, its stone slick with rain. She hadn't meant to come here, hadn't even thought about it consciously, but here she was. She'd expected it to be dark, locked until after the holidays. The lights were on, a soft golden glow spilling from the tall windows. Calling her in.

She wasn't trying to get answers. She just wanted to breathe.

She hesitated, rubbing her wrist where the dream's scar still stung faintly, then pulled a cigarette from her coat pocket and sat on the frosted steps. She lit it, exhaled slowly. She knew it was a bad habit—she'd been doing it since eighteen, lifting them from Ailin's desk when his nerves were frayed enough not to notice. It calmed her the same way it calmed him.

Weren't adults supposed to be role models?

"Those can kill you, you know."

Piper jumped. The voice was smooth, and calm in a way that made the skin on her neck prickle. She turned to see a boy standing near the library steps. He looked like a secret the clouds hadn't meant to drop.

His hair was white as untouched snow and tousled like he had walked through a storm. His pale skin shimmered faintly against the dull Dublin morning. His face was sharp, sculpted with cheekbones like blades, and lips too perfect to belong to a teenager. He looked unreal. Impossible.

His sunglasses were round and dark, covering his eyes completely, reflecting the grey world around them. It wasn't sunny, and yet he wore them like armor. Like he couldn't afford to be seen.

"Can I try?" he asked, gesturing toward her cigarette.

Piper hesitated, confused. "Didn't you just say these are bad for me?"

He smiled slowly, as if he'd already heard this conversation before.

"You're not scared. So why should I be?"

He stood utterly still, and yet something about him *pulled*. Like gravity bending inward. There was something strange— *no, wrong*—about him.

She held the cigarette between two fingers, unsure why she offered it, only that it felt like a challenge. He turned his head *toward her*, as if he sensed her hand before it moved.

"Here," she said, hesitant.

He didn't reach yet but stood there. Listening maybe. Then slowly, he reached out, his fingers missing the cigarette, brushing them along her hand. Immediately, something cold and brittle coiled up her arm like frost laced with static. It wasn't painful, but sharp.

She startled and looked up, just as the dark glasses on his face slipped, ever so slightly, down the bridge of his nose, enough to reveal his eyes. They were pale, glazed over, and had no iris.

He wasn't avoiding her gaze. He couldn't see her because he was blind.

"Will you hand it to me?" he said, confirming her theory, unfazed by the touch that rattled her whole body.

"You can't see," she said softly.

"Yet here I am," he murmured, hand out waiting for her to guide the cigarette to it.

Piper stood up and placed the cigarette in his outreached hand, carefully refraining from their skin to touch each other again. Whatever that feeling was, had pulled something inside her.

In his other hand, something lean and silver gleamed, easily mistaken for a walking stick. It was carved from some silvered braid, bound in odd loops like a helix, tapering to a point at one end. Iridescent feathering coiled near the grip—peacock-like, but unnatural. Embedded across the feather's edge were tiny stones. No—*eyes*. Hundreds of them watching. Some sleeping.

"What is that?" she asked, unsettled. She didn't even have to explain *that* for him to know what she meant. What a strange yet intriguing boy. He was perceptive to the point that it made her think: *What is the true meaning of eyes?*

She watched as he ran a thumb over its spine, thoughtful. He was remarkably swift and intuitive for someone who couldn't see the world around him.

"A thing I carry."

She frowned. "What is it for?"

"Balance," he said at last. "When the ground isn't what it seems."

His tone was even, like a truth he didn't care if she understood. It made her more uneasy. He raised the cigarette to his lips but didn't inhale.

"You're supposed to inhale," she said shyly.

He turned his face toward her voice. "Am I?"

"That's the point, isn't it? Get that momentary high... To feel something?"

"No," he said. "I think it is to *erase* something."

She blinked.

"People don't smoke to feel alive," he continued. "They

smoke to kill something inside. Slowly. The difference is that some of them know it."

He put his lips to it again but still didn't inhale.

"Then what are you doing with it?" she asked. What a strange situation going on right now. She looked around.

Was I being punked?

"I am keeping you from taking more from this life than the little you already have."

That answer hurt more than it should have. *Little?* She was an adult.

She reached out, maybe to take it back, maybe to make him stop, but as her fingers closed over the cigarette, the ember flared, singeing her skin.

"Ow!"

She dropped it by reflex, but before it hit the pavement, he caught her hand with exact pressure, like he *knew* where she'd be.

"Don't reach for what you don't mean to take," he said, thumb resting lightly over her burn. "Pain is honest. Most humans aren't."

When she finally yanked her hand away, the sting was gone, something else taking its place. Just below her thumb, a faint spiral had formed.

It wasn't red or blistered like a true burn, but ashen. The ash from the cigarette had seared into her skin, pale as smoke. Its very own tattoo.

"What did you do to me?" she whispered, her voice accusatory.

"Nothing," he said quietly.

"Then what is this?"

He didn't answer, continuing to stand there, unblinking behind his dark glasses, as though the silence was the answer.

She studied his face, trying to make sense of him and of how someone who couldn't see *moved like he could.* Of why he *felt* so familiar and yet so untouchable.

"How can you see me?" she asked.

His head tilted slightly.

"Some people watch. Some people look. Some people *see*."

That didn't answer her question. "And you?" She couldn't believe she had to clarify.

"I listen. I feel."

He stepped back, and she noticed how the silver object in his hand didn't tap the ground. He didn't need it. Not the way blind people did.

"Are you... here for *me*?" she asked. It was the only explanation. He was intentional in coming up to her. *Why*? A shiver ran down her entire spine as she waited for his answer.

"No," the boy replied. "You're walking toward something. I just happen to be here."

"Where is *here*?" She wondered out loud but was scared to know what he'd say. She didn't feel like his answer would make sense to this world. Of course, it didn't.

"Closer than you think," he said cryptically, then asked, "What are you searching for?" He tilted his head slightly, reading her expression without seeing it.

"Searching for?" Why did he sound like Colik right now? Another shiver ran down her spine.

"What book are you looking for? Unless I am mistaken, one comes to a library to search for a book," he said, sounding amused.

"Oh, right. Yeah, I'm looking up dreams," she answered, feeling oddly defensive.

"*Dreams*," he repeated thoughtfully. "Any specific dream?"

She hesitated, unsure whether to share or not. Something in his expression, curiosity, perhaps, drew her in. "I've been having weird dreams, I guess. Trying to figure out why."

"Weird dreams? In what way?"

"I think I am lucid dreaming... or something like it. Or dreaming—in another place," she replied, feeling silly saying it out loud now. "It's this old idea where you can control your dreams, possibly live among them. I know it sounds stupid. Crazy, even."

"That's not crazy," he said, his voice steady. "Sounds like the *perfect* dream to me." His eyebrows lifted with a strange mix of interest and intrigue.

"Maybe," she murmured, then eyed him cautiously. "What are you looking for?"

"Ironically enough, I too am looking for a rather unique book on dreaming. More a journal if you will," the blind boy said, his voice smooth but uncertain. He was eyeing her through his sunglasses rather inquisitively. She saw it in the way his eyebrow rose as his dark glasses stared at her. Then, after a pause, he added more firmly, "If you come across something like that, I'd be curious to know."

"You want to know about dreaming, too?" she asked, her skin prickling.

He tilted his head slightly, amused. "Don't we all?" he said, with a soft smile. "Dreams hold mysteries—secrets. The reasons we dream, the symbols that haunt us. Why wouldn't someone want to understand that?"

She stared at him; caught in that strange gravity he carried.

That made sense, I guess.

"Why do you want this umm—journal?"

He leaned back, balancing on that long silver cane of his.

"Just because I am blind here," he continued, "doesn't mean I can't see elsewhere."

Piper's breath caught. The way he said *elsewhere* felt heavy. All too meaningful and super cryptic.

"I, too, would like to know what's real, and what's just a dream. The lines aren't always clear, are they?" he added.

"No," she murmured. "Apparently they are not."

She watched as his fingers traced the spine of the cane, or staff, she wasn't sure what to call it. The metal shimmered faintly where the light caught it, and for a second, she saw what it truly was: three silver strands twisted like rope, frayed slightly at the base, where the handle curved into what looked like a spindle. It reminded her of something from a myth. An artifact. Or *something*.

"Why do you carry that if you don't seem to need it?" she decided to ask.

He didn't answer right away. His hand stopped, resting gently at the top of the shaft. When he finally spoke, his voice was barely above a whisper.

"It is called a distaff."

Piper blinked. "What's a distaff?"

"A tool for severing..." he said cryptically. "A story belonging to the Fat—" but his voice trailed off with no clear intention to finish that sentence.

"Fates?" she asked. "Like in Greek Mythology?"

Piper's heart started racing as she thought about the Ollopa train that Colik had said was made by the gods. Would he know about that?

He shrugged, giving her nothing.

Piper's eyes lingered on it, but when he clearly wasn't going to offer more on it, she pivoted. "You said you were looking for a journal," she tried again. "What is in this journal?"

He smiled without smiling. "A script. From before the gods rewrote the rules. Before law became something humans were forced to follow, instead of something that was woven for us."

A script? Of the gods...

A strange chill passed through her. "What do you mean?"

He shrugged, as if brushing away smoke. "Nothing important, only that there were once laws that governed more than human waking. Laws that bound thought, emotion, and dreams. The Oneiroi knew them before even humans gave names to dreams."

Piper's pulse spiked. *Oneiroi.* The dream gods. This was all getting weirder by the second.

He stood then, drawing up the distaff with a grace that was impossible for someone who couldn't see. Yet he moved like he could see everything. Again, like he didn't need eyes to *know*.

"Just let me know when you come across that book," he stated dryly. "Or anything of the sorts. You will know what I mean when you find it."

Piper gave a hesitating nod. He sounded so sure she would find it...

This strange boy's mysterious pull grew deeper with every word he spoke. The way he talked to her was like he knew her, had met her before, yet, for the life of Piper, she did not know him. She knew she would have remembered someone like him.

The bell tolled, announcing the ninth hour of the day. Rising to her feet, she headed toward the front door, eager to escape.

"*βιβλίο*," the blind boys called behind her.

"Pardon?" she asked, half-turning. "It means book in Greek," he clarified, his eyes glinting with the hint of a mystery. "They say the books with the biggest secrets are the ones no one wants you to read, but what's the fun in that?" he questioned.

Piper weighed his words, feeling that he could help her piece together the fragments of her dreams, if she were to ask. She refrained as something in her gut warned her to tread carefully. She was also afraid to.

He suddenly turned and began to walk in the opposite direction from the library.

Odd, she thought. *Was he not going to the library too?*

A beat passed. "I don't even know your name," she called out after him this time.

He stopped, half-turning, his white hair brushing against the collar of his coat. "Steele."

She froze. That name was fitting.

"Well—I'm Piper," she said, the name catching awkwardly in her throat.

He gave a small, amused tilt of the head. "Piper..." he repeated, and gave her the faintest bow, pretending this was nothing more than a passing encounter on a grey Dublin street. "Happy hunting, Piper. I have a feeling we'll be meeting each other again soon."

Then, without a sound, he disappeared into the dark between buildings. There was no sound of footsteps. No tapping of a cane. Nothing to prove he had ever even been there.

CHAPTER FOUR
THE WORD BIBΛ´IO

The doors to the Dublin Library and Archive were open, though no one waited at the front desk. The space was dimly lit, quiet, and softly humming with the scent of ink and dust. Piper almost turned back but a subtle pulse of the new strange scar made her step inside. It was the kind of place that didn't pretend to be anything more than what it was: shelves of forgotten things and space to think.

She moved deeper into the stacks, her fingers trailing along spines as she searched for specific words. *Βιβλίο. Oneiroi.* The blind boy's voice lingered in her mind, low and deliberate.

Somewhere between Greek dictionaries and folklore collections, a tug in her chest quickened. She slowed, scanning the shelf, and that was when she saw it.

It wasn't even properly shelved, but more dropped there, as if having slipped between the worlds and landed there by accident. A small, leather-bound book, half-hidden behind a warped copy of *Dublin Myths & Folklore* and Homer's book, *The Iliad.* The worn cover read: *The Dreamer's Mind: A Study into*

Lucid States and the Greek Gods of Sleep. The author's name looked to have been scratched out.

When she cracked it open, the scent of dried lavender, something earthy, and metallic, rose to meet her. The script inside slanted elegantly, the ink faded but steady, each line precise as though whoever wrote it had been certain of every word.

She turned a page. Then another, until her eyes snagged on a smudge in the margin. It was someone's handwriting, faint enough to nearly disappear. She brought the book closer to the light.

"Βιβλίο. Oneiroi." The same words. Followed by a fragment in English: *"Not just control. A secret to the ages."*

Her pulse quickened. The note was crooked, rushed, as though written in the middle of some urgent thought, or in the dark.

She sank into a creaky chair in the far corner, the kind that rocked on uneven legs, and the moment she settled, the book settled too. It fit against her palms, meant for her to read.

"The lucid state of dreaming is not merely awareness," the passage began, scrawled in aged ink. *"It is a waking within the unawake. It is a breach in the barrier where sleep no longer binds, and truth no longer hides."*

A *breach.*

Piper's breath caught but kept reading.

"In this state, one may drift beyond the confines of mortal sleep, past the stage of REM where memory, emotion, and myth intertwine. This in-between, hidden within the folds of deeper dreaming, is where titles once whispered return from ages passed. Dreamers. Oneiroi."

The words rang in her chest like bells.

"The Silver Age," she continued, *"was the last great dreaming. An age where the Silver Children—born of dreams and human flesh —could bend the strands of reality, slipping between truth and falsity freely. They moved through the Gates of Horn and Ivory with ease,*

unbound by the moral weight of waking. Like demigods, they had the control to live an immortal life within their dreams."

Piper's eyes traced the curling letters, their ink sharp and freshly penned.

"Back then," the next line read, *"dreams were not illusions. They were memory. Blueprint. Law. What was imagined could be made. What was feared, undone."*

A strange warmth pooled in her chest, like something half-remembered pressing forward. Steele mentioned law.

In a more personal hand, a script slanted and urgent, added later, was a note that struck harder than the rest:

'Human laws echo the dreams they've forgotten. – H.'

She read it twice. Three times. It was written to be a conflicting thought from someone who read this leather-bound book. Yet it felt truer than anything.

Her fingers grazed the margin beside it, tracing where the scribe had pressed too hard. She turned the page and hurriedly continued reading, as if she were on the brink of getting caught doing something illegal.

"The gods feared such freedom of human children made of dust and dreams," the next page read. *"So, Zeus sealed the Gate of Horn. He fractured dreaming for mortals and rewrote the dust that once tied gods and humans alike."*

Her eyes scanned the ink-stained page, her breath catching as the next words appeared. *Gate of Horn.* Her new scar itched as the word repeated in her mind.

"Like Hercules, forged in strength but bound to mortal labors. Like Perseus, gifted with divine tools only to be accused by the gods later. Like Cupid, stripped to choose between the gods and mortal love. Like demigods and the gods who loved humans, these dream-born children were the first to be exiled."

Piper's pulse quickened. "These weren't just stories. They

were warnings," she whispered, then turned the page again, hands trembling.

"Those who were born of both dream and soul, of mortal longing and the god's design, were permitted to live, never to control. Their dreams were too wild. Their hearts too loud. And their strands too unpredictable."

Again, that same thin line of script slanted at the bottom margin. Barely legible, handwritten, and different from the rest:

"When a god fears a mortal, they do not kill them. They immortalize them elsewhere— So they can be forgotten more quietly. - H.'

Who was H?

Piper's pulse fluttered, her finger instinctively grazing the ashen mark on her hand. It was a half open fish shape curving into the middle with a slash, carefully sketched into her skin. Like *that* made sense—

A voice broke her thoughts and the silence around her.

"Excuse me, dear. Can I help you?"

Piper jumped, her fingers tightening on the book. A middle-aged woman with a mane of red and purple-streaked curls stood nearby, her expression kind, but sharply observant.

"I—uh—I didn't know anyone was here."

The woman tilted her head. "I wasn't meant to be. I just came to pick up a few things. I suppose fate has its own calendar."

Piper held up the book, suddenly defensive. "I was just reading this. I was going to put it back."

The woman's eyes flicked to the title, and for a second, her expression faltered.

"Ah. *That* one."

"You've read it?" Piper asked.

"Years ago," she said. "When I still believed in all *that*."

Piper blinked. "What do you mean?"

The woman looked away for a beat, then back again. "Believe it or not, I used to believe that there was a *dream* world too. Before I saw what they became."

The new scar on Piper's hand itched like fire.

"So lucid dreaming is real then?" Piper asked slowly. "The Silver Age. I had a dream about it, I think. Or partially."

The woman—Himyla, as her name tag read—studied her more carefully now, like she was searching for a lie in Piper's face. "Some people say dreams are just reflections. Harmless. Others say they're doors. That once opened, they don't close the same way."

She stepped closer and gently took the book from Piper's hands. The librarian's gaze drifted to Piper's thumb, her eyes widening. Piper pulled her sleeve over her scar.

"It is true—" Himyla said under her breath.

"What?" Piper asked, her heart skipping a beat.

"Nothing." Her voice snapped back into politeness. "We just don't get many readers wondering about Mimics anymore. Or really at all."

"Mimics," Piper repeated. The word felt heavy in her mouth, and the woman's words sounded purposefully cryptic.

"A Mimic is a sort of Dreamwalker, if you will. They believed dreams weren't just messages," Himyla continued carefully. "But places. They would try to cross into them. It started off as simply lucid dreaming, but Mimics...they didn't just try to experience the dream, they tried to live in them...and some of those who tried...they—they didn't return."

"And you think that is real?" Piper asked, pulse racing. "True?" Could the Ollopa train be part of some *Dreamworld*?

Himyla's lips parted, but she hesitated. "I think some doors should only open from one side."

Piper wasn't sure how to interpret that. How did this woman know so much? What was a Mimic really?

She was about to ask when the librarian broke her thoughts.

"I will walk you to the front. I must close soon. Tomorrow is Christmas Eve after all."

Piper stood, reluctant. "Right. Sorry. I'll go." She hesitated a beat longer, then added, "I recognized you. From Olympus House. You brought bread for us… Thank you."

Himyla's expression softened just a touch. "It wasn't much."

Piper thought about the oddly familiar *book* Himyla had in her arm at Olympus House, curiosity tugging at her. "That book you had, the tucked under yo—"

"Come back after the holidays, if you like," Himyla interrupted. "I am the librarian, if you need help finding a book *another time*," She repeated. There was an edge to her tone now. It sounded guarded and uneasy.

When they reached the front of the library, the librarian moved behind the checkout desk and patted a small stack of books down, checking they were still there. The one on top snagged Piper's attention immediately: the same worn brown leather, the same red velvet ribbon tied around its pages. *Now,* she was sure. The librarian had the book from the Ollopa train.

"What book is that?" Piper had to ask again. It was more than a coincidence now.

Himyla followed her gaze. "Just checking these in," she said hesitantly.

Piper frowned. "I think I've seen that one before." Her voice was sharper now. Braver. "The one on top."

Himyla's expression tightened, fear flickering in her eyes. "No. You couldn't have."

Piper already knew that she had.

"βιβλίο?" she blurted, the word Steele had mentioned tumbling out. Her pronunciation was clumsy—*viv-lee-a*—but the color drained from Himyla's face.

"Where did you hear that word?" she demanded.

Piper ignored the question. "Why does that book look like the one I saw in a dream?"

The librarian's mouth opened, then closed again. Her hand settled protectively on the book, not yet moving it. Her silence confirmed everything.

"That's the *Book of Godspells*, isn't it?" Piper pressed.

Himyla's shoulders fell, barely, but it was enough to crack her composure. She didn't answer right away. Her fingers stayed curled over the ribbon-bound spine as if letting go would open something she couldn't contain.

"This is," she finally started. "The book sought out by the Mimics."

"Looking for a Dreamworld?"

Himyla's eyes flicked to hers. "I didn't say *looked*. I said *searched*. Obsessively. Desperately. Like it was more than a dream. Like it was calling."

"You talk like you knew one of them."

"I did." Himyla's jaw tensed. "He was my closest friend. Once."

Piper's pulse jumped. "What happened?"

Himyla didn't answer at first but lifted the book gently and pressed her palm flat on the cover. "He believed there was a place beyond even lucid dreaming. Not REM, but something deeper. He called it the REMembrance layer. It was a stage of sleep so rare most never touch it. For those who do…they don't come back the same."

A pause and then a breath. "He found a way in."

Piper froze. "And?"

"Like I said, he never came back." Her words were flat, brittle, like glass about to break. "He said there were myths buried in that layer. A place the gods abandoned. A world where memory lived as matter. The Mimics believed those myths weren't just stories. They were *gates*."

Piper swallowed hard, the scar on her hand beginning to pulse faintly beneath her sleeve.

"He said if dreams were echoes of truth," Himyla continued, "then the REMembrance was the place where humans can be immortal."

A chill spiraled up Piper's spine.

"I watched him go," Himyla whispered. "He marked himself first. Just like——" She stopped, her eyes darting to Piper's hand through the sleeve. She had already seen it. "Just like *that.*"

Piper instinctively tucked her hand behind her back.

"That's where he drew the *Reverie*," Himyla continued, her voice strained. "That is what he called it. On his thumb. Repeatedly. As if he were sketching a memory he couldn't name. The same mark appeared after he vanished...in the dust he left behind."

Himyla's breath stilled, then went on as if she had been waiting ages to get this off her chest. "He went looking for the world the gods tried to erase. Said it was older than Olympus. That it had rules—*laws*—the Oneiroi obeyed before the Olympians ever wrote theirs. He thought if he could recover those laws, he could remake reality. He was wrong."

Had *she* written the book Piper had just read?

"What happened to him?" Piper whispered.

Himyla looked away. "He became dust. At first, it shimmered like starlight. Over time, it started turning gray. To ash."

"Did he die?"

"I don't know," she said tightly. "He said he could transmute, that if his dust was here, he would reincarnate back here when he was ready to come back. He has never come back, his dust slowly turning all to ash. Like he is not just gone, but *in-between* worlds."

Piper clutched the edge of the shelf for balance.

"You're trying to go there, aren't you?" Himyla said, more

certain now. "You've seen it. Felt it pulling, but you can't follow his path."

Piper shrugged, slowly. "My dreams... They're not dreams. I think I've already been there."

Himyla stepped forward. "Then you need to stop. Right now."

"I can't."

"You *must*. That world doesn't just take you. It *rewrites* you. You start unraveling. Piece by piece. First memory. Then motion. Maybe will. Until there's nothing left but dust. Like him." Her tone was pleading.

Piper hesitated. "What if I'm already unraveling?"

Himyla's lips parted, but no answer came.

"I need that book," Piper said, not believing that dust meant he had disappeared elsewhere. That was absurd. "It's what ties any of this. I need to learn more."

Why did Steele want the *Book of Godspells*? Or was that even what he wanted at all? Something in her gut told her it was *exactly* what he wanted.

Himyla closed her eyes, pressing her hand to the book like it was a coffin. "He said the same thing. Tore it apart, page by page, looking for the laws before law. The first dreaming. The forbidden truths. When he found them...he disappeared. Both from himself and then this world."

Piper stepped closer. "What was his name?"

Himyla tightened her lips, as if trying not to spill a secret.

The silence that followed was thick. Aching. "Please," Himyla said. "Don't go looking for that world. If you really cross to *there* or cross again...you may never fully come back. If you find him...I do not think he will be the same as what he was when he left this world." She shivered. "If his studies are correct, he will no longer know what it means to be human, and that scares me for *you*."

Piper didn't speak, her thoughts a mix of fire and fog.

"You still have a choice," Himyla added, her voice trembling. "That so-called *Dreamworld*... I am afraid it is not a place for humans to find themselves."

Himyla went around the desk now and started pushing Piper back to the front door.

"It is a place to lose yourself," Himyla whispered. "And I am afraid that what is worse is if you do find *him*."

She opened, and cold air swept in.

"Go. While there is still a *you* left to return to," Himyla warned, then turned before Piper could say anything back. The library door clicked shut behind her.

Defeated, Piper walked away, her mind reeling with what was, what had been, and what could possibly be... All in her dreams.

It was late afternoon when Piper slipped through the back gate of Olympus House, her boots crunching faintly on the frostbitten path. The sky sagged low with a pale drizzle, the kind that clung instead of falling, and yet, like every winter afternoon, Penelope was in the garden.

She knelt among the rosebushes in her worn green coat, scarf loosened at her neck, bare hands working with a patience that had outlasted entire seasons. She clipped away blackened leaves, brushed snow from petals that bent under its weight, coaxing life from things the cold had every right to claim.

Piper lingered in the doorway, reluctant to break the stillness. The garden wasn't grand, but in the hush of winter it felt sacred.

Most of the roses by the fountain had dulled into muted crimsons and silvery whites kissed with frost. Except for one. A rose turned entirely black. Its petals curled inward like shadows folding into themselves. She blinked and it was back to its frosty white.

Piper thought of the book she had held at the library— *The Dreamer's Mind*—its faded ink, the words about a "breach" where sleep and waking no longer obeyed the same rules. She thought of the other book too, the one Himyla guarded with trembling hands, the *Book of Godspells*, red ribbon bound like a warning.

She watched as Penelope touched the once black rose without fear, whispering, *"I see you."* For a moment, Piper wondered if she meant the rose or her. The weight of it pressed harder than frost, harder even than the memory of Himyla's voice when she said the Mimics searched for that book: *"obsessively, desperately...like it was calling"*.

Maybe Piper was like this rose. She was darkened and caught between survival and surrender. Maybe the Dream-world she'd stumbled into at the library was calling her, too.

She stepped back before Penelope could notice, imprinting the sight of the frost, the roses, and the once lone black bloom. Just as the books had felt like they were meant for her hands, so too did the silent pull toward the so-called *Dreamworld*.

CHAPTER FIVE
THE SILVER GIRL

T he day passed in a blur, Piper's mind caught between what the blind boy had said, what she'd read in the library, and what the librarian had told her. Every word, every strange connection tangled together until she couldn't tell what was myth and what was memory. By Christmas Eve, the city had gone quiet beneath the falling snow, and Piper found herself wandering the streets alone, trying to outwalk her thoughts. She kept to the edges, avoiding the children laughing and running past with ribbons and bells. Having *aged* out, Penelope and Ailin thankfully didn't make her following strict rules anymore.

When dusk came, she slipped quietly back through the doors of Olympus House. The familiar scent of boiled cabbage and old floor polish greeted her like an unwelcome handshake. She took the stairs two at a time, careful to avoid the creaky boards she knew by heart. Right turn, short hall, closed doors. Five more steps. Left. Then right again. The place was a maze of narrow corridors and shadowed corners, the kind that made you feel watched even when you were alone.

The walls were an off-white dulled by years of neglect,

their edges faintly yellowed near the ceiling. The air was thick with the scent of dust from books no one read anymore, a smell that clung to her hair long after she left the building. The windows were tall enough to promise a view, but too narrow to offer escape.

Her room was the smallest in Olympus House, a leftover cell meant to hold rule-breakers until they "calmed down." Penelope let her claim it at eighteen, when she was supposed to move out and start her own life like normal eighteen-year-olds. Instead, she stayed. Her life was anything but normal.

She told people it was by choice, but really, she just couldn't afford to leave. The room wasn't much—just a bed, a crooked shelf, and walls that listened—but it felt like hers.

She dropped onto the thin mattress, staring at the ceiling where sunset bled in through the blinds. The stillness didn't last long.

A knock.

She closed her eyes. "Yeah?"

The door creaked open, letting in the faint scent of Ailin's cologne, a sharp cedar, and paper dust from the stacks in his office. The owner of the house leaned just inside the frame, acting like a guest in her space.

"Just wanted to check on you."

"I'm fine," she said, the words too quick.

He didn't leave. "It is okay that you're still here," Ailin said softly.

Her stomach sank. She knew he meant that she didn't have to rush, that not everyone needed to have life figured out by twenty. They had been through this before, but that only made her feel smaller.

Her cheeks burned. "I should be doing something," she murmured. "Making something of myself. Not just..." She gestured vaguely to the room, to the ceiling that had held her for years.

Ailin's voice was calm. "You don't have to run ahead just because everyone else is. Life isn't a race, Piper."

It felt like one to her. One she'd already lost. Every reminder that she was still under this roof felt like a chain tightening. She had no money, no direction, and no purpose to her name. Just a body in a borrowed room once used for isolation.

She forced a shrug, though her voice wavered. "Yeah. I guess."

No rush sounded like *no escape*.

He lingered, his eyes on her like they were having a staring contest. Done with the conversation, Ailin, slowly moved back into the hallway. The door closed with its usual soft click, leaving her in a silence so heavy she could hear the faint hum of the old radiator.

She lay back down, the smell of dust still in her nose, her muscles coiled as if the walls themselves were leaning inward. It wasn't that she hated this place. Staying here just felt like she was giving into a version of her life that everyone else had decided she should have.

In the waking world, there was nowhere to go. In her dreams, there *was* somewhere else. Piper had never been so sure of it until now.

She shut her eyes.

I am not here. I am there.

Piper opened her eyes to somewhere else entirely. The ceiling above her bed was gone. So was the bed, the floor, and the faint creak of Penelope's slippers in the hall.

In their place stretched a forest that stretched endlessly, each towering trunk sheathed in silver bark that shimmered like frozen moonlight. Threads of light pulsed faintly beneath their mushroom top surfaces, veins of starlight running through them. Their bark glittered with silver flakes, and their star-shaped leaves flickered in hues of deep gold and ember, each carrying its own trapped fire.

The air was thick with floating dust, silver motes suspended mid-drift and unmoving. Somewhere ahead, a river curved between the roots, glowing from within. The current pulsed with starlight, like it had swallowed constellations whole and was carrying them away to someplace unseen.

She was in the dream with—

The girl made of molten silver was waiting.

She stood across the riverbank, framed by the strange light, her frame slight, but her presence heavy. Sixteen at most in appearance, her stillness carried an ancient patience. Her hair was white, threaded with veins of living silver that caught the dim light and refused to give it back. Her skin glimmered faintly like the heat-shimmer rising from metal just pulled from a forge.

A robe the color of stardust fell around her in layered folds, draped so loosely it looked to be made of molten smoke. Strands coiled and uncoiled around her. The robe's hem trailed into the glowing water, the silver threads dissolving into light. She stood over her reflection, inspecting it, as a craftsman inspects their work for flaws.

"Piper..." The girl's voice reached across the river, each syllable deliberate, peeling her name apart. "Piper..."

Piper's lips parted. "Why are you calling me? I didn't—" She stopped herself, surprised to find that this time she could speak.

The girl's mouth curved faintly. "Sometimes you don't have to call. You just ache and the worlds listen."

Piper tried to step forward, but when she moved, the forest moved with her. Every tree, every root shifted just enough that her feet never left the spot she'd started from. That part of her dream hadn't changed.

"Who are you?"

The girl lifted her gaze slowly, and Piper flinched. Her eyes were the color of moonstone, but it wasn't the color that struck her. It was the weight in them. A child's eyes should not carry such ages. Even teenagers.

"I am what's left," the girl made of silver said. "Of something beautifully made and broken by fear. I'm a Silver Child, from the age before Dreamers had laws. Before the gods locked the gates. Before they erased us."

Her voice dipped lower. "Zeus made sure of that. Said we were dangerous. Said we could undo the order he bled to create."

Piper's brow tightened. "Why would *he* fear you?" She couldn't believe she was speaking about Zeus as if he were real.

"Because I was the Cloner." She lifted her wrists and red strands fell from them.

Cloner?

"I could split the strands of dreams as the Fates weave the strands of life. We could give mortals second chances. We could make dreams last longer than the gods wanted them to. Zeus wanted endings. He wanted limits and we refused him."

The red strands quivered between her fingers like something alive and angry. "So, he punished us. Hunted us. The ones he didn't destroy, he locked away. I've been here ever since, watching ages of dreams and gods pass by."

Her pale eyes found Piper, and something in their focus made her feel skinned to the soul.

"You're not like the others," she said softly. "You're still warm. Your strand is unclaimed. Do you know what that means?"

Piper shook her head, her throat too dry for words.

"It means he would hate you too," the girl said, her voice

softening into something friendly. "Because you're dangerous, whether you want to be or not. You could unmake what he's built. You are strong enough to make your own rules."

The words slipped into her like water through cracks, finding all the hollow places she'd never been able to fill.

Piper stilled.

"You don't belong in your world," the girl continued. "Not really. I can feel it on you—the way you've been waiting for something you can't name. You've been told that waiting makes you nothing. In the Dreamworld, that means you're ready."

The girl waited. Piper swallowed hard. "I don't know how to help you," she finally breathed.

"You already are," the girl whispered. "You must finish what was started. Follow the Motif River. It will take you to the Elphiates. That's where I am. What is left of *us*."

"Elphiates?" Piper repeated, tasting the unfamiliar word.

The girl's eyes widened with what could be tears, or just a molten brightness Piper didn't understand. "Promise me. Come before they do."

"They?"

From somewhere deep in the forest, a low note rang from a lyre. It was so beautiful it ached, but so sharp it warned. The Silver Girl clearly heard it too because she stiffened, her gaze darting toward the dark beyond the silver trees.

"They know."

The words were not out loud this time but spoken in Piper's mind.

"What—"

Before Piper could finish her words, or even a full train of thought, the Silver Girl's hand lifted, a red strand unspooling across the space between them. She reached for Piper like a lifeline—

The red strand snapped.

Piper jerked upright in bed, lungs burning as if she'd broken the surface after drowning. Raindrops whispered against the window.

The dream was already slipping away, except for one thing: A warm tingle at her wrist.

She looked down. Faint but precise, a spiral of red dust curled like a bracelet just removed. It shimmered in the dim light.

"It was just a dream," she said, though the words fell empty in the quiet.

Dreams didn't leave physical marks.

She yanked her sleeve down, but the Silver Girl's voice stayed, wound around her thoughts like a thread.

Follow the Motif River. Come before they do. You don't belong in your world...

CHAPTER SIX
THE LETTER P

Piper lurched awake from the faint *clink* of something hitting glass. She blinked into the dark, listening. Another pebble tapped the pane.

A whisper floated up from below, stretching her name in the dark: "Piiiper."

She threw back the blanket and crept to the window, unlatching the distorted frame. The hinges groaned in protest as she pushed it open. Down in the yard, moonlight caught on a familiar face—Morry Ovid—standing at the base of the old oak, hand poised with another rock.

"Piper, Piper, wherefore art thou, Piper?" Her best friend called softly, lifting his arms in mock tragedy. "Deny thy Olympus House and refuse thy bedtime."

She stifled a laugh. "You're insane."

"I'm committed," he corrected, already grabbing the lowest branch. "And if you don't come down, I'm climbing this tree like the good old days... barefoot, middle of winter, and risking hypothermia just to see your face after a week's voyage away."

"You'll break your neck trying that at this age," she hissed.

She was unable to keep from smiling as she tried to keep her voice down and get on to him.

He grinned up at her. "Woah, woah, I am not *that* old!"

Piper laughed in whisper as her heart tugged at the memory—fifteen years old, sneaking out at midnight to race across the roof or hunt for constellations they'd made up names for. They weren't teenagers anymore. They were adults. She had 'work' in the morning. The idea of shimmying down an oak tree should have sounded ridiculous.

"Come on," he urged, voice low and warm. "I'm not here to talk about classes or responsible life choices. I'm here to steal you for one night. Roof races. Chocolate raids. Maybe even another round of Penelope and the great teepee incident. You know—like in the good old days."

She groaned. "She still hasn't forgiven *you* for that."

"Exactly," he said, his eyes glinting. "If you are true to your word about leaving here soon, you need to get out of the house. Must make it count." On any other occasion, she might have been offended, but she knew what he meant. Since he went to university, they hadn't done something like this. Act young again.

She hesitated for a sliver of a moment, arms braced on the sill, weighing sense against the ache to feel that wild, roof-breathing freedom again. The choice was over before she admitted it.

"Fine," she said, disappearing from the window. A moment later, she stepped out the front door, a coat thrown over her pajamas.

Morry was waiting in the darkness, his smile crooked.

"See?" he said, holding out his hand. "No tree-climbing necessary."

"You're still ridiculous," she muttered, taking it anyway.

"Yeah," he said, leading her toward the dark yard. "Ridiculously charming."

They stood before the small graveyard they'd found years ago, hidden behind a tangle of ivy and a wrought-iron fence that no one bothered to mend. In the heart of Dublin, it felt oddly apart from everything. A place that existed after midnight. They came here sometimes, for reasons neither of them ever said out loud.

The night was cold enough that their breath lingered in the air. Above, the new moon slipped in and out of thin clouds, silvering the frost on the fence.

"Climb over," Morry murmured, glancing at the padlocked gate.

Piper arched a brow. "You're serious?"

"Always." His grin was all trouble. "Now step on my knee."

She gave a reluctant shake of her head, but when he bent down, she didn't resist. His hands slid briefly to her waist as he lifted her over, his touch light but certain. She landed less than gracefully, the damp winter grass soaking into her pajama pants. Before she could brush herself off, Morry hurdled over in one clean motion, landing beside her without a sound.

"Still got it," he said, that easy charm rolling off him.

They wandered in among the gravestones, the ground uneven beneath their boots. Names had worn away, some stones leaning at precarious angles. A few graves had been claimed by wildflowers, their frost-tipped petals trembling in the wind. The air smelled faintly of earth and something older, like the inside of a locked vault that hadn't been opened in ages.

She hadn't even noticed he was carrying a backpack when Morry pulled out a bottle of wine, already uncorked. "For the occasion," he said simply.

"The occasion being…?" she asked, eyeing it.

He just smirked and handed it to her. "Drink first, questions later."

She took the bottle but didn't lift it yet narrowing her eyes. "I thought you were out of town."

"We cut it short this year," Morry said with a shrug. "Mum's side was in London before Christmas—very proper, very British. Spent a few days here for Christmas, then spent New Year's in Edinburgh with Dad's family. Bagpipes, whiskey. The whole lot, you know."

He eyed the bottle. "Now drink."

The label read *Phantom*. It was a tangle of black branches vanishing into fog. *Ironic*, she thought, given where they were.

She raised it anyway and took a sip. The wine was warm and sharp against the cold, cutting straight through her chest. Morry walked past the tombstones like a labyrinth, winding and weaving as any clearly tipsy young adult would.

"I don't know why you always want to come here," she said, following his steps.

"I like it," he replied, eyes skimming the graveyard like he was mapping it in his head. "It's quiet. No one bothers us. I like…" he trailed off, his gaze sliding back to her, "…watching you here."

Her pulse stumbled, but she looked away before he could see it in her face. "That's creepy," she said lightly.

"Probably," he agreed, taking the bottle back and drinking deeply.

They kept walking, weaving between the stones. Morry read the names aloud in a half-whisper.

"Brandt Elias. Liora Morrin. Caelum Reed." Each name sounded like it belonged to someone she might have known in another life.

"You ever think about it?" he asked suddenly.

"About what?"

"That we're just…two people who'll end up names on stone one day. Maybe no one will come read them."

Piper met his gaze. "You've been drinking too much."

"Maybe," he said, but didn't look away. He smiled that half-smile that kept her guessing, handed her the bottle, and said, "Your turn."

"Okay, I took it. Now tell me."

They were nearing the last tombstone in the row, the one that had yet to be engraved. Piper's boots brushed frost-bitten grass as she slowed, waiting. Morry trailed a hand along the stone's cold surface.

"Poor letter P," he said with mock solemnity. "Whoever gets this spot, may the gods above or below bless their soul."

"Morry…" She arched a brow. "The suspense is killing me."

He glanced up at her, a flicker of something unreadable passing over his face. "Do you know what today is?" His voice had shifted. It was quieter, less of the showman he usually was.

Piper frowned, glancing at the sky. Midnight had probably come and gone. "Christmas," she said, the words tasting more bitter than she intended.

He shook his head, lowering himself to sit on the damp grass. The cold didn't seem to bother him. He sprawled back against a tombstone, arms open against the earth, the kind of careless pose only Morry could make look intentional. "Nope," he said, patting the ground beside him. "Sit."

She hesitated—her light coat was no match for the wet, winter ground—then sat, knees pulled tight to her chest.

"So what day is it?"

"It's the day we met," he said, his gaze steady now. "Five years ago."

Her heart stuttered. *Five years.*

Piper remembered the day she met Morry like it was yesterday…

She was fifteen, standing outside the back door of Olympus House with a jump rope in one hand, freezing in the damp December air. The cold bit through her sleeves, but she lingered, staring at the glow of Dublin's streetlamps over the stone wall surrounding the grounds, wishing she didn't have to live here.

"Oi," a voice called from the alley.

She turned, startled, to see a boy—she later learned he was sixteen—leaning on his bike, scarf crooked, and hair damp despite the cold. His autumn eyes, even then, were sharp and searching, like he'd already decided they would be friends.

"You live here?" he asked, nodding toward the building behind her.

The question made heat prickle in her cheeks. She tightened her grip on the jump rope. "Why?"

He shrugged. "Just asking. I think my cousin stayed there once." Piper knew that couldn't be true but decided not to say that out loud.

"Good for him," she muttered, looking away, wishing she'd worn gloves, or better yet, that she'd gone back inside before anyone saw her.

Instead of pressing, he grinned and stepped over a puddle, closer to her. "You know, from the outside, it looks like where Dracula lives. Do you have lights in there? Do you have red and black robes? Please tell me you at least have a talking bat."

A laugh slipped out before she could stop it. "It's not Transylvania."

"Shame," he said, leaning on the handlebars. "Guess I'll cancel my enrollment form."

Only then did he glance at the jump rope in her hand. "Jumping alone?"

"I prefer it that way." *That was a lie.* "Usually." He had a nice bike while she had an old jump rope. How appealing she looked.

He nodded but said nothing about it. "So, you're stuck in there?" he asked, tilting his head toward the lit windows of Olympus House.

"Sometimes."

"Well, if you're ever looking to get unstuck..." He gestured toward his bike.

For reasons she didn't understand then—except maybe that he'd made her laugh when she wanted to hide—she said yes.

Shortly after, she followed him into the city until her curfew, and from that day on, it no longer mattered that she didn't have the kind of home other children did, because she'd found the one person who made her waking world feel like home.

Back in the graveyard, the memory slipped away.

"How do you even remember the day?" Piper asked softly.

"Because it changed everything," he said simply. He smirked, softer than usual. "Why else do you think I dragged us out here in the middle of the night with a bottle of wine in a vaguely gothic atmosphere?"

She shook her head, hiding a small smile. "We've never celebrated it before."

"I know." He tipped his head back, eyes on the starry sky. "I wanted to this year. Before everything changes. Before we *really* must grow up." He winked at her, which made her blush.

"You've been saying that a lot lately," she said. There had to be a thousand stars out on this night.

"Because it's true," he replied. "I'm twenty-one in March. You turned twenty in September. You keep talking about how *next year* you'll finally go—travel, leave Olympus House, see the world. Yet, you're still here. No offense." He hesitated, his gaze catching hers. "So, I thought… Maybe tonight we could steal one more night of being fifteen. Just you and me. No plans. No future. Just the way it was for the past five years."

Her chest tightened. She wished they could go back to those kids running around Dublin, where the city was theirs alone. Then again, back then, she *was* trapped. At least now it was her choice.

"I used to think you told me all those dreams of yours just to pass the time," he said. "That they were an escape from being stuck here. Now I think…" His gaze dipped to the frost-laced grass, then back to her. "Those counseling sessions…" He stopped, and she knew why.

That was not a fun time. He knew how long it took her to stop having nightmares from the fire that put her in Olympus House in the first place. He always listened, but never said anything about any of it. It was like he was trying to keep from sharing too much of his own past experiences, though she wasn't sure how their past lives could have been similar at all. He had a real family. Piper did not. Maybe that *was* why he didn't speak about it.

She swallowed hard, caught between wanting to deflect and wanting to tell him what she had been dreaming recently. She had told him about her dreams for years, but more recently, she was nervous that he wouldn't see her the same way.

"Morry—"

"I've been buried in books at Trinity," he continued, voice soft. "Plato says the soul remembers truths from before we were born. Kant says reality is just perception. And lately—"

he gave a short laugh "—I keep thinking about your silver-eyed girl, the lion having its mane cut, those stars that change shape when you look at them. The way you describe them. It is always the same, every time. That's not how dreams work, Piper. That's how memories from trauma work."

Her breath caught. She'd never thought he'd remembered all those details.

Morry leaned forward, elbows on his knees. His autumn eyes shone in the dark.

"You know what Aristotle said about dreams? That they're the mind's way of showing you truths you ignore when you're awake. Freud thought they were wish fulfillment. Jung said they were messages from the deep—symbols guiding you to where you need to be."

She gave him a look, a knot forming in her throat. "You've been doing too much reading."

"Too much studying, you mean. I had to learn all of that to pass my Foundation Scholarship Examination, and trust me, *that* was a beating, so bear with me. What I am saying is that when I put those theories against your dreams, they all fit. Every one of them."

For a moment, they just looked at each other. Close enough for his shoulder to brush hers if either of them leaned in. Neither did at first.

Then Morry tilted forward, slow but certain, and before she could think better of it, his lips grazed hers. Piper let it happen, just long enough for warmth to spark, but then she pressed a hand against his chest and pulled back.

He gave her a crooked grin, though it didn't quite reach his eyes. "It's not like we haven't done that before."

"Yeah," Piper said, her voice sharper than she meant. "Look how that turned out. We didn't speak for months. You said we were just friends."

Something flickered across his face, the smile faltering, then gone in a flash. "Everyone has their three loves. I guess I am just the first, but timing seems to never be on our side." He winked, fixing the awkward moment between them like he always did.

Still a long silence fell between them.

"I wanted this night," he finally spoke up, leaning back against the cold stone, "because when things do change, and Piper, I feel change is happening soon. It is just a gut feeling…" he shrugged, "I don't want us to change. Not entirely. Not our relationship. *Not this.*"

He pointed around them. He was being so sentimental, which was unlike him. He was the fun lighthearted one. She was the serious one.

She eyed him up and down, but he was already facing the night sky, relaxation on his features. She tilted her own head back, letting the winter sky consume her. The stars were endless.

There was another long silence before either of them spoke. "See the Big Dipper?" Morry traced the shape in the air with his finger. Piper nodded.

"Most people stop there, but if you follow it, you find the Little Dipper. I always thought of them as mother and son. She's big, bright, easy to find. Where he is smaller, quieter, but still tethered to her by that same patch of sky. They're apart but connected. Can't have one without the other."

She glanced at him, the way his voice softened when he said it.

"I don't know why," he continued, "but I've always felt connected to them. Like they are more than just stars, you know? Like they are always watching over me. I notice them every time I look into the night sky."

He leaned his head back until it rested against the stone. "What about you? What's your favorite constellation?"

Piper thought for a moment, her breath clouding in the cold. "The black stars," she said finally.

He frowned, half-smiling. "There's no such thing as black stars."

"Not ones you can see," she clarified. "The ones you know are there anyway. Hidden in the spaces between the bright ones. The ones you feel. You just know they are there even if you don't see them."

Morry followed her gaze into the dark, saying nothing.

Piper didn't tell him that in her dreams, those dark spaces weren't empty. That sometimes in the distance of her dreams, the black stars moved, intertwining themselves into shapes no waking eye could follow.

She didn't tell him that she was starting to think those stars weren't missing at all but were waiting to come out of the darkness.

Those parts of her dreams she kept to herself.

CHAPTER SEVEN
THE RED EYES

"You have to come back."

The voice came before the world did. It was an echo that pulled Piper out of a darkness deeper than sleep. It felt weighted.

When her eyes opened, the silver forest had returned. Silver lit bark shimmered on towering trees, the glowing river curling nearby in its endless loop. Ash drifted down like stardust, catching in the branches before dissolving.

Time here didn't move, but it waited. So did she.

The Silver Girl stood barefoot on the far bank, her stardust robe clinging like mist, the quicksilver seams along it pulsing faintly. Piper had seen her before—in other dreams, in other nights—but something was different. Urgency had replaced stillness. Her hands trembled at her sides, and her pale eyes, which were unreadable before, were stricken with something close to fear.

"You came back," Piper breathed, the words tangled with awe and apology.

"I never left," the girl replied. "I knew you'd return."

"How could you know that?"

"Because your strand is tied to this place. To *us*. Whether you understand it all." Her voice thinned. "And the more you wake, the more the tether frays."

"I had to wake up," Piper said.

"No." The word was sharp. "You *chose* to."

The air between them shifted, heavy.

"You always choose to leave," the Silver Girl said more quietly now.

"I didn't think I had a choice," Piper whispered.

"You do. You are more than a human." The girl's gaze cut into her. "You're a Dreamer and Dreamers don't have to wake."

The word *Dreamer* hung in the air like a brand. Colik had said it. The Routs were one themselves. Here, from her, it felt heavier—like it carried weight beyond a name.

"I don't even know what that means. I am not a Dreamer."

The girl didn't say anything, but turned her eyes toward the river, where its surface changed.

A frost-covered garden shimmered into view. Penelope, kneeling in the cold, brushing snow from roses that looked too far gone to save. Then chalk drawings appeared—spirals, stars, and her name scratched over and over in cracked sidewalk script by small, determined hands.

"They remember you," the Silver Girl said. "Even when you forget yourself."

Piper's chest tightened.

"They talk about you," the girl continued. "As if saying your name will keep you from fading. As if you're still there."

"I *am* still there," Piper whispered. "When I'm awake."

"Yet you are here when you're asleep."

The river shifted again. Penelope was still there, but the image flickered, rippling into another scene. A shadowed figure leaning close, speaking her name. The features blurred, unformed, as if the dream itself didn't want her to see too much. A faint warmth weaved through her chest, a pull that was achingly familiar, though she couldn't place it.

"Why me?" she asked. "Why am I tied to *this*?" She still wasn't sure what *this* was.

"Because you heard me," the girl said. "Because you felt the pull. You aren't just dreaming, Piper. You are searching. That's rare. That's hope."

Her voice dropped lower. "You're not only being pulled by me. Someone else in your world is reaching for you. If you don't follow it—if you don't help—bad things will happen. To both worlds."

The forest groaned.

"Please," the girl made of molten silver said, her form fraying at the edges, the glow in her eyes dimming. "Promise you'll come back. Promise you'll find me before this age falls apart too."

"I don't even know how to stay here," Piper said.

"You'll need help," the girl told her. "In both worlds. Someone already knows. When the moment comes…they may be the one to bring you back."

Her throat tightened. "Who?"

The girl was already fading, her body scattering into silver dust.

"If you wait too long," her voice warned faintly, "the strand will break. I will come apart and so will you."

Then she was gone, the silence folding over the forest like a closing book.

Piper's breath came fast, the echo of the girl's voice still ringing in her ears. It was urgent. Trembling. Pleading.

Promise you'll find me before this age falls apart too. The words clung to her like the mist curling between the silver-barked trees.

"I'll come back," Piper whispered into the empty air just as the dream faded.

Piper woke slowly, her body frozen for a breath before her eyelids flickered.

The first light of dawn slipped through her eyelids, drawing her up from the dream of the Silver Girl. She'd tried to forget it, to bury the call that still echoed faintly in her chest, but it clung to every fiber of her being.

She blinked against the pale winter light. The sky was rinsing itself into soft silver, and frost curled over the edges of nearby tombstones. Morry was still asleep beside her, his breath steady, a curl of black hair fallen over his eyes.

For a moment, she almost woke him in a panic. Then she remembered that no one at Olympus House was checking her bed. No rules to break anymore, no curfew to race home to.

She sat up, her coat pulling at the shoulders, and nudged his arm gently. "Morning," she said.

He groaned and rolled over, blinking into the frost-bright air. "Already?"

"It's Christmas," she said. "We both have things to do."

Morry stretched. "Yeah. Guess we do."

They didn't rush, cutting through the back streets of Dublin, the city half-asleep, and the air so cold it made their breath spiral like smoke. The frost hadn't lifted, only thickened, curling around the lamplight and swallowing their footsteps.

"I had another weird dream," Piper said at last, her voice carrying in the stillness. She decided maybe she could tell him.

He glanced at her. "Oh yeah?"

"It was different this time. There was the same Silver Girl I've seen before, but she spoke to me. She said that I could choose to stay in that world if I wanted. Said I had to find her… in my dreams."

He didn't speak right away.

"I think she's trapped," Piper went on. "I think she was pulling me in. Like she's been waiting for me." Saying it out loud made it sound ridiculous, but the chill that ran through her as she said it was real.

Morry slowed his pace until he stopped. "You're serious."

"Of course I'm serious."

He looked up at the early morning sky for an answer. "Piper, I wanted you out here to get some air, not…" He trailed off. "I thought maybe if you got out of that house, you'd remember what dreams we had as children… not now."

"*I am* remembering," she said quietly. "That's the problem."

His mouth tightened. "You don't think it's strange? Dreams pulling you while you're awake. A girl made of silver calling you. That's not—"

"Normal?" she said, sharper now. "No, but it's still happening."

He met her gaze, and for a moment she thought he might argue. Then he sighed. "I don't think you're crazy. But dreams bleeding into your life like this. That's not something I can explain anymore."

They walked again, slower, until the crooked gates of Olympus House came into view.

"You remember when we were sixteen?" he said suddenly. "That dream you told me about when you were a child, about the lion with the mane being cut off."

She nodded, suddenly feeling like that dream had resurfaced recently.

"On your eighteenth birthday, you told me how that night you dreamed of the snake in the glass room, coiled around a white, glowing tree staring at you from all directions."

A prickling ran up her arms.

"I think they really are *just* dreams Piper," he said. "The lion, the snake, this Silver Girl—they're also symbolic. The lion guards what shouldn't be known. The snake whispers what shouldn't be spoken."

He stopped at the gate. "Them repeating just means that your dreams are trying to tell you something. Not *about* another world. About *this* one."

Piper's lips parted, but she didn't argue. For some innate feeling, she didn't agree with what he was saying, but she listened to him as if she did.

"Maybe they're mirrors," he went on. "People dream about what they can't say when they're awake. Maybe your brain's sounding an alarm, telling you something's wrong."

She swallowed. "The train was made from the gods," she murmured.

Morry frowned. "What train?"

She didn't answer.

He stepped closer. "Piper, promise me you won't lose yourself in this when you do finally choose to leave Olympus House. Don't let these dreams take you somewhere I can't follow."

She nodded, though deep down, she already knew she couldn't stop it.

He tried to smile. "I guess if you do stray too far, stay grounded long enough for me to catch up, alright?"

"I will," she said softly, but truthfully. If anything was keeping her grounded here, it was him.

He hugged her, a warmth against the cold morning. She held on longer than she meant to.

"I should go," he said. "Mum will bring the whole kitchen to flames if I don't go help."

She watched him walk away, swallowed by ice and mist. Then she turned toward Olympus House, its cracked walls and rusted gate waiting for her, when all she wanted was to leave it behind.

It was still barely morning, the sky a dull gray pressed against the windows. Piper slipped quietly through the back door of the food hall at Olympus House, her breath catching at the familiar creak of the hinge. Her fingers trembled as she pushed into the drafty corridor.

The old instinct to be quiet, to move like she was breaking a rule, crept back in, though there were no rules for her anymore. Still, her body remembered. She'd learned to avoid the common room in the mornings, where the younger children played, where Ailin taught, and where Penelope sometimes read by lamplight.

She rounded the corner when voices drifted from the kitchen. Low and urgent, it was the kind of whispers that made her freeze. Nosiness taking over, she pressed herself against the wall, breath shallow, listening.

"I think she is ready to leave." Ailin's voice was quiet but firm.

"She's not ready," Penelope's voice snapped. "And I don't want her to leave."

"She can't stay here forever." They were talking about her.

"I'm trying to keep her safe."

"Safe from what?" Ailin challenged.

Penelope's pause was sharp enough to feel. "You know what. You saw what happened that night."

Piper's pulse quickened.

"She can't build a life in these walls," Ailin pressed. "She needs to figure out where she's going, what she wants. She's already restless. The longer we hold her here, the more it's going to feel like we're hiding something."

Penelope's voice hardened. "We *are* hiding something. For her sake."

"Penelope—"

"Don't," she warned. "You weren't the one holding her when they pulled her from the flames."

Flames. Piper's stomach tightened. She tried not to remember even the little bit she did of that night.

Ailin's tone softened. "I know. That was sixteen years ago. She can't live in the darkness of that fire forever."

"It wasn't just a fire," Penelope whispered.

"No, it wasn't."

There was silence.

"What are you not telling me, Ailin?" Penelope's voice was more tense than Piper had ever heard it before, even when scolding the children.

Ailin was silent for a beat before speaking again. "Her mother died giving birth. Her father…he didn't die. He left. Maybe he came back that night. Maybe it was him in her room. We don't know if it was a man at all."

Penelope's breath hitched. "What did you just say?"

Piper could hear Ailin hesitate.

"You told me both her parents were gone," she said, her voice trembling with disbelief before hardening into anger. "You told me she had no one."

"I found out later," Ailin admitted quietly. "When I filed her papers for Olympus House. Her mother's death certificate was there, but no record of the father—just a note, unsigned. I didn't want to tell you because I know what she means to you."

Piper's heart thudded in her chest.

What the hell?

Her father had been alive but left her. The fire hadn't been an accident and the figure with red eyes—real or dream—had been there when she was a child. She'd had nightmares about red eyes before, only now remembering it.

More silence.

Then a chair scraped against the floor, and she jumped a little. "You should have told me. You should have *told her.* She's spent her whole life believing *someone* might come back for her." Penelope's voice was forcefully hushed.

"I thought it was easier for her to believe that," Ailin said, his voice fraying. "Easier to think someone cared enough to return." He drew a slow breath, then lowered his tone, the weight of memory pulling it down. "The fire…it doesn't make sense. The reports said it started in her room, but there was something else. A dust storm. Black sand in the air and in the corner… someone watching. With red eyes, though I think that had to be some typo in the file. It stated, *'The red eyes were gone the moment the ceiling caught flame.'*"

Penelope gasped. "How would that even be in the report? Who could have written that in there?"

Piper had her hand over her mouth so she wouldn't gasp out loud.

She sensed more hesitation. "That's what unsettled me. The line wasn't typed. It was handwritten, like someone added it later. Barely legible, scrawled in ink that didn't match the rest."

Piper heard Penelope sigh. "Someone *wanted* that note there."

"Or wanted it found," Ailin said grimly. "Either way, it wasn't official and that worries me."

"You think whoever it was…came for her?"

Ailin didn't answer. He didn't need to. The silence said enough.

"I've always wondered what was looking for her," Penelope finally whispered. She sounded exhausted. "Someone was chasing us that night. I felt it."

"We may never know," Ailin said, just as quietly. "If she leaves without knowing the truth, we can't protect her. I don't even know if we can now."

Piper's chest tightened as their words sank in. It felt like the walls had leaned closer, like someone—or something—was coming to claim her, and she was terrified of who that could be. If it was true, if something had been after her that night, what would it want with her?

Those dreams of hers felt too real now. Too vivid to ignore. She'd always told herself they were just dreams, nothing more, because Penelope *convinced* her they were. Now she knew why. What if they weren't? What if whoever, or whatever, was still waiting to finish what it started?

She stumbled back from the door before they could hear her. The hallway tilted under her feet as she moved away from the kitchen, past the stairs, until her knees buckled outside her bedroom.

She slid down against the cold wooden door.

Penelope's love had always been a shelter. Tonight, it felt like a lock, and Ailin, the key turned against her. She knew they meant to protect her, but what if they couldn't? What if she was the only one who could?

Piper's stomach tightened, her breath catching as tears blurred her vision. Their words—the fire, the storm, the eyes —echoed until they no longer sounded like fear, but like a call.

Everything led back to the one place that had ever felt like it was truly hers: Her dreams.

There was a sudden white flash, a lightning strike behind my eyes, and then, silence.

My eyes fluttered beneath closed lids, rapid and restless, still tied to the rhythms of waking life. My mind was slipping deeper and downward, past the edge of sleep, past dreams, past even thought.

I was falling and floating all at once. Not dreaming. Not awake. Somewhere in between.

I couldn't feel my limbs or my weight, only motion. A gentle, invisible tug, as though a string was laced through my being, pulling me in every direction. Each strand was a whisper, calling me. One strand pulled stronger than the rest. It was red, trembling, and insistent, so I followed it.

The world around me unraveled into starlight. The air shimmered with constellations, shifting and alive.

Orion blinked out.

Pegasus galloped across a field of black.

The Little Dipper tipped forward, spilling light like water.

Then they vanished, and in their place came visions, scattered scenes stitched from memory or myth.

The Ollopa train glided by on glowing tracks through the heavens, its windows burning with faces I'd never seen.

The jagged roof of Olympus House glistened like a mirrored slate in the clouds.

A crow perched on the broken clock tower, cawing into the wind.

Penelope smiled from behind her computer, her eyes weary and exhausted.

I reached for them, but they too scattered like dust, untouchable.

Were these memories? Echoes of the waking world? Or dreams unraveling from my past?

Everything was moving. Time pulsed in strange rhythms. A moment stretched like a lifetime, then vanished in a blink.

The stars bent toward me, folding all around me, until for a moment, I was part of them. My shape stretched across the heavens, my skin dissolving into a thousand points of light. My veins became the glowing lines between constellations. I could feel the red strand weaving from my burning wrist through my very core, binding my dust to the map of the sky.

I began to come apart. My bones, my breath, every cell peeled away into dust. My body was scattering outward, my human form unmaking itself, the pull of gravity loosening until nothing held me but the red strand.

It led straight ahead, into a doorway of curved horn and swirling ash.

I crossed, every grain of me swept through into a place where the dust was denser, stranger, and aged.

It rushed into me like breath, filling the spaces where my own dust had drifted away, shaping me into something both familiar and foreign— somewhere in between.

CHAPTER EIGHT
THE REFLECTION

Piper braced herself for the familiar jolt of awakening, but to her astonishment, a quiet calm filled her instead. Her skin still hummed with starlight, the red strand still burning faintly beneath it. Tingles ran throughout her entire body as if the stars themselves had sewn her back together. Her boots sank into a carpet of crystal moss, cool and whispering against her skin. Tiny motes of light floated upward.

When she inhaled, a sharp, clean scent filled her lungs, carrying something faintly nostalgic, like the first night she ever looked up at the stars and believed they might be looking back.

Suddenly, her body flickered, and she found herself back in the woods of this strange new *dream* world.

"I did it," she breathed with a half-laugh, half-gasp, shoving the waking-world conversation she just overheard from her mind like it was something she could physically push away. She had gotten used to that.

She looked up, and the black-and-silver trees bent slightly toward her, their long trunks curving, acknowledging her arrival. The entire forest breathed with slow, celestial rhythm.

The gold-flecked river murmured softly in its endless curl, but the Silver Girl was not there. That was a first.

She couldn't move, still rooted to the dream like the air itself had bound her, but she didn't fight it. Instead, she breathed it in, the taste of metallic and moonlight catching at her tongue, the delicate sting of drifting ash brushing her skin. Along with a smile, a shiver ran through her, having known that she'd crossed some invisible line, and there would be no easy way back. Or desire, since it felt harder to get—

"What are you doing here?" a voice asked, breaking her thoughts.

She turned to see the boy—or rather the hot, irksome young man—from the Ollopa train hovering astride a translucent, stingray-like beast, its silent wings undulating through the air. Together, the beast and Colik were a regal storm cloud.

"Do you always drop in unannounced, or is this just a hobby of yours?" Piper asked, unapologetically. The creature made no sound as it circled above, but its presence filled the clearing like lightning just out of reach.

"I could ask the same," Colik said. "You seem to be making it a habit of slipping past places humans don't belong."

"And it happens to be your job to stop me?"

"My role, yes." His smile faded. "It kind of is." The creature circled overhead.

Piper wasn't expecting that response. "You were sent to retrieve me?" she pressed.

"You catch on quick."

"I'm not cargo."

"And I'm not a shepherd," he said, brushing dust from his sleeve. "Yet, here we are." He sighed and dismounted his beast. The ground rippled faintly under his boots, dust curling upward as his feet hit the ground.

The beast hovered close, casting a glassy shadow over

them both. Its massive fin-like wings barely moved, but Piper could feel the pressure.

"You just happened to know I was here then, *huh?*" she asked, her heart racing. He was circling her like a vulture on foot, and she didn't like it.

His jaw tightened. "I wasn't expecting you."

"So, you admit you were waiting for me?"

"I didn't say that."

"You didn't *not* say it."

He gave a slow exhale, stepping closer. The beast floated behind him like a ghost, glowing veins pulsing faintly beneath its skin. It was both stunning and terrifying.

She tilted her head at the creature. "Hiding behind a pet now, are we?"

"It's not a pet. It's a loyal guide. Like I'm supposed to be."

Her smile turned razor-edged. "Oh, *you're* the guide? Comforting."

"You really are sharp."

"Years of practice," she replied. "Mostly from surviving idiots."

"Then this will be fun."

"You're enjoying this," she accused.

"Define *this.*"

"This back-and-forth. You said shepherd, so I'd say you are trying to wrangle me like a lost sheep."

He smirked. "If the sheep is heading for the lion's den, then yeah."

The words sent a strange chill through her. He stepped closer, and again, something lifted from her skin. A shimmer, a breath. Something less than air but more than thought.

"What are you doing?" she whispered.

He blinked. "What?"

"Never mind."

He didn't press.

"Why are you here, really?"

His voice was low. "Because if I don't take you… Someone else will."

"So, you're telling me that *you are* the nice one?"

"Relatively."

The stingray-beast dipped lower behind him, its shadow falling over him. The dust on the ground shimmered.

"Where would you take me?"

"The Citadel."

"Sounds ominous."

"Not if you cooperate."

"Oh, that clears it up." She scoffed. "Let's go. I am ready!" She rolled her eyes.

"Humans," he muttered, and smiled sarcastically. "This wasn't how it was supposed to go."

"What does that mean?"

"I thought I'd find someone broken, ready to wake up. Like I said…" His eyes held hers. "Not you."

"Flattery won't work either," she said.

Silence.

"Piper, you are not supposed to be here," he finally spoke, his features telling her had some crazy revelation in his head. Him saying her name did things to her she did not want to admit out loud.

"Maybe I get to decide that, thank you very much."

Colik let out a slow breath, pinching the bridge of his nose like he was debating what to do with her. "This would be easier if you were some sleepwalker, but no, you have to be difficult." He looked her up and down again. "That is what we call you humans who dream normal dreams, if you didn't catch on."

"I did." She did not.

Long silence.

"I'm not going unless I choose to."

"I gathered that much," he muttered, finally meeting her eyes again. "And that complicates things."

"Then ask me. Politely."

He laughed. "You think I'm built for polite?"

"You could pretend I have a choice."

His smile softened. "You do."

"Prove it."

Colik gave a low growl and turned to his stingray beast. "I'm here because something's missing in your world. We can help you find it. And if you can't... I'll help you back." He grunted and slipped his fingers through his white, silky, looking hair. Piper turned away but hesitated at his words. That was too close to the truth.

As she watched his features, something in his eyes softened. There was a flicker of conflict, but that was all she needed to see or hear to give in.

Her gaze dropped to her unmoving feet, her voice softening with dry sarcasm. "Well then, Colik, first hurdle... How do we get me to move?" She tried to take another step, but the world didn't yield. The ground beneath her shimmered faintly, like it was waiting for permission.

Colik looked at her, at her feet, then back to her eyes. "Guess we start with that," he said with a smirk. "Do you want to move?"

"Yes..." she answered slowly, unsure of the counterproductive question. She *wanted* it to be. She didn't know this world and what it could possibly do for her. Or to her.

"Then say it like you mean it and feel the frequency around you. That's how it works here," he said. "Desire, not logic."

"Like magic?"

"We call it frequency while humans call it *magic*." He put the word magic in air quotes.

Ignoring him, Piper took a deep breath and tried to imagine her legs unlocking. The image wasn't just a thought, but a pull, like something deep inside her was answering.

She closed her eyes. "I want to move."

"Then move."

"How—" Her body had already acted. She exaggerated the motion and toppled forward slightly, her foot catching in the soft moss. Before she fell, Colik's hand found her arm, steadying her. Again.

She didn't thank him this time.

"How…" she repeated, and Colik gave a quick laugh.

The moss under her boots glowed faintly, a silvery pulse trailing behind where she had stepped. The Dreamworld was accepting her now.

She took another step.

"It worked! I moved!" she exclaimed, the words slipping out with a smile she hadn't felt in a while. It was hard to find reasons to smile at Olympus House. It just was that way of living.

Another step. Then another. Like a child learning balance for the first time, she tested the world, and the world bent to her desire.

"Now will you trust me?" Colik asked, eyes wide. He lifted both palms beside him in a gesture of mock innocence.

Her heart fluttered—once, twice. Darn him and his looks, his eyes and his smug, maddening confidence.

Finally, she exhaled. "Okay."

His brow lifted. "Okay, what?"

"I'll go," she said, brushing past him.

"You will?"

"Don't make it weird," she said. "If I fall, I'm blaming you and your beast."

Colik smirked again, moving into step beside her. "You won't fall."

"Why not?"

"Haven't you caught on? Because I'm watching."

"Creepy."

"Dutiful. Maybe even protective."

"Still creepy."

Colik turned and started walking. His laugh echoed through the dream air, the beast trailing behind him—silent, loyal, and watchful.

Piper hesitated for a heartbeat before following. She tried to ignore the awe tugging at her chest. As much as she hated to admit it, wandering alone here would be naive. Or just stupid. When Morry went off to university, she promised him that she wouldn't do anything stupid.

If only Morry could see this place.

They walked in silence along the edge of the silk-like river, its waters glowing, and its depths unclear. The air itself hummed, like a steady echo of some celestial heartbeat. Every leaf above her shivered with secrets. Every shadow moved, aware of their passing.

Piper felt more alive and seen than she had ever felt in her waking world.

The starry sky pulsed faintly overhead, bending gently around them. Just behind Colik, that strange stingray-like beast drifted low, its wings rippling like silk slicing through air. Fluid. Soundless.

Colik hadn't acknowledged it once since dismounting, but still it *followed.*

She slowed her steps, letting distance form between them. "How are you doing that?"

He didn't look at her. "Doing what?"

"The beast. It just follows you."

Colik finally turned, expression unreadable. "It doesn't *follow.* It obeys."

"Tomato, *tomato.*"

He tilted his head. "Excuse me?"

"Nothing." Piper smirked.

Shaking his head, Colik continued, "Dray is called an atmospheric beast. Dream forms born from dust, the same way memories form from experience. They remember who shaped them and obey those to whom they feel most loyal to."

Piper stared at the creature. Its translucent skin shimmered with glowing veins, and now that she was looking closely, she noticed the way it curled slightly toward *her*, sniffing something only it could sense.

Colik gave the slightest nod, and the beast *withdrew*.

"That *Dray*... It knew I was here, didn't it?" she said softly.

"Of course it did," he replied, brushing his coat sleeve where a strand of silver dust clung like static. "It feeds off your dust print. All dream-forms do, in some way. This one is mine."

"Dray," she repeated. "Why, or how, is it yours?"

"Dray recognized what I am."

His look towards her wasn't cruel or cold, but something deeper. Something aware.

"And what *are* you?" she whispered.

Colik didn't answer, but behind him, the beast lifted its great wings, its light pulsing in time with Colik's *breath*.

She shook her head, trying to think this all through rationally. She needed a few moments to try and ground herself. She took a deep inhale and exhale, Colik watching her like he had never seen anything like her.

A few breaths later, Piper finally asked, "How was I able to suddenly move like that?" Her eyes strayed away from the sting-ray beast, Dray.

Colik glanced sideways at her. "In this world, the impossible is simply possible. We call them sleepwalkers who believe this is a dream and wake up. They never try to come back because it was a dream. You didn't and that is rare."

He paused. "Dreamers have gifts like the gods. The power to will something into existence with nothing but desire, choice and divine enforcement."

So, desire meant choice. Choice meant *power*.

Piper blinked, letting the words settle like the subtle dust brushing her skin as they walked on.

Divine enforcement, she repeated in her mind. Something stirred within her bones.

"Why help me then? *A human?* What do you get out of this?" Piper asked, her voice breathless, betraying the curiosity and something else that had been building.

"You know, you ask a lot of questions."

She raised a brow. "You are the only one around here I see that may have answers," she exaggerated looking for someone else around her. "Unless Dray would like to try?" She smirked.

He stifled a laugh at her theatrics. "Fair." Then, with a dip of his chin, he added low and teasing, "*Pipes.*"

Piper blinked. "Did you just—did you just call me *Pipes?*"

Colik burst into laughter, unbothered by her glare. "Oh, come on. That is golden."

"No! That's awful is what it is!" she snapped, cheeks burning. "I'm not a plumbing system!"

He held up his hands in mock defense. "It is meant to be charismatic. Pipes, like Piper, but sassier and louder." He gave her a look that suggested he might be enjoying her flustered reaction a little too much.

Her mouth dropped open. "You're exasperating."

"And yet," he leaned in slightly, eyes glinting, "you're still walking with me."

She crossed her arms, trying not to smirk, but failing. His multi-colored eyes moved from her right green eye to her left. Then his expression fell, the humor fading into something more serious. "I'm choosing to help you because, like I said..." he said slowly, "from what I know about humans, you wouldn't fight so hard to be here if you weren't searching for something you couldn't find in your world."

"How do you know I am fighting to be here?" she asked, holding his gaze. He gave a sneer of a smile, causing her chest to tighten. Something about the way he said it was so certain, and quietly reverent. It made her feel seen, and not in a good way.

"Well, *Pipes*," he started, ignoring her question as if the answer was obvious, and stepped closer until she could feel the warmth of him through the chill breeze, "Why not let me show you what you've been missing in my world?"

Then, with a slow, knowing wink, he turned and started along the river again, leaving Piper breathless, her pulse racing, and the nickname *Pipes* echoing like a dare in her mind.

"How much time has passed?" Piper asked after what felt like hours of wandering. She didn't know if it had been hours, days, some lifetime?

Time *felt* different here. It unraveled in slow motion, feeling soft, silent, and seemingly endless. She kept circling back to what Himyla had warned. Her dust. Her body. The lifeline to the waking world unraveling. Was she already gone? Was she walking in a dream while her real self-turned to ash?

Colik paced beside her, silent. He always stayed a step ahead, but far enough from the river, like he feared its pull.

"You're still thinking in hours," he murmured, eyes forward. "In time."

"Well, yeah," she muttered. "Time matters where I'm from. It dictates the path of my life."

"Time—*the moon*—or humans?" A small smile curved his mouth. It was more melancholy than amused. "Time doesn't live here, Piper. Not like you understand it. There's no sun to chase. No ticking clock. Just frequency. Resonance. Pull."

"Pull?" she echoed.

He lifted his hand, and the air quivered. It was soft and harmonic. A second heartbeat beneath the surface of everything. It moved through her bones.

"This world moves by remembrance. A form of memory dreaming," he said. "When a thought sharpens—when you hurt, or hope—it shifts. That's how the Reverie counts time. Not in hours or minutes. In frequency of moments."

Reverie, Piper mouthed. Himyla said that word. Her eyes moved to her scar. That was what this world was called. She caught herself smiling, despite the eeriness of how she got this mark on her thumb.

Colik looked up through the mushroom top trees, and her eyes followed. Through the branches, a red moon frayed. It was vast, low, and pulsing with a rhythm she could feel in her teeth when she held her gaze on it.

"That's the Blood Moon," Colik said, following her gaze. "Its cycle isn't bound to the day or night like in your world, but to the rise and fall with the frequencies. Each moon pass pulls certain moments toward us and pushes others away. It measures frequency of moments with each cycle."

Piper found herself holding her breath, listening. The Blood Moon's throb was faint at first, like a distant beat, then she realized her own heart had started keeping pace with it. It was a perfect, quiet sync. The longer she matched it, the slower her heartbeat was. Like the moon was trying to slow her down.

She tore her gaze away. "So, if I wake up…?"

"Maybe not even a breath will have passed," Colik replied. "Depends on how many Blood Moon cycles have passed compared to hours there. I have never been to that world to know the correlation." He gave a casual shrug. "In other words, you won't know until you wake up. Do you know how much time passes in *normal* dreams until you wake up?" Piper shook her head. "Same goes with this Dreamworld. A different stage of dreaming, but a dream none the less."

Giving a silent nod, Piper's gaze followed the fall of the leaves, drifting downward until it caught on the ribbon of water winding through the woods. The river's surface mirrored the flickering sky above, but its current moved slower, heavier, as though carrying something unseen beneath.

There was that small, electric wonder she thought she'd outgrown lingering in her chest. She wasn't a child anymore, yet her mind moved with the same tentative awe as if she were seeing a world for the first time. There was that memory from a dream. Again. The girl of silver, standing on this rivers' bank, her form bright and blurred all at once, calling Piper's name like it mattered. She was glad the Silver Girl wasn't there.

Piper's fingers curled against her palm. She wondered if she should tell Colik, but some part of her feared that talking about the Silver Girl out loud might pull her closer.

"That river is called the Motif River, and this part of the Reverie," Colik said, watching her confused gaze at the riverbank, "is called the Broken Woods."

"Because something is wrong with it?" Piper asked, shaking her head at her previous thought. She would tell him about the Silver Girl when it felt appropriate.

"Because everything that finds its way here becomes broken."

She swallowed hard. The moss beneath her feet glowed faintly underneath her hand-me-down boots. Flowers unfurled in slow motion, with petals of silver, blush, and ash. Every sound was a hush. Every breeze, a whisper.

She glanced sideways again.

Colik was still silent, his eyes looking around, watching, or being all *dutiful* as he described it. She held back a scoff and turned her attention to the river again.

"You know *motif* is a word in literature in my world," she pointed out. "It is a recurring element in a story. An image, symbol. Something that reminds the reader of something important."

"Lovely." Colik nodded slowly. "This river," he said, voice low, "repeats everything. Thought. Memory. Longing. It connects all layers of the Reverie. Some Dreamers say it flows *through* frequency of time. Others say it *is* frequency of time."

She stepped closer to the bank, each stride a slow surrender, then crouched, her knees pressing into the soft ground, fingers hovering just above the surface. It wasn't cold. It wasn't even wet. Her reflection surfaced in the water, showing the girl she feared she had become. The face staring back was hers yet dulled—eyes hollowed by years of waiting for something that never came, lips pressed thin from swallowing truths no one wanted to hear. Her shoulders sagged with the weight of growing older and still an orphan, time itself having abandoned her alongside everyone else. The waking world had left her lost, worn, and unsure if she was meant for anything more.

Still, Piper wondered, was she a passerby or could she belong somewhere outside her own world?

Her skin in the reflection began to loosen into particles, drifting away like ash into the current. It should have been horrifying, but it wasn't. The image was lighter now, beautiful even, all that weight in the reflection she carried, finally lifting.

Her breath trembled.

This wasn't just a reflection, but a premonition or false presence. A life without the slow rot of longing. Without the constant strain of wanting something just out of reach. It wasn't the grass-is-greener lie. It was no grass at all—no seasons, no time, no ache. Just the stillness of knowing she'd never have to carry such internal weights again.

Her pulse slowed to match the river's rhythm. She leaned closer and the pull deepened. It whispered of what could be, and what she could become if she stopped fighting and simply let go.

"Is this what death feels like?" she murmured, staring. "Not an ending, but a... perfect self-reflection?"

Behind her, Colik's voice was quiet, but with no softness in it. "That's what they all think. Just before the river takes their name."

She tore her gaze from the water to him. "You think I'd disappear?"

His eyes were steady as he answered, "No. You'd still walk and breathe, but you wouldn't be you. You'd be the dream of yourself—a thing without hunger for more, without love for living, and that is much worse. The river will put you in loop, longing yourself. Like Narcissus."

Her eyes fell back to her reflection, to the unscarred, unshaken version. She looked complete. Untouchable. For one terrible moment, Piper wanted this version of her more than she wanted anything else.

Her hand twitched toward the water. The hum climbed higher, until it became unbearable, the river sensing her making a choice.

She remembered Morry's voice—low and earnest—telling her not to disappear. She remembered Penelope's laugh, the one that lived in her bones more than her memory.

Colik's hand steadied against her back, oddly patient.

With a sharp breath, she pulled away from the water's edge, drawing herself upright. The hum dissolved. "I'm not Narcissus."

CHAPTER NINE
THE POLARIS HUNT

The silence started to bother Piper again, and her feet —small, worn, and used to cobblestone and city sidewalks—began to ache. The ground here was not rough, but it still felt strange beneath her thin boots. Her shoes were secondhand, like most of the clothes she owned back at Olympus House.

"I want to be a Dreamer."

Colik didn't slow. "*The* Dreamer," he said, "is not the same as *a* Dreamer."

Her steps faltered. "I didn't know there was a difference."

"You have no need to know that." He glanced sideways.

She clenched her hands. "Then why say it? You are the one who brought it up."

She saw his mouth move, mumbling something under his breath, but she couldn't catch it. "Because knowing changes things," he said slowly. "If you change too quickly, this place will finish you before it has even started."

They continued in silence, the woods pulsing faintly around them. Every breath Piper took felt less hers, if that was even possible to feel.

Then Colik spoke again, his voice quieter. "A Dreamer is a

sort of guide. We have different Guilds of Dreamers. Like the Routs on the Ollopa Train, we protect lone sleepers—*humans* —from crossing too far and if they cross too far—the sleepwalkers—we ensure that world is just a dream."

"Too far from what?"

"From remembrance. From the waking world. Humans call it REM. Dreamers call it REMembrance. Same rhythm, different truth. What you should have not remembered."

She blinked. "How does that have to do with me not remembering the Ollopa train?"

"I told you that you weren't meant to wake up here," he said. "No one like *you* are. The Ollopa train is supposed to pass through humans. Not stop for you."

"It didn't pass. It stayed. I stayed."

"Exactly." He looked ahead, the set of his shoulder's sharper now. "Something went wrong."

The words settled over her like a weight. *Something went wrong.*

"You know when humans forget dreams?" he asked without waiting for Piper to answer. "That's us. That's what we do. We blur the lines so you don't follow them too far you can't come back from it. Can't wake up. The gods are why you dream. The Dreamers are why you wake up. When a Dreamer fails…"

Incredible. Scientists couldn't even explain it. Here it was being explained, so—or not so—simply.

"What happens when a human goes too far?" she asked. She couldn't believe she was talking about humans in third person as if she weren't one, but here she was.

His pace quickened. "If a human gets trapped in a nightmare for too long, it can kill them. Not because the dream is real, but because the body forgets how to wake."

Piper swallowed. "And if it's not a nightmare?"

Colik glanced at her, eyes dark. "Then it's worse."

"How?"

"Because a beautiful dream can be just as fatal. You stop wanting to return. Your soul settles here. Slowly. Quietly. Like sleepwalking off a cliff."

Her heart pounded louder.

"It becomes a death by choice." Colik met Pipers eyes. The only way to truly kill someone who has passed REM is to kill them in *both* worlds."

"A death by dreams," Piper breathed. Colik nodded.

"That, Piper, is the tricky game of divine and mortal dreaming."

They stopped walking, and around them, the Broken Woods stopped with them. Colik turned to face her. "Do you feel the stillness of the woods?"

"I do." Piper breathed.

Colik gave a grim smile. "Imagine that stillness in the human world. Imagine what humans would do to themselves if they had to walk each moment with that stillness."

"They couldn't," she answered truthfully.

Humans didn't do too well with silence. Noise was their drive. What drove them mad.

"Exactly. Yet here you are. A human taking in the silence."

"It is breathtaking," Piper whispered.

Eyeing her, Colik shook his head. "You like it here, don't you?"

She nodded. "I feel like I could belong."

His jaw flexed. "That's how it starts. You *feel* seen. Whole. Heard. You're not yet being replaced. That happens slower than moments, all at once and never at all until you have become the very thing you didn't know you wanted to become."

She flinched, the sharpness in his voice slicing through her thoughts, and she couldn't help but notice how determined he was to make this world sound uninviting. When she lifted her gaze and let the moment breathe, she realized she was standing inside the very thing she'd been missing her whole life—a place alive with wonder, humming softly beneath every surface, as if waiting for her to finally see it.

"What is that?"

"A mortal dreamer choosing to stay." His eyes shadowed.

"I want to stay. I am not scared. I have nothing left for me in my waking world."

He didn't look at her. "Wanting something doesn't make it safe. It makes it seductive. Possibly even obsessive. You saw how you reacted to the Motif River."

Her breath caught at the latter words. Is that what this world was? A world seducing humans to the luxury of beauty within their dreams?

"You said Dreamers are guides," she pressed, shaking away her thoughts. It only made her want to be here more. "So, guide me."

He shook his head and kept walking, slipping deeper into the dreamy grove where the air hung thick yet strangely agile, folding around him in ways that made Piper feel as though the world itself was shifting to let him pass.

"Why can't I be awake here?" she finally asked. "Why is it so bad for a human to stay here? Choose this world?"

"Because this place wasn't made from your dust. It was forged by gods. Patterned and precise. The longer you try to bend yourself into this world, the more you fracture."

"It feels real."

Colik turned, eyes flashing. "So does drowning—until the last breath is gone."

She looked down, the moss beneath her shoes dimming.

"Are humans and Dreamers really so different? You look like me…" she hesitated, squinting at him. "Minus the white hair, the mismatched eyes, and that whole sharp-tongued, I-could-kill-you-with-a-sentence vibe," she thought dryly.

"We are," he said, "You forget. We remember. You live in different ages and time. We live in frequency and echoes of dreams."

Piper looked down, her thoughts spinning. Maybe that was the difference between them — humans let go. Dreams didn't. *Dreams remember what we try to forget.*

They kept walking, but for the hundredth time, after a long stretch of silence, Piper couldn't help but ask, "Do you think I *could* ever be a Dreamer?"

Colik didn't answer right away. His gaze looked past her onto the shifting shadows between the trees, as if weighing her question against something he wasn't ready to name.

"Maybe," he said finally, his voice low. "Maybe you already are."

The words made her chest tighten, a strange mix of dread and hope tangling together. "What does that mean?" she pressed.

Colik gave the faintest smile, too brief to trust. "You'll see."

More walking. More silence. Piper had never been good with silence. It was not one of her virtues, unless she was angry enough to need silence to calm herself down.

"I know we're headed to the Citadel"—*how could a place sound so exciting without knowing anything about it?* — "Wouldn't it be faster to ride that creature of yours? Dray, is it? It looks big enough to carry us both," she suggested, pointing to the creature that had made itself known again sometime back.

"We can't both ride it. An atmospheric beast is loyal to one Dreamer at a time, to its dying breath," he explained, a mischievous glimmer in his eye. "I doubt it would allow you to ride it, even if given the choice."

"Why not?" she argued.

"Because it follows Dreamers and those with the sincerest of hearts," he teased, winking at her, which made her cheeks flush. "Something that humans never seem to master."

"Oh, please!" Piper rolled her eyes. "What a false thought for a poor creature. Hiding that monstrous soul deep down, aren't you?" she joked, and he let out a mock laugh. She liked this lighter side of Colik.

"Seems you will never know, *human*." He nudged her playfully, but his eyebrow raised, surprised by her joking accusation. Then he went back to a serious look as if realizing what he was doing—playing nice with a human.

Even though it had been a joke, she had never despised the word *human* more than she did in that moment, not when it suddenly felt like a boundary drawn between them that she wasn't ready to accept.

Another long span of silence fell between them before she found herself asking her next question.

"The Broken Woods... Is there a story behind its name too?"

Piper saw Colik sigh. She was learning words for the first time, untainted by doubt, and unashamed to ask. The world was new, and she wanted to know everything.

"That's just it. No one really knows, but whenever one leaves the woods—they, it, whatever *it* is—becomes broken," Colik explained, causing a shiver to run down her spine. He had said that before, but she didn't get it. Much like she didn't get the entire Dreamworld.

"Are you saying something on my body will break?" she asked, her voice small. Colik shook his head.

"If you leave the woods with just a broken bone, then you have hardly been scathed by the woods' true fate."

"Then what could you mean?"

"Piper, you are *in* a Dreamworld. Physical things hold little value or importance here. Your mind, feelings, and memories—those are the *stars* here," he explained. She nodded, pretending to understand, though still confused.

"You're in the woods now."

"So are you."

"That means that you risked something being broken to find me?" she asked, incredulously.

"Find you? I told you that I didn't know it was *you* I'd be finding…it is much more than that… Don't worry about me," Colik replied quickly, his pace quickening again. "Do you ever listen?"

She frowned, suddenly annoyed at him.

What was it with him?

Silently, ignoring him, she turned her attention back to the Broken Woods. Everything around them appeared so beautifully whole, yet Colik insisted that all who entered were affected by its fate.

She wondered how something could break that was already broken.

Suddenly, Colik's demeanor shifted entirely, and he stopped abruptly, extending his hand to stop her, too. His eyes darted around, wild and primal, like a hunter scanning the underbrush for unseen threats.

"What is it?" Piper whispered.

"Someone, or something, is following us," Colik murmured, his voice low and tense.

Then, before Piper could fully grasp what was happening, he hurled both against the ground.

"Ouch!" Piper cried out, the impact hurting her fragile and lean frame more than she wished to admit. She wanted to tell Colik that orphans were not made to withstand much weight, that their meager diets stripped them of excess muscle, but the opportunity was cut short.

"Stay low!" Colik hissed, urgency thick in his voice. Just as he fell on her, she caught a glimpse of a massive creature—a hybrid of polar bear and lion, its shimmering white and silver fur gleaming in the dappled light—leaping over them. It landed with a thundering crash that sent vibrations rippling through the ground, turning to face them with an imposing presence just a few feet away.

"A Polaris," Colik whispered, his elbows bracing against the woods floor on either side of her, his face hovering a little too close to hers. Piper held her breath, a mixture of terror and fascination consuming her as her eyes observed the creature.

"Don't move," Colik instructed, his lips barely parting. The Polaris raised its great head, nostrils flaring as it drew in the scents swirling around them. Suddenly, a beam of light burst forth from its mouth, illuminating the surrounding woods like a searchlight, but the vibrant foliage cloaked them safely. The leaves were enormous, far larger than they appeared from the heights of the treetops.

The creature prowled through the underbrush with unsettling grace, its thick, snow-like fur glistening. It blended seamlessly with the trees' silver-etched bark. Its massive paws pressed into the soft ground, leaving deep impressions.

"They are practically blind, so they only sense what stands out. As long as we remain hidden among the underbrush, it won't be able to detect you."

The Polaris moved with an intimidating elegance, gliding over the leafy terrain as it instinctively scanned the surroundings for any hint of movement. Piper could see the muscles rippling beneath its silvery-white fur, tense and ready to spring into action. It paused, inhaling deeply, its nose twitching as it searched for the faintest trace of life.

It finally took several steps closer in their direction, its head lowered, ears pricked, and alert. The creature's eyes darted around, absorbing every detail, sending a shiver down Piper's spine.

"Hold your breath," Colik whispered, urgency lacing his tone. She nodded, swallowing hard in compliance.

As the Polaris prowled, she could hear the soft rustling of leaves getting closer. Their breaths mingled, barely audible as they remained hidden beneath the protective canopy of leaves.

With a sudden gust of wind, the Polaris paused, nostrils flaring as it inhaled deeply, detecting a new scent swirling through the air. The creature turned its head high, then back toward them, momentarily confused by the direction of the smell. Its sharp, glistening teeth were visible when it snarled.

Out of nowhere, Piper heard what must have distracted the Polaris. A faint whoosh approached rapidly, followed by the high-pitched whoops and hollers of distant voices. They both lifted their heads slightly. Two fast-moving entities darted and dove through the trees, their forms barely noticeable as they blended with the Broken Woods greenery.

"Yeeee-ha!" cried a voice, echoing through the air like a cowboy chasing a stampede.

The high-pitched laughter came from children, their wild hair flowing behind them like colorful flags in the wind. They rode on the same creatures that Colik had called atmospheric beasts.

She could see exhilaration and mischief in their faces. The long, flowing tails of their steeds trailed behind, creating a mesmerizing dance of color and movement that blended seamlessly with their surroundings. These atmospheric beasts appeared even larger than Dray, twice the size, yet just as translucent and shimmering. The children who rode them couldn't be over sixteen, their childish laughter ringing through the trees like a calling. There were two of them, swooping around and zipping past the Polaris, their hands twirling what looked like bright red glistening ropes.

With a whoosh, the powerful creatures surrounded the Polaris, catching it off guard. No longer fixated on the scent coming from the brush, the beast roared, rearing up on its hind legs, swiping at the daring duo. With wild hair streaming behind her, one child expertly swung the red rope above her head, preparing for a daring capture of the Polaris's neck. The other child darted around the back, moving perfectly in sync with his shimmering beast. It was a thrilling dance amongst a childish game.

The Polaris slashed, but one child's creature dodged the

Polaris with breathtaking poise. The child's eyes were focused, determination etched across her face as she readied her lasso again.

Piper glanced slightly at Colik, who also looked taken aback by the extraordinary scene before them. Did he know who these children were?

Piper's eyes darted back to the flying children, just as the one coming from the back tossed the red rope. With a flick of his wrist, he bound the Polaris' back legs with his bright lasso. Together, the two children calculated their strike, and before the Polaris realized what was happening, it was down.

Piper watched in awe at the children's playful yet expertly precise game.

"Dreamers, Dreamers, come out to play," called the child who had roped the Polaris from behind. His smile was wide and playful, as though the entire spectacle was a performance meant just for them.

Colik immediately pushed himself off her, leaving her stunned at having him on top of her, the ferocious beast threatening her, and witnessing a fantastical rodeo unfold before her eyes.

Colik extended a hand to help her up. She took it, feeling warmth radiate as she climbed to her feet. The boy's creature lowered itself, its majestic gaze meeting theirs while maintaining a careful distance.

The child was unlike anything Piper had ever seen before, except maybe in her imagination when reading about the lost boys in *Peter Pan*. He looked like a child who had chosen to live out his nights in the woods—a true wild child.

He was thin and fragile in appearance. His upper body was bare, revealing intricate patterns that twisted and curled like the branches of the woods. His hair was a chaotic tangle of dark strands resembling twisted branches, with bits of shrubbery peeking through, forming a rustic crown atop his head. Delicate wings, like a pixie's—if that was even possible

—sprouted from his upper back, shimmering softly in the dappled light.

His attire was a playful mishmash of stitched fabrics in shades of silver, white, and green, blending perfectly with the surroundings. He had browned smudges covering his cheeks, like he had just been frolicking through the underbrush.

"I didn't know the Scirges were such wranglers," Colik said, a smile brightening his face. Relief washed over her. He at least knew them.

Scirges?

It was the girl who laughed, a sound like tinkling bells. Piper couldn't possibly understand what was amusing right now.

With a nimble leap, the boy hopped off his atmospheric beast, landing with the effortless grace of a cat. "Cyril, at your call!" The boy said with a salute, his eyes on Colik.

Watching him, she thought of Morry.

How would she possibly tell Morry about this that would make him believe her? It was all too much to believe herself.

Slyly, Piper pinched herself to make sure she was, in fact, not really dreaming. Then again, she was.

It was all still so confusing.

"We don't just fall, Dreamer. We crave a challenge and, of course, any chance to play," chimed the girl, who had successfully wrangled the Polaris by its neck. With a confident grin, she leaped gracefully from her own stunning atmospheric beast, glowing with a greenish hue.

"Who is this?" the girl asked, her gaze sliding from Colik to Piper as if introductions were a mere formality. She was small and delicate, though her face looked older than her years. Moss clung to her skin in deliberate and decorative patterns that both clothed and camouflaged her. Dark, tangled hair framed her like the rough bark of the trees, and tiny, translucent wings fluttered faintly at her neck. Patches of green and silver stitched together in curious shapes wrapped her darkened limbs and waist, wearing the shrubbery as accessories. Her smile was soft, but her moss-colored eyes sparkled with a mischievous light.

"I am—" Piper began, but Colik stepped forward, claiming the space between them.

"A mortal dreamer," he said, his tone warm but deliberate. "Taking her to the Citadel to help get her back to the waking world."

Piper held her breath. She assumed—*hoped*—he was lying.

The two children froze. Their eyes darted between Colik and Piper, wonder and unease flickering across their faces.

"She's *human*?" The girl whispered, as if the word itself were dangerous, and looked up at Cyril. "Humans don't come here. They can't."

Cyril's expression faltered, curiosity overtaking fear. "Are you sure she's not one of us?" he asked, stepping closer. "She looks—different. Fragile, but awake."

Colik said nothing, but his jaw tightened.

The girl glanced from Cyril to Piper again, her voice dropping to a quiver. "Could she be *the* Dreamer?"

Cyril's gaze flicked to Colik. It was sharp and questioning, but he didn't speak. The silence that followed felt like it could shatter.

Colik's mouth curved, with the kind of smile that wasn't quite pride and yet carried the weight of it. "I found her," he said softly, each word deliberate, as though he were naming something rare. Something no one else had dared to touch.

Cyril's eyes widened with revelation. The girl Scirge took a step back, her hand half-raised, caught between shock and excitement. Piper, standing in the middle of it all, wasn't sure whether she'd just been claimed or condemned.

The girl's tone was caught between awe and giddy relief. "From Morpheus' promise?"

Piper frowned. "What promise?"

None of them answered her.

"If she's *the* Dreamer," Cyril said, grinning so wide it looked like it hurt, "then maybe she is one of us. A Dreamer of falling!"

The girl clasped her hands together, eyes bright and searching Piper's face like she wanted to believe in her more than anything.

"Do you know what that means? It means *hope is back.*"

Piper's breath caught. *Hope.* It sat in her chest like a spark, small but stubborn, warming a part of her she'd almost forgotten.

"Falling?" Piper asked with unease.

The girl grinned. "We Scirges don't touch the ground unless we choose to. The air remembers us."

Colik's hand pressed lightly against the small of Piper's back, protectively.

"I'm Colik," he said at last, stepping in front of Piper with quiet pride. "This is Piper."

The Scirges smiled as if a long-awaited answer had finally arrived.

"Ooohhh, I've never met a Royald before!" the girl exclaimed. Her eyes sparkled like dewdrops. "I'm Eda."

Piper blinked. *Royald?* She turned to Colik, but he didn't meet her gaze.

"Royald?" she echoed, barely above a whisper.

Colik remained composed, but there was tension in his jaw.

"Of course, we recognize a Royald," Cyril stated, giving a slight head bow. "At your call, Colik," he repeated.

Piper stiffened, and Colik's tone shifted as he turned to Cyril. "Why was that Polaris here? You hunted it like this has happened before."

Cyril nodded, eyes narrowing. "The third one. The Polaris's are following something they shouldn't. Dust is unnaturally stirring."

Cyril exchanged a quick glance with Eda. "The Fray's strands might be unravelling," Eda whispered.

Piper frowned, her gaze shifting to each of them. "The Fray?"

Again, they ignored her. She might as well not have been there.

"They answer to the Royalds," Cyril said carefully, still eyeing Colik. "So, either you summoned it, or it sensed a human nearby." He moved his gaze to Piper.

Colik's expression darkened. "It was here before us, I could tell." He shook his head. "Still, I will speak with Lulu."

"Lulu?" Piper repeated, her voice louder than she intended.

"Piper," Colik snapped.

Piper winced.

Asshole.

The Scirges flinched and the Polaris stirred. Its body thrashed against the red ropes holding it, the bindings cracking under the strain.

"I think we'd better get out of here. Those ropes won't hold for much longer," Cyril said, his gaze now fixated on the massive silver-white creature.

They all turned to go, but Piper's thoughts reeled.

Polaris. Royald. The Fray.

Colik was royalty and didn't tell her.

What the actual f—

"Hop on to Folla," Eda said to Piper, pulling her out of her thoughts. She gave a sharp whistle, and a green hued atmospheric beast materialized beside her, floating just high enough for them to mount it with ease. Eda gracefully climbed onto the slimy, stingray-like creature, then extended a hand toward Piper. She didn't even suggest Piper ride with Colik on Dray.

What made the two creatures different?

"Where are—" Piper began, but Colik silenced her with a

sharp look. It was unclear whether he was trying to protect her or simply controlling, but it was pissing her off her regardless.

She scoffed and accepted Eda's hand. With a gentle tug, Eda helped her mount onto Folla while Colik watched with a tight expression, clearly torn between stopping her and shocked that she followed through.

Yep, asshole.

"Colik, I see you have your own beast," Cyril pointed out as he effortlessly hopped back onto his own. To no one's surprise except Piper's, Dray suddenly appeared beside Colik. He climbed on to his beast, but his eyes remained on Piper.

Once Folla and Dray were out of the way, Cyril skillfully untangled the red ropes that had restrained the Polaris, freeing its neck and hind legs.

"That should teach it to come back here for some moments. The one thing a Polaris hates more than anything is physical restraint," he called out to no one in particular.

Free from restraints, the Polaris turned its head, scanning the branches around it. Just as a surge of panic ran through Piper's very core, fearing the creature might come after them again, it leaped higher into air with astonishing speed, fleeing.

"Though dangerous, the existence of a Polaris is a testament to the adaptability and strength of this world," Eda shared, seeing Piper watching it go with unease.

"It is beautiful," Piper breathed.

"Indeed, it is. A beautiful servant to a potentially dangerous master."

"A dangerous master?"

"They serve the Royalds, but some say the Polaris chose the wrong master," Eda replied. A visible shiver coursed down her spine.

"Who is the right master?" Piper whispered, but Eda shook her head, as if shaking the thought out of her mind.

Then she turned her head toward Piper and smiled widely. "Are you ready?"

"Ready for—"

Before she could finish her question, Eda added with a squeal, "Hold on tight!"

Piper quickly grabbed Eda's waist covered in moss, as the atmospheric beast shot up in the air. She tightened her grip to avoid being thrown back as they sped through the air, much faster than she had anticipated.

Whether Eda was guiding it or the beast knew the way, the ride was swift and exhilarating, carrying them to wherever they were headed. Piper dared a glance behind her, noticing Colik carefully following on Dray, his unwavering gaze fixed on her like an unyielding storm.

"Your beast—why can I ride it when Colik said I couldn't ride his?" Piper yelled over the gusts of wind. It was odd sitting behind a child on a flying stingray. It felt like she was back on the carousel in Dublin with one of the orphan children again. That feeling of nostalgia made her stomach churn.

"The atmospheric beast is one of the oldest creatures in the Dreamworld. They are loyal to one. Did Colik share that with you?" Eda answered loudly. Piper had to turn her head to hear her correctly.

"Yes!" Piper yelled in reply. The Scirge giggled. "I can hear you fine, Piper," she called out behind her, making Piper blush. "There is something about being true to one with the sincerest heart," Piper went on, focusing on her voice level.

"They're not just creatures," Eda said, her voice steady over the wind as Folla glided through the air like a sliver of ribbon. "They're a kind of test. A reflection. They choose those who truly believe in this world—not just with their dust, but with their souls. If a beast leaves its Dreamer, it means that Dreamer has lost their way. Lost sight of what this world really means."

Piper squeezed her calves, tightening onto the creature's soft, pulsing surface. Folla's body shimmered around her, translucent and cool, lit from within by streaks of soft color of the wood's greenery. It was the strangest and most stunning thing she had ever ridden—if "riding" even described the weightless glide of it all.

"Why can I ride Folla?" she asked again.

Eda faced ahead, quiet for a moment, then replied, "When an atmospheric beast loses its Dreamer, it doesn't die. It loses its purpose momentarily, like shedding its skin. What remains is something ancient. Eternal. It becomes semi-transparent—ethereal and reborn. In that form, it gains the strength to search again, to choose a new Dreamer worthy of its loyalty."

Piper's eyes widened. "So, they choose?"

"Always," Eda nodded. "They're never tamed, never trained. They choose you, like dragons. You know what dragons are? The difference is, they don't breathe fire. They breathe the very breath of the world. All nature's soul lives in them."

Dragons?

Piper swallowed hard. "You said something remains. So, they can't die?" She decided to ask, ignoring the dragon part. There were no such things as dragons.

"In a way," Eda said. "It's skin can bypass decay. Folla is reborn again and again, but its loyalty is only ever to one during its span of life. If it chooses you, even for a moment, that means something. A rebirth of sorts."

"Then how did it choose me if it chose you?"

"Because I did…" Eda replied with a wink. "And that means something too!" she cried out just as Folla dove. Piper squeezed Eda, her heart jolting at the quick maneuver.

So, Colik was just *choosing* for Piper not to ride Dray.

Asshole.

Suddenly they surged upward again, the beast's wings

curling and rippling with every pulse. Piper gasped and clung tighter.

Colik moved parallel to them on the right while Cyril met them on the left. There was a strange buzzing sound as the three translucent creatures broke through to the open sky.

Piper could see, as clear as day, the eerie red reflection shimmering among the mushroom tops and reddish leaves. The leaves weren't red, but the moons color gave it that hue. The Blood Moon, larger than any moon or sun she had ever seen, hung on the horizon.

The three beasts flew in perfect formation, their synchronized movements a testament to Eda's words about their natural influence in this world. Their sleek bodies gleamed in the twinkling light, their long tails trailing behind like the tail end of a shooting star.

Then, within a split moment in the open air, a large shadow loomed *over* them. It was immense and shapeless, curling like smoke but heavier than sky. The Blood Moon dimmed as the world beneath them shifted to grey.

"Eda…" Piper whispered.

Eda's shoulders tensed.

The shadow thickened, eating the light. A new scent filled the air—bitter, metallic, and dry. Piper's chest tightened, the new air slowly putting her in a chokehold.

"A dust cloud. It's not supposed to come this far. It is ash-filled. Something *is* tearing through the Reverie." Piper could barely make out all of Eda's words through the thickness.

"What is?" Piper cried out, her words dry from the odd dust in the air.

"Chaos."

Piper's heart skipped a few beats. Somewhere, behind them, she heard a snap. It sounded like glass breaking underwater.

Eda twisted in her saddle and looked back at Piper with sudden urgency. "Hold your breath!" she snapped.

"What?"

"Now! Don't breathe it—don't even taste it."

Piper obeyed, sucking in a quick gasp and sealing her mouth shut. The dark cloud rolled in like a tidal wave of burnt pages and forest fires. Tiny flecks of grey and black floated in its mix. It wasn't mist or dust.

Ash.

The air itself started to distort. Folla's wings stuttered, struggling to push through gravity.

Piper's eyes watered. Her skin prickled. The ashy dust didn't necessarily burn her, but it did not welcome her either.

The atmospheric beasts suddenly dove back through a break in the treetops, slipping beneath the dark clouds that trailed them like an eye of a hurricane. In harmony, they let out a high-pitched screech, their calls sharp and melodic, echoing through the trees.

She heard Eda let out a long sigh.

"You can breathe in again, Piper." It took a moment before Piper could breathe properly again.

"So, where are they taking us?" The wind tugged Piper's voice backward as her hair whipped across her face.

"Where else...home!" Eda shouted back, her tone back to its playfulness again.

Something knotted in Piper's chest.

Home.

The word shouldn't have stung, but it did.

She stared at the back of Eda's wild silhouette, then into the blurred trees flying by them.

How long had it been in her own world? An hour? A night? Days? Time felt fractured here. Colik had said time wasn't a thing here, but had anyone in her world noticed she was gone? *Was* she even gone?

A sudden weight settled in her gut. What was her body doing now? Was it just lying there, unmoving? Sleeping? Or was it truly a pile of ash? Was she dreaming? Or had she been forgotten already?

The whirling thoughts came again out of nowhere, like something had triggered her fears to surface.

No, she shook her head at herself while the beast leveled out, slowing its speed. The dust clouds had dispersed.

If the Motif River showed her a true image of her world, then her body *wasn't* there.

Right? Colik had compared it to dreaming a normal dream. She guessed she'd figure out all the questions when she went back. *If* she went back. *Could* go back.

The wood's palette shifted, and Piper's wandering thoughts quieted. Ahead, a vast, glimmering body of water opened to them, still as crystal.

Its surface reflected the red-tinted sky with such lucidity that Piper wasn't sure where the world ended and the dream began. The beasts glided lower, their tails leaving small, delicate tremors that spread wide and slow across its surface. A series of joyous howls and trills vibrated through the beast's body, sounds that echoed through the air, celebrating their return.

On the edge of the vast body of water, they folded in their wing-like fins and landed in a hidden cove. The water shimmered dark and held still, half-covered in fog. Thick tree trunks rose from the marshy ground, their roots twisting as if guarding something secret.

Eda swung off her beast, but before she could reach Piper, Colik was already there.

He didn't say anything, just offered his hands up to her. Piper hesitated a moment before lowering herself into his grasp. His fingers wrapped around her waist, gentle but unsure, like he wasn't used to holding someone but didn't want to let her fall.

The moment her boots touched the mossy ground, he

didn't step away. He stayed close as if waiting to see what she would do with the space he hadn't given her.

The air around them smelled of damp leaves and saltwater. Strange glowing bugs drifted through the twilight, blinking like stars caught in a slow rhythm.

Colik stood beside her quietly, guarded, but his gaze never left her. Not watching so much as searching, as though he feared she might shift into something unfamiliar if he blinked. Or disappear entirely.

There was something in his silence. A softness he hadn't meant to show, tangled with confusion he couldn't quite hide.

It made Piper fight a grin.

Just ahead, half-concealed by hanging vines, stood a stone figure. It was carved from pale green rock, soft with moss. The statue was of a wild-looking man with horns curled from his tangled hair, hooves instead of feet, and a flute resting at his lips. Though frozen in stone, the statue's smile was maddeningly alive.

"Who's that?" Piper asked, softly. The air was much calmer on the ground.

"Pan," Eda replied, bouncing in step with her. "God of the Wild. Guardian of the natural in this world. The old Scirges believe he protects our kind. Or tests us, depending on who you ask."

Piper stared into the god's stone eyes. They danced, despite the stillness, causing her stomach to turn.

Past the statue, the woods thinned and the world opened. Before her stretched a vast crystal-like terrace suspended in mist, carved into tiers that spiraled around a central spire of translucent glass and iridescent light, much like the colors of the atmospheric beasts. The air shimmered with drifting motes of silver dust. Great panels of lucid crystal arched overhead, their interiors laced with green vines glowing faintly from within. Wind flutes carved into the higher spires sang hollow notes as the breeze slipped through, filling the space with a strange, daunting melody.

It was beautiful and wrong. Not because it didn't belong, but because Piper didn't. The feeling struck her like a familiar ache, the same way she'd felt standing in the halls of Olympus House: surrounded by wonder, but not quite a part of it.

"This is Kryvos Hollow," Cyril noted, coming around to the other side of Piper. "Home of the Scirges—the wild children of the Reverie."

The crystalline terraces shimmered with laughter as Scirges darted across glass bridges, their bare feet leaving temporary trails of light.

Kryvos Hollow should have felt different—wild and alive —but instead there was that same invisible weight, like time had hardened around her before she'd ever had the chance to live freely. The children here *wanted* to be part of this place, to belong to something untamed and shining. At Olympus House, no one had wanted to stay. They all dreamed of leaving, of being chosen. Perhaps that was the difference. Or maybe Piper had always been the odd one out. She had dreamed of leaving Olympus House, while the others had learned to belong. Maybe this was all a false hope. A curse to never feel home where she was, only where she wasn't.

She stood there a moment longer, bathed in refracted light, trying to remember why she'd wanted this world at all.

Damn it, if she didn't at least try to find a place in it.

"I'm…" she began, but Eda caught her eye.

"You wear the human years heavy, Piper," Eda said softly, like she could see straight through her. "We don't, not here. We keep our child moments as long as we can, especially when the gods try to strip it from us. Maybe stop trying to grow up so fast. The Reverie gives you back what's been taken, if you let it."

Piper said nothing. Her throat had gone tight.

Above, glass bridges swayed in the wind. Piper's gaze

followed the nearest bridge as it curved around the trunk of a massive tree. A low, distant rumble stirred the air, muffled but aroused.

Piper turned her head toward the noise. The mist swallowed everything behind them, yet her heart stuttered anyway. Unfazed, Eda skipped ahead, with Cyril close behind.

"Is that…?" she began.

Colik's jaw tightened. "The Polaris is on the hunt again." The way he said it made her skin prickle. She didn't like the sound of that.

Her eyes lifted to the fog-veiled sky hiding the marshy entrance of Kryvos Hollow, half-expecting to see silver fur catching the dim light, a mouth smoldering like embers, and those orange eyes fixed on her.

"On the hunt for what?"

Colik's gaze didn't waver. "Not what," he crooned. "*Who.*"

The air around her tightened.

"Me," Piper breathed, catching on.

He didn't correct her, but stepped just slightly ahead, like armor. "You need to understand, Piper that the Polaris appears when there's a threat of unfamiliar dust."

Her breath caught. "You mean human dust."

It started to all make sense. Eda's shock. Cyril's secretive looks. Colik's hesitations. Humans were an anomaly here. Maybe even dream taboo.

"Yes, I do."

CHAPTER TEN
THE SCIRGES GAME

Pan was just the guardian to the crystal-terraced city, a place half treehouse, half prism, and wholly alive. It kept unfolding the closer they got.

Eda and Cyril stayed a step ahead of Piper and Colik, their wild hair whispering against the moss-lined steps that spiraled upward through mist and more faint, chiming tunes. Piper gripped the silver railing, slick and cool beneath her palm, as the stair swayed ever so slightly, suspended between roots, cut-glass and reflective light.

Below, the marsh faded into masked water and distant outline. Above, cliffs unfolded into a crystal treehouse city, roots of quartz and branches of light woven together in living patterns. Hammock-like canopies swayed between vine-draped ledges, rippling gently in the wind, carrying the scent of salt and dew with each slow, swaying breath of the air. In a few of them, Piper saw Scirges curled within the crystal strands, fast asleep.

As they climbed higher, quartz spires rose like trunks, catching the Blood Moon's glow. Piper glimpsed movement within the vines and walls: A hand spun red straw into glinting strands, another figure pressed two stones together until they fused into a black-and-silver coin, and laughter drifted from a terrace carved into glasslike bark.

"Don't look down if you are scared of heights," Eda shrieked behind her, giggling after as if a joke.

Piper did not look down.

At last, the stairway opened into a vast canopy bathed in more shifting light. Scirges darted through the air, weaving between crystal limbs and swinging from vine to vine with wild precision.

"Welcome to Kryvos Den," Cyril announced, holding his arms out to present the spectacle around her.

Piper stopped, feeling slightly dizzy. From this height, she could see far across the Broken Woods, the mushroom tops forming a second forest below, a soft, shimmering ground where the Scirges moved like flashes of wind and light. Something deep within her stirred. Whatever this place was, she had crossed into the part of the Dreamworld where the real adventure began.

"What does *Kryvo* mean?" Piper asked, fighting the nerves and excitement in her voice. For once, she had someone other than Colik to ask.

Eda grinned over her shoulder. "It means *fall* or *falling* in Dreamtongue, depending on the context. This—" she swept her finger around the room, mimicking Cyril, "—this is Pan's design. He built a fort in the trees, for when the gods call another war."

"What war?" Piper echoed. She felt Colik stiffen beside her.

Cyril's smile faded and gave Eda a glare.

"If she's a human here, she deserves to know." Eda's voice sharpened. She turned to Piper again, her expression softening just enough to let the words through.

"Piper, what you need to understand about the gods is that

there is *always* going to be a war. In one form or another. They never forget what was taken from them. They never forgive it, either. They just wait for the next reason to avenge it."

Cyril gave a short shrug, then piggy backed off her words. "Pan was the guardian to the Silver Children in the Silver Age. After the Reverie was created and Zeus imprisoned them, he swore no child here would share their fate. He has protected the Scirges since."

Silver Age. The words rang through Piper like an echo she couldn't place. She'd seen that name before in the book at the library, buried in a line about gods and their failed creations. Steele spoke of it. The Silver Girl… was it all a cry for help?

Piper tensed up. Maybe she was misunderstanding them both. Maybe they just wanted the same thing everyone did here—to be left alone by gods who never stopped sparring. For the first time, she felt something that wasn't fear or questioning wonder toward them. It was pity.

Eda twirled a vine hanging from the air idly. "Some of us just never want to grow up."

Piper hesitated. "So, the Silver Children were just…"

Colik's head snapped toward Eda. "Stop," he said sharply. "You're telling her too much."

The Scirges nearby had turned, their gazes sharp and protective. Piper was right not telling him about the Silver Girl.

Cyril ignored him. "They were Zeus's final attempt to grant human immortality," he said, tone measured, as though reciting forbidden history. "After mortal heroes like Hercules and Perseus, Zeus thought that humans earned the right to stand among the gods, not beneath them. Mortals could never climb Olympus, so he offered them another way: a path to eternity through dreams, and from it, the Dreamworld was born. He chose the bravest among them—their children, their bloodline—and remade them in silver if they were to pass

REM. Like the Titans and the Giants before them, they grew too strong. Too proud. They stopped worshipping, and instead they tried to rule."

Piper couldn't believe it, and yet it all fit. The stories. The symbols. The myths. The gods *were* real, and she was standing in the aftermath of their wars.

Colik stepped forward abruptly. "That's enough. I'm a Royald, and I said stop." His words rang with authority, the kind that made even the air hesitate.

Cyril didn't flinch. "Not here, you're not," he said evenly, meeting Colik's glare. "Not until Blaze sees her. Then you can take it up with him."

Who is Blaze?

The words landed hard, and for a moment, Colik just stood there, the weight of its truth pressing against his pride.

Cyril's gaze still didn't waver. "This is my home, Royald. If you don't like what's said here, you can leave." He glanced toward Piper, his tone softening. "She can make her own choice to stay or not."

Colik exhaled slowly, retreating a step back. His features went taut but did not argue.

"Where was I," Cyril began again, his tone reverting to its lightness, as if he hadn't just clashed with a Royald. "Right. Lengthy story ever so concise, that's how the *Guild of Dreamers* began. We are humans who died in the waking world, chosen by the gods to serve here. With the help of the Oneiroi brothers, we wake up humans using their dreams before they know that this world exists to them."

Piper eyes widened.

Noticing, Eda stepped closer, placing a soft hand on Piper's arm. "It sounds sad, I know," she said, her voice gentler than before. "For children who die too young in the waking world, we must believe it's better to dream here than to face true death."

Eda's gaze flicked between Cyril and Colik before settling back on Piper. "That's why you, *human*, could be a Dreamer."

The word *human* hung in the air like a dropped stone. Around them, the Scirges froze. Those swinging from vines slowed to a halt. A pair perched along the upper terraces leaned forward, whispering. One small boy even climbed down from a glowing branch, his wide eyes fixing on Piper.

She felt the weight of every stare before she dared to move. Heat climbed her neck. They were all looking at her, as if the word had marked her. She'd been listening so closely she'd forgotten there were others in the den at all.

The murmurs grew louder among the Scirges.

"Human?" someone echoed from above.

"A new Dreamer?" another whispered, the word carrying through the crystalline air.

Piper swallowed hard, wishing she knew which one she was.

"See…" Colik growled.

"She's different," a Scirge whispered.

Gasps rippled through the terraces, echoing faintly off the crystal cliffs.

Colik shook his head, but Eda stepped forward, her voice bright and unafraid. "This is Piper. She rode Folla."

There was a collective gasp, then the den went wild.

"She rode an atmospheric beast?"

"That means—"

"Could she be—?"

"—*The* Dreamer?"

"They said she is a human!"

Scirges began to circle her, hesitant but drawn. Piper instinctively stepped closer to Colik.

"If you were all once human, why would they be shocked that I'm a human? That I'm here?" Piper's voice came out smaller than she intended, tight with confusion and something close to fear. She needed them to get away from her. She needed space. Air.

Colik opened his mouth as if to answer, but the words caught behind his teeth. His jaw flexed, his anger simmering just beneath the surface. She could feel it radiating from him, that same controlled fury as before, but this time, he did not react. Cyril's words still held him in place.

Eda leaned into her, like a protective blanket, her eyes glinting with excitement. "We have been wondering who could be the one from Morpheus' promise."

There it was again, that promise.

From an upper terrace, a boy stepped into view. He looked like the others, except for the dust-lit antlers rising from his head. From this distance, Piper couldn't tell if they were worn or part of him.

"Is it true?" he asked softly. "The Dreamer could be walking among us?"

No one answered. Piper's stomach twisted tighter each time she heard the word. She didn't even know if she could be a Dreamer, let alone whatever kind they thought she might be.

Sensing her unease, Cyril clapped his hands sharply. "Alright, that's enough staring! You were all humans once. It's not like she's a new star in the constellation cloud."

A few Scirges laughed nervously, the hum fading back into the bones of the den, but the glances that lingered on Piper said the thought hadn't entirely gone away.

"Go on, go play!" Cyril called, flicking his hand in a gentle shoo. The Scirges drifted off, but not before stealing one last curious glance at her.

"Come on," Cyril said, beckoning to her and Colik. He offered Colik a subtle nod, a quiet signal that whatever had bristled between them was now settled.

"We'll show you the best part."

Cyril led them along winding paths carved through crystal roots and hollowed trunks draped with glowing vines. Eda skipped after them, practically vibrating with excitement, as if they were about to see something extraordinary.

And how extraordinary it was.

The path widened into a massive clearing, revealing a coliseum carved out of the trees and open sky. Vines as thick as pillars spiraled upward, braided with tree trunks shot through with crystal. Its railings twinkled with facets that caught and fractured the Blood Moon into cascades of color. The seats were carved from luminous crystal, veins of light running through them, pulsing softly beneath the feet of Scirges leaning over the edges.

High winds swept through the arena in great, spiraling currents, carrying patches of silver dust that danced between the tiers suspended among the towering crystal spires. Rope bridges of spun glass stretched between each tier, trembling with every passing gust. It felt as if the wind itself was trapped within the coliseum, circling restlessly, searching for a way out.

Eda spread her arms out, like a performer on a stage. "This is Pan's ring. He built it for us to learn moves like the woods do—how to be quick, quiet, and untouchable—so when danger comes, we can protect our own. For reasons you now know." She gave Piper a wink. "Oh, and to practice the act of falling."

"Why falling?" Piper asked, trying to shake off the sudden chill that had settled over her. She hadn't put the two and two together until now. The Scirges *chose* to fall.

"Most human children dream of it," Cyril explained. "The drop, the rush; the part right before you wake. We live there. We're the wild children of the Reverie. We fall, and we catch humans who dream of falling."

Eda's laugh rang out through the wind. Piper's stomach tied in knots.

A dozen atmospheric beasts circled below them, their skin refracting the light and their wings cutting through the growing wind with ease.

"You have to train to be a Dreamer?" Piper asked, dumb-founded.

"Of course," Colik chimed in, his tone short.

"Train?" Cyril grinned. "We play. That's the point. Pan believed growing up makes you slow and cautious. Afraid. We learn how to be quick enough to escape. Even a fall."

Colik's expression was unreadable as he looked over the arena. "Quick, but not untouchable."

The Scirges either didn't hear him or pretended not to.

A streak of silver light abruptly blurred past, and a girl no older than fourteen crouched on the back of an atmospheric beast, hair whipping behind her, eyes alight with mischief. Coming around again, Piper watched her lean low as the sting ray looking beast skimmed past them, calling out, "Well? Are you playing or not?"

Piper blinked. "Playing what?"

Colik, beside her, didn't hold back. "The Scirges game."

"What...game?"

"The one they think matters," he said, low enough for only her to hear.

The beast circled a third time, darting just above the crystals and branches, the girl's laughter spiraling down like chimes. The air around Piper buzzed with a strange, expectant pressure.

"Come on, Dreamer!" she called again, laughter bubbling in her throat. "Let's see if you can fall correctly!"

Piper watched the beast circle around her repeatedly, her heart racing faster by the moment.

"This is insane," she whispered, feeling lightheaded.

"Insane would be an understatement," Colik said, his gaze fixed on the circling beasts. "Welcome to the Dreamers of falling."

Cyril's grin widened, teeth flashing white against skin silvered by windburn. "The game is called Kryvo i Kross. *Fall or Fate*. You and your partner—we call them twins—will ride an atmospheric beast, fight the windstorm to a ring, and trust that you or your partner will not fall off your atmospheric beast."

Before Piper could question his sanity again, Cyril lifted his chin toward the sky. "The game isn't ours originally," he said. "It belonged to the Twins in the Stars, Castor and Pollux."

Eda was already nodding eagerly. "They invented it long before the Dreamworld ever had Guilds or laws. Legend says the brothers carved a path through the night sky itself, chasing the same falling star. One held the light while the other steered through the darkness. They trusted the storm, trusted each other...and so their constellation was born."

Cyril continued, voice lowering. "They called it *the Crossing of Fates*. Two stars tied together, daring the fall." He motioned to the arena. "When the Scirges first learned to ride the atmospheric beasts, we felt the old pattern under our feet. The way the wind folded. The way the storm tested you. It was the same pattern the Twins carved above us. So, we took their game from the sky and made it ours here in the Reverie."

Eda leaned in, buzzing with anticipation. "That's why we call partners twins. It's not about blood. It's about trusting someone enough to fall with them and rise with them too."

Piper blinked. "You call that a game?" Voluntarily joining the Defense Forces of Ireland sounded better than that.

"Game. Training ritual. Same thing," Eda said with a skip toward the edge. "You play, you learn, or you meet your fate."

Colik's boots scuffed behind her. "They are serious."

"Lovely," Piper whispered, folding her arms as her pulse quickened.

"Who will she—" Eda began.

"Me," Colik cut in.

"An anchor to a flame," Cyril said with a sly, knowing grin.

Piper turned sharply. "Wait—what does that mean?"

Colik met her eyes, unreadable. "It means if you slip, you'd better hope I'm paying attention."

The girl who'd been circling them dismounted and joined Cyril's side. This close, she could tell that the silver of the beast had a tint of brownish yellow, just like her rider. She had striking bronze skin, amber eyes, and silver-threaded cornrows that...

Piper flinched from recognition. The silver in her hair reminded her of the Silver Girl. How close were the Scirges to the forgotten Silver Children? How much of their blood still sang in Scirge veins?

"The purpose of this game is to what exactly?" Piper said through clenched teeth, trying to keep her knees from shaking.

Colik stepped closer and wrapped his hand gently around her forearm, his middle finger grazing her skin. Warmth steadied her. Her eyes darted up, but his didn't meet hers.

"You know those nightmares where the ground rushes up and you wake before impact?"

She nodded. "That's only the surface of the fall. A true nightmare dives deeper." His hand slipped away. "That's where the Guild of Dreamers comes in. They stop the fall. The Scirges—" his voice drifted, "they guide the humans who dream of falling. They fall with them, keeping the dream from turning so dark the sleeper can't find their way back."

"You mean—"

"Turning so far into a true nightmare they never wake," he finished.

Eda rolled her eyes. "We're getting dramatic now."

"It happens." Colik glared at Eda, her rolled her eyes back at him.

Cyril laughed lightly, breaking their tension. "We Scirges must also trust the fall. To feel it. To remember it. If we forget what falling feels like, we lose the ability to guide humans out of it."

Piper swallowed. This wasn't a game. It was a test. A question. Would she trust this world? Would she choose to fall?

Suddenly—maybe because of Aisling. Maybe because of the kids at Olympus House. Maybe because she wanted to matter—she knew her answer.

"How do you play?" Piper asked.

Eda squealed.

"Holin?" Cyril prompted to the girl who had dismounted off the circling beast.

The young Scirge lit up like she'd been waiting her whole life for this question. "The twins—you and Colik—ride the beast through the heart of the windstorm and shatter the silver ring of the Kross Eye before the other twins do."

Piper tilted her head. "That's it?" She was clearly being sarcastic.

Holin snorted. "You make it sound *boring*. It is not boring. It is *brilliant*! Two riders, one swar, one fall."

Her grin widened as the wind howled overhead, tossing her silver curls. "The Eye opens for a breath. Miss it, and you fall through the clouds. If you trust your partner…" Her gaze flicked to Colik. "You might just fly, and you try again."

Piper frowned. "Swar?"

Cyril motioned to a rack of slender blades. "Dream-metal forged from stardust that fell and never rose. It is what you will shatter the silver ring with."

"Comforting," Piper muttered.

"Oh, it gets better," Eda chimed. "Each pair has one swar." She mimed a looping tether. "The anchor steers the atmospheric beast through the windstorm, while the flame cuts the silver ring."

"All about trust," Piper mumbled, her heart beating faster. She didn't know how to guide a beast mid-air or how to use a sword—or *swar*, or whatever the hell they called it.

Holin offered a small, steady smile. "This place doesn't ask for mastery, Piper. Only surrender. Let the wind catch you, and it will."

Piper exhaled slowly. "If I can't?"

"Then you learn how far trust can stretch," Holin said simply. "Like Colik said, hope he is paying attention." It was clear who was the anchor and who was the flame here.

"Come to the stables! You must pick your atmospheric beast."

Piper swallowed hard, her eyes shifting to Colik. He shrugged with an innocent smile.

Shit. This is happening.

They were led to the stables, which was a loose word for a metal ridge open to the sky. Dozens of atmospheric beasts perched along the ridge, their bodies rippling like airborne stingrays made large as small dragons. Their wide, fin-like wings unfurled and fluttered, catching the wind with a soft, sail-like shine. A few snorted, scattering sparks from their gill-like vents, the sound high pitch and child-like.

Sleek and immense, they glared with pale starlight along their smooth, iridescent hides. Their needle-tipped tails curved in slow, deliberate spirals, trailing a faint spray of silver dust behind them like comets shedding.

She recognized Folla, the one Eda rode, and of course Dray, Colik's beast. Up close, she finally saw what she had missed before. Each creature carried a faint tint beneath its silver iridescent skin, a whisper of color melding through their sheen.

Folla's hide had a mossy green hue, the same warm shade as Eda's eyes. Drays, by contrast, was a hard silver grey, and now that Piper stood close enough, she saw the truth in the wings and tail. They were not just sharp as ice. They were tinted with the exact cold hue of Colik's single blue eye.

Piper's jaw parted slightly at the sight.

Cyril tossed Colik a silver blade so thin it looked like it

might cut the air itself. "The swar. It burns when you clash, and cuts when you fail. Don't drop it."

Colik's handed the swar to Piper. "I am well aware of how a swar works." It was cool to her touch, and yet she felt a burning sensation run through her as her skin met the metal.

"This," Eda said, pointing to the coiled band of red strand wrapped around the swar's handle, "is what will tie to both of your wrists. It is why we call you twins. If you fall, you fall together. And fail as one."

Piper hesitated as Colik extended his wrist in silent offering. The swar stirred in her hand, as if recognizing the choice, she was about to make. When she looped the strand around his wrist, it curled on its own, coiling into a slow spiral of red light. The glow pulsed softly, like a heartbeat that wasn't hers or his but something between them.

Then the swar responded to her. Part of the red string slithered free from his wrist, leaping like a live current, and wrapped around hers in one swift motion. It didn't stop at her skin but sank deeper, lacing through her veins until she swore she could feel its pulse merging with her own. It felt less a connection, and more a claiming.

She tried not to react to the warmth that brushed through her fingers when her skin grazed his. The instant the strand sealed around both their wrists, a thin, luminous tether unfurled between them, pulsating in the air, as if they were now breathing from the same breath.

Piper jolted in place. The sensation was hauntingly familiar, an echo from somewhere beyond memory. She had felt this before—maybe in a dream or maybe in another life—but the recognition struck hard and uninvited. The déjà vu was so strong it made her dizzy, as though the swar had been waiting for her, written into her blood long before this moment.

"If the red string ever unties," Cyril said, his voice calm but carrying a quiet warning, "it means you've been disarmed. In real use, one Dreamer is tied to one swar, and the strand loosens when the bond between them and the swar fails and the dream-metal refuses to hold."

He tapped the red strand between their wrists, and it flickered faintly.

"For this game, we've branded it, which means the dream-metal has been shaved down so it won't drink as deeply from the dust in your wrists. It keeps the bond loose, so you won't snap apart by mistake."

Piper glanced at the thin, loosely hanging strand between them.

Cyril nodded at the slackness. "It isn't meant to tighten here. If it ever does…" His eyes flicked between them, something unspoken tightening the space. "That happens when the swar decides your fate is shifting. When it tightens, it never does so gently."

Piper grasped the swar tighter, her hand squeezing around the metal handle.

"Try not to tug," she tried to joke with Colik

"Try not to fall," he said, matter-of-factly.

What in all the gods…

Instead of mounting Folla, Holin hopped on her own beast, then helped Eda on after her. They both looked at her, expectantly. "Ready to play?" Holin pressed.

What harm was one game?

Cyril's voice followed like a shadow. "In exchange for a place for sleepers' rest while the dust cloud settles, we ask that you play the Scirges game."

Piper looked at them. Eda and Holin smiling. Cyril with an eyebrow raised. Colik staring her down with a look that was starting to get creepy. They were all watching. All *waiting*.

Piper's throat tightened. She thought of Olympus House. Of the children who were never picked. Of wanting to feel *part* of something, just once.

"One game?" she asked.

"One game," Colik answered for Cyril.

Piper swallowed hard, the wind tugging at her hair as if pressuring her too. She drew in a breath that trembled at first, then steadied.

"I'll play."

Holin erupted into a shout of victory, and Cyril's hands came together in one sharp clap, his gaze sparking like struck flint.

Eda smiled behind Holin. "So, it begins!"

"Great!" Cyril said, grinning so wide his freckles nearly disappeared. "Now, pick your atmospheric beast. Your beast is more than a mount. It feels every doubt you have. Even the smallest flicker."

He tapped two fingers to his temple. "Lose trust in your partner, and the beast will feel it. It will stop trusting you as a pair..." Cyril lifted his shoulders in a helpless shrug. "It will make its own choice to fall. Both of you. Your fate in the game is over before it even begins."

He motioned toward the ridge of massive, starlit creatures. "Beasts are loyal to one rider. For this game? The twins work as one."

Piper followed his gaze. "Fall or fate," she mumbled.

Cyril's grin returned, fierce and childlike. "Exactly. Now Piper, choose your be—"

"—Not Dray," Colik cut in quickly.

Piper gave Colik a confused look, not sure if he was joking, then huffed and rolled her eyes as she faced the creatures again.

Dray is loyal to one.

They hovered before her like living shards of a dream made flesh. Their wings beat slow and powerful, stirring the air with the hush of distant storms. One creature gleamed with a faint wash of sea-glass green, while another drifted through the air in a soft purply-pink glow, its light blooming around it like a suspended mist.

None of them looked at her. Their slit for eyes slid past her as if weighing her dust and finding it wanting. One by one, they turned away, wings folding back, tails curling in quiet dismissal.

Piper's chest tightened.

Right. How do you choose a beast if it won't even look at her.

Then she felt a prickling along her spine.

A third creature, half-hidden behind the others, drifted up above the first two. Its ray-like hide shimmered with an emerald hue, deep and shifting, like light moving through forest glass. It was beautifully shaded and dangerous, and its eyes locked on hers.

It was ready to play.

The beast drifted forward, wings unfurling in a slow, reverent sweep. As it approached inches to her face, the air around her began to vibrate. The thrum pressed into her ribs and settled there, matching the rhythm of her heartbeat. At her side, Colik drew in a sharp breath, the sound quiet but unmistakable.

"That one," Piper whispered.

"Yes," Colik affirmed.

Eda and Holin both saluted Piper with matching, mischievous grins before Holin's beast launched into the air. The creature released a low, playful screech as the girls slipped into their dual nest-like makeshift saddles, already splitting through the windstorm brewing with effortless, practiced ease.

"It's harder than it looks," Colik said, swinging onto the beast Piper chose in one smooth motion. He settled into the saddle of braided ivy, unbothered as the beast's comet-tail whipped once beneath him in a testing lash. He held steady. "You'll be fine."

Piper stepped closer toward the emerald-hued beast, as to not let the red strand between her and Colik loosen. Her palm brushed its nose, its skin cool and impossibly smooth, like polished stingray hide. The beast breathed out a soft thunder, and the saddle reshaped itself along its spine, unfurling vine-straps and luminous petals in a silent, unmistakable invitation.

Cyril stepped toward her with a conspiratorial grin. "Let me help you onto your beast." He reached out, but before his hand could even graze her back, Colik's voice cut through the air.

"I have it from here." It was calm, controlled, and territorial.

Cyril lifted both brows, chuckled under his breath, and backed away. The red swar between her and Colik pulsed once, sensing the decision.

Only then did Colik extend a firm hand down toward Piper. "You'll need to put both arms around me," he said, his voice low and careful. "Your dominant hand has to hold the swar against my side."

Heat curled low in Piper's chest. She stared at his outstretched hand, at the confident line of his shoulders, at how the emerald glow of the beast caught in the white of his hair. The cool wind tugged at her clothes, urging her forward…but the pull in her chest was stronger.

She placed her hand in his, and an instant spark skittered up her arm. He drew her up with surprising strength, guiding her into the make-shift saddle behind him. She slipped into place, her hands coming to rest at his waist, tentative at first, then tightening when the beast shifted beneath their weight.

The red swar-tether between them brightened for a moment. She pressed it tight against his side with her dominant hand like he said. Her cheek hovered just shy of his back, close enough to feel the warmth of him. His scent was pine touched by winter frost. It was clean, sharp, and edged with a danger she couldn't name.

Their beast hovered to the edge of the towering ridge, wings stretching wide. The arena's windstorm roared up to meet them. Piper held on to Colik, fingers locking tighter around him.

"Both twins ready?" Cyril called from above, perched atop his own atmospheric beast. A small horn was pressed to his lips, the sound carrying his voice across the coliseum.

"Ready!" Eda shouted from somewhere Piper see.

Colik turned his head just slightly, enough for her to see the curve of his smirk.

"Are you ready?"

Piper swallowed hard. "Not even a little."

"Good," he said, the smirk deepening. "That's how all the best games start."

CHAPTER ELEVEN
THE SLEEPER'S REST

The air split as their beast launched off the ridge, and Piper's stomach dropped. It was like a roller-coaster plunge with no bottom, no end, and pure freefall. Nothing like the steady glide she had felt riding Folla to Kryvos Hollow. That had been smooth and predictable. This was anything but. This was wild and *fast*.

Colik sat in front of her, the wind clawing through his white hair as he steered the beast into the storm of winds. Piper pressed her thighs against the creature's slick sides, trying to anchor herself while her right hand clutched the swar and his waist with every ounce of strength she had.

The wind didn't just hit them. It *turned* on them.

One moment they were diving cleanly into the currents, and the next the entire storm lurched sideways. The sky tilted. The beast banked hard left without warning, its massive wings slicing through a violent crosscurrent that felt like a physical shove.

Piper's scream tore out before she could stop it.

Her grip slipped. The swar in her hand seared hot, reacting to her fear.

"Hold on!" Colik shouted, shifting his weight in one fluid,

practiced motion. The beast twisted under him, muscles rippling against the air.

A wall of wind slammed into them. Piper's body snapped backward, the red strand and her arm around Colik keeping her from being flung off into open sky.

For a terrifying heartbeat, they were sideways—*truly sideways*—the world a blur of emerald wings, silver clouds, and the dizzying drop beneath them.

Colik reached back blindly, catching her thigh and pulling her tight against him. "Lean with it, Piper! Not against it!"

She forced her body into his, mirroring his posture, pressing her cheek between his shoulder blades. As soon as she shifted, the beast responded. The strain in its wings softened, the violent tilt easing into a controlled curve.

The storm still roared around them, but the beast was no longer fighting it alone. They were part of its arc and its momentum.

She saw flash of metallic light ahead.

The silver ring.

That was too easy, and she was right. Before she could fully register it, the wind twisted again, sharper than before, clawing at them with a force that felt intentional.

"Ready or not," Colik's voice rose above the storm, "the wind is about to test you.

Whatever that flash of metallic was had disappeared in a snap. Instead, the wind sucked downward in a sudden, vicious funnel, dragging their beast toward the drop like an invisible hand closing around their wings.

Piper's stomach lurched violently as the beast pitched nose-first into a controlled spiral.

"Colik—!" she choked out.

"I know!" he snapped, though not at her, but at the storm, at the beast, and at the impossible angle they were dropping toward.

The emerald beast fought to level out, its massive wings

cutting through the downdraft with deliberate, powerful strokes. It wasn't panicked—Piper realized that now—it was *working*, adjusting, and reading the storm with instinct.

Even so, her pulse hammered as the sky spun around them in a blur of silver lightning and churning clouds.

"Colik—" she gasped again, her fingers slipping on his waist.

He reached back, catching her forearm with a firm, grounding grip. "Piper. Breathe."

"I am," she lied, voice thin.

"Trust the beast," he said, steady and calm despite the chaos. "It knows the fall better than either of us."

Another jolt of wind hit them, but the beast shifted instantly, tilting its wings to carve through the current with controlled, practiced precision. The atmospheric beast had a coiled strength, choosing its movements with purpose.

Piper swallowed hard, pressing closer into Colik's back.

"Trust me!" He cried over the gush of air. "Lean where I lean. Move where I move."

The beast surged forward as if answering him, folding into the storm with a confident dive.

Piper's grip slipped again as the wind pushed against her, the beasts slick skin offering nothing to hold onto. Her knee slid. Then her hip. She felt her balance tipping.

The storm roared, seizing her with cold fingers of wind. Her body tilted backward, weight pulling her off the saddle.

The world went upside down, and she felt herself falling off the saddle. The windstorm opened beneath her, and the swar in her hand burned white-hot, snapping tight in warning.

Colik whipped around so fast she barely saw it. His hand shot out, snatching her arm just as she slipped past the saddle's edge.

"Piper!" His voice cracked through the storm. "Lean forward. Now!"

He hauled her back against him, her chest slamming into his spine. The red strand between them buzzed with tension, vibrating like a live wire. It strained again, sensing how close she was to being lost.

"Listen to me," Colik said sharply, his breath ragged. "You must move with me, or you will never learn to fall. You will never learn to be a Dreamer."

To be a Dreamer.

Piper forced herself to breathe, pressing her right ear against his back as the beast spiraled upward. Her hands locked around him again, his body a solid shield against the storm, and slowly her senses began to return.

In. Out.

She matched her breath to the rise and fall of him until she could feel his heartbeat, fast and steady at the same time, guiding hers back into rhythm.

"I'm ready," she breathed into his back.

She felt Colik exhale then, a deep quiet breath that told her he had been holding tension he would never admit aloud.

He leaned left. She leaned left with him.

He shifted right. She mirrored. He angled his body upward, muscles coiling, and the beast responded, wings snapping wide. With a violent surge of strength, it tore out of the funnel, banking hard with a triumphant screech that rattled her bones.

Piper gasped, chest heaving.

Colik didn't turn, but she felt the slight drop of his shoulders, the release of tension. "Good," he said, voice low. "You listened."

Her voice trembled. "I almost fell."

"You didn't," he answered.

They barely had time to steady themselves. A sharp whistle split the air and Piper twisted to find the source, but the storm's glare blurred everything.

Colik stiffened beneath her. "Incoming."

From the left, Eda and Holin burst through the wall of clouds, their beast streaking. It cut across the sky in a blazing arc, straight toward them. The silver mist split open as the two beasts shot toward the same target. The silver ring of the Kross Eye bloomed ahead of them like a shiny prize.

Eda and Holin angled their amber beast upward, laughter echoing as they surged ahead.

Colik leaned into their beast, guiding the emerald creature through the spiral.

"Piper, the swar!" he shouted.

She gripped the glowing red strand, heart hammering. The ring pulsed and Piper raised the swar, aiming to slice through the silver halo—

She wasn't alone. Eda was there too. Close. Too close. Their beasts collided in the same stream of current, wings brushing. Piper's aim jerked to the side. Instead of striking the ring cleanly, her blade arced toward Eda's swar.

"No—!"

Piper braced for impact, but Eda didn't move like anyone else. At the last possible instant, she folded the air around her. Her body tilted in a way that defied every law of gravity, the sky itself bending to make room for her.

One heartbeat she was there—hair wild and laughter sharp—the next, her entire form dissolved into a burst of light and wind. The spot where she'd been exploded outward like chalk dust scattered by an invisible hand. Then, as quickly as she'd vanished, she reappeared, already balanced on her beast's back as it bolted away, grinning like a phantom who'd cheated death.

"Missed me!" she called, voice ringing through the storm.

Colik smirked, seemingly unbothered.

Piper gasped. It wasn't just a dodge. It was like watching someone take control of the fall itself, turning a stumble into flight. It made the impossible look like child's play.

"What was—" Piper started, but Cyril broke her question,

having flown up to meet both of their beasts, unbothered by the storm.

"Oi!" Cyril's voice boomed like thunder. "Cut that out right now!" Cyril's eyes were burning at Eda as he pointed a finger at her. "Gravity breaks during a game? Are you trying to get us all severed by the Fatales? Because that's how you get locked in the Room of Lockes, Scirge."

Eda dropped her eyes like a scolded child, but her smirk didn't vanish entirely. "Sorry, Cyril," Eda said quickly, her voice singsong. "Didn't mean to float the rules."

Some of the Scirges on the crystalline ledges watching snorted with laughter. A few even clapped, but Cyril wasn't amused.

"You're not invisible, no matter how good you are at vanishing into clouds. Every time you pull one of your tricks, you are noticed. Next time, it won't be me shouting! It'll be the Fatales slicing you out of the air themselves."

Eda went quiet, though the light behind her eyes didn't dim.

Colik leaned toward Piper and seeing she had already seen too much, muttered, "That is the Scirges little secret... they fall, but never have to land."

Piper gave him a sidelong glance, completely forgetting about the game for a moment. "What?" Her hands tightened around him again as their beast jerked away from the crowd.

"Scirges," he said, eyes flicking toward Cyril as he flew off, followed by the other team of twins.

"They don't just break rules. They break gravity. Drift midair, bounce off walls, fall through barriers... It's why they're impossible to catch, if they don't want to be."

"Sounds more like magic than a game."

"Sounds dangerous to me," Colik said, shrugging. "And that's the problem. They're not supposed to show it. Not in front of a human."

Suddenly, Colik dropped his weight hard onto one side,

pulling the beast into a violent, banking dive. Piper clung to him, arms locking around his waist, her cheek pressed to his shoulder as the wind screamed past.

The amber beast skimmed inches above them, so close Piper felt the heat of its wings flash across her back. The emerald beast jerked from the turbulence, its body tilting in midair.

"Piper, lean right!" Colik barked.

She did, too fast.

The beast overcorrected, spinning them sideways. The sky flipped. It was a storm above, then below, then above again. Her vision blurred. Tears stung her eyes from the wind.

Eda and Holin weren't finished. They looped around in a sharp hook-turn, aiming to slice between them and the silver ring ahead.

"They're cutting us off!" Piper shouted.

"Then we don't let them." Colik's voice dropped to something dangerously calm. "Hold on, Piper."

He steered them straight into the next twist of the storm. The storm opened before them like a giant mouth, its winds whipping in violent spirals that carved rings through the sky. The silver ring of the Kross Eye flickered in and out of view, blinking through the chaos like a pulse of light.

Another flash of amber tore past on their right. The other twin's beast spun upward, leaving a trail of sharp, star-born dust in its wake.

"They're going for the Eye!" Piper cried.

"So are we," Colik answered.

The emerald beast roared, the sound low and deep, echoing through Piper's bones. It shot forward, matching the storm's spiral, climbing higher until the air thinned and the clouds tore open to reveal the *Kross Eye*. A metallic ring suspended in living storm light, pulsing silver. Open for only a breath.

"Now!" Cyril's voice called distantly from somewhere far below. "Shatter it!"

Colik leaned forward sharply. The beast dove beneath the ring's spinning edge, its wings slicing cloud. The other twin's beast was already climbing into position, Holin shouting commands over the storm.

He lifted one hand from the reins. "Piper," Colik called out, reaching back with one hand, palm up. "The swar."

Her heart lurched. "Is that part of the rules?"

He turned his head just enough for her to see his one silver-gray eye fixed on her. It was confident.

"Trust me."

The storm roared around them and the other beast streaked closer. The silver ring ahead flickered with silver light, moments away from closing.

Piper swallowed hard, then placed the swar into Coliks waiting hand. The moment his fingers closed around the swar, the tether between them blazed, light coursing through it like molten glass. Piper gasped, heat pulsing from her wrist to her chest. Their dust synced. Their breaths synced. Their fear synced.

Colik lifted the swar, its blade-like length shimmering in the storm light.

The amber beast lunged for the Kross Eye at the same instant. The ring began to close.

"Colik!" Piper shouted.

"Lean into me and hold on tight!" he answered, and she did without hesitation. The emerald beast responded instantly, banking so hard her vision blurred. The twin's beast attempted the same move, but the storm slammed into them, knocking them out of line.

A perfect opening.

"Now!" Piper cried, surprising herself.

Colik raised the swar, its tip ignited with red light. The

ring snapped half shut, and he slashed, the blade striking the heart of the Kross Eye.

A sound like a bell made of starlight cracked through the arena. Silver shards burst outward, scattering into the storm like shattered constellations. The shockwave hit them, a blast of wind and pressure that nearly threw Piper backward.

Cheers erupted below them, the Scirges' cries wild and echoing. The windstorm itself answered, thunder rolling like applause. They had won *Kryvo i Kross*.

The beast angled downward in a graceful arc, preparing to land back at the ridge. The remnants of the silver ring flickered behind them like a dulling moon. Piper could see the swar still pulsing against Colik's hand, but the red string coiled around her wrist tightened.

Piper flinched. A strange tingle pricked up her arm.

"Colik," she whispered, lifting her wrist.

The red strand was moving. It wasn't just glowing but tightening, drawing in on itself, twisting tighter around her skin. One coil snapped so sharply she felt the sting, like it might snap entirely.

"Colik," Piper said again, voice breaking. "It's too tight."

Colik's head whipped toward her. His eyes widened with a kind of fear she'd never seen in him. The strand constricted further, trembling as if deciding whether to snap or bind.

"No," he said, not to her but to the swar itself. His tone shifted, suddenly hard and commanding. "Not here. Not now."

He reached across the saddle and caught her hand. The moment his palm touched hers, the red strand reacted violently, tightening once more—so sharply Piper gasped—and then it collapsed, loosening all at once as if recoiling from itself. Its blade flashed, the heat draining instantly from it. The red strand fell slack against her wrist for a heartbeat before curling back into place. The air around them went cold.

The emerald beast faltered mid-flight, wings shuddering

once before leveling out. The game was over, but the silence that followed wasn't victory. Not anymore.

Piper's pulse roared in her ears.

"What just happened?" she whispered.

Colik didn't answer. His eyes swept the storm, then the sidelines, scanning the crystalline ledges as if searching for someone. Or something. The swar still glowed faintly in his hand.

He pressed his heel into the beast, guiding it toward the landing arch.

Piper looked down at her arm. Its red string was wound around her wrist again, but near her skin it had darkened, shifting from bright red to a dull, iron-like color.

When they landed, Colik dismounted first, then turned to help her down. His hands were careful—too careful—and lingered longer than they needed to.

She met his eyes. "You didn't answer my question."

"I don't know exactly." He exhaled once, sharp. "I will admit, I should have not taken your role and cut the ring myself," he said quietly. "I interfered, and the swar...reacted. Nothing for *you* to have to worry about."

As promised, Cyril led Piper and Colik toward a hidden corner of the Kryvo Hollow where glass and greenery intertwined. Lanterns shaped like flowers hung low from curved crystal branches, each one glowing with a cluster of tiny, winged creatures that shimmered like molten fireflies. Their light drifted lazily over the narrow path, painting their faces in hues of green and gold.

Colik's hand stayed firm at the small of Piper's back while they crossed the narrow vine bridge between two glowing mounds. His gaze hadn't wavered from hers, not since the red strand unraveled from their wrists and Cyril reclaimed the swar.

Beneath them, mist and foliage blurred together into a silver-green haze. When Piper made the mistake of looking down, her stomach dropped, and her grip on the vine railing tightened until her knuckles whitened. She could fly...but bridges. She hated bridges.

"You alright?" Colik asked softly, his breath warm against her ear.

"Fine," she muttered, jaw tight. She didn't dare linger on the tingles that ran through her when his breath touched her skin.

"I'm sure you are."

They followed Cyril up a spiraling ramp where the crystals grew denser, wrapping the walls in glassy veins of light until the passage opened into a hollow at the top of the mound.

"The best of the best for a Royald," Cyril stepped aside and motioned them in, "and well...*Piper*." He said her name like it held its own importance. As if that would have happened.

He winked at Piper all the same. Colik stiffened beside her.

At least he didn't call her the Dreamer again. Because what if they were wrong? What if she wasn't one of them at all? Would they send her back? Or worse, imprison her like the gods did the Silver Children?

The thought pressed against her chest until it hurt.

"You can rest here until the dust cloud settles," Cyril stated, giving Colik a nod of respected acknowledgement.

The chamber inside was breathtaking. Light filtered through translucent walls streaked with vines that bloomed faintly in the shadows. At the center rested a circular bed of moss and soft fern.

Piper glanced toward Colik, brow furrowing. Was the dust cloud *that* bad?

"With that dust stirring above the Broken Woods," Cyril added, his gaze flicking to hers, "we wouldn't want a human wandering about. Especially you, Piper."

Colik stepped forward, his tone smooth but firm. "This will do. Thank you."

"At your call, Royald. I do ask that you speak to Lulu about the Polaris." Cyril gave a small bow, a grin tugging at his lips.

Colik nodded. "Of course."

Cyril turned back to her. "I am eager to see the path you make here for yourself, Piper." Then, without another word, he backed toward the arched entrance, letting the hánging vines fall behind him like earthly curtains as he slipped out of sight.

Silence settled the moment he left, the crystal chamber humming in slow, steady breaths. Piper's heartbeat thudded too loudly in her ears, every beat reminding her how close she kept coming to wanting something she didn't even understand.

"Still fine?"

She nodded, but her body betrayed her with her tight shoulders and shallow breath.

"No, you are not," Colik said, settling onto the moss-and-fern bed as if it had been carved for him. "You've gone quiet, and that is rare for you."

The bed's base was cradled by curved shards of translu-cent crystal, each one glowing from within. Tiny roots spilled down the sides, threading into the crystalline floor and pulsing in slow, soft intervals.

"Come on," he said, patting the space beside him, his tone a mix of coaxing and command. "Try it. It's safe."

She narrowed her eyes. "Safe. That is not comforting coming from you."

He smirked, but the expression faded as soon as it appeared. "You can trust me," he said, quieter this time, as if the words cost him something to speak.

Something in that contradiction—the way he moved toward her and away from her simultaneously—tightened something deep in her chest.

Against her better judgment, she stepped onto the glowing moss bed. It shifted fluidly beneath her feet, and she immediately slipped, falling forward onto her hands and knees as her hair swung wildly into her face.

"Smooth."

She glared through her hair, cheeks hot. "You're impossible."

"Only when it works."

They reclined together, shoulders brushing, the moss bed swaying gently with their breaths. The contact startled her more than it should have. Morry had brushed her shoulder in the graveyard once, leaning in, but it had felt wrong.

This didn't.

This felt dangerous.

Above them, the canopy drew back as if the trees themselves had peeled open the sky. Constellations arched overhead in silver geometry, with veils of colored light weaving between them. No yellow. No gold. Just blues, greens, violets, and molten silver.

"Why aren't the stars yellow like in the waking world?" she whispered.

"Because yellow means illumination," Colik replied. "Revelation. Answers. The Reverie shows what the dust permits."

His gaze dropped to her wrist, where the red strand had darkened as if listening.

"Sometimes the constellation cloud knows before we do."

"The constellation cloud," she echoed.

"Yes, what you humans call the sky."

"Hmm."

He returned her "hmm" with a soft, teasing smile that made her heart flip. "The stars can be yellow or gold. You simply haven't seen them in the right light yet."

She turned toward him, only to find him already watching her. Watching her closely. Watching her like he was memorizing her breath.

"What?" she whispered, her heartbeat stumbling.

"You are rare."

"So are you."

"Not like that."

A tense, quiet moment followed. The sky shifted overhead.

"You'll need sleeper's rest," he said. "Given you're a human."

"You don't?"

"Not like you. Dreamers do not sleep the way humans do. This world is already sleep. Thought becomes rest here. Want takes the place of need." His gaze lingered on her face. "You must not will your body to sleep. Not yet."

"If I fall asleep here…"

"You will lose this," he said softly, and the way he said it made her throat tighten. Did he mean lose this world. This sky. Or lose him.

"That's why sleepers use ties," he added, voice velvety and steady.

"Ties."

"Someone to keep you anchored while you rest. So, you do not slip out of the Dreamworld by accident."

"You would tie to me?" she whispered. "You would keep me here?"

His knee brushed hers. Warmth sparked through her body like a struck match.

"Yes. A tie works two ways. Me here, holding you. Or your world using you to pull someone back."

Her breath caught. "Steele has been…"

Colik froze. He blinked once, sharply. "I will not rehash that."

He sat up slightly, shifting away without distancing himself. Then his eyes dropped to her mouth and stayed.

Her breath hitched. So did his.

"You're staring," she whispered.

"I'm deciding."

"Deciding what?"

"Whether I should," he murmured, and his fingers brushed hers.

Then he leaned in, slowly and carefully. Their mouths were nearly touching. A hair's breadth away. Her lips parted, ready, wanting.

Then he stopped. Just before he kissed her, his breath shuddering, as he pressed his forehead against hers for a heartbeat.

"I can feel it," he whispered, voice trembling. "Your heart. The way it beats." His eyes fluttered shut. "You feel the connection too. The emotions flooding between us. Humans and Dreamers are not meant to share this. It is forbidden. It is unnatural." His voice cracked, quiet and aching. "It does not stop me from wanting to get close to you. Even for a moment."

She didn't breathe.

Colik exhaled shakily, pulling back just enough that she saw the war behind his eyes.

"I cannot kiss you, Piper," he said. "Not yet. Not until I know your place here."

Her heart dropped.

"But," he added quickly, his eyes brightening with something hopeful, "if the Royalds can figure out what you are meant to be, if they can understand your role in the Reverie, then maybe…" His smile, small and unsteady, held a hope he tried to hide. "Maybe you can become a Dreamer. Or more."

Her breath stilled.

"If that happens," he said, excitement flickering through his voice, "I will help you. All of it. Sleepers rest. Learning the dust. Navigating the Citadel. Everything. When you wake up, we will go to the Citadel and unravel this together."

She swallowed hard, unsure whether she was falling into something impossible or being offered something too fragile to hold.

"How do I rest?" she asked.

He softened, truly softened, in a way she had not seen before. His hand found her wrist. His thumb brushed slow circles there.

"I will keep you from slipping back," he said. "I will hold the Dreamworld to you for as long as you sleep."

Her chest tightened. His touch was warm. His voice was quiet.

"Okay, I trust you," she whispered. Her eyes closed without meaning to, and sleep pulled her under.

The last thing she felt was the brush of his thumb on her pulse and the almost-kiss that echoed in the space between them.

Piper jolted awake, slamming against her bedroom door.

For a heartbeat she couldn't move. Her body wasn't frozen so much as confused, caught between sleeping and waking, as if the instructions to breathe, blink and stand had scattered. She felt everything at once and nothing clearly, awareness drifting inside a shape that didn't feel like hers.

Then her body caught up.

A violent shudder tore through her, every nerve sparking like it had been ripped apart and shoved back together. Her bones felt as though they'd been poured into her too fast, her skin struggling to contain them. She felt the scrape of her dust dragging into place, fragments of herself slotting back together in a rush that left her gasping.

"Piper!" Penelope's voice came muffled from the other side, followed by a sharp rattle of the knob. The door pressed inward, catching on Piper's weight. "Are you in there? The children are becoming wild. Come help me, please!"

Children. Wild.

Piper's heart was still running at the dream's pace. Then, too quickly, her body settled, everything snapping into place within a few blinks.

She was back.

She hadn't kissed Colik, but she would have. He was the one who leaned in first. He was also the one who stopped it, hot and cold all at once, like a boy who didn't know what he wanted or was too afraid to admit it.

How was she back?

The memories of the Dreamworld were sharp and blurred all at once. She realized too late that she hadn't been resting. She'd been forgetting. The dream had been feeding, and he hadn't stopped it. Her body ached as though she'd dragged herself up from somewhere deep and dark just to stand here again. She could still feel the ghost of his touch on her wrist. Could still see the way his gaze had lingered, close enough to mean something, far enough to obey some secret he was unwilling to share.

"Piper!" Penelope's voice cut through again, the door bumping her shoulder this time.

"I'm—" Her voice cracked. She cleared it. "I'm coming."

She pushed herself upright, stepping away from the door so Penelope could swing it open. She stood there in her patchwork shawl, hair pinned messily, and one hand braced on the frame. Worry etched her face, but it was the brisk kind.

"How long was I gone?" Piper asked slowly, trying her best to hide the panic in her voice.

"Gone? The children said they saw you go to your room maybe an hour ago?" Penelope then brushed her own words away with her hand. "I know you have the day off, but it is our traditional Christmas movie night," she announced. "The children are antsy, and I'd like you to be on popcorn duty."

Piper nodded, hiding every shock she had in her mind, though her pulse was still caught between worlds.

Only one hour?

As Penelope turned away, her voice trailed down the hall. "No more hiding up here! I am begging you to help contain this chaos!"

Piper lingered a second longer, her gaze catching on the faint outline her body had left against the door. It wasn't just a shadow. It was dust. A thin, ghostly imprint burned into the wood, the kind the librarian had warned her about. Proof she hadn't simply woken up. She had broken apart, had turned to dust, and then reformed. The evidence clung there like a quiet accusation.

She lifted her hand, staring at her fingers, half expecting them to sift away into grains right then and there.

With a low, involuntary grunt, Piper brushed the back of her hand across her face, willing away the fog clinging to her mind, then started down the narrow stairs of Olympus House. Each step creaked in the same familiar way, the warm light spilling up from below as if she hadn't just been somewhere else entirely moments before.

Why was she back?

The scent of butter hit Piper before she reached the kitchen. Penelope was coming around the counter, shaking a dented pan over the stove, kernels rattling like rain against metal. The children's laughter echoed from the sitting room, loud and restless.

"Perfect timing," Penelope said, passing her going out as she was coming in. "Bowls in the cupboard and mind the salt… Last time you had them licking it off the popcorn like it was all there was to eat."

Piper reached for the largest bowl, her limbs still heavy from the way she'd woken.

Grunting again, she moved to the far counter for space, half-aware of the cold that seeped in from somewhere nearby, until she noticed it. The back door was open. Winter air curled in, lifting the hair on her arms. Beyond the door, the garden lay silver from the frosty air.

"Piper."

Her name, low and steady, rolled across the frost. She froze, her hand still on the cupboard handle.

Steele stepped into view, his coat dusted with ice, his cane catching a shard of light from the trees. His expression was unreadable, his presence sharp enough to make the open door feel like a mistake.

Something was different about him. He looked thinner than she remembered, the angles of his face more severe, like something was being slowly subtracted from him. The frost on his coat hadn't melted despite the kitchen's warmth, and when he exhaled, his breath didn't cloud the air the way hers did.

"I've been looking for you."

Piper's voice scraped out. "Steele?"

He stopped just beyond the doorway. "I need the Book of Godspells. Now."

Her brows knit. "I don't—"

"Don't play dumb," he said, a flicker of impatience in his voice. "You've been to the Dreamworld. You are tied to it now, whether you like it or not. I need that book before it's too late."

Her pulse jumped. "Even if I had it, why would I give it to you?"

"Because if you don't, I'll lose more than just my place there." Something shifted in his expression, brief and unguarded, like a door blown open by wind before being slammed shut again. "I am not supposed to be here, Piper. Not in this world. What it did to me—what I did to someone else—the book is the only thing standing between that cost and something neither world survives." His jaw tightened, the words clearly costing him. "Without it, what I sacrificed will not hold. And when it breaks, it will not break quietly."

He said nothing more. He didn't need to. The frost still clung to his coat. His breath still didn't cloud.

Before she could answer, Penelope's voice carried from down the hallway. "Piper, are you coming? Please spare me on Christmas day!"

She forgot it was Christmas.

"I—" Piper glanced over her shoulder, making sure Penelope wasn't about to walk into the kitchen. "I don't have it," she said quickly, turning back to Steele. "I don't know what you want me to do, but how did you know—"

"I want to know where it is," he interrupted and stepped closer, paler looking than before. Without warning, his hand closed around her wrist.

Piper jerked back, but not before the sudden rush of light-headedness hit, like something inside her had been drawn out. Just as quickly, the sensation ebbed, leaving her heart pounding.

"Aha." His eyes sharpened. He let go, stepping back with a smirk that didn't reach his eyes. "I'll come back, and you will tell me where it is."

Her voice steadied even as her stomach twisted. "Again… why would I do that for you?"

"Because I can help you get back there." His tone was matter-of-factly.

Her breath caught. "You can—"

He was already turning away. Where the stone met the dying grass, he paused, looking back once. "For good faith, I will tell you this: someone there has been taking your dust."

Her chest tightened. "How would you know?"

"Because I, too, have exchanged my dust for yours." His smirk deepened. "You have less now than you did when I saw you last."

He lifted his cane in a mock toast, then stepped into the shadows of the trees, and was gone.

Piper stared at the empty doorway. The frost his coat had shed lay on the outdoor mat in a thin scatter of white. It wasn't melting.

She glanced down at her wrist. In the dim light, the faint spiral scar on her thumb glimmered. She rubbed at it hard, willing it to fade, but a chill spread from her fingers upward instead.

It was slow and heavy, sinking deeper than both vein and bone.

CHAPTER TWELVE
THE WAKING WORLD

Piper made it through Christmas. Then New Year's came and went like a sigh in the wind. Still, time didn't feel real anymore. Minutes stretched into hours. A few days turned into a few weeks. The world moved forward, but Piper stayed stuck, adrift between what had happened and what she couldn't make happen again. She couldn't get back to the Dreamworld, no matter how much she tried.

What unsettled her most wasn't the wanting. It was the math of it.

She had been gone—truly gone, dust scattered across another world entirely—for what felt like days inside the Reverie. Long enough to ride an atmospheric beast, survive a game in the sky, and cross the Untold Brine. Long enough to be almost kissed by a Royald and start living a new life she quickly was getting used to. It was new and scary, but the Dreamworld made her feel more alive than her waking one.

In the waking world, no one had noticed her gone.

Not Penelope, who had knocked on her door once and accepted the silence. Not Ailin, who had assumed she was out on one of her walks. Not the children, who had chalked her absence up to her usual habit of disappearing into herself for days at a time.

She thought about that more than she probably should have.

Colik had tried to explain it once, standing beside the Motif River with the Blood Moon bleeding overhead. Time there didn't live the way humans understood it. Not hours or days, but frequency of moments. A single Blood Moon rotation could swallow what felt like a month inside the Reverie and return less than an hour to the waking world. Or the reverse—a breath inside the Reverie becoming days of stillness in Dublin, her body lying somewhere between sleep, dust and absence while the world moved on without her.

The trouble was she still didn't know which one had happened. She had come back after only one hour by the clock on her nightstand, but she had no way of knowing how many Blood Moon rotations had passed inside the Reverie in that time. No way of knowing how much of herself she had left behind.

What she knew was this: nobody had looked for her.

Not because they didn't care, exactly, but because she was Piper. The girl who stayed. The one who had always been there, quiet and present and predictable, folded into the background of Olympus House like old furniture. Her absence fit so neatly into the shape of her usual silence that it hadn't registered as absence at all. She could disappear into another world entirely, and the most the waking one would do was leave her porridge to go cold.

She returned to the library more than once, heart thudding with fragile hope each time. The wooden door was still locked, and a yellowed sign taped to it read: "CLOSED UNTIL FURTHER NOTICE."

No explanation. No one inside and no Steele.

Every night, when the lights clicked off and Olympus House fell silent, she lay awake staring at the ceiling.

Wondering if it had all been real.

Wondering if Colik had intentionally let her wake up.

Wondering if she'd ever hear Eda's laugh or feel the wind of the Broken Woods against her skin again.

It wasn't just her mind that missed it. Her body did too, in ways she didn't have words for. A low, persistent ache had settled into her bones, not painful exactly, but present. Like a hunger that food couldn't touch. Like something inside her had grown accustomed to a different kind of gravity and was quietly, stubbornly refusing to adjust back. In the Reverie she had felt lighter. Not weightless, but unburdened, as though the world there had no interest in holding her down. Here, Dublin pressed on her like it always had with its cold stone, grey sky, and particular heaviness of a life that didn't quite fit. She noticed it most when she climbed the stairs, or lifted her arms, or simply stood still too long. Her body felt like it was remembering a place her mind kept trying to forget.

All the while, a taste of dust lingered in the back of her throat. A reminder.

For what, Piper was dying to know.

The cheap desk lamp hummed faintly above Piper, its light pooling across the desk in a small, warm circle. A stack of library books lay open—anything she could get her hands on about Greek myths, constellations, and dreaming. She wasn't reading so much as circling the same lines repeatedly, pencil tapping against the margin.

It was the last Friday of Morry's winter break, so he was still gone, unfortunately. Not for her of course, since she didn't have classes to return to, deadlines to meet, or anywhere she needed to be that mattered. Just the Olympus House common room, this desk, and too much time thinking about the Dreamworld.

Piper dragged a fingertip down a page about Nyx, who she recently learned was the Goddess of Night. Ailin had her once follow a curriculum about Greek Mythology, but oddly enough, the Gods of Dreams or Night were not a part of it. Still, the words felt far away, like something she used to know but couldn't quite reach anymore.

The door to the common room squeaked open.

"Piper?"

Penelope's voice was gentle. She stepped inside, wrapped in her worn cardigan, a mug in one hand and a stack of papers under the other. Her cheeks were pink from the cold, hair falling loose from its clip.

"I thought you might want some tea," she said, setting the mug beside Piper. The steam curled sweetly upward. It was black tea with honey, just the way she liked it.

"Thanks," Piper murmured, not looking up.

Penelope hovered, eyes scanning the open books. "You've been keeping busy," she said, but Piper said nothing. She was still mad at her and Ailin for keeping all those secrets she overheard, even though Penelope didn't know she knew.

"I'm glad you're here. It's been nice having someone around who helps. Who is familiar with the routines and makes the place feel full."

Piper's stomach twisted. "You don't have to say that." She was repeating what Ailin had told her before Christmas.

"I mean it," Penelope pressed on. "Not everyone's path is clear right away. There is nothing wrong with needing time to find where they fit."

To Piper, there. Every word of comfort was a reminder that she'd never left. That while Morry was off chasing degrees and non-fiction stories, she was still here, stuck between who she'd been and who she felt like she was supposed to become. Until she woke up from the Dreamworld.

She forced a small smile and lifted the mug. "Yeah. I know."

Piper's jaw clenched, her chest tight. Looking at Penelope, all she wanted to do was ask about the secret she and Ailin had kept. She didn't because a piece of her hoped Penelope would eventually tell her. She had too…

Penelope adjusted the folder under her arm, her voice dropping low. "Sometimes it isn't knowing that saves us, Piper. It's patiently waiting and we both know that you aren't the most patient…" Her voice trailed off, her tone playful.

Piper didn't react.

Penelope lingered a few seconds longer, then turned for the door. "I'll be downstairs doing inventory. Let me know if you need help with your assignment."

"I won't," Piper said, too quickly. The soft sigh behind the door caught her anyway.

When her footsteps trailed off, Piper sat motionless, her eyes fixed on *Nyx* and *Astraea* in the open book. Astraea, she had read, was the Keeper of Stars.

Her pencil trembled, stilled just above the page. None of this was simple anymore. Astrology. Her dreams. Steele's demand for the *Book of Godspells*. The reason it mattered… Why *she* mattered. It was a knot tightening around her, and she knew she couldn't untangle it alone.

Piper hadn't planned on seeing anyone. She was there to look for more books now that the library was open again, but when she stepped into the back alcove of the Dublin Library, she saw him.

Morry sat slouched in one of the deep leather chairs beneath the domed ceiling, pale winter light striping across his shoulders. His jacket hung from the armrest, his boots stretched out in front of him, and in his lap lay a large book she didn't recognize.

She hesitated, clutching a small stack of books against her chest. "Didn't think libraries were your thing," she said finally, sliding into the chair across from him.

"I don't hate them," he said without looking up. "I just like finding the books no one else bothers with. The ones passed down through so many ages that they are almost forgotten."

She smiled faintly. "That sounds about right."

He looked up, and his eyes fell on the spines of the books in her hands—*Gods and the Divine Power*, *The Myths of Night, Dreams and Stars*, *Mapping the Heavens that Don't Want to Be Mapped*. A corner of his mouth lifted. "You've been busy I see."

"Just trying to make sense of some things."

"Looks like you're either starting a thesis for a class I didn't know you were taking or losing sleep again." The latter words were hesitant.

"Maybe both."

Something softened in his expression. He closed his book and leaned back, studying her.

"Can I help with anything? Not as a mockery or anything serious. Just two friends figuring out the cosmos."

She arched a brow.

He shrugged with nonchalance. "I could use a break from pretending my life's sorted out. Besides," his tone gentled, "we used to be good at this. Just talking. No expectations."

For a moment, she couldn't find words. The offer sounded simple enough, but there was something else beneath it. Something that she was scared to bring up again. Morry was her best friend.

She nodded and set her books on the table, next to him. "All right."

They quickly settled into a quiet rhythm. Piper pretended not to notice how easily Morry slipped back into her waking world or how natural it felt to sit across from him again. Still, she wanted to go back to *that* world.

Was that wrong?

The library was nearly empty, golden light spilling across the worn carpet. Morry started reading aloud from one of her books, his voice low, loud enough for her ears only.

"'Nyx stretched her veil across the heavens, weaving constellations into the dark so mortals might remember their beginnings. Yet not all stars were born of wonder. Some were woven in vengeance. When Zeus silenced the Silver Age and bound its children in shadow, Nyx took her grief to the sky. They say she threaded a secret—a darkness meant for him alone—one for one"'

Piper's pencil stilled. *One for one,* she thought. She had no idea what that could mean. When she looked up, Morry was watching her, the faintest smile in his eyes.

"See?" he said quietly. "Still a pretty good team."

A woman emerged from between the shelves. It was Himyla, the librarian. Her eyes swept from Piper to Morry, then to the books sprawled out on the oak table in between them.

"I don't believe we've met." Her eyes were on Morry, her smile warm but deliberate.

"I'm Piper Knell." Piper spoke up, straightening in her seat. "I met you right before Christmas… He is helping me with an astronomy prerequisite." Given their last conversation, she felt like she had to defend the texts she had open in front of them.

"Oh, yes, yes. I remember you." Himyla nodded, but didn't look pleased at the recognition, her gaze quickly passing to Piper before returning to Morry. For a moment, her expression went blank. Then her head tilted slightly, asking again, "You are…?"

"Morry Ovid," Morry answered evenly.

Himyla studied him briefly, but whatever she was looking for, she didn't find it. No spark of recognition from him, no startled catch of breath, nothing like the way she'd looked at Piper. Her gaze snagged on to the book *Mapping the Heavens that Don't Want to Be Mapped,* open to a page about the Greek myths scattered among the constellations.

"Stories like these," Himyla said quietly, her tone unreadable, "spill farther than the pages ever claim. The stars hold fragments of ages. Of waking and of sleep. Mortals have always searched for such places beyond their dreams, hoping to find something more than nightmares waiting behind their shut eyes."

Her lips pressed into a line, a pause weighted with something unsaid. "Remember—myths are safest when they stay myths. Keep your inquiries…educational."

Piper's hand froze on the pencil. Why wasn't she continuing her rambling tale like last time? Morry needed to hear it. From her, not from Piper.

"Even the Mimics?" she asked softly.

Himyla's gaze flicked to her, sharp and fleeting. "It's when you forget they are stories that they begin to trouble you." She adjusted her glasses, the gesture oddly deliberate. "Take care with it."

She turned and left. No further warning. No goodbye.

Piper sat frozen, the air heavy with what had been said, and heavier with what hadn't.

"What was *that* about?" Morry asked finally. He looked flabbergasted.

Piper's gaze was on the page the librarian's had been. "Probably nothing."

She didn't turn the next page right away. Her hand stayed where it was, pressed lightly against the paper, holding it closed against something. Her eyes, though fixed downward, were somewhere far away. Somewhere she knew Morry would never follow if she didn't tell him now.

Himyla's footsteps faded into the hush of the library, her shadow swallowed by the shelves. Piper waited until the last trace of her presence was gone before she spoke up, her voice unsteady.

"She's wrong, you know."

Morry didn't look up from his notes. "About what?"

"About it being just myths." Piper's thumb dug into the edge of her desk. "It's all real. It's happening. To me."

That raised his attention. Slowly, he closed his book and leaned towards her. "Piper—"

"No, just let me—" She stopped herself, swallowing the knot rising in her throat. "I've been holding back, and best friends don't do that. I haven't told you everything about the dreams."

Her voice softened. "Because they're not just dreams, Morry. They're places—whole worlds. I'm *in* them. I can feel the ground beneath me, smell the air, taste things. You can't tell me that's just my brain making it up while I sleep."

He stayed quiet, and it gave her room to keep going.

"There's this fort for wild children," she said, the words tumbling faster now. "High up in the trees. The Scirges live there—they guide humans when they start to fall in their dreams. That's what the Dreamworld is for. Why we dream. Or maybe *how*." She gave a shaky laugh. "I'm still not sure about the semantics but it makes sense why science can't explain it because the gods built it. They control it. They just don't want us to know."

Her hands moved as she spoke, sketching invisible lines in the air, as if she could anchor the images before they slipped away.

"They ride these atmospheric beasts, Morry. Enormous creatures that are translucent, with wings that slice through

clouds and hold steady against the wind. You should see them
—" She stopped herself, her voice softening to a whisper.
"There's this boy…who knows about that world. His name is
Steele."

The name lingered between them like a breath that
refused to exhale.

Morry's brow furrowed. "Steele?"

"He's not like the rest of them," she went on, voice trembling with something between awe and fear. "He's blind. Born
from the Silver Age, I think. There's something dangerous
about him, but I don't know what yet."

Heat rose to her cheeks. She reached for the open
astronomy text between them and tapped the page, her finger
landing on a sketch of constellations. "Even here. Nyx and
Astraea. The space between night and day, *waking and dreaming*.
It's exactly where I've been living, Morry. I am telling you.
The gods aren't just myths. They're—"

"Piper." Morry's voice cut through her words, quiet but
firm. "Stop."

She blinked at him.

"Alright…" He ran his fingers through his hair. Piper knew
that was his sign of distress. Oh no, maybe she shouldn't
have—

"I *want* to believe you," he said slowly, breaking her
thoughts. "I do, but dreams… They're meant to *feel* real.
That's their trick. They take what you've read, what you've
seen, even what you've felt, and they stitch it together into
something solid. Something that convinces you it's more than
it is."

"This isn't—"

"Please." His eyes were steady, but there was a tension
behind them, like he was afraid of something. "You're
searching for something in your dreams, I get it. But you won't
find it there. Not what you're hoping for. Not answers that can
explain or take you back *there*."

His eyes told her what he meant—he was implying her old home, the place before Olympus House, but that wasn't what she was searching for. Not anymore.

She stared at him for a long time, the words lodging sharp in her ribs. "So, you don't believe me, do you? You still just think they're just dreams."

"I think…" He leaned back slightly, his voice dropping lower. "I think you're trying to find a place to make up for a world that was cruel to you. Maybe even *trying* to live in two places in fear that one will never be enough for you." He sighed deeply. "The grass isn't always greener…even in your dreams, Piper."

It was the same cadence Himyla had said to her the first time she went to the library. It had the same weight behind the words, and Piper heard it instantly. She wasn't sure whether he knew he was echoing her, but it hurt way worse coming from her best friend than from a random librarian.

Her chest tightened as she asked, "I am not going to be able to convince you, am I?"

"As your best friend, I am saying maybe you should stop letting something you can't control decide what you do when you're awake."

The sentence landed heavy, like a door clicking shut.

Piper swallowed, but it didn't help. "You sound just like her," she murmured.

"Who?"

"No one." Her voice was flat. She wanted to tell him that he was wrong. Make him see that she had found things that felt more alive than anything in Dublin ever had, but the words felt too fragile. Too easy to break if she spoke them aloud again. It was as simple as that. He didn't believe her.

"Let's pivot to my educational studies, shall we? I am almost at my time limit," Morry teased, trying to lighten the mood.

Piper met his autumn gaze, at the innocence in his eyes, and forced a weak smile. "Alright."

Morry slid one of his textbooks toward her, the worn cover stamped *Philosophy and the Human Mind*.

"Help me annotate chapter twelve?" he asked, his tone careful. Too normal.

Piper nodded, but the words on the page blurred. Instead of reading, her gaze drifted to the constellation chart beside her, to the faint outlines of gods she now suspected might exist.

Beside her, Morry turned a page, the rustle of paper a small, cold sound in the unnatural stillness between them.

And for the first time since she'd woken from the Dreamworld, Piper wondered what she might lose *here* when she finally found her way *back there*. If she ever did.

I felt it before I saw it. Dust slid out of me, grain by grain, tugged by something I couldn't fight. My chest hollowed with every pull. My breath scattered into darkness.

The shadows moved first. They weren't shapes, not really, but hands made of smoke, curling around my arms, slipping between my ribs. Each touch stripped more of me away, and beneath it all came the faint hiss of dust leaving my skin.

Then the floor turned to glass, cold and clear and merciless. Beneath it, a serpent stirred. Its body was black as oil, coiled in endless rings, scales glinting like shattered mirrors. It rose from the abyss with a slow, deliberate grace, vast and godlike. A monster born of storms.

The serpent wound itself around a tree growing in the center of the room. It wasn't any tree I had seen. It looked like something from a greenhouse I had never entered, alive with vines and pale, trembling leaves, every branch glowing. It pulsed like a lifeline, its roots pressing against the glass as if desperate to break free.

The serpent tightened its coils, and the glow of the tree flickered, waning with each constriction until only a faint pulse remained.

That was when my dust began to burn.

Tiny sparks flared beneath my skin, glowing like embers beneath glass. They drifted from me one by one, rising through the air in silvery currents before sinking into the tree's veins. The moment they touched, the branches brightened, light surging through them like breath.

The storm serpent recoiled. Its scales scraped the glass, a harsh sound that filled the room. It hissed, coils tightening around the trunk as the light spread. The air trembled with its fear, or maybe mine.

My dust kept pouring out, unstoppable, drawn toward the tree. The serpent's body shuddered as if the glow burned it.

I didn't know if I was saving the tree, or if it was saving me.

CHAPTER THIRTEEN
THE DEAL

The nights had begun to haunt Piper more than the days ever could. During the day, she could fold herself into routine, wear her practiced indifference, and surround herself with faces that didn't dig too deep. In the dark, there were no distractions, only memories and silence.

If she did dream or fall into nightmares now, she never remembered them. All that lingered was the feeling of being tugged at from the inside, pulled toward something, or consumed by things hidden in darkness.

It had been a week since her tiff with Morry, and he'd buried himself back in his studies. Piper lay in bed, the hush of Olympus House pressing in, the air heavy with the smell of old linen and rain through cracked windows. All she could think about was leaving. She could walk out tomorrow, taste the night air, pretend it was the same freedom she'd felt in the Dreamworld, and tell herself it was enough.

Where would she even go?

Her restless mind spiraled until the hollow spaces swallowed her whole. Just when she thought the night couldn't press any heavier, a sound split the silence.

A *thud.*

Not the creak of old floorboards or the sigh of wind, but something heavy. Someone was downstairs.

Piper froze, her heart pounding as she listened. Another sound followed, this one quieter, like a footstep. Someone was coming up the stairs.

If Deeno sleepwalks into her room again…

The footsteps sounded heavier, coming from someone more considerable than a borderline malnourished hundred-pound child sleepwalking. She scrambled to her feet, creeping toward her bedroom door. She cracked it open and stepped out into the dark hallway. A shadow danced on the walls, faint and flickering.

"Piper."

The voice was low, rough, and unmistakably male. Her stomach dropped. She recognized it.

Steele.

She barely had time to react before he appeared at the end of the hallway, his silhouette against the faint glow from the stairwell. His black sunglasses locked onto her, intense and purposeful.

"What the hell…" She whispered. She quickly motioned him to step into her room, which he did with ease, the darkness not phasing his spatial awareness of things. Or blindness.

The door closed before she spoke again. "Steele," Piper hissed. "How… Did anyone see you?" This was creepy on so many levels.

"Don't worry," Steele reassured her, carefully stepping further into her room, but not directly toward her. "It's midnight. Everyone's asleep." His voice was calm, but a tension radiated from him like a warning bell. Piper moved over to her nightstand, subtly grabbing the alarm clock. It was the only tangible thing she could use as a weapon, if need be.

She noticed Steele smirk, but he said nothing.

"You can't be here." Her voice rose slightly in panic. "You have to go…"

Steele shook his head. "No, Piper. *You* must go back."

"What are you talking about?"

He stepped closer to her. "What happened before you woke up?" The question caught her off guard.

"I was at the—" She hesitated, lifting the alarm clock up in a defensive position.

"The Reverie. I know. What happened?" Steele pressed, cutting her off.

"I was with the Scirges and then…" She faltered again, her voice catching as the memory of her body trying to fall into a sleeper's rest came back.

Steele's features softened slightly. "Fine, don't tell me. I can sense it on you…" He stepped closer to her and inhaled. It was like her very essence breathed life into him.

He lessened his grip on his cane as she moved to the side of the nightstand, putting more distance between them as quietly as possible.

I could kick out his cane in front of him and knock him out in the head. The door is about—what—maybe six feet. Easy bash and dash.

"Sense what? The dust?" She remembered what he said before about—

"Someone is taking your dust…and…" His cryptic smile chilled her spine.

"What?" she demanded.

He didn't answer her. Instead, he paced around the room, which felt even smaller with him in it. It became some silent dance, him moving one way, her dodging him another way.

"I need that book, Piper." Steele's voice was sharper than before. The features behind his dark glasses looked intense, shadowed with an emotion she couldn't quite place. "You are the only one who can get me what I want."

Her throat turned dry. Suddenly, it all clicked together like pieces of a shattered mirror reforming: His nudging her toward the section on the gods. His pointed interest in her discoveries about dreaming. The mentioning of some *journal*.

It wasn't a coincidence. It had never been a coincidence…

Her pulse quickened. Colik had said the *Book of Godspells* held secrets about the gods and humans and their connection. Himyla acted fearful of it, and now, Steele wanted it.

What could he do with it?

"Let's make a deal," Steele said, his tone shifting again. It was smooth and coaxing.

Piper's instincts screamed at her to say no, to stay away from him as much as possible. The alarm clock stayed raised in her hand, ready to strike, but the promise of answers held her captive.

"What kind of deal?" she asked cautiously.

"Promise me you'll get the book," he said, his tone deliberately calm. "Then I'll tell you why I need it and help you return to *that* world."

The words hung in the air, heavy with both promise and threat. Every part of her warned not to trust him. Steele radiated danger, a web of charm and half-truths spun tight around every word, but the pull of the Dreamworld was stronger. The way the Scirges had spoken of the Silver Child —as if the gods had made them the villain instead of the victim—haunted her. The answers buried there, answers she had been chasing for what felt like her whole life, burned too bright to resist.

"Deal," she replied before she could second guess herself again. She lowered the alarm clock by her side. The time caught her attention: 11:11 P.M.

His lips curled into a grin, sending a shiver down Piper's spine.

"So where is it?" he asked her, and she looked back up at him. Did he really think she already had it?

"I have to get it."

"Where is it?" he repeated, his words more forceful. He had stopped pacing, his black sunglasses staring hard at her.

She hesitated a moment. "The librarian has it. I saw her with it, but she wouldn't give it to me."

The silence that fell between them stretched, taut and suffocating. Piper could feel his speculation simmering just beneath the surface of that pale skin of his.

Finally, she broke the tension. "I told you where it is, and I promised I would get it, but I can't and won't get it at three in the morning, so now you tell me why you want this book so bad. What is it?"

Another long pause.

Then Steele slightly tapped his cane on the floor as if striking an idea. "How about I tell you a story instead?"

"What kind of story?"

"A fire—to the past."

Her stomach dropped. No twisted in knots.

"What…" Her heart raced. Her eyes watered.

Fire…

Taking her reaction as an answer, he put the hand without the cane out to her.

"Take my hand."

She shook her head aggressively. There was no way he could know anything about the fire… She hardly remembered anything about it—

"What more do you have to lose, Piper?" His question broke her panicked thoughts but proved that he knew something that she wanted to know.

Heart pounding a million beats per second, she slowly put her empty hand in his. Her whole body tensed. A warm, burning sensation filled her, like the blood in her veins was speeding up, twisting her insides.

"Now look into my eyes," he whispered.

Piper tried her best to look through the black lenses and see his eyes, but she couldn't see anything. Not at first anyway.

Then, using the hand with the cane, he pulled down his glasses, and she could see everything. His eyes were red—

The hospital stretched before her, sterile and moonlit, though the light felt wrong. It had already caught fire. Beds lined the corridor like forgotten cradles, all empty but one: near the window, where a four-year-old girl lay curled beneath a blanket, her lashes trembling while she dreamed. The smoke had not caught up to her yet to wake her up.

Then came the scream.

The door burst open, and a young nurse, smeared with ash and shaking with urgency, stumbled into the room. Her eyes locked onto the child, and whatever fear lived behind them, it never reached her voice as she knelt by the bed. "We have to go now." She wrapped the girl in the blanket tighter as if hiding her from something watching from behind the flames.

The hallway was filled with smoke, and though the nurse coughed and blinked against the sting of it, she didn't slow. She opened door after door, searching for something she refused to leave behind. Every room spilled more chaos, fire dancing along curtains, tiles raining from the ceiling like broken bones, but still, she pressed forward, holding the girl close and shielding her from what she didn't yet understand.

At last, she stopped. A boy stood at the end of the hall, his face pale, his auburn eyes wide with shock that rooted him in place. When the nurse reached for him with her free hand, he took her hand without hesitation, as if he had been waiting all along to be saved.

Together, the three of them ran, not toward safety, but through the burning hall, because the building no longer offered any. The fire was not chasing them. It was consuming the building they had already lost. A ceiling tile shattered above them, and part of it struck the girl's exposed hand wrapped around the nurse's neck. She cried out, but with a breath that turned inward.

Embers clung to their clothes, and their footprints left trails in the ash. The nurse kept moving, guiding them through what were no longer hallways but a path of dust and flame burning in their wake.

Neither the nurse nor the boy looked back, but the little girl did. Her eyes widened as a wall of fire rose behind them like a god taking shape. From its heart stepped a figure born of white ash, his wings fractured, his eyes burning red enough to scorch whatever met their gaze.

He bent forward and blew——not to extinguish the flames, but to still them——and for a single breath, the fire froze.

His gaze shifted between the girl in the nurse's arms and the boy fleeing beside her. A flicker of confusion crossed his pale face——

"Nooo!" Piper shouted as the vision went dark and she was back facing Steele. Her hand went up to her mouth to keep from waking everyone. Steele stared at her, his dark glasses back over his eyes.

That girl was her.

Speechless, Piper closed her eyes, trying to hold the memory in place before it slipped away again. She had seen everything. Felt the panic. Saw the nurse's determination and her unbearable need to protect.

It was the girl who haunted her the most. *Her* eyes. *Her* trust. The way she followed without question. The boy running next to the nurse while she was in her arms. Both running blind into a fire.

How did Steele see that? This was the first time that memory came to her…after all these years——

The red eyes.

"It was *you*. You are the one with the red eyes that was added later in my file. But——" She was scared to press further, but Steeles silence confirmed it all.

Tears formed in Piper's eyes. Her heart wasn't just pounding, but racing out of control, like a war drum in her ribs. She bent over, coughing, trying to breathe, but it was like ash was stuck in her throat. Her knees buckled, and she staggered toward the bedframe, clutching it to keep upright.

"How did I see that?" she gasped. "How did *you* show me that? *Why were you there?*"

Steele didn't move. "That was the story of a little girl found alone in a hospital with no family. Eventually taken to Olympus House."

Her vision blurred. "Why were you there…" she repeated.

"How do I not remember that until now?" Piper's mind was jumbled, and her words were following suit.

"It is called remembrance," Steele answered with a practiced calm. "Some truths don't live in your waking mind. They hide. It is a space where memory does not die but retreats. A pool of forgotten truths, born from pain too great to bear. It's the dark water that feeds nightmares."

"It's mine. That was *my* memory."

"It was also mine."

Piper's stomach dropped. "How were you there?" she asked for a third time, sounding like a broken record.

Steele smiled. "That was me who helped still the fire. I am why you lived. Why you survived that unfortunate night. I also *updated* your file to include the most accurate details."

"What the hell do you mean?" Her question was now a demand.

"I told you." He was extremely calm, which infuriated Piper. "I've exchanged your dust with mine."

She shook her head. "I never——"

"You never what?" he questioned, eyes narrowing. "You don't even know what that means. How could you deny what you've already unknowingly given? I had to find a human in this world that carried dust and you——" He stopped, took a breath, then pivoted his words, "It's called a sandtie. When one being exchanges dust with another, a tie is formed between their strands."

As he spoke, something shifted. Piper blinked, and the room glitched. For one breathless instant, Steele's skin cracked like porcelain, silver strands glowing beneath. His glasses slipped down his nose, and she saw what lay behind them: white eyes with a red-coated ash for corneas. Silver wings—burnt, ruined, and skeletal—flickered behind his shoulders like a mirage.

Deep in his chest, just beneath his ribs, a dark light pulsed —raw and glowing.

Her body jolted backward and everything snapped back. Steele stood before her as before, seemingly unchanged. Her heart was screaming now.

"What—what *are* you?" She could hardly get words out.

For a long time, Steele didn't respond. Then, quietly: "You know what I am. You have known since you researched it in the library." *A Silver Child.* She hadn't been positive, but now she knew she was right.

"Do you know what happens to silver when it's left out of its element too long?" he asked. "It tarnishes."

She had no words.

He glanced at her. "Due to an unfortunate event… I have been ripped from my world. That world, and you are the only one who can help me get back."

Piper took a deep breath, hoping it would calm her pulse.

"What in your right mind would make you think that I would help *you* back? Help you with *anything* after that!" she snapped, not caring now if she woke anyone up. He needed to leave now.

He didn't flinch. "I am trapped here, and the longer I stay, the weaker I become. I had no choice but to tie myself to something still touched by *dreams*. I was there that night because of you, Piper Knell."

"*Me*," she breathed.

"Yes," he whispered. "Now, why *you* or how, those questions I do not know, but I had to isolate you. You'd been touched by the Dreamworld, and I needed you to be alone so that I could ration the dust you had until you were old enough to help me back."

What!

"So, you were using me as your own emergency dust bag? What a sick—"

"I am not the only one taking your dust," Steele cut in. That stopped Piper.

They both stood there, and silence filled the room again. She looked down at the crooked wooden floorboards, trying her very best to process it all and quickly.

"Then who is?"

"I'll be honest with you," he started, tapping the cane once, the sound dull against the floorboards. "I don't know. I can't even explain why you're able to pass between the worlds. You shouldn't be able to. Humans these days…they've forgotten how to dream with that kind of cosmic force. It does mean someone *marked* you. You have a tie to that world, and it wasn't made by me."

Piper squeezed her hands into fists to keep them from shaking.

"If someone's taking your dust," Steele continued, his voice dropping, "it means you have something someone wants. If that's the case, then it's already happened before. Whether you remember or not."

Her mind reeled. She didn't want to know who *else* had taken her dust. She wasn't ready to ask.

"Take it back," Steele said abruptly.

"Take it…back?"

"Dust is power. The more someone has of yours, the more control they have over you. It's not always used to harm, but it is inevitable that it will change you."

Says the one who tied himself to her like a parasite.

"You said before, if you don't get the *Book of Godspells*, you'll lose more than just your place in there."

"Yes," he said too quickly. "Without it, I lose my way back completely. I'm not from here, and this world decays me unless I'm anchored to dust born of my own world. That's why I went to the hospital. That's how I found you. When your human dust clashed with the dreamdust in you—"

He trailed off, but she already knew.

"It caused the fire."

"Yes. We call it revishing," he explained, "but I never thought it could happen here. Not in a place so sealed off from the Dreamworld."

There was another long silence, but this one was heavier. Piper stood, holding the quiet in her fists like it might split open with pressure.

"I still don't understand something," she said at last.

Steele raised an eyebrow over his shades and nodded.

"I told you where the book is. Who has it, so you can go retrieve it yourself. So why are you still here? Why do you need me? To feed more dust off me?" The latter words were daggers.

He smiled.

"I told you. You are the only one who can help me back," he stated. "The book is here, but it's not enough. Not without something to bind me back to where I belong. You and a black flower."

Of course, there was more to this deal…

"Black flower? Like a rose?" She thought about the rose turning black in Penelopes Garden. Or what she thought was it turning black. She honestly wasn't even sure anymore.

"It contains enough stardust to anchor a Dreamer, but it's rare and volatile. It grows in forgotten places."

"Let me guess, in the Reverie?"

Steele nodded.

"You trust I would get it for you?" Her tone turned sharp.

She wanted him to hear it. She wanted him to feel how little she trusted him.

"I trust you want to get back there," he said softly, "and right now, I am your only way."

She hated that he was right.

"Fine. Finish your deal. Send me back and I will find the black flower root for you," she said carefully, deliberately not promising she'd give it to him when she did find it.

His smile deepened. "Don't you love making deals?"

"Just tell me how to get back, will you?" she asked, her tone still sharp, but her heart racing in excitement. She was going back!

"At your call."

Steele stepped forward, and the cane in his hand twisted, then shimmered. "This belonged to one of the aged ones." His voice dipped lower, reverent.

Without warning, he held it out toward her. "Grab it," he said. "It will recognize your dreamdust."

Piper hesitated, every bone in her body quivering. "Now what?"

Steele looked down at the distaff, then at her hand slowly wrapping around the distaff. "Now all that's left is the touch of return."

Suddenly the room shifted, not physically, but in sensation. The air thickened. Her vision blurred. Steele—ever the white devil with a cause—reached up to remove his glasses again.

"Look into my eyes," he whispered.

"Why, if I am alr—"

Steele cut her off. "Because your dust knows the way better than your mind ever will. Now look."

The air shattered around her, and she fell *through* him like sand through glass.

CHAPTER FOURTEEN
THE REVISHING

Piper woke to motion. A cool breeze brushed her face, and the steady rhythm of someone carrying her—strong arms, and a lean chest—grounded her before thought caught up. The world smelled like pine, flowers and dust.

Her eyes snapped open to find Colik's face hovered above her, jaw tight and eyes scanning the trees.

"Put me down," she barked, and he did, immediately and without grace. She landed hard; her legs unsteady as they found the ground of the Broken Woods.

"So much for a thanks," he muttered.

"I am back!" she exclaimed, ignoring him. She looked around, trying to catch her breath, making sure it all was how it looked before.

Suddenly, panic struck her, and her eyes shot back to Colik. "Why did I go back to my world? How is my body still here when I *was* there?"

"I couldn't hold it." His voice was clipped, but he did not stop walking.

She caught up to him after double-checking her legs wouldn't give out on her. She felt weak, like something had just tried to pull her body in multiple directions all at once. "You started convulsing… I thought I lost you to death by sleep."

"I felt like I was being pulled apart."

He nodded, jaw clenched. "Because you were."

She stared at him.

"The sleeper's rest caught you," he said, softer now. "It's supposed to hold your dust here, but something was holding your dust there too… You were flickering, like something was trying to claim you in both. That is not normal…"

She blinked. "What do you mean?"

"I kept you tied. Just enough to stop you from fading completely."

Her stomach dropped. "Tied?"

"Not fully. Not like…" He shook his head. "It doesn't matter."

"No, say it. What did you do to me?"

He finally met her eyes. "I used the sandtie. It anchored a part of you here. It's the reason you were able to get back here. I didn't have a choice."

Piper's pulse slammed against her ribs.

"There's always a choice," She whispered. If she had learned one thing here, it was that.

Colik slowed his steps. "If I hadn't, you wouldn't be standing here. Trust me."

"So now what? I'm *tied* to you, too?" He eyed her, surprised by her question.

"Too?"

Piper didn't clarify.

"No. Not fully," he said quickly, shaking his head. Then, quieter: "Not unless I let it deepen. How do you know about that?"

She stared at him. "Why not?"

"I told you before. A Dreamer can't tie to a human. Not without consequences. Piper, how do you even know that?"

"If they do?"

His voice lowered, rough as stone breaking. "Then one becomes one. Mortal dust and dream dust don't run side by side—they fuse. The mortal side vanishes, and the divine forgets it was ever divine."

The woods pressed in, silence too thick for comfort.

"I didn't ask for any of this."

"I know," Colik said. His eyes flickered with something unguarded. "Neither did I."

Her throat tightened. "Then stop treating me like I'm a liability."

Colik's gaze burned into hers. "You're not. You're a risk. And risks change everything."

Piper stepped away from him, her face burning. "Is that why you're really taking me to the Citadel? Because I'm a risk that you must what? *Contain?*"

He didn't answer.

"So that's it?" she snapped, her heartbeat rising fast. "I'm just the latest human you have to rid from the Reverie?"

"No," he said with a grim look on his face. "You're something I don't understand and that terrifies me more than anything else in this world. Now tell me how you know about a sandtie," he demanded.

Piper met his stare and held it until something sharp jolted through her chest. The air tightened, shrinking around her like a closing fist. Her breaths turned shallow, ribs straining against the pressure. A prickle swept over her skin, cold and electric, and her hands began to tremble. Then came a burn, searing and alive, the spiral scar on her hand flaring as if it remembered something she didn't.

"Piper?"

She didn't answer but turned and pushed through the moss-soft ground of the Broken Woods, her boots making no sound but her heartbeat roaring in her ears.

The woods leaned in around her, their shadows catching

the red moonlight, her thoughts scattering into a thousand jagged edges—Steele's grip, Colik's reaction, and the sandtie's pull. She could feel the heat building before she knew what it meant.

She tried to process everything Colik had said about helping her staying here, but her mind struck like a storm. His words swirled within her, clashing with the fear she had yet to fully allow herself to feel. It was overwhelming. The shift between worlds. The uncertainty of her existence here. Her emotions threatened to spill over, no longer contained by the carefully constructed walls she had built over the past sixteen years, ever since she could remember *anything* tangible.

She felt suffocated. She needed space, a breath of fresh air, anything to hold her steady.

Without a word, she turned and began to walk the other way, the trees around her strangely quiet, her footsteps soft on the damp floor of the woods. Each step fed the storm stirring inside her, thoughts swirling faster like a wildfire building up deep within. A strange heat grew inside her, turning her fear and confusion into something feral, and suddenly out of control.

"Piper!" Colik's voice rang out from behind her. She stopped suddenly, spinning around to face him, shock flashing in her eyes.

"What!"

Colik's eyes widened at her. "You must calm down." Calm down?

The nerve of him.

"Excuse me?" she snapped, her voice shaky with uncontained frustration. The look on his face—his eyes wide with worry—was unsettling. He knew something she didn't, and that realization rooted her in place.

Smoke rose from the ground.

She didn't notice the odd feeling under her feet, until she did. There was a prickling heat beneath the soles of her boots and when she looked down, thin trails of smoke rose where she had just walked.

The woods were on fire.

Panic struck, she took another step, and her heart pounded as a flame crackled, following that step. It wasn't the woods that was causing the fire.

It was me.

Heat poured from her skin like a furnace unleashed. She had turned into a match. Each step left scorched foliage blackened by the force of her emotions. Panic welled up, her fists clenching as she tried to hold back the blaze inside her. The more she struggled, the hotter she burned.

She couldn't control it even if she wanted to.

"Look at me, Piper!" Colik's voice cut through the line of small but violent flames rising around her, urgent and steady. "You must cool down! You need to control your feelings!"

She stepped toward him, but the flames continued to form with her every move. The air crackled between them, so tense it might ignite the entire woods in one big swoop.

Desperate, she stomped down, hoping to put it out, but each step only fed it. The flames leaped, licking at nearby trees and spreading fast.

"I'm setting the woods on fire!" she gasped, her voice breaking, the heat warping the air around her. Panic crashed through her, blazing as fiercely as the flames. Breathing was getting hard. Deep down, she sensed a wild blaze driven by all her pent-up feelings—*the frustrations, fears, confusion, being trapped and lost.* There was no stopping it...

"LOOK AT ME!" Colik bellowed, aggressively enough that Piper forced her gaze onto his.

Skillfully, he maneuvered around the moving flames to reach her, eyes locked on hers, no longer calm, but tired, and desperate. The smoke clawed down her throat, filling her lungs until each breath became its own battle.

"What's happening to me?" she whispered, her voice splintering as she collapsed to her knees. Her fingers dug into the scorched earth, pressing so hard her nails bent, desperate for something to hold onto while the fire tore through her from within. The sensations were unbearable, yet the pain itself felt tolerable, as if beneath it something darker stirred. It hurt, but it called to her. She wanted to feel it, to draw it in, to make it hers.

Colik dropped down with her, his hand seizing hers more roughly than before. "Breathe, Piper," he snapped, his tone edged and impatient. His touch was cold against her burning skin, not quite in the soothing way, but it pinned her in place. "You have to fight it."

She couldn't. Her muscles shook so violently, her bones could splinter. Her vision warped, the edges of the world curling with fire, the sky and ground both spinning. She sucked in another breath, only feeding the inferno raging inside her chest. The dizziness dragged her under.

She collapsed forward, gasping, her body caving in.

"Piper—" Colik's voice cut through the roar, harsh and frantic now. He grabbed her shoulders, hauling her body upright.

"For fuck's sake," he hissed, the words ripped from him like a curse. His face was tight, his multi-colored eyes intense. "Look at me!"

She blinked up at him, tears searing tracks down her ashy-streaked cheeks. Her lips trembled, ready to apologize, to beg for help, but the fire inside her flared again, choking her words.

And then his mouth crashed against hers.

The kiss was not gentle. It was desperate, furious, and necessary. Cold collided with fire, shocking her system like a plunge into freezing water. Piper gasped against his lips, her entire body jerking as his icy calm poured into her veins, colliding with the fever tearing her apart. She clutched at him like she might explode if she let go, her fingers curling into his tunic, nails digging deep.

The flames around them wavered, flickered, and one by one, collapsed into ash. Her fire broke under his kiss, the inferno giving way to shivers. Her body shook violently now from the sudden plunge of cold washing through her.

When he finally pulled back, his breathing came out harsh. He stared at her like she was both fragile and infuriating, like saving her had cost him something he hadn't meant to give.

Piper sagged against him, her lips tingling, her skin faintly glowing like dying embers. "What did I just do?" Her voice was shredded.

Colik exhaled hard, running a hand down his face as though she had drained the last of his patience. "It's called revishing," he said, voice flat, clipped. "It means to set fire."

Her stomach dropped. "Is that...has—?"

"No," he cut her off sharply, shaking his head. The anger in his voice was quieter, but no less real. "No, Piper. That's not normal. Not for a human, not for a Dreamer. You don't just set the fucking woods on fire."

Her chest hollowed out at his words. She turned her head, staring at the blackened forest around them. The trees stood like burned witnesses, and above them the Blood Moon glared down, its crimson glow casting her destruction in merciless light.

"Why—how—"

"You revished because the dreamdust is clashing with your human dust. It doesn't know which is which. It is why I told you humans don't come and go from this world. It is *dangerous* in more ways than one." He looked up her and down with furrowed eyebrows, then stood up.

Her throat worked, but no words came. She wanted to apologize, to explain, but she had no explanation. Only the truth that the fire had been because of her. *Again.* Steele said the same thing about what caused the fire at the hospital.

"I thought you'd be fine. You were fine when I was carrying you. I—" Colik held out his hand to help her up. She grabbed it, his touch steading her, but his voice carrying little softness. "We need to get to the Citadel."

His hand didn't leave her back as they started walking again. His presence pressed against her like an anchor, holding her upright as if she might collapse again at any moment.

The fire was gone, but its ghost lingered—the burnt moss, the charred bark, and the faint, acrid sweetness that caught at the back of her tongue. She didn't look back.

Piper refused to speak, embarrassed about what she did, what to say and what to even think about that kiss. It was forced, but deep down, she felt something under the surface. Longing? Desire?

Her pulse hadn't completely slowed from it. She could still feel the phantom of his mouth on hers, the way his coolness had sliced through her panic. It had worked. It had *calmed* her. She knew it hadn't been *for* her, and that knowledge sat in her chest like a splinter.

Every so often, Colik would glance her way, and not in the way someone stares when they're drawn to you, but in the way someone studies a weapon to see if it's still loaded.

"You're quiet," he said finally.

Her gaze stayed forward. "Just trying to calm down so I don't burn the rest of the woods down."

His mouth curved, though it wasn't quite a smile. "Smart."

Longer silence.

More walking.

They reached a narrow pass where the woods thinned, and the light from the Blood Moon poured over them. The smoke curled into waves of crimson haze, brushing across their faces like strokes of paint.

"Piper," he said, her name was low and rough, like he wasn't sure he should speak it at all.

Her pulse stuttered. There was a pull inside her that was strange yet familiar, like a dream she'd half-lived once before. When he stepped closer, the air between them grew thin. His gaze flicked from her lips to her eyes, lingering just long enough to make her breath catch. For a heartbeat, she thought he might kiss her again. This time, she would choose to kiss him back.

She watched his eyes trace the tremor in her jaw, and then, "I know you know about the sandtie."

The words snapped her back. He wasn't trying to tempt her this time. He was making sure she wouldn't revish again.

She hesitated, then gave in. If that is how he wants to play this. *Heartless.* "Steele warned me. Said someone was taking my dust." She decided to keep out the part about Steele taking her dust too.

Colik froze, eyes narrowing. "Steele?"

The way he said the name made her throat tighten. It was the same reaction Morry had when she'd told him.

She nodded. "A boy. White hair. Blind. He's the one who helped me get back here, so I don't know why you think you're the reason I am."

Colik slowed his pace, his expression unreadable. "I don't know that name."

"He knows about the Reverie," she said quietly. "About the sandtie." She held his gaze, refusing to give him more than he'd given her.

"No." He shook his head once, then again, more sharply.

"He told me someone here was draining my dust."

Colik's mouth opened, then shut. The sharpness in his posture softened into something darker and unsettled.

"He shouldn't exist," Colik said finally, more to himself than her. "Not in the waking world. Especially not if he knows all that."

"What are you saying?"

"I'm saying it isn't possible. A Dreamer can't cross into the waking world. Not unless..." His gaze swept the woods, wary. "Unless he isn't just a Dreamer."

Piper's stomach twisted. She knew what Steele was, but she wanted to see if Colik did. He had been quiet and hesitant when the Scirges spoke of the Silver Children.

"Then what is he?"

His jaw clenched, like the truth itself tasted bitter. "Maybe a Silver Child," he said at last, voice low. "Or what's left of one."

Her breath hitched. That was what she feared.

"I thought they were all contained."

"They were. Or so we believed." His tone darkened. "If one made its way into your world—and he's helping you?"

"Yes," she said. "He helped me get back here."

"No, Piper." His voice sharpened. "You don't need him to get back here. Not when I tied to you like that during sleepers' rest. He targeted you, and I want to know why. He's dangerous."

She didn't blink. "Are you saying I shouldn't trust him?"

"Of course not," he said through gritted teeth. His gaze softened when he saw the panic rise in her. "Piper... I'm not trying to make you lose control again, but if there's a Silver Child manipulating dust in the waking world—using *you*— then this Dreamworld is in more danger than I thought, just by you being in it."

She swallowed. "What about you? Do you want something from me too?"

He went still. "If I had taken all of your dust," he said, voice rough, "you wouldn't be standing here. I had to pull you back when you started to fade."

"At what cost to you? You said there was a consequence for a Royald."

"Don't worry about me." Colik looked away, scanning the woods before turning sharply. "We move."

"Why?"

"I saved you," he said quietly, "but I also made you visible to every creature that follows dust. Steele has done the same to you there."

Piper didn't follow right away. "You keep telling me being here is dangerous," she called after him. "Maybe I'm just waking up to what I actually am. To my purpose."

Colik stopped, glancing over his shoulder. "You think this power makes you special?" He let out a low, humorless sound. "It makes you the biggest target. It will catch up to you eventually. It always does."

Power? She said nothing of the sort.

She took a step to follow him when the ground shifted beneath her heel. She stumbled, catching herself against a tall stump slick with cold bark. The woods inhaled sharply around them, silence pressing in. Under her palm, the stump pulsed once.

Then came a voice, rising through the wood and into her chest before rattling her ears.

"GET OFF."

Piper let out a startled cry and lurched backward into Colik's shoulder. His muscles tensed beneath her weight, steadying her before she could stumble. His eyes snapped instantly to the stump, his hand at the hilt at his side, daring it to speak again.

Was that a swar? How had she never noticed that before?

"What was that?" Piper panted, heart pounding against her ribs.

Colik's jaw flexed. "I am sure it is not what I think it is."

Like ice cracking on a still lake, the voice slithered again through the hush. It was deep, metallic, and impossibly old.

"CRUEL WORDS FOR THE DREAMER."

The stump's bark shifted, folding in on itself with scales of living wood until a slender form emerged like molten shadow given shape. He unfolded slowly into a creature of obsidian black, marbled with veins of bronze that pulsed faintly like embers beneath ash. Translucent wings, quivered in the dusky half-light, catching the absence of wind and turning it into a spectral tremor. He stood half-hidden among the sculpted folds of bark, the leaves overhead draping him in veils of muted green that swayed without movement.

His eyes found Pipers. They were bronze irises as ancient as sun-forged metal, shimmering with a quiet fire that might scorch her from within. Piper froze from awe at a beauty so possibly terrifying that it threatened to undo her with a single look.

"The Bronze Gink," Colik breathed, each syllable measured as though naming a curse. "A Fatale." His eyes were as wide as hers.

Piper blinked, her throat tight. "Like one of the Fates?" She recently read about the Fates, the goddesses who controlled the thread of life. She tried to remember each Fate. Clotho spun birth, Lachesis measured...destiny, and Atropos —Atropos cut death.

Colik met her gaze with grim solemnity. "*Like* the Fates, yes, but not them. Where the Fates deal in life's certainty, the Fatales deal in dreams' fragility." He turned his gaze from Piper back to the being formed of bark and bronze. "The Bronze Gink doesn't weave strands like the once Cloner, nor sever them like Solari. He is the counter, measuring the weight of a dream. When a dream grows too heavy, he decides when it must unravel."

The creature shifted, perching on a slender branch that spiraled into place beneath him. The wood groaned in protest but held firm. Rings of glass and bronze adorned each finger, inner swirls of bronze and gold flakes reflecting smothered sparks of light.

"FEW SEEK ME. FEWER DESERVE TO."

The words rang like the last toll of a bell, and the surrounding trees leaned closer. Colik stepped forward, boots sinking into moss. "We aren't seeking you." Piper wasn't sure if that was meant to be a question or a statement.

The Bronze Gink tilted his head.

"THE WILD STRAND WRITHES."

The words pressed against Piper's skin like a physical weight. She felt, absurdly, as though she were being judged… *No, measured.*

Colik's eyes narrowed. "Who bears the wild strand?" His eyes shot at Piper, then back at the Bronze Gink. A ripple of shadow crossed the Bronze Gink's form, gold veins flickering like lightning beneath midnight glass.

"I SEE WHERE DREAMS HIDE. STRANDS ARE COMING UNBOUND. DANGEROUSLY SO IF WRONGFULLY OPENED."

Piper's breath hitched. The Bronze Gink's gaze drifted, landing on Piper, sharp and knowing. His bronze irises were bright, molten and relentless.

"STRANDS PULL FROM THE WAKING WORLD. WHAT COMES WILL NOT ABIDE BY REVERIE LAWS."

Colik's posture stiffened. "What will come?"

The Bronze Gink's form shimmered, gold pooling along his limbs until it looked as though he might melt into pure bronze metal. He leaned forward, wings trembling faintly, and began to recite something that sounded both dangerously distant and utterly sacred:

"IN THE FIRE—
TO THE PAST.
INTEND TO BIDE HERE,
A NEW WORLD,
IN THE DARKNESS,
THE FIND IS SHE.
MY ROOTS,

THE TRANFIGURATION—
ALL HUMANKIND,
EVER IN THE EMPITNESS.
IN HIGH IS,
MAN TO MAN,
BIRR AND SMEDDUM."

Without warning, the Bronze Gink began to dissolve. His gold-veined limbs fractured like brittle glass, flaking into specks that drifted soundlessly through the still woods.

His wings shimmered once, then shattered, his final breath crystallizing into molten gold. His bronze eyes dimmed last, like dying coals. In less than a heartbeat, he was gone, leaving only a damp stump.

"What in all the gods' names does all that mean?" Piper asked. Half of it sounded like gibberish.

Colik exhaled slowly. "He just spoke the Gods of Dreams' foretelling," he answered slowly. "Morpheus' Promise."

There was that promise again, for the third time. In it were the words: *in the fire— to the past.*

Steele recited that to her. He *knew* this foretelling. He knew this world. And it was being spoken to her, too.

"What *is* Morpheus' promise, Colik?" she asked again, pushier. No one had ever told her a thing about it, only kept saying it around her.

"The Fatales don't appear unless it is vital," he muttered to himself, now pacing. "And even then...not like that. Not to one who does not belong here   a human..." He looked up at Piper, noticing her again. "No offense."

Piper stared at the stump, limbs shaky. She took offense but didn't say it. This was what Eda had warned about. What Colik was too afraid to admit happened.

"I've never heard it in full," he kept on. "Not in all my ages as a Dreamer and from the Bronze Gink? That's like a god giving you a knife and saying, 'Careful, this cuts dreams.'"

"Why is it so important?"

"It is *the* telling of who *the* Dreamer is. Who the gods put in the Reverie to protect it from, well, *everything*. Especially the gods. A sign of *hope* that there won't be another war of the gods."

She turned from the stump to face him, but his eyes were already on her, searching—not just looking at her, but through her. "Now you are here and the Bronze Gink came."

There was a long, uneasy silence between them.

"You're not telling me something," Colik finally said pointblank.

"I'm not—" she said quickly. "I don't understand all of this either."

"That's not an answer."

"No," she snapped. "But it is the truth."

He stepped closer. "Do you know what it means for someone to carry a wild strand? It means their dream isn't written entirely. It can break things—and not just here," he tapped the side of his temple, "but in the waking world. *Your* world."

"I didn't ask for this!" she barked. "You think I want your creepy woods, your weird laws, or Dreamers who speak in riddles? I just wanted an exciting place to find a purpose!"

Colik stared at her, cold and unreadable. Something cracked behind his eyes—pull, warning, maybe apprehension.

"We have to get to the Citadel," he said stiffly, already turning.

"You already said that."

"I need to report this."

Piper scoffed, but her body tensed. "Report *me*, you mean?"

"The promise," he shot over his shoulder. "If Morpheus' Promise has been spoken in full, they need to know. Blaze and Lulu will want—"

"Oh, *now* I am just some message in a human body?"

He stopped walking but didn't face her. "The message is the promise. You're the ripple."

Heat flushed through her. "Or maybe," she said, stepping closer, "The Bronze Gink shared the promise to me because I'm more than that."

That made him turn. He looked at her fully, not as a passenger or a problem, but as something else entirely.

"Trust me, they will want to talk to you about what you are," he said after a long beat, his voice cautious. She raised an eyebrow. "The Royalds. Blaze—the King. Lulu—the Queen."

She tilted her head. "You?"

"Think of me as a knight."

"Like the one who saves people?"

He didn't flinch. "No. The one who handles what can't be saved."

Piper flew her hands up in the air. "Your role, quite literally *is* to hand me over to the King and Queen!"

That heat started rising again inside her. She took in a deep breath, pushing it down best she could.

"I've told you… Not until I understand what you are." His voice was cool steel. "When we reach the Citadel, I'll do the talking. Let them believe I am still in control."

His words lodged in her chest like a thorn, one word in particular, jabbing her outright.

Not *who*. *What*.

CHAPTER FIFTEEN
THE LAVYRINTHOS

"Wait," Colik demanded suddenly, and his arm shot out, halting Piper mid step. She followed his gaze, not sure what they were halting for. He still pissed her off, but those rising emotions eventually settled.

The trees in front of them began to thin, pulling apart until a hole opened in the woods. The trunks bent back with a deep groan, their branches twisting away to clear a path that hadn't been there a moment ago. Two huge antlers pushed through the gap, curving toward each other until their tips met, joined by a thin line of glowing amber sap that pulsed softly. Faint dream-markings ran along their edges, not carved but grown, and a perfectly crafted gate of horn and vine stood before them.

Piper stiffened.

It didn't belong in the middle of the Broken Woods. It belonged in a myth. In the space between what was remembered and what was real. It opened with a humming and pulsing like its very own entrance to a new dream.

Her breath faltered.

"It's like the woods were hiding it," she breathed. "Hiding *this*."

"They were," Colik replied. "The Broken Woods don't just curse. They protect. They've been guarding this gate since the moment you first set foot here."

She stepped closer, heart pounding. The path ahead glowed faintly, each stone lit with starlight. The sky had descended to pave the way.

"What is it for—exactly?" She saw the gate, sure, but why would the woods be guarding this from her?

Well, besides her revishing…

"This is the Gate of Horn. Beyond it lies the Lavyrinthos and past that… the Citadel."

She blinked. "The Gate of Horn. That is *also* from Greek myths." Both the Silver Girl and the librarian mentioned the gates.

He nodded. "One of two gates the Gods of Dreams carved into the veil between worlds. The Gate of Ivory sends false dreams—illusions, fantasies, visions that mean nothing. The Gate of Horn…"

He looked at her, something haunting in his gaze.

"The Gate of Horn delivers *true* dreams. Dreams that *reveal*. That cross over."

"So, this isn't just a path." Her pulse skipped.

He stepped beside her. "No. It's a choice."

"If I go through…"

"You don't just walk this Dreamworld," he said, "You *live* this dream."

She looked again at the glowing trail, at the vines curling around the edges like veins. Her hands trembled. "I'm scared," she admitted.

Colik didn't turn. "I would be more concerned if you weren't."

Piper stepped closer to the gate. The air hummed against her skin. She looked behind her at the Broken Woods, then at Colik.

"How about the fate of the woods? When will I know *that* fate?" she asked.

"You won't."

"Why walk into the woods, knowing you might never come out the same?"

He didn't hesitate. "Because you already *aren't* the same. The woods don't break anything new. They just reveal the fracture that was always there. Hence why I said… a broken bone would've been the easy way out."

She studied him, at the way he held himself like he was bracing for impact. "What about you? What will it do to you?"

She saw something flicker in his eyes. *Was that pain?*

"Do to me? Who knows. You heard the promise, but you shouldn't have. Which means if this goes wrong—" his eyes shifted to the gate, glowing like a wound in the air, "—it is on me."

Then, without another word or a glance back, Colik stepped through the Gate of Horn, his form swallowed by stardust and clouded shadow, leaving Piper alone at the edge of this newfound fate. He didn't offer his hand, and that hurt more than it should have.

She stood still, and the heat inside her stirred again.

Was this how it was for Narcissus? Not love of a reflection, but of a world where the ache was finally quiet?

This gate… It wasn't just showing her a different realm. It was asking her to choose between walking in a dream and *living* in a Dreamworld.

She could still turn back and beg Colik to help her back to the path she knew—back to Olympus House and to the real world where her name had always been an afterthought.

The dream—this *truth*—was not calling from the other side. It was already inside her. If she were to step forward through the Gate of Horn… Then she was no longer just surviving. She was *answering*.

Answering the call of dreams that broke her sleep. Answering the cry of the Silver Girl begging to be free. Answering the promise for Steele, who was abandoned from his world, too. Answering for the part of herself that had always known there was more to her life than being silenced, unsure, and misunderstood.

That, perhaps, carried a cost. A choice and a truth.

Not the truth of the so-called gods who claimed to shape this world. Not of the Royalds sworn to protect it. Not even of Colik's sharp tongue, his half-spoken hopes, or the promises that clung to her like dust.

The truth was that she *could stay*, if she wanted. She could choose a purpose, if she just so dared to step through the Gate of Horn.

The moment Piper stepped beneath the arch of twisted horns made from roots, bone, and the fading glow of dying stars that refused to collapse, everything changed.

Colik had called this place the Lavyrinthos. Above her, arches of ivy laced with silver rippled open like ribs drawn wide. Ancient roses, the color of bruised dusk and forgotten gods, unfurled in slow, sacred motion. Vines curled along the ground, tracing gentle spirals. The air was thick with the scent of florals, dust, and something overwhelmingly sweet.

The path narrowed as Piper stepped deeper. Ivy curled thick across the stone walls, their leaves twitching, and for a moment, she thought it was the wind, but then the vines unfurled. The air shimmered. Spores lifted off them, delicate and glowing, scattering like powdered red moonlight.

"Poppyseeds." Colik's curse broke the silence.

Her jaw cracked with a sudden yawn. Then another. Her legs went weak, heavy as wax. "What—what is this...?"

The world around her started to blur.

Colik caught her wrist, tugging her close with a hard grip, steadying himself as much as her. There was strain in his voice. "The Lavyrinthos scatters them to turn humans back. To make you sleep. To drown you in memory."

She sagged against him, eyelids sinking. "I can't—"

"Yes, you can." His breath seared hot against her ear. He turned his head and, with a fierce exhale, blew the drifting seeds away from her face. The haze broke instantly. Piper gasped, head slumping against his shoulder like someone waking from drowning.

Her pulse thudded fast. His arm was firm around her, but she could feel how tightly his muscles wound, how badly he didn't want to let go but did.

"Why is it always humans? Why are we always so wrong?"

His answer came softer than she expected, but ragged, like he hated giving it voice. "Because when humans find their way in, they don't come back the same. They become uncontrollable and that is the gods' own nightmare."

Suddenly, the ivy shivered, and a sharp rustle split the silence. There was a loud crunch, and leaves dragged like bone across stone.

Colik shifted instantly, pulling her behind him in one smooth motion.

"Stay close," he hissed.

Piper's chin lifted stubbornly. "Don't tell me what to do." He was acting dramatic.

"Then at least don't move," he retorted. Though his stance was iron, his voice was thinner, drawn tight like he was expecting something bad to happen.

What could possibly go wrong now?

Then she saw him. A boy no older than six or seven stood motionless, only a few paces away. His eyes were pure black, like glassy marbles, any light in them having phased out. His mouth was too tight it looked sewn shut, though no strand bound it. It was cracked. He looked majorly dehydrated.

Colik stiffened. Piper looked to him for reassurance, but there was none. She moved closer to him.

"It is you," a voice said. It was high pitched, though she never saw the boy's lips move. The sound hung in the air, like it traveled on the wind itself.

Colik moved forward cautiously. "Come again?"

The boy did not move. "You walk as Phobetor," he whispered. Then his head tilted toward Piper. "You do too."

Piper's stomach dropped. Colik froze but said nothing. Did he know what the boy meant?

A new voice broke the air, firmer. Older. "Please excuse my child. He is speaking what he does not know how to speak about."

From the shadows behind the small boy stepped a woman. Dark hair streaked with silver, her gaze carrying the same depthless black, but tempered with a sliver of warmth. Her lips barely moved, but her words, when spoken, were hushed and heavy. She placed a hand on the boy's shoulder, pulling him back toward her with quiet authority. Concern sharpened her features. Or fear.

"Do not heed to his stories. For we do not fully ever get its entirety." Her eyes lingered on Colik with warning and pity, before she turned to lead the boy away.

They drifted rather than walked, figures dissolving into the trembling ivy.

Piper's voice was hushed. "What did he you walk like Phobetor? Like the God of Dreams?"

Colik's jaw worked, but no words came at first. Then, he pulled her closer to him. "They are Shades," he answered at last. "They shouldn't be here. Not this close to the Citadel. Not in the Lavyrinthos." His voice was taut with suspicion. "They should be…farther out." He trailed off, head shaking.

His eyes flicked to Piper, then back to the mother and boy walking off in the other direction. "I think we should follow them," he said slowly, then turned toward them.

"What? Why?"

"The Shades are another Guild of Dreamers, like the Scirges. Their dreams are tangled closest to nightmares." His voice was low as he began walking after them. Piper hesitated for a second before trailing behind.

How many Guilds of Dreamers were there?

"But this is a Dreamworld?" she prompted more as a question than a statement. Maybe she was naive, but— "wasn't a Dreamworld supposed to not have any nightmares?" Then again, the Scirges told her that dreams were technically nightmares too.

"Who do you think helps rid of these nightmares?" Colik eyed her wearily. "There is also the Dreamless—those whose dreams have entirely disappeared."

She shrugged, having never thought about that before. In fact, before this Dreamworld, she thought both dreams and nightmares were just, well...*were*. To know or think—she still didn't know what all to believe—that they were controlled and prevented by the gods—that was the last thing she would have ever believed to be true until now.

"Dreamless?" Piper repeated, the word hanging heavy.

Colik nodded once, grim. "The worst fate a Dreamer can fall to. Empty. Hollow. No dream. No nightmare. Nothing left to call their own. A skin wandering the Reverie, cursed by silence." His eyes darkened. "It's almost always a Shade. Who else dares walk so close to the edge of a nightmare?"

Piper shivered, watching the last of the ivy settle from the Lavyrinthos, the silver leaves folding back to expose a new path, one that was damp and smelled like seaweed.

"Again, why are we following them?" she asked.

Water began to seep through the soil, spreading outward

until a body of water shimmered before them. Piper was certain it hadn't been there a moment ago.

The woman stopped at its edge. Without looking back, she lifted her chin and began to hum, low and mournful. The water stirred, and from its depths, a boat rose. It was translucent and glistening, shaped from something both soft and primordial.

"It's a piece of the Plaas," Colik said, catching her wide-eyed stare. "We call it a ploat."

"A boat?" Piper repeated uncertainly.

"No. *Pl-oat*," Colik corrected, slowly enunciating the foreign word like it held sacred weight. "Boats are made. Ploats are born."

"What's a *Plaas*?" she asked.

Colik tilted his head toward the Shade, watching the mother as she began lifting her son into the ploat. The boy's frail frame weighed nothing in her arms. When the woman stepped in after him, the ploat dipped slightly into the water, adjusting itself steady.

"After you," Colik urged.

Piper hesitated, eyeing the vessel. Could something so strange—so *alive*—really hold them all? Before she could make the choice herself, Colik pressed a hand gently but firmly against her back. She stumbled forward, her foot landing on the spongy surface with a jolt.

Colik gracefully stepped in behind her, steadying her with a firm grip as she wobbled.

"You think you can survive this world without me?" he snickered, a smile curving on his face.

"Let go. I can manage," she muttered, though her voice betrayed her nerves. He released her, but she could feel his eyes still on her.

The Shade woman hummed again, and the ploat began to drift. It didn't cut through the water, but *glided*, the water itself welcoming it. Piper reached down to touch its side and recoiled in awe. The texture was soft, warm like flesh, but pulsing faintly beneath her fingertips.

Colik joined her at the edge. "The Plaas is a creature of the Untold Brine, a never-ending body of water of the Reverie," he said quietly. "It flows between all dream waters. No one has seen a living Plaas in ages. When it sheds its layers, sloughs off parts of itself, the Guilds of Dreamers use the cast-offs for various purposes."

"Like a fossil?" Piper asked.

"Not quite. More like the discarded shell of a crustacean. When the *Plaas* finally dies, it leaves behind its Plastrof, the conch-shaped chamber where it once lived. That shell, or Plastrof, become vessels, sanctuaries, or armor. What you're standing on now is a fragment of that creature."

Piper imagined it: *a crab shedding its shell, yet the shell not left to rest. Instead, another life drifted in, moving within what was no longer its own. And the body is used elsewhere. Yes—something like that.*

She stared out across the water. "We're going there. To the Plastrof?"

Colik nodded. "I believe so."

"For the third time—*why?*"

He gave her a small smile. "If our road to the Citadel were simple, this world wouldn't be doing its part."

"Doing its part?" she echoed.

"This world is alive, Piper. It tests. It listens. Nothing here happens by accident. There are no coincidences, only choices and moments."

His words struck her. They were mystifying yet oddly grounding. She wanted to press him more but held her questions close.

As the ploat slid forward, the shore behind them faded like mist. The waters of the Untold Brine shimmered, catching the light in glints of silver and crimson. Beneath them, icy-white circles drifted like pale moons under the surface.

"What are those bubbles?" she whispered.

"When the needle-leaves of the Broken Woods fall into the Untold Brines waters, and dust from the constellation cloud spirals down, they birth these frozen disks."

"Ah. Do those bubbles have a name?" There she went again, with the million questions.

"Spirits, we call them." The word hung in the air—*Spirits* —like it meant more than simple shapes in water.

Just then, a flicker beneath the surface caught her eye.

"Look!" she gasped, pointing. The excitement filled her again, the way it had when she first met Colik here. It was the beauty and magical aura that made her fall in love with this world. That, and the possibility of her fitting in, floating in the air.

From the depths, a creature burst upward with silver hair that looked like a mermaid woven from starlight. Her scales shimmered in sea-glass hues, and her laughter was the chime of distant chimes before she dove again, vanishing in a spray that kissed Piper's cheek.

All around, multi-colored jellyfish emerged, their tendrils trailing light through the darker depths of the Untold Brine. Then came winged fish, leaping in arcs, their wings sprawling trails of sparkling dust, like glitter, in the air as they soared.

Piper leaned over the side, eyes wide. "It's… magic," she whispered.

"No," Colik said softly behind her. "It is dreaming. Magic has rules. This?" He gestured widely. "This just *is*. If anything, you could call it *sinew*—the work of a god's divine cosmic power."

"Sinew?"

"Divine godly power."

So true power was a thing here after all.

Beneath them, the water shimmered brighter with every nautical mile, as though the Untold Brine itself were waking up at the ploats touch. Like a reef suspended in the sky of the sea, giant plants unfurled below in vibrant shades of blue and silver, their petals swaying with the current and glowing like sunlit glass. Within the reef, a sound rose from the depths. Melodic voices. Singing. A soft, celestial hum that wasn't just heard but felt. It tugged at the back of Piper's heart, pulling up memories she couldn't place, and emotions she didn't understand.

"Sirens," Colik said behind her, his voice hushed in awe. "The original ones, if the stories humans tell haven't changed entirely."

Piper turned sharply. "Haven't changed? Sirens are the ones who lured sailors to their deaths?"

Colik nodded. "You think your world is the only one with versions of stories, do you?" He gave a joking *tsk, tsk,* before continuing, "before the stories softened them into temptresses with harps, they were daughters of a Muse and a river god. Cursed for failing to save Persephone from the underworld, they sing to call what they've lost back to them."

The silver-haired beings swam upward, revealing scaled torsos and limbs that shimmered like glass beneath the liquid light. Their hair flowed like spun mercury, and their eyes were wide, beautiful, and unblinking.

"How dangerous are they?" She had read the stories, but looking at them, they seemed...mesmerizingly harmless.

Colik's gaze remained fixed ahead. "The Sirens call to you when they sense you want something they can give you. Beware, sometimes, wanting what they can give is the most dangerous thing of all."

As the Sirens sang, something sharp and soft stirred inside her—a woman's voice, a lullaby half-remembered from her earliest days, and a pull of belonging she hadn't touched in years.

Suddenly, a face rose from the water, just beneath the ploat's wake. Its features were delicate, sad, and achingly familiar.

"Piper..." it whispered.

The name curved through the air like a question and a promise. Piper leaned over the edge, captivated. The voice wrapped around her mind like warm water. She didn't know if it was hers or someone else's, but she wanted—no, needed —to hear it again.

"Piper…" the voice breathed again, vibrating through her bones. She leaned further, heart hammering. The colors pulsed again, subtle but firm, steering her, though she couldn't say how.

"Look up," Colik's voice cut through the trance. She jerked upright, and ahead, a colossal black conch shell rose from the side of a distant undersea cliff. Its spiral wound inward endlessly, a living coil of obsidian, and faint light pulsed along its ridges, the shell itself pulsing with breath.

She turned back to the surface of the water, searching for the face, the song, the silver eyes. The Sirens were gone, only the faint shimmer of disturbed water remained. The echo of her name still hung in the air, fading with the ploat's waves as they slowed.

For the first time, the Shades next to them moved. Their motions were eerie and eager, a restless energy rippling through them as the ploat drifted toward the cavern mouth of the enormous spiral shell.

"Welcome, Piper, to the home of the Shades."

CHAPTER SIXTEEN
THE SHADES DREAMS

The Plastrof was not a shell. It was a frozen memory of one.

The Shades guided Piper and Colik through a corridor where every breath felt sharp enough to cut lungs. The room ahead shimmered beneath vaulted arches of black stone veined with silver frost, where chandeliers of ice hung like suspended galaxies, their light fractured into a thousand shimmering prisms that danced across the onyx marble floor. Ash-gray ridges threaded in the walls, like smoke caught in marble that shifted with their movements.

Piper's teeth instantly started to chatter. It was frigid.

This cold place was a cathedral of silence. Just like the Shades. Stars did not twinkle here. Instead, pale specks drifted like dying embers in a cavern, freezing before they reached the floor. The tables, chairs, even the vines curling along the walls were carved from the same black stone. When Piper brushed her fingers against one, a faint hum reverberated through her bones. She pulled her hand away quickly, a shiver running down her spine.

Colik did not sit. He leaned against the wall, his silhouette long against the marble-black surface, his posture a coil of tension. The Shade woman's gaze lingered on him a moment before she lowered herself gracefully to the floor across from Piper. Her dark form folded into the faint shimmer so well that it was difficult to tell where she ended and the silver-ash stone began. Her eyes, pale and glinting, were fixed on Piper with quiet intent, as though studying not just her presence but the dust that breathed from her skin.

Outside, the murmur of Shades moving along the passageways continued, their steps hard and unsteady, carrying too much weight for their frail, darkness-wrapped forms. They looked the most *human* of all the Guilds of Dreamers at first glance—figures with normal shoulders, faces, and hands—but the longer Piper stared, the less certain she was. Their skin carried the pallor of ash, color having been drained away, and shadows clung to them as though stitched into their very outline. Their eyes were the worst. Dark, yes, but not empty. Each gaze shimmered with a faint orange tint, a low ember burning at the center of the dark.

They were Dreamers, Colik had said, but twisted by their work. Their very essence was very much *Dreamers of Nightmares*.

The boy Shade vanished for a moment, his mother following close behind. More Shades passed, slowing down at the entrance of their cove. They would nod at Colik. Piper noticed, and something heavy settled in her stomach. They knew him. They saw her.

When the mother and son Shade returned, each carried a steaming cup of water and handed them to Piper and Colik. She took it with a faint smile. Warmth rose in her fingers and chest immediately at its touch.

"What is your name?" the Shade woman asked Piper gently, but uneven.

"Piper," she replied hesitantly.

The woman's lips pressed together. "Hmmm..." The sound was neither idle nor thoughtful. It felt like a swearword, as though her very name had been judged and found wanting.

The Shade turned to her boy, then back again, her expression trembling between reverence and desperation. "Could you…" she faltered, voice cracking. "Are you able…"

Colik stepped in at once, clearly understanding what she was trying to say. "No. Don't ask her that. She can't." His fists curled, voice like iron. "It's against Reverie Laws."

The Shade's gaze never wavered from Piper, but her next words struck at Colik. "You would know that best, *Royald*. Yet even you sound like you've forgotten—the choice does not belong to you. It belongs to *her*."

Piper's throat went dry. Colik glared at the Shade, fury flashing in his eyes, but then stepped back, just as he had when Cyril warned him. Even as a Royald, there was a kind of mutual respect among Dreamers, an unspoken law that kept – or in this case forced— their tempers in check.

The Shade's voice shook when she spoke again. "The boy is too weak to hold dreams when he must rid nightmares from humans. It is breaking him. He has never seen a complete dream, only fragments. That's why his words come out in pieces, half-formed, like the stories he sees but can never finish. He is fading, *Piper*." The way she said her name made Piper's heart ache. "He is forgetting how to exist. I would give him my own dreams if I could, but mine are nothing more than the echoes of human nightmares."

Piper's heart stuttered. She looked at the boy, at his ashen skin, and eyes dimming from all color. He didn't speak, yet when she knelt closer to him, he met her gaze, seeing a sliver of hope from someone who had no reason to have any hope at all.

Colik's voice rasped low. "Piper, don't. You don't owe them anything. They chose to be a Shade."

The Shade groaned, her black-orange eyes locking on Colik. "I did—until the chaos stirred. He didn't choose this. Do you know what children this age are like? Have you ever watched them laugh, dream, or play?" She looked back at

Piper." Tell me, *human*—what would you give if it were one of them fading before your eyes, and you knew you could save them?" The way she looked at Piper was like she knew her past. She knew she would fall for this.

"It's not supposed to work this way," Colik cut in, but did not step in between Piper and the boy Shade. "Giving away a dream—*your human dream*—it's not like handing over a toy. Even human dust. It is a part of you, Piper. A strand of your own very making. If you stretch a strand too thin—"

The boy Shade put out a hand for Piper to take.

Piper's eyes stayed on the boy, her hand wrapped around his, cold and rigid as if she were holding an icicle. She couldn't walk away. Not when she knew what silence felt like —waiting for someone to bring hope back into her life. Not when she had once been that child. Not when she could still see the faces of the children at Olympus House who would have begged her to help him.

Piper nodded at the woman Shade, then to the boy. He lifted her hand to his cheek, and at once, something stirred. Not from him, but within her.

It started with laughter, mine maybe, or maybe the fields. The wheat around me swayed, gold rippling in waves that didn't care about wind or direction. The sky flipped colors every few heartbeats, gold below, silver above, then silver below and gold above. None of it made sense, but it felt right.

A lion cub bounded beside me, its fur glinting like sunlight and honey. When it sneezed, dandelion fluff burst from its nose and drifted after us in glowing little clouds. I laughed until my ribs ached.

Then I saw it—a snake slipping through the wheat like a ribbon unspooling from the air itself. It looked back at me with what I swear was a grin before slithering off again. The cub gave a tiny, brave roar, and I ran after it too, chasing the green shimmer across the field. The ground stretched, folded, then twisted. Each step felt like running up, not forward.

Then we were at a tree that glowed from within. Its bark was clear as glass, pulsing with soft light that hummed under my fingers when I touched it. The cub nudged me, like I was supposed to lead. I climbed, higher, until the world below blurred into a sea of wheat and light.

At the top, a raven waited. Huge and patient, its feathers shimmered like oil in moonlight, and where they fell, stars bloomed in the air before fading. It tilted its head, and I understood without words.

"I only need a few," I said. My voice didn't sound like mine. I plucked one feather, then another. Each turned into a silver thread in my hands, and when I pressed them to my back, warmth bloomed. Something unfurled inside me, soft, weightless, and right.

The cub roared from the ground. The raven gave a single approving croak. The tree whispered something I couldn't catch, and from a distance, the snake slipped into a shiny hole.

"Fly, if you can," the Raven crooned, though not unkindly.

So, I did—

The dream poured into the Shade like light forcing itself through a shattered window. As Piper's hand touched his skin, a shimmer passed through him. The color returned to his cheeks, and his breath deepened.

She smiled, until—

The warmth in her hand began to burn. No, sting. Panic twisted in her gut, as the warmth was suddenly being replaced by something colder. Darker.

It was the same dream, but different. The field shimmered, the wheat bowing like it remembered me. The lion cub bounded beside me, sunlight catching in its fur. I reached for it, but something in the air shifted, turning darker.

The cub grew as it ran, paws striking harder, heavier, and its play turning frantic. Its fur deepened from honey to rust, then to red. The gold of its mane dulled to ash. Someone was cutting it, with slow and deliberate snips that echoed through the field. The cub didn't fight. It only looked at me with wide, glassy eyes that didn't understand why I wasn't helping. There was no laughter.

Then I saw the snake again. Only it wasn't small anymore. Its body shimmered with cracks of lightning, its skin peeling off in great, wet folds that steamed where they touched the ground. The sky darkened, clouds coiling as if drawn to its motion. Its new skin was black and silver, its eyes twin storms.

"Run," the lion said, or maybe it was just the wind. But my legs didn't move. The serpent uncoiled, rising higher than the glowing tree had once stood, its breath hissing as loud as thunder.

Then I was climbing again, not up, but down. The glowing tree was gone, its bark blackened and hollow. Light leaked from its cracks like dying fire. I could hear the raven above before I saw it.

It wasn't waiting this time. It was screaming. Feathers fell around me like shards of darkness. When I looked up, it was already diving, claws outstretched, eyes white as frost. I tried to shield myself, but it landed on my back, its weight a sudden, crushing ache.

It tore at me, ripping and pulling until I felt my skin give. My wings, the ones I'd made from its feathers, tore free in its beak. The warmth that had bloomed there before turned cold. I reached for them, but the feathers disintegrated into dust before they touched my fingers.

"Fly, if you can," the serpent hissed from below.

I tried. I really did. But when I leaped, there was no air, only a newfound silence—

"NO!" Colik's voice tore through the nightmare. He yanked Piper's hand back, and she collapsed backward, gasping for air. The boy's color started to fade instantly, his body curling once more into a sad stillness.

Her skin burned with cold sweat, her limbs trembled, and something deep inside her still pulled tight, as though the bad dream refused to let her go.

The Shade mother's hand gripped Pipers, making her jump. "Please," she whispered, voice soft and fragile. "Just a little more... Just one more dream."

"I. Said. No!" The Plastrof quivered with the echo of his voice, shadows rippling in the corners of the onyx crystalline walls as if afraid. Colik stepped between the Shades and Piper, every word humming with barely contained power. "You're letting him take too much."

He gripped Piper's arm away from the Shade and pulled her behind him—gentle, yet unyielding.

The Shade's eyes shimmered with grief. "He just had to live..." she whispered. Her son looked up at her, faintly smiling. As if that was all she wanted to see, she gave a small bow to Colik, then Piper.

"I must tend to him," she murmured, clutching the boy in her arms. Her trembling stilled. "Just for a moment."

When she turned back to Piper, something had changed. The fear was gone. Her gaze was distant, too peaceful, as though she had suddenly crossed into some other place.

"You'll still be here, won't you?" she asked softly. The

words sounded rehearsed, like an echo from a dream. "There's warm water. Bread—*yes*, I'll get bread."

Her tone carried no trace of pleading, only a fragile certainty, like she was remembering something Piper hadn't said. Before Piper could answer, the Shade smiled, then stepped back into the Plastrof wall with her child. They dissolved into the dark.

Silence followed, heavy and uneven.

Colik's hands were still shaking. "You almost gave everything," he said finally, his voice cracking through the quiet. "You don't understand what this could mean."

Piper's throat ached. "I was just trying to help."

He turned to her, eyes sharp and bright with something close to fear. "You gave him a dream; Piper and he tried to turn yours into a nightmare."

The space between them felt thinner than the bitter air itself.

"That wasn't a tie," he said, stepping closer. "That was a dream remembered. If any other Shade learns what you are —*what you did*—they won't stop with a plea. They'll devour everything you've ever dreamed."

He tore his gaze away, shaking his head. "I'm finding a way out," he muttered, backing toward the wall. "Without Shades. Without risk."

She reached out, but he was already gone, his last words trailing like smoke.

"Stay here. Don't move."

Then he vanished too, swallowed by the same dark as the Shades.

Piper stayed still for a long moment, listening to the quiet that followed. One breath. Two. Then something inside her shifted.

No.

The thought was sharp and raw. She didn't trust him. Not fully. Maybe not ever.

I don't need him, she thought, steadying her breath. *I made my choice.*

Crossing into a new feeling herself, Piper slipped through a different passage, her boots pressing softly into the icy path, each step echoing in the hollow silence that stretched ahead. The walls around her were sculpted from glassy black ice, smooth and translucent like the inside of a dark, frozen wave.

The crashing of the Untold Brine roared faintly in the distance. It sounded constant, wild, and unbothered. Here, deeper in the body of the Plaas' shell, the sound was muffled, and distant. Everything moved slower. Threads of light flowed within the ice, drifting like captured auroras, and when she passed too close, they flickered. The tunnel itself was aware of her presence.

The air carried the scent of sea flowers and salt, laced with something faintly sweet. The smell stirred emotions in her that felt like distant memories. Penelope's roses in the frost. Morry's laughter trailing through cold streets of Dublin.

She breathed in every bit of it, getting comfort from the familiarity, until she realized she was going in circles. Or at least, she thought it was the same tunnel she had just been in, and yet it could have been somewhere else entirely. Everything felt twisted here.

What choice did she really have but go back to find Colik?

Somewhere ahead, a faint light spilled around a bend in the tunnel. Piper slowed, listening. For a heartbeat, she swore she heard footsteps echoing behind her.

She quickened her pace and followed the light, emerging into another cavern within the Plastrof's coils.

This one felt different.

Stalactites hung like glass teeth, catching the faint glow of the ceiling, pinpricks of light shimmering like fallen stars trapped in stone. Piper hesitated at the mouth, her breath catching, then stepped further in, her boots crunching on wet rock until the floor sloped into black water.

She crouched, fingertips brushing the surface. The water mirrored the glow above, as if constellations had been drowned here long ago.

On impulse, she tugged off her shoes and slid her bare feet into the pool. A shiver raced through her, sharp and biting. It was the kind of cold that woke you up, daring her to feel.

The ripples spread outward, scattering the reflections until the stars fractured, breaking and reforming across the surface. The water welcomed her, sliding up her calves. It was cool, startlingly so after all the times she had steeped in fire. The chill didn't just touch her skin, but sank deeper, seeping through the heat that had clung to her for so long. It threaded into her bones, whispering relief, quenching something she hadn't realized was still burning.

Don't forget why you wanted to come back here, she repeated in her mind.

It felt like it had been forever since she'd been alone like this. Was she stupid for returning? For believing there was something waiting for her here in this impossible world of Dreamers and Royalds and *chaos*? Every step forward just pulled her deeper into something she didn't understand. Something meant for her, despite being a human.

She *did* miss her world. At least the simplicity of her life. The heaviness of real things, of trees that didn't breathe and wind that didn't hum. Of rain on windows, curled blankets, and the scratchy couch at Olympus House. Of Penelope's firm hand on her shoulder. Of Morry's smirk right before he said something rash to make her smile.

A lump formed in her throat.

In her waking world, she was invisible. An orphan even at twenty. Abandoned at four. At least she *knew* how to exist there. She had a routine. She had become comfortable with being comfortable.

Here, she wasn't sure who she was supposed to be. She

was being tugged in all directions, but something in her gut told her that they would *eventually* align.

Her fingers skimmed the surface of the water. It rippled outward again, distorting her reflection. Her face stretched, starting to unravel.

Like in the Motif River. Like when she came and went through the two worlds.

Suddenly, something in the water stirred, and she realized she wasn't alone. She hadn't noticed him when she came in, but on the other side of the water hole, a silhouette was half-submerged against the ledge.

He sat with his elbows casually holding himself up, head tilted slightly, dark hair curling damp against his temples. The upper half of him was bare, broad shoulders tapering to a frame she couldn't help but notice, but there was nothing showy in it. Just quiet confidence. He brought a comfort to the water, like it belonged to him.

He wasn't asleep because there was a clear intention in his stillness. So, was he watching? Waiting?

She froze, torn between carefully sneaking away and asking him to help her out of the Plastrof.

"Care for a swim?" His voice carried easily across the water.

Her instinct was to draw back, to keep the distance, but her eyes locked with his. They were *emerald*, the kind of color that held even in darkness.

"I didn't mean to disturb you," Piper said, softer than she intended. She should have left then and there, but his gaze had her pinned.

"You call it disturbing," he said, amusement flickering in his voice. "I was the one hoping to disturb you."

She couldn't think of a single thing to say.

Piper squinted at him, searching for some clever reply, but her mind went blank. Her stomach fluttered, but from nerves or something else, she couldn't tell. Was she afraid of him, or drawn to him?

In the silence, he suddenly moved toward her, the water lapping lightly at his chest. It was then she noticed the strange markings along his wrists and forearms. From this distance, they looked like red slashes, but she couldn't tell. Maybe they were intricate tattoos inked in red.

She stayed where she was, breath holding, which quite literally made her feel lightheaded.

Where was Colik?

To her surprise, the boy offered out a hand, not forcefully, but as a sincere invitation. "The water cools more than skin, you know," he said slowly.

She just stared, words caught somewhere between thought and breath, which was a first.

After a beat, he added, "I dare you."

Her gaze flicked to his hand, then to the faint curve of a smile tugging at his lips, not mocking, but gentle. Finally, she exhaled, slow and measured. His eyebrow lifted, just enough to let her know he'd noticed.

"That fire in you," he said plainly. "You carry it like the world is on your shoulders."

Eda had said something like her, but when he said it, it didn't feel like a burden. It felt like a confession.

Her mouth opened, but still no words came, so she closed it again.

Had she become some mute?

There was something about him that made her scared to talk now that he was this close. It was that little voice in her head that said run, while the beating of her heart said to stay. What would Colik say if he saw her with him?

He moved closer to the edge, directly in front of her feet still dangling in the water. She could tell he was purposefully holding back from touching her. That restraint gave her voice back.

"How would you know the heaviness I carry?" she asked, quieter than she meant to.

The boy, who looked about Colik's age, laughed. It was a low, unguarded sound that rippled through the cold air. His gaze traced her features before locking on her eyes, green meeting something darker, and for a heartbeat, neither of them looked away.

His pupils widened. She knew exactly who.

"Let's call it *dreamer speculation*."

She nodded, pretending to understand though she hadn't the faintest idea. He shifted beside her, moving from in front of her feet to her side, the cool water rippling between them.

"If you are not going to joining me, how about you turn around," he said evenly, "unless you plan to keep staring while I get out."

It wasn't teasing, exactly, it made Piper's heart skip a beat.

"Why—" but before she could finish, her head turned fast behind her as he leaped up, a flash of a bare body following. Her eyes tore away before she saw anything, but she couldn't hold back the gasp that followed.

Fixing her gaze on the cave's obsidian stone steps, she heard the soft shift of movement.

"Hand me that cloth," he said.

She saw what he was talking about, reached for it without looking at him, and threw it behind her.

"*Humans*," he said lightly, "always so careful about when they dare to look…and when they pretend not to." He snickered.

"Or maybe we just know we don't want to look," she shot back, though the words were thinner than she intended. Still, she couldn't help but wonder how he knew she was human. Was it written that plainly on her?

A pause, then, "I am decent."

She hesitantly turned back toward him, finding him wrapped neatly, posture relaxed, droplets of water tracing down his shoulders. There was no arrogance in the way he stood there, just a calm certainty, as if he was used to being studied, and not minding it.

"That heat rising in your face…this water would've helped," he said, mockingly.

She raised a brow, then stood up. "I think I'll survive." His mouth curved slightly, but he didn't press.

He was about seven inches taller than her, though the water made him seem closer. Those red marks were, in fact, red scars.

She swallowed, trying to not let her gaze linger. "I should go."

"If that's what you choose…" he said, though there was a note in his voice that made it sound like he wasn't convinced.

She turned to leave the way she'd come, but after a few steps, she paused. With a quiet sigh, she slowly turned back to him. "Do you know a more—*umm*—discreet way out?" she asked with an innate pout. She hated to ask but needed to leave before Colik found her. Or the Shades.

The mysterious boy with emerald eyes gave a devilish grin. "I thought you'd never ask." He came up to her, making Piper catch her breath. "Come," he said. "I'll show you." Something in his tone told her it wasn't just about finding an exit.

He turned and led her toward the opposite wall through which she came in.

Colik won't find her now.

Even from behind, Piper noticed the way he moved, like night poured into human form. Unlike Colik, whose confidence carried the faint tremor of something breakable.

No, this boy was fluid and unhurried, its shadows folding around him with every step. He was assured, controlled, but dangerous.

They reached another arching passage in the Plastrof's shell and another. It never ended, but then on what Piper felt to be the final turn, a breath of cooler air swept her face. The passage darkened, and figures appeared from its depths.

Two Shades.

They must have been waiting, and drifted closer, their pale faces with black eyes cocked as though scenting Piper. *A human.*

The pull came swift and merciless, tugging from her chest, and her thoughts spilled loose and dizzy. One Shade placed a hand on her arm, and immediately her knees weakened. She swayed, caught in their silent hunger.

The boy with emerald eyes didn't stop them. He didn't even turn around.

She was unraveling, warmth draining from her bones, and her vision dimming. It felt the same as when she tried to give the boy Shade dream, except it seeped through her skin a lot faster.

"That's enough." His voice cut the air, slow but deliberate.

The Shades hesitated, still getting closer to her, as though curious to see whether he meant it.

Only then did the boy move. Swiftly coming to her side, his hand closed around her arm, breaking the Shade's grasp and pulling her into him. Her lungs seized as air rushed back, sharp and cold. Her palms met the hard line of his chest, her head spinning.

"Not this one," he said, each word edged with command.

Finally, the two Shades recoiled, melting back into the folds of the shell with dark obedience. Silence fell, heavy, but her heart thundered on.

She was still pressed against him when his emerald eyes found her gaze, assessing, and amused.

"You continue to bleed human dust like that to a Shade," he breathed, words brushing her skin. "You will tempt even the gods to take it."

Her pulse stumbled. "You—"

He turned, stride unhurried, and she had no choice but to follow. The passage curved once more, but this time no Shades waited in the folds. Instead, the dark shell opened into a view that stole her breath for an entirely different reason.

What she expected—the open waters of the Untold Brine —was gone, but the land stretched unfamiliarly anyway. A pale river wound its way through a shimmering basin, where sand met slick glass like the Untold Brine had frozen mid-motion. She recognized the Motif River, flowing with shimmers as ever before. In the far distance, beneath the wavering curtain of the dream-haze, the Blood Moon hovered, massive, red and watchful.

"It's where the Reverie leaves what it no longer wants," the boy said softly. "The Forgotten Land."

Then, glancing back at her, his mouth curled. His dark-ened emerald eyes had lightened again. So had his demeanor. "Don't like it?"

"No, it's just…" Her words died, caught in the strange hush that draped the space. "Thank you for saving me back there."

His eyes widened for a moment, then he tilted his head, his dark hair shifting with the motion, "Your face says other-wise. Do you always wear your thoughts like that?"

"For showing me out," she said quickly, ignoring his ques-tion. She knew he wouldn't like the answer. "Ummm…" she faltered, realizing she didn't get his name.

"Just call me *Shade*." His eyes were back to being unreadable.

He studied her for a beat longer, then let his gaze drift toward the path. "It's the only way to leave without the other Shades noticing. Convenient, isn't it?"

Piper narrowed her eyes. "But you're a Shade?" So were the ones he saved her from.

It came out half a question, half a statement.

That earned her a sharp-edged smirk. "Perceptive. Are you saying that matters? Would you have preferred I didn't save you…because *I am* a Shade?" He stepped away from her, deeper into the curling, black-speckled shadows of the conch-like tunnel they had just exited. Then he stopped.

He turned slightly, just enough for his gaze to catch hers again. For a breathless moment, he did nothing but stare. The air shifted between them. It prickled over her skin. His eyes sharpened to curiosity. Or cautionary.

He inhaled. "You're bleeding dust."

Piper stiffened. "You said that already."

His smile faded. "Giving it away so easily too…" He went on, his hand twitching at his side. "But I won't take it. Not even a taste."

"Why?" she asked, her voice barely audible. "Isn't that what your kind does?"

A pause stretched between them, the silence brimming with tension. This time, because of him, not her.

"I'm not—," he said finally, then stopped himself. "Before you ask why I helped you…" He looked away, something tightening in his jaw. "Don't."

The words weren't cruel, but they carried weight and finality.

She took a step back, feeling her spine press against the cool curve of the shell behind her.

"You should be careful who you trust in this world," he kept on, voice dropping and backed away even more. "You'd think *humans* knew that by now."

She caught herself nodding, listening intently. She knew the sudden chill that slid down her spine had nothing to do with the air. Before she could figure out what he meant, he vanished, swallowed by the folds of the Plastrof like the other two Shades.

She scoffed, more to herself than at him. She had been around enough Shades to last her a lifetime. Even as she turned to face the open land that had called the *Forgotten Land*, the echo of his presence lingered behind her like a new shadow.

CHAPTER SEVENTEEN
THE VALUE

P iper had stumbled upon a headland crafted from a geologist's dream. The ground formed a mosaic of stones—amethysts, emeralds, and peculiar iridescent gems. Their jagged edges twisted into natural arches, while others into spires.

Small openings exposed minerals gleaming in hues of turquoise, violet, and gold—colors so vivid they were unreal. Colors that she hadn't seen anywhere else in the Reverie. Most everything in the Reverie were white, silver, and black, while the Blood Moon cast its restless glow, washing everything in a faint red-orange shade.

Piper followed the Motif River, its current whispering to her in a tongue she craved to understand, every ripple tugging at her feet as though urging her forward.

It was like she was walking on the edge of two worlds... and perhaps, she was.

The river's murmur deepened as the path widened toward the Blood Moon, though the moon itself remained the same, close enough to feel yet impossibly distant. She knew she had found the path the Silver Girl wanted her to follow.

Follow the Motif River. It will take you to the Elphiates.

This place felt untouched by even the Dreamers.

Out of the corner of her eye, Piper saw a swift fluttering movement beyond the rocks and stones. Kneeling to get a closer look, tiny creatures toiled tirelessly amidst the vibrant minerals and gemstones. No larger than her thumb, their skin was a liquid mercury, limbs quick and nimble, and eyes gleaming with elation and cleverness.

She watched, fascinated, as one of the little creatures used its sharp, gleaming teeth to gnaw at the outer edge of a particularly tough amethyst. Its movements were quick and deliberate, each bite slowly chipping away to uncover the rare crystal hidden within. Others worked alongside it, their tiny hands prying open more rocks and stones to expose sparkling amethyst veins and shimmering quartz clusters. They moved with such purpose, as if unlocking a treasure chest only they knew existed.

One of them turned from the rock to Piper, its eyes sharp with a strange protectiveness. Then it grinned, jagged teeth glinting with bits of stone, before darting into a crack between the crystals. Piper smiled and let it go.

As she walked, the Motif River darkened, its silver gleam fading into a cool, nightshade glow that deepened with every step. The air grew heavier, the soft blue sparks thinning through the mist ahead.

She followed them, breath shallow, until the darkness opened into a waterfall of living light pouring into a vast pool below, each droplet bursting into constellations before vanishing into stone. The water roared, and the air folded in on itself.

Piper stumbled forward, swallowed in a flicker that tasted of salt and iron. Her vision splintered into fragments—wings, dust, flames—and when her feet struck ground again, the river was gone. So was the waterfall.

She had crossed into somewhere completely unknown. A place Piper couldn't have imagined belonging to the Reverie.

The Blood Moon hung low, its ember light smothered behind smoke.

The Dreamworld was no longer beautiful. It was a place worthy of nightmares.

Fields of gold rippled in the distance, yet the wheat moved like liquid, stirred by no wind. Above it all, the sky churned into a celestial storm of midnight, bleeding with slashes of dulled silver and aged bronze flakes. It was dust clouds. Broken trees made of ash and musky wood towered in mourning rows, and in the wheat, silhouettes wandered aimlessly.

Fear filled Piper's entire body, hesitating each new step forward. She could feel the ground mourning the dreams lost here.

The path narrowed into a metal bridge spanning the gorge where the Motif River fell. Its rods were warped, ancient, and skeletal in their design. Across the bridge, a castle formed of blackened stone and molten bronze.

From the shadows on either side of the bridge, two forms emerged, their bodies silver dulled to ash, color having been stolen by the ages. Wings clung to their backs, fractured and featherless, bones jutting through what remained of the membrane like shards of glass. Rusted gold braces circled their wrists, each inscribed with symbols long eroded and chains snaked from their ankles into the cracked stone below. Their eyes held shape, but bronze rims burned around the corneas.

One leaned forward, its movements scraping the ground like nails on a chalkboard. The other raised its head just enough for the faint shimmer of its ruined wings to catch the dying light. They were silver ghosts rusting away from what they once were.

Piper's stomach tightened.

One raised its limb, its bony fingers leveling at her.

She froze.

"You've come to the Elphiates," the first said slowly, its voice grinding through the stone beneath her feet.

"Where one walks backward through forgotten ages," whispered the other, even slower, "and stirs the bones of memory to see what still remembers."

Piper's stomach twisted. The air around her turned corrosive. It scorched down her throat, metallic and harsh, leaving her eyes stinging.

"What is your value?" The voice was dry and brittle, like parchment curling over flame.

"I am…" Her voice cracked, hollow. She had never been asked that before, but she didn't like it. "I'm here to—"

The sentence fractured. Her mind raced with reasons: to find the Silver Girl, to follow get away from Colik, to figure out her purpose here as a human. None of those were value worthy…were they?

The rusting ghosts tilted their heads as one, and their voices braided into a single echo:

"You were not lost to chance," one intoned.

"The dust remembers what the flesh forgets," answered the other.

"Morpheus marked your dust when the world was young—"

"—and so you were never meant to wake human."

The words fell like chains around her chest.

Then, slowly, they turned toward one another. Their arms rose in tandem, and from the cracked stone beneath their feet, two swars surged upward. They were rusted, blackened, and veined with old red strands whose gleam faded by the moment.

"Another strand drawn," murmured one, driving its swar into the stone next to it.

"Another debt remembered," replied the other.

The other swar went into the stone and a soundless pulse shook the ground beneath her feet. The cold followed immediately, not just brushing her skin, but seeping into her bones. It wasn't the dryness of the weather but of her life. Of her past. The dull birthdays no one celebrated, the quiet of empty chairs no one filled, and the silence that always followed when no one came to claim her as an orphan at Olympus House.

She gave a stiff nod, and the ghostly guardians moved aside as one, their limbs jerking in perfect unison like puppets with invisible strings. They didn't speak. They didn't breathe but parted just the same.

It wasn't any standard bridge. It stretched forward, arching into the void ahead as though the Dreamworld itself had bent to make way. Brass and ash gleamed beneath her feet, fused into ribs of metal and bone that curved outward like the spine of a fallen god. The surface was cold and its sheen dulled, flaking to reveal veins of pale marrow beneath.

The air brushed against her where silver touched ash, murmuring the ghosts of what this place had been. Bright once. Sacred once. Alive once. Now hollowed, the Elphiates bled color into the dark, their light grown old with remembering. Beneath the archway, the Motif River turned in a slow, dreaming current—not of water or flame, but of something born from the breath of gods forgetting this place.

She stared at it, and it stared back. The current didn't flow so much as it dragged. Her foot hovered over the first plank, and it trembled beneath her weight. It was not enough to break, but to remind her that this place didn't tolerate hesitation.

Piper hated bridges.

As her hand brushed the railing, heat flared into her skin. It wasn't comfort, and it wasn't kindness, but it felt familiar, and that made this all worse.

She stepped forward—once, then again—and the bridge groaned. Beneath her, the river churned with smoke and shadow. Shapes shifted in its depths, unformed and restless, longing for her fall. The Blood Moon bled its color across the world, staining the iron spine beneath her feet. When she reached the center, her breath faltered. The air grew too heavy, too sharp, and her lungs burned with the weight of forgetting to breathe.

When she dared to look back, nothing was there. The world behind her had vanished, swallowed by the silver fog that wore its mask like a secret. Colik's warning carved into her:

"Trust me and survive this Dreamworld. Or don't—and let it take the last of your humanity."

Her hands clenched the railings of the bridge.

"What does he even know?" she whispered to herself but hated the way it broke.

Solitude was no stranger. It had been sewn into her bones back at Olympus House. This wasn't loneliness that trembled through her—it was hope. Terrifying, uninvited hope. The kind that made her think someone might be waiting on the other side of this bridge. At fifteen, she would've called that a dream. Now, it felt dangerous to believe.

Now, hope was more dangerous than despair.

The bridge ended without ceremony. No gate, no elaboration, just stone and clay beneath her foot. Her knees buckled, heavy with something she could not name, and she fell to the ground, gasping.

Ahead of her, the castle pulsed once with light, as if expecting a guest. Its spires rose like black glass and obsidian, jagged against the star-swarmed sky. Roots of reddish-brown trees clawed toward its gates, their autumn leaves trembling in colors too vivid for the ash-choked air. The walls rippled faintly, the base of the fortress seeming to grow from the earth itself, dissolving into the wheat fields, its arch framed by glowing carvings. Silver-white flowers clung stubbornly to the stones at its entrance.

Just before the gate—large enough to admit a dragon—rows of small green plants bloomed with pale lotus flowers, their petals slick with dew that shimmered like sleep. Beneath them, seeds glittered like pomegranates, pulsing faintly. Alive. Piper's stomach twisted. She pinched her nose and sprinted past before the scent could reach her lungs, before it could coax her into forgetting.

She knew about *that* myth. And was not going to risk it after what happened in the Lavyrinthos.

The pillars had no handles, only carvings of lions, serpents, and peacocks that climbed higher than she could see. Their shapes were disturbingly familiar. Steele's distaff had borne the same marks. Why the hell was she here? What made me think her think she could take this world on alone?

Everything in her screamed to turn back, but there was no turning back.

Fear had knocked, and Piper chose to walk straight toward it.

CHAPTER EIGHTEEN
THE ROOM OF LOCKES

Piper passed the gate, bracing herself for darkness. Maybe a black hole, a void, or something jagged and final. Instead, she entered a vast chamber of gilded cages. From the vaulted beams above, massive birdcages hung in slow suspension, faded in gold; their once-brilliant metal dulled by time. Each cage was large enough to hold a human, and from its crown hung a golden lock, glinting faintly where the light touched.

Within some cages, faint movement stirred.

Figures.

Some lay still, sleeping, while others paced within the confines of their gold-plated prisons. The chamber breathed with them, as if a cathedral of forgotten souls.

"Piper."

One voice cut through the rest. It wasn't spoken aloud, but pulsed inside her chest like a second, evasive and all-consuming thought. It was both a plea and a command. She stumbled a step forward and the chamber answered her. The rough stone floor smoothed beneath her feet, a path unraveling from where she stood. Moss and crystal curled aside, and a faint silver light led her toward one cage suspended higher than the rest. Its glow rippled, sensing her approach, and the silhouette inside shifted—long limbs, a bowed head, and silver hair drifting as if the cage was filled with water.

"Do you hear me?" Piper whispered.

The voice came again, clearer, echoing through her veins. *"Come closer."*

The other cages shivered in protest. A chorus of hands pressed to the bars, of silent mouths stretched wide, and of eyes burning in the dark. The one silver path drew her on, each step tightening the pull in her chest.

The air thickened as she neared the last cage. The bars were too beautiful to be cruel—gold braided with silver veins that pulsed with each step closer. This was the only cage that had some silver, opposed to being gold. Within, something moved.

Piper stopped. Her pulse echoed the rhythm of the cage's glow. She reached out, the air searing her skin with heat.

The figure lifted its head, and silver eyes opened.

The breath that left Piper was ragged, tearing from her lungs. She knew those eyes, had glimpsed them before. In her dreams by the river. In warnings she hadn't fully understood.

The Silver Girl.

Her skin was etched faintly with glimmering cracks, as though her body was carved from porcelain and threaded with starlight, just barely holding it together. The cage pulsed with her heartbeat, every pulse resonating with her own.

"Piper." The voice inside her chest was unmistakable, soft but relentless. *"I knew you could find me. That you would."*

Her fingers brushed the bars. The heat was immediate, searing past skin to settle in bone. The Silver Girl raised her hand, palm mirroring Piper's through the gold, but when their fingers nearly met, the pain struck deeper and Piper tore her hand away.

"Why are you in there?" Piper asked, her voice trembling. Even as she said it, she knew.

Her lips never moved, but the words carved themselves into her. *"You know why. I can see it in those pretty little green eyes of yours. That is not why you are here…to ask why."*

All around the room, the other cages shook violently, as if sensing danger. Fists struck the bars, and voices rose in a cacophony of desperate pleas. Piper couldn't look away. The sound warped, like a dream gone wrong, muffled and distorted, as though someone had twisted the frequency inside her ears. The words weren't ones she knew, yet some part of her felt she should have.

The Silver Child leaned closer, her silver eyes burning into Piper. *"Free me Piper like you have always wanted to free yourself. If you do…everything will change for the both of us."*

The path beneath her feet pulsed once.

The Silver Girls hand trembled on the bars.

"You have power here you've barely begun to touch," she said softly, her voice smooth and unhurried, slipping into Piper's mind like silk through water. *"Free me, and I will tell you everything, your past, your truth, and the destiny written for you among the stars."*

Piper's heart thudded against her chest. The voice didn't echo in her ears so much as *inside* her, brushing the corners of her thoughts like fingers tracing wet glass. For a moment, she wanted to believe her, to reach through the gold and let whatever truth waited spill out.

Something in the girl's eyes stopped her. They gleamed too steadily, too knowing, like mirrors reflecting someone else's design.

"I don't even know who you are," Piper said, though her voice came out smaller than she meant it to. "Or why I should trust you."

The Silver Girl tilted her head, the faintest smile curving her mouth, as if she'd been expecting that answer all along. Her smiled deepened, soft like a child, but wrong in a way Piper couldn't name.

"Trust is a fragile thing," she purred. *"It isn't what binds this world together. Choice is."*

Her fingers brushed the bars again, unflinching this time. The gold hissed beneath her touch, yet she didn't move.

"You've already been chosen once, haven't you? Only ever told half the truth."

The words slid beneath Piper's skin like a shiver. "What do you know?" she whispered, more desperate than she would have liked. "How do you know anything about me?"

The girl's silvery eyes brightened. *"Because I heard your name spoken by——."* She stopped, looking around as the cages around them groaned, their glow dimming to a dull, feverish red.

Piper's heart thudded. The girl's words pulled at her, threading through doubt and longing until her fear began to blur.

"By whom?" She didn't care that she sounded desperate. First Steele. Now this Silver Girl. How did the Silver Children know her life more than she did?

Piper lifted her hand toward the bar. The heat should have warned her, but it didn't. All she could see was the Silver Girl's gaze, bright and pleading, a mirror of something she couldn't name but felt she'd lost long ago. Their fingers were an inch apart.

Then——

"Piper, don't!"

The voice struck through the room like a blade.

She turned just as a gust of wind broke through the gold light, scattering dust and feathers of ash. Colik emerged from the shadows on Dray, his expression twisted in shock. Hovering in the air next to her, his eyes caught the glint of the cage and widened with something between fury and fear.

"Step back," he snapped, his voice low but trembling. "You have no idea what she is."

The Silver Girl's lips curved faintly. *"He would say that,"* she whispered, for only her ears. *"He's forgotten what he is, too."*

The sound of her voice made the air hum. The gilded bars trembled, light bleeding from them like cracks in glass.

"Piper," Colik said again, softer this time, his hand outstretched. "Please. Don't touch her."

"She is just a child." Piper whispered, her eyes moving from the Silver Girl's to Coliks, then to Dray.

"If you know anything about the ages of gods, you will know the children are the most dangerous. The true monsters," Colik whispered, his tone as desperate as hers.

The Silver Girl tilted her head, studying him as if he were something already broken.

"Monsters," she echoed softly, for only Pipers ears. *"That's what they called us when they locked us away. Children, too wild to control. Children who dared to dream beyond the gods."*

Her gaze slid to Piper, and the heat from the cage pulsed stronger, matching every heartbeat. *"You know what it is to be abandoned, don't you? To be left behind by the ones who were supposed to love you?"*

Piper froze. The words pressed too close.

"What is this place?" She whispered.

"The Room of Lockes. Piper—you shouldn't be here," Colik said, voice low. "You didn't let her touch you, did you?"

"She says she needs me to free her."

"No," he snapped. "She wants to tie to you."

"I chose to come," Piper said, her voice low and very much afraid.

"You think you chose," Colik growled, his voice rough with something that sounded like grief. He didn't move. His eyes stayed locked on the Silver Girl, but his feet never touched the flickering path Piper stood on. It shimmered between them, gold and ghost-light, as if warning him away. Or maybe he was simply afraid to cross it.

"Her power was never force," he said quietly, as if to himself. "It's always been suggestion. That's what made her dangerous then...and what makes her even more dangerous.

She is what happens when a dream is broken and no longer controllable." Piper thought about what Eda said about children being dangerous…Was that true?

The Silver Girl's expression softened into something pitying. *"Oh, Colik,"* she murmured in Piper's mind. *"He speaks of me as though he remembers. There is a reason he is the knight."*

Piper looked at Colik, searching his face for some sign that he could hear her, but his eyes told her he couldn't. The light beneath her feet wavered, uncertain, as though the ground itself couldn't decide whose side it was on.

"I was born into silence," the girl said softly. *"They buried me in gold so the gods wouldn't hear me cry. You and I, Piper—we're not so different. We're both forgotten things."*

"Piper," Colik warned, hovering as close as possible without entirely cowering over her on Dray. "Whatever she's saying to you, don't listen."

Piper couldn't look away. The Silver Girl's eyes gleamed like mirrors of starlight, and the words wound deeper.

"Free me," she whispered.

The air went still. Even the other cages fell silent, their voices swallowed by the weight of her promise.

"You're afraid of her," Piper said to Colik, her voice unsteady. Conflicted.

"I'm afraid of what she'll do to you," Colik whispered, his voice cracking. The sound made her chest ache.

The Silver Girl's voice slipped back into her thoughts like a thread of silver through silk. *"He fears what you can become without him."*

Piper's breath caught. "What did you become?" she asked, though she wasn't sure whose question it was anymore. Hers or the Silver Girl's.

"Piper," Colik begged, his words barely reaching her.

The Silver Girl smiled, her eyes burning into Piper's. *"A god's regret."*

The lock on the cage pulsed silver beneath Piper's fingertips as she touched it again. The heat dulled, the air stilled, and for a breathless moment, nothing moved. Then the Silver Girl lifted her hand, her pale fingers rising to meet Piper's through the gold.

~

The Silver Age glowed like a dream poured into silver light. A hundred children with molten skin ran barefoot through meadows of silver grass beneath lavender skies, their laughter ringing like windchimes. They leaped from cloud to cloud, the air it's playground, shaping dragons from mist, weaving stories like dreams remembered, from thin air.

FLASH—

The meadow dissolved into marble and thunder. Zeus stood at the dais, his eyes storm-bright, Athena at his side, and Hermes crouched below in silence. The Silver Child stood before them, silver dust clinging to her fingers, radiant with the naive hope that they had summoned her in praise.

"You can remain free, Hazel," Zeus said, his voice a weight heavier than chains, "if you agree to serve. You will be the last Silver Child while this age ends."

Hazel's breath hitched. "Serve?"

"To be a Fatale," he decreed. "A Cloner of strands. You will take the red threads spun by the Fates themselves and weave human dreams, feeding the Fray so it does not starve." His words cracked like lightning across the Olympus throne. "This is so humans do not stray. You will not let wild strands pass the Gate of Ivory. If you disobey, you will be contained in the Room of Lockes."

Hazel's lips trembled. "If I refuse?"

"Then you will be locked away like the others."

Her silence was taken as consent.

FLASH—

Hazel's hands worked feverishly, cloning strands like a robot dressed in silver skin. At first, she obeyed, but compassion soon outweighed command. She began to slip strands past the Gate of Horn, crafting wild dreams, giving mortals the freedom to wander beyond REM.

Hazel tried to free others like herself. Silver Children who longed to live as dreamers again, one in particular who whispered thanks as she wove them a strand of escape.

It did not last.

Zeus's fury split the sky. Hazel was dragged, her silver blood streaking the marble, her wrists bound in chains that burned against her skin. The role of Cloner was torn from her, stripped strand by strand until her hands were left empty and shaking in the Room of Lockes.

She had been banished. No longer a Fatale. Forever contained with the rest of the Silver Children.

In the midst of it all, Hazel's silver eyes cut through the memory, finding Piper's——

~

The vision shattered, but the weight of it stayed lodged behind Piper's ribs. She stumbled back, gasping, because it wasn't just memory. It was *remembrance.* Like what Steele had showed her.

They both were Silver Children.

The Silver Girl clutched her chest like she'd been stabbed, and Piper clutched the cage bars harder, trying to hold onto reality. Zeus had called her Hazel.

Hazel.

That was the name of her stuffed bear, the one she whispered secrets to when Olympus House felt too dark to breathe in. The one lying on her bed right now back in the waking world.

"You saw it. You know what they did to me. You know what they'll do to you. I can keep you from them." Hazel's voice reverberated through Piper's head.

The other cages shook violently, their captives wailing, fists pounding against their cages, but none burned like Hazel's. None reached her so wholly. So piercingly.

"Why me?"

The stone path Piper was standing on suddenly trembled, and beside her, Colik *struck.*

Piper screamed as Dray swooped low in a blur of silver

light. Colik leaned over and seized her wrist, dragging her away from the cage—away from Hazel's reaching hand.

"Please," Colik said, his voice mournful and tense. "Trust me."

He pulled her against him until she was in his lap, the Silver Girl's cage vanishing from sight beneath a rush of wind and blinding dust. Dray's wings unfurled like storms breaking, the beast shrieking as it climbed through the chamber's hollow air.

"Let me go—" Piper gasped, twisting in his grip.

"You don't understand what she is," Colik shouted over the roar.

"I do!" Piper cried back. "She's me!"

The word *me* trembled like a chord pulled too tight. She could still *feel* Hazel, like a hand tugging inside her chest, drawing her down. Every beat of her heart throbbed with it. The air between them stretched thin, a current of dust and longing, as though the world itself were trying to pull her back to her.

Dray burst through the roof of the Room of Lockes, the force of its wings shattering the black glass overhead as it ascended through the hollow spires of the dark palace. As they flew further away, the air outside shifted, from a suffocating heat wave to a cold, sharp breeze threaded with starlight and ash.

Still, Piper reached back, fingers trembling toward the shrinking palace below. "Hazel—" she whispered, though the wind tore the word away.

Her chest ached. The pull didn't fade, but *tightened*, like something deep within her refused to let go.

Colik's grip on her waist tightened, trying to hold on to both her and his atmospheric beast. "Just wait," he whispered, his voice raw. "The tie will break once we are out of the Elphiates."

It did. Dray's wings spasmed mid-flight as the beast shot

past the borders of the Elphiates, tearing through the last veil of darkness and dust clouds. The familiar stars of the Constellation cloud wavered above them, trembling as gravity tried to reclaim its hold.

Something inside Piper snapped, a soundless break felt rather than heard, like a strand being cut. The pull vanished, but the world lurched.

This was nothing like Kryvo i Kross.

There, the fall had been controlled, practiced, and playful. Here, it was feral. Unforgiving and uncontrollably terrifying.

Dray screamed. The beast's wings spasmed again, light flickering along its translucent veins. For one breathless moment, it hung suspended in the air.

Then Dray dipped hard.

The silver haze below surged upward to meet them, and Piper realized that a tie hadn't *just* snapped between her and Hazel. A tie had snapped between *Colik* and Dray too.

They were descending fast. Too fast. Piper felt sick to her stomach.

"*Ne kryvo!*" Colik cried out, slamming his heel into Dray's side, its fins slicing through the air like torn sails catching the wind, but the movement wasn't smooth. Something was wrong.

Dray's form trembled, and its trajectory faltered. It wasn't just straining but *resisting*. Its body glowed, flickering silver-blue in chaotic pulses, split between instincts it couldn't reconcile. Colik had told her Dray answered to one. Now it had two.

"Dray, *ne kryvo!*" Colik roared again, desperate.

The beast's fins snapped once, trying its best to keep level, but then they folded, collapsing inward with a sickening crack.

Like a dying star folding into itself, gravity claimed them without grace. Tumbling, twisting, and shattering through the air, Dray plummeted. There was no control left, only speed, a spin, and terror within all three of them.

The air howled like something cruel, tearing at Piper's

skin, her hair, and her breath. The world spun in sickening, silver-edged loops.

Colik clutched her, his arms locked around her like he could stop the sky from swallowing them, but his grip trembled, a look of terror on his features.

Beneath them, Dray thrashed wildly, its wings tremoring out of rhythm, the weight of two riders breaking its shape apart. Its cry tore through the air, guttural and raw, a sound that pierced through Piper's ribs like a blade forged from mourning. It wasn't the cry of a beast in pain. It was the cry of something being split in two.

They nosedived faster, the Reverie smearing into a storm of colors merging into one as they fell, then soared, fell harder, then rose again. Each motion was more violent than the last, as if gravity and flight couldn't agree who they belonged to.

Piper's stomach lurched while Dray's body convulsed mid-flight, its tail lashing, wings faltering against the pull of nothing. Piper's vision stretched, elongated, and warped with every new descent.

This was nothing like the Scirges' game. There, the emerald beast had moved with purpose and clarity, carrying Colik and her through the wind as if it could feel their trust.

Here, the air felt like a mouth closing around them, and Dray was falling straight into its throat.

"*Dray!*" Colik shouted, letting go of Piper and placing both palms on either side of his crying beast. "*Hold—HOLD!*"

There was nothing to hold onto.

Piper's mind fractured into an instinctive, silent, and sharpened plea: *Please. Please, don't let us fall.*

She didn't know if she was speaking to Dray, or to the stars, or to anything that might still be listening. Something answered. Dray's body rippled. Its limbs seized. It's tail coiled. Then it's wings, once limp, flared open like sails catching divine wind. The air tore past them in sheets of starlight, the blur sharpening into blue, blue bleeding into silver, and silver burning into the searing white of the Constellation cloud.

Dray dove, buckled, then pushed until they were no longer falling. The air steadied beneath its wings as it fought for balance, moving faster than before, as if desperate to regain control.

Dray still didn't seem to know who to serve.

The beast twisted through the air, its muscles straining, its tail slicing against the wind. The world tilted, one moment a threat of plummeting, the next a trembling climb, and each conflicting motion pulled harder at its form. Blood roared in Piper's ears, and the horizon blurred as her vision began to fade. Her grip slipped. Her consciousness frayed.

They hit hard, the landing anything but smooth. Piper's eyes opened again as she slammed onto marble steps, sliding across cold stone, her breath ripping from her lungs. Her vision burst with white and silver, pain sparking across every inch of her scraped skin. She coughed hard, throat raw, but alive.

Blinking through the haze, she forced her eyes to focus.

They were no longer soaring on Dray. No wings. No fins. No starlit shape carving through the skies. Only a shimmer of silver dust, already breaking apart and drifting upward, swallowed by the brilliance of the heavens.

When her vision cleared, the world before her made her freeze.

A castle. It had to be the Citadel.

It rose higher than her mind could measure, carved entirely of luminous white stone, its towers pierced with four enormous spires that glittered like frozen fire. Silver lace threaded through every arch and balcony, catching the drifting clouds and constellations above until the whole palace was aflame with radiance. Colossal, winged statues lined the double metallic gates, their stone feathers so vast they could have sheltered whole villages beneath them. A shimmering white staircase spread before them, wide enough for an army to climb.

Beside her, Colik stirred, dragging himself upright with a rough exhale. His hair clung to his brow, his chest heaving, but he too was alive.

Piper swallowed hard, feeling impossibly small under the weight of so much grandeur. The Citadel loomed like the dwelling place of gods, and the golden doors at its heart glowed as though sunlight itself waited on the other side.

Piper blinked again, disoriented, her chest heaving with both pain and grief. Why had Colik's atmospheric beast—his companion, his creature stitched from dreams and loyalty—obeyed *her*? Dray had listened to *Piper's* voice in the chaos.

She heard movement beside her, slow and shuddering.

Colik sat up with a grunt, one hand clutching his side. When his eyes lifted, when he saw the sky and the outline of dust, he froze. Then he broke.

He collapsed forward, catching himself on trembling arms. His hands pressed into the ground, as if trying to pull energy from it, as he had none.

She watched him shake his head, his body following like a cold chill. Then he turned to face her, his eyes full of rage. Helplessness. Loss.

"You *took* Dray!" he roared at her, voice raw, cracking like glass. "You damned it from obeying me! *To save you!*" He slammed a fist into the ground. Then repeatedly. His knuckles bloodied, his voice unraveling.

Piper stared, wide-eyed, using all her strength to keep the water behind her eyes from forming real tears.

"I—"

"Dray was mine," Colik gasped, more to himself than her. "The beast was… the one thing that listened—*really listened*—not to the gods. Not to the Royalds. To *me*."

His head dropped. His shoulders curled in. He looked like he might cave in on himself.

Piper didn't move or breathe, because in that moment, Colik wasn't the Royald who'd journeyed through the entire Reverie with her. He was just a boy who had loved something fiercely and lost it.

Because of me.

He didn't say her name. Didn't look at her. He didn't have to because his silence was heavier than a thousand curses.

He dragged a hand through his hair, then spoke so softly she thought she imagined it. "I knew something was going to break in the Broken Woods," he whispered. "I just never imagined it would be a human girl, unravelling the one part of me I thought was unbreakable."

Piper's stomach twisted painfully. "Colik…"

He lifted his gaze to her, and the hurt in his eyes was sharp enough to cleave the world in two. "You are the last thing I expected to fracture anything inside me. Let alone him."

Her heart lurched. Right then, she would have given anything to undo it. The moment Dray had listened. Because maybe—just maybe—Colik wouldn't be looking at her like he wished he had never saved her. Not on the Ollopa train. Or during *Kryvo i Kross*. Or even in the Room of Lockes, but never at all.

A sound in front of them made both of their head's whip towards its direction. It was footsteps. Quick and measured.

A figure stepped out from the double metallic gates, his silhouette cutting sharply against the crimson-constellated sky. He was small and aged, draped in a deep purple cloak that spilled from one bare shoulder and flowed down his body like velvet. A brooch fastened it at his chest, shaped like an open fish with a single slash through it. It reminded Piper of the scar on her hand, except the mark on hers was curved, not slashed.

Despite his silence and hesitation, he was unmistakable flamboyant. Both his cheeks and sandals sparkled, and his nails were polished to a mirror-like purple sheen. He wore far too many rings, and when he tilted his head, the jewels caught the light like tiny galaxies of amethysts. A feathered half-mask clung to the side of his face, as though he wore it purely for drama.

When he spoke, his voice rippled like harp strings dragged through a cloud.

"The Royalds are calling," he announced. He didn't acknowledge Pipers fearful gaze or Colik's cruel one.

"Patryk," Colik breathed, his expression changing, like he had just been caught in an illegal act.

Patryk's smile was small and uncomfortable. Apologetic almost. The smile of one who has had to deliver death, truth, and lies all in the same breath, and grown utterly indifferent to which was which.

"And this time, *my dear Dreamers*... There will be no distractions."

CHAPTER NINETEEN
THE ROYALDS

The moment Piper entered the Citadel, the world shifted from otherworldly to heavenly. The staircase before her rose like a cresting wave, frozen mid-surge, its surface a smooth silver stone and pale marble.

Arched ceilings rose above her, carved in stone with every constellation imaginable. The floor shimmered like frozen tidewater. Candles hung down from the beams above with small sliver chains you'd see subtly on a woman's neck, their flames cool and blue. They didn't merely glow but shimmered, making the air itself glisten and ripple, as though the entire room existed inside a star of enchanted, steel blue light. Balconies twisted up the walls like vines, and little hidden spaces peeked out. It was a theater made for gods. The air was cool and perfumed with something floral, but not earthly.

Then she saw them.

At the top of the stairs, where the twin staircases met, stood—

"My Royalds." The one named Patryk spoke and gave a small bow as they all three stopped at the foot of the steps. Standing closely next to her, Colik looked unamused.

Piper stared up at the two Royalds, poised like living

constellations, each standing on a separate landing, and each crowned with a delicate circlet of laurel leaves.

The male was the highest. His hair was dark brown, falling just above his collar in soft, restless waves that caught the glow of the torches on the staircase railings. His clothes, black as midnight and tailored close to his frame, were laced with delicate gold stitching that shimmered faintly. The fabric moved with him, quiet but commanding, the kind of grace that made stillness feel intimidated. Though his laurel headpiece was pure gold, his eyes were not merely grey but the color of storm light, trimmed with silver like the edge of an owl's wing. They were ancient, unblinking, and fixed directly on her.

The woman stood one step down, and regal in the way a panther might be if she wore perfume and diamonds. Her gown was black lace, stitched with threads of molten gold that curved along her spine in the shape of a serpent, the train pooling to the bottom step. Her hair, white as frost, spilled over her shoulders, and her laurel headpiece beamed the color of molten silver.

Piper's heart stuttered, her body caught between awe and fear. There was something *wrong* about her, as if perfection itself had been forged out of suffering. Her autumn-colored eyes held striking beauty and menace, and every curve of her mouth suggested she'd already had an impression of Piper. It wasn't a good one.

Piper glanced at Colik, who stood lower in every sense of the word. His stance was too controlled, his clothes noble but not enough to disguise the strain, and no laurel headpiece of any color around his head. His eyes flickered with restrained irritation, especially when they landed on each one of them.

She wasn't sure if she had sensed it wrong back at the Kryvos Hollow, but now it was undeniable. Colik did not like this order of hierarchy among the so-called Royalds.

In this moment, Piper didn't know if she herself was

supposed to bow or run. All she knew to do was stand still and be ready for whatever was to come next.

"Welcome," the male said, his tone warm, but formal and practiced, like a king who had greeted thousands before. His gaze fixed solely on Piper.

Discreetly, Piper smoothed the front of her ugly, old sweater.

"What is your name?" Blaze asked. She knew his name because Colik had said it before. *Blaze.*

He looked to be in his late twenties, while Lulu was somewhere in between the ages of him and Colik. Blaze carried the weight of many ages behind his poise.

Talk about an old soul.

"Piper," Piper answered. The name came out uncertain and small. Her name felt unworthy to be spoken aloud in a place like this. In front of someone like *them.*

Blaze raised an eyebrow, studying her openly.

"Again—welcome, Piper." He spoke her name with an inflection that made it sound ceremonial and yet, knowing. "I am Blaze. Royald of the Reverie. King of the Dreamers' Belt."

He was handsome in the way Colik was a boyish *hot*, like the different between sunlight's heat and starlight's divine perfection. She wondered if they were even related. They shared little resemblance, yet something in the curve of their features, too precise for mortals, spoke of godly blood. Piper had thought Colik was beautiful, until she saw the other two Royalds.

Piper gave a small curtsy. "Nice to meet you."

Next to him, Colik barely moved. Barely *existed.* He didn't react to her voice or to Blaze's presence. He stood beside her like a statue, his jaw tight and his hands clasped loosely behind his back.

The woman laughed lightly, but there was no genuine warmth behind it.

"You're a pretty thing, aren't you?" the female said, her autumn eyes slicing into Piper with judgment.

The comment caught Piper off guard, and she stiffened. Colik did nothing.

"Hardly," Piper blurted out, her voice brittle.

Lulu raised a brow, not amused. "I beg your pardon?"

Heat rushed to Piper's cheeks. Colik had said her name was Lulu but said nothing about how intimidating she was. Or stunningly beautiful.

She glanced at Colik, waiting—*no, hoping*—for one of his usual disarming remarks, but still, he didn't speak. He was staring at the marble floor like *it* was offending him.

Coward.

It was Blaze who stepped down a step, giving Lulu's comment a dismissive wave.

"Human humor," he said wryly. "We may never understand it, but it seems that you two have had quite the adventure," he added, his tone shifting. "The Guild of Dreamers are in a frenzy about potentially having *the* Dreamer among us."

He descended another step, his eyes transfixed on her.

"Tell me, Piper. How is it you walk this world with such ease, when you are, by all definitions we know, *human?*"

Piper glanced for the third time at Colik for support. Though not offering any, Blaze raised another hand, stopping him from answering even if he had tried. So much for all the 'let me do the talking.'

He wasn't doing a damn thing!

Piper looked back at Blaze. "I don't know," she started, her voice uneven. "I've been dreaming of this world lately. Every time I feel lost…When I want to escape…I find myself here." She felt like a child saying it loud, but it was true.

"Lost in what world?" Blaze asked, his tone genuine.

"My waking one," she replied. "The real world."

Blaze narrowed his eyes. Not with suspicion, but *with curiosity*, like a riddle piece he didn't expect to come across.

"What exactly makes you feel lost?" he pressed.

Lulu raised an eyebrow; her voice velvet dipped in venom. "You mean *why*."

Blaze cut her off with a quick glare in her direction. "No. I mean exactly what I said. Go ahead, Piper."

Piper hesitated and looked again to Colik. Still nothing. His arms were crossed, his face set. He was deliberately looking at a high arch in the ceiling. Anywhere but at her. Like this had just been an assignment. Or strictly *business*.

Piper's stomach flipped. Suddenly, every touch, every word in the Broken Woods, every soft glance…the kiss. It all felt further away. Almost non-existent.

"I…I feel like something's changed in me," she said, her voice growing shaky as she met Blaze's gaze. She had never been in front of anyone important, let alone *royalty*. "Since these dreams started, I don't feel the same. My mind feels tired. Like it's being pulled too far in too many directions. Or I'm slipping." She gave a heavy sigh. "It is like my world is forgetting me. Or maybe… I'm forgetting it."

Silence.

Then Lulu spoke. "You think you belong *here*?"

Colik glanced Lulu's way. "She's here, and that is what matters." His tone was clinical. Sounding like a warning.

Piper tensed beside him. That was all he had to say? That she was *here*. Not that she mattered. Not that she deserved answers. Just that he had brought her here.

Blaze watched the exchange like a silent judge.

"Hm," he mused. "Then we'll see if the world agrees."

Piper said nothing. Neither did Colik.

In the silence between them, the space stretched thin, a fragile thread between what they had been and what they had become in such a short amount time. Or moments.

Then Blaze nodded empathetically. "May I share something with you?"

Piper nodded. Lulu rolled her eyes. Patryk stood still as

stone on the other side of Piper. He hadn't moved once since introducing the Royalds.

"We all lose ourselves—Dreamers, humans, even gods," Blaze said as he slowly descended to the final stair. "Sometimes, that loss isn't a tragedy. Sometimes it's design. A necessary unraveling that forces us to remember what was buried inside us all along."

Colik's voice sliced in, sharp and unexpected. "Why are you telling her this?"

"Because we all feel it, Colik," Blaze replied without looking at him. "Across different worlds. Even as different pieces of existence."

"Well, that's poetic," Lulu drawled. "But it still doesn't explain how she is still *here*." She looked at Piper with a harsh gaze. Was that jealousy behind the elegance she saw?

"So, what, you just *dream* your way here? Just close your eyes and *poof*—welcome to our world?"

"When I really want to be here," Piper admitted. "Yes. That tends to be when it happens."

"Interesting." Blaze stepped down to the ground level, and Patryk gave a reflexive bow while Colik straightened subtly beside her.

"You surpass REM each time," Blaze said slowly. It was a statement, not a question. "You're not dreaming like a human." His grey-eyed gaze moved from her right eye to her left. "Now, Piper—how are you doing that?"

Every word he spoke was measured and deliberate, holding the kind of control only a man carved from composure could possess.

"I…"

"She—" Lulu began.

"Shush, Lulu," Blaze snapped, his tone as final as thunder.

Lulu's jaw tensed, her gaze flicking to Colik. He, too, gave her nothing.

"There's this book," Piper said suddenly, her heart racing. "I think it might be connected."

Blaze's expression sharpened. Colik held in a breath. Even Patryk shifted slightly beside her.

"A script?" Blaze asked.

"No… Or I don't know. It's more like a journal that was blank when I opened it. It's called the *Book of Godspells*."

Colik's head turned toward her—finally—but the tension in his face only tightened.

"There's this boy in my world." The words came out like a flooding gate. "He is blind. His name is Steele, and he knew about the Dreamworld. He knew about the book."

Blaze leaned forward, calculating. "You're saying…a book in your world can bring humans to ours?"

"I am not sure," she said truthfully. "A librarian has it. Said it was safe. Said no one could use it, yet Steele acts like it can bring him back here."

"This *Steele* doesn't have the book, does he?"

"No."

"It's never come here with you?"

"Once, on the Ollopa train."

Blaze's face darkened. Colik's fists clenched at his sides. No one spoke.

Piper stood beneath the silver inlays of the Citadel gleaming like silent verdicts. Her breath came in shallow bursts. She hadn't meant to say so much. Or had she? Did she say something wrong?

Blaze turned slowly from Piper to Colik.

"You thought silence was better than speaking up about *that*?" he said, his voice suddenly cold. "I already must learn about what happened in the Reverie from the Harold and now a *human*?"

The Harold?

Colik stayed silent but there was shame in every line of his face. Blaze looked back at Piper.

"Do you believe you are *the* Dreamer?" he asked.

Piper flinched. "What?"

"Some believe you're Morpheus' promise. You cross worlds unscathed. You've spoken to a Fatale. You've seen a book from the gods. So, I'll ask again. Do *you* believe it?"

Colik shifted beside her. Lulu stilled.

Piper swallowed. "No. I don't even know what that means. I'm not a promise. I'm just...lost." The words hit her like a gut punch. The truth was undeniable. She was still lost, only in a different world.

A long silence followed, then Blaze turned away from her completely.

"She's not bound by our laws," he stated. "She crosses between worlds meant to remain sealed from each other. That book, that boy... It's not the foretelling. It's a fracture."

He looked again at Colik. "She's a liability."

Piper's chest tightened like a fist closing inside her ribs.

"Until we understand her connection to it all..." Blaze said, turning to Patryk. "We must first contain it."

"Contain?" Piper whispered.

"Boygle," Blaze called out into the room without hesitation.

From the shadows, another creature emerged, draped in silvered armor, its helms crowned with vast antlers that sparked with threads of light like stars caught in branches. Its face was hidden, masked in burnished metal. Each step it took was metal striking marble.

The Boygle did not speak. It did not need to. Its arrival was judgment; it's silence was a verdict already written. It stepped behind Piper, while Colik instinctively stepped back, both movements small but telling. That was when she realized.

"No—wait!" Piper cried out. "I didn't do anything wrong! *You* brought me here—"

"*Colik* brought you," Blaze said coolly. "As usual, he let his feelings outpace his judgment. Or duty."

"I made a call," Colik snapped, but his voice cracked. "Maybe it was the wrong one…but she's not a threat. Look at her!"

Piper winced.

"She doesn't *have* to be one," Lulu said somewhat softly. "Sometimes, just being what you are is dangerous enough."

The Boygle's hand, not of flesh but plated silver, closed over Piper's shoulder and pulled her back.

"Where are you taking me?" Piper shouted, twisting under its grip. She winced at the hard metal digging into her collar bone.

Blaze didn't turn when he answered. "The Willows will silence your dreaming. For some moments… that is mercy for a human."

"No!" she cried, thrashing. "You can't do this!"

"I'm sorry," Colik said beside her. It was the first sympathetic thing he had said since the Dray incident.

She glared at him, furious and betrayed. "Monster," she spat.

The Boygle's grip tightened, the metal like an ice burn on her skin, causing her limbs to buckle. Breath fled her chest as her strength drained in a terrifying rush, leaving her trembling beneath the faceless helm.

"Piper—" Colik started toward her.

Blaze glared, and Colik stopped cold.

Still, her eyes pleaded with Colik for something—*anything*—but his silence sealed her fate as the Boygle lifted her, and Piper's body sagged beneath its weakening hold.

She was given nothing.

CHAPTER TWENTY
THE WILLOWS

When Piper's eyes opened again, she found herself lying on a surface so soft it could've been made from clouds. The walls, floor, and ceiling were all mirrors, reflecting endless versions of her. There was no corner to hide in, no shadow to escape to. Just her. Multiplied and trapped.

At first, panic clawed at her chest. The emotion inside her stirred, crawling up her throat as she sat up from the cloud-like bed in some mirrored cell. Then she looked. *Really* looked into her own green eyes, and she didn't recognize the girl staring back. When had she last looked in a mirror?

Her eyes were sharper, edged instead of innocent. Her smile—or what she could force into the shape of one—was crooked, like it had learned not to trust its own joy. Her face was still flushed from fear, cheeks warmed by the searing frost-bite the Boygle's armored touch had burned into her, a cold fire she could still feel beneath the skin.

What struck her most was everything else. She was still bony, the kind of thing that came from years of being an orphan who ate last and slept lightly. Yet her skin—always pale like any Dublin girl—had shifted into something sharper, not quite ivory, but an undertone too luminous to be natural. Not Irish pale. Unworldly pale. Dream-pale.

Her hair…

She brushed her fingers through it, startled by the way it caught the light. It wasn't just blonde anymore. It was a strange mix of icy white at the roots and sun-bleached along the ends, like winter and summer had fought over her, and both refused to let go.

It made her look like someone who belonged to neither world. Someone who was becoming something else.

"You have a pretty smile." A voice cut the silence between her and her reflection.

Piper startled, twisting toward the entrance.

It was Patryk.

He stood in the doorway with a plate of food in his hands, eyes wide and restless. Filled with a random assortment of cheeses, olives and meats, the looks of it alone made Piper's stomach growl.

There it was again. *Pretty.*

"What is this place?" she asked, ignoring the compliment. Orphans weren't trained to receive flattery. Especially not her.

"The Willows," he said quietly, then, after a moment, "are you hungry?" She knew the name of this place—Blaze had said it—so his answer was no help to learning more about it.

Piper gave a dry chuckle. "So, you're not planning to starve me. That's comforting."

She watched him blink, clearly unsure how to take that.

"Is that a yes?" he asked.

"Yes," she admitted, her stomach growling again in betrayal. She didn't know how long she'd been down here— even moments felt slippery in the Reverie—but her body hadn't lost track. Did she pass out when the Boygle took her? If so, why hadn't she woken up in her world?

Patryk's gaze dropped to her right wrist. That's when she

noticed a gold-plated brace encircling her skin. It was so light she hadn't even felt it.

He placed the plate of food gently on the mirrored table beside her bed, but she didn't reach for it. Eating in front of someone who looked like he hadn't eaten himself felt wrong.

"What is this?" she asked instead, her eyes flicking from the untouched food to the shimmer of gold on her wrist. It matched the ones she noticed the Royalds wore, even Colik. It hadn't mattered until now. Patryk had one as well.

"That," Patryk began softly, eyeing her wrist, "isn't jewelry. It's a safeguard. A brace to shield what lurks in the deeper layers of the Dreamworld." His eyes were looked guilty. "With this, you can walk the Reverie without being pulled back to your waking world. It anchors you here."

The words fell like a stone in her chest. No one had *asked* *her* if she wanted to stay.

"If I want to go back?" she asked, trying to keep her voice calm though she felt anything but.

"Then we remove it," he said quietly. "If…or when."

Her fingers drifted toward the cuff, tempted to rip it off. Something in Patryk's face stopped her. She refrained and looked around, trying to process it all.

"Does this also protect me from the nightmares?" she asked, thinking of the boy Shade, and the Silver Girl showing her memory in the Room of Lockes.

Patryk gave a small nod. "It dulls their pull. They're drawn to uncertainty, Piper. To minds split in two and your dreams…" He trailed off, eyes flicking to the mirrored wall as if someone, or something, might be listening.

She wanted to be furious. To scream. When she looked at him, she saw no power behind his words. Just a pawn playing along. Just like her.

No, her anger didn't belong to Patryk. It belonged to the one who had made this choice for her. She knew exactly who *that* was.

"Do you work for the Royalds?" Piper pivoted the subject, softening her tone. Patryk had said *we*, like he could remove the brace if he wanted. She needed to know where he stood, and if he could be an ally. Even if he *were* one of them.

"Yes," he said, his voice shifting into something more formal. "Harold to the Royalds. Retainer to the gods." So, *he* was the Harold that Blaze spoke of.

"Retainer?" she repeated. It sounded ominous.

He gave a small smile. "Not what it sounds like. I'm not a servant. I'm the messenger. The keeper of each world's boundary. Like Hermes, but between worlds…and with better style, *of course.*"

"Of course," Piper repeated, giving a weak laugh. She needed that.

"I walk between Olympus and the Reverie. I retain messages, translate laws, keep watch…and ensure nothing crosses between those worlds that shouldn't."

The way Blaze said he had learned about their adventures from the Harold…

"You knew I was here, didn't you? That is why Colik went to the Broken Woods?" Piper's brow furrowed. She understood what he meant when he said *worlds*: Not the human world, but the space between dreams and gods. He was a gate-keeper of sorts, not for mortals, but for the gods. He knew things about *all* worlds.

Patryk looked around again as if being watched before giving a subtle nod. Strangely, it comforted her. In his own careful way, he was telling her he hadn't reported her to the gods. At least not yet.

Her eyes widened. "Then you *also* knew about the *Book of Godspells?*"

He hesitated. "I know *of it*, yes," he admitted. "I know it cannot be read by just *any human*, and not without some obvious consequence."

"Is the book that bad?" She didn't get it, and given the look she was giving Patryk, he clearly knew that too.

His voice grew hushed as he spoke. "I've heard whispers. Of others like *you*, whose dust bishoped. They didn't belong to either world. Someone always noticed. Someone always wanted them silenced."

"Bishoped?"

What the hell was that?

Patryk looked at her in shock. "*Bishoping* is what is happening to your body. It is when your body folds into itself like a star turning to dust and reforms into something else when it meets a space it is not used to. The Reverie does not run like Earth. I'd thought you'd understand that by now…"

Piper shook her head. *Bishoping*. She wondered if Himyla knew that term. She turned to Patryk. "What happened to those who tried to bishop?"

"They all ended badly," he answered. "Twisted. Forgotten. I was told never to speak of them. Warned by those who… watch everything." His voice was low.

Was everyone afraid to speak of the gods?

She leaned in. "Then why are you telling me this?"

Patryk looked straight at her. "Because it seems that someone has already tried to reach you, Piper and Blaze are terrified they might succeed."

Before she could answer, a new voice sliced through the room. "Patryk."

The mirrored door had opened again, and Lulu was standing in the doorway. Piper grunted.

"You and your noises," Lulu said, her voice melodic. "Humans truly have become a strange species, grunting like animals when silence would simply do."

She stepped in, and Piper stiffened. Lulu owned the air itself. Her presence drew all the light. All the attention. Even the walls went tense. Patryk shrank beside her, visibly uneasy.

"Patryk, leave us," Lulu ordered, not sparing him a glance.

Patryk gave Piper one last glance, his eyes carrying a quiet warning. She met it with a small nod, and a comforting after thought flickered in her mind: maybe she could trust him. Maybe, just maybe, she could have a real ally here.

Then, without a sound, he slipped through the mirrored frame like a coil of violet smoke.

Piper's stomach rumbled, but she left the plate untouched.

"Came just to mock me?" she asked, facing Lulu.

"I came to understand you," Lulu said smoothly. "Your defiance is amusing."

"If you want understanding, ask questions instead of barking orders." The words that came out even shocked Piper. She had never spoken up like that before, but she was proud of herself for doing so.

Lulu circled the room like a lioness. "Very well, then. Tell me... Who is this boy? The one who helped you back. This *Steele*." Lulu seemed too interested. "Who is he? What does he look like? What does he want with you?"

"He's just—"

Lulu cut in. "Is he human?"

Why did she care so much?

"I don't really know... He implied he was from the Silver Age."

Lulu froze. It wasn't just surprise on her features. It was *terror*.

"Lies," Lulu whispered.

"I am not."

"Impossible," Lulu hissed. "The Silver Age is *sealed*. That age is *gone*. No Dreamer survived its fall—not whole anyway. Or caged."

Piper blinked. "Like the Silver Girl?"

Lulu's eyes widened further and stepped back as if Piper had uttered a forbidden spell. "How—" she started, but Piper's face apparently told Lulu all she needed to know. Patryk had known and told the Royalds.

"So, it is true. You two really did have an adventure," Lulu said quietly. "She is not just some *Silver Girl*. She's a Silver Child. Do you know what that means?"

Piper didn't respond, but Lulu didn't wait for her to.

"They were born in-between. Humans given the freedom of gods. They tore the original fabric of this world—the Silver Age. Do you understand? They weren't Dreamers. They were weapons. Unpredictable. Untied. They thought they could walk through Olympus and the Reverie like they belonged to both, but they belonged to neither. *Humans* will never belong in the god's world, even if gifted immortality."

A long silence fell between them.

"Hazel wasn't locked away because she was broken," Lulu said, back to her usual sharp tone. "She was locked away because she couldn't be controlled. Because she nearly undid something that would have ruined..." She trailed off when she noticed the sudden shift in Piper's expression.

"What *is* that look?" Lulu sounded appalled, and yet, still looked flawless. Piper, on the other hand, looked confused.

Hazel.

There it was again. Familiar. *Too* familiar.

Her pulse hammered. How could a Silver Child share the name of her old stuffed bear? Maybe it was nothing. Maybe it was another coincidence. Another dream bleeding through. The name clung to her like dust in her lungs, refusing to let go.

Piper shook her head, trying to scatter it. She wasn't ready to explain that. Not to the Royalds, and not to herself. Because if the name had followed her here, then maybe it hadn't belonged to the bear at all.

"Then why give me this?" she changed the subject, lifting her wrist and motioning to the brace. Her voice was steady, but it felt like a bluff.

Lulu studied it for a long moment. When she finally spoke, there was a spark of excitement in her voice. "Because Blaze is afraid," she said, watching Piper closely. "We all are, of what you are, or what you might be opening the door to."

Though she tried her best to keep a poker face, Piper suddenly understood. It wasn't the Willows that were containing her. It was the brace. Not just to anchor her, but to restrain her from leaving this world.

"I'm just a human," Piper said quietly, her voice barely carrying. Saying it aloud didn't help make sense of anything. It only made her feel smaller. Out of place. As if saying it could convince the others, or maybe herself, that she didn't belong in any of this. That this was yet another disappointing world to live in.

Lulu turned to one of the mirrored walls, but didn't meet her reflection, like she couldn't bear to see herself.

"A human," Lulu said softly, "and dreams. They pass. They forget. But you…" Her eyes narrowed. "You're not doing any of those things. And then to know of a Silver Child?"

Piper's brows drew in. "What do you want from me?"

"To know if you are one of us," Lulu replied, her eyes burning into hers. "Or the cause of this growing chaos."

Piper's pulse skipped. "Growing chaos?"

Lulu didn't answer her but stared through Piper with a look that wasn't just of fear. It was sorrow, fury, and memory all braided into one long winded expression.

Then, like a small flame blown out, Lulu blinked, and the mask slipped back into place. Cool. Composed. Untouchable.

"Eat," she said coldly, looking at Lulu's plate of food. "You'll need strength."

"For what?"

"To dine with us," Lulu said. "The Royalds. Perhaps we will share some petaled wine. A tradition reserved for the rarest of guests."

"Why?" Piper asked, suspicious.

"If everything you say is true," Lulu whispered slowly, her

voice cooler than stone, "then everything the Dreamers have built, everything the gods have buried, has begun to unravel again." She turned toward the door, then added wistfully, "I'd very much like to savor a glass of petaled wine while the Reverie still has sweetness left…a drink that someone your feeble size will not do so well with on an empty stomach."

She stepped into the doorway, one hand lingering on the frame. Then she paused, tilting her head just slightly, an amused glimmer returning to her eyes.

"Oh, and I will have a change of clothes brought down here for you," Lulu said. "You are no longer just a human girl trying to find herself, Piper. You are something the Dreamers are starting to notice."

She motioned vaguely toward Piper's dress and the brace.

"That is not how you dress when you are noticed around here."

She began to turn, then added with a single raised brow, "Honestly, if Colik has kept you around this long, you must be more than human. He barely tolerates his own kind, much less a mortal." She laughed lightly. "He's many things, but he is not sentimental. So, whatever you are, it is certainly not ordinary."

With that final sting of a compliment disguised as an insult, Lulu was gone.

Piper wasn't sure how long she'd been confined to that cell, but after Lulu left, silence returned like a weight. Her mind throbbed with everything she'd just learned, but hunger won out. She devoured the food without thinking, barely tasting it, then collapsed on the cloud-soft bed. Her eyes squeezed shut. At least the mattress cradled her, and her stomach no longer tried to eat itself. It wasn't freedom, but it was something close to peace. For now.

With the brace, she could sleep in with peace, right?

Still, the oppressive presence of mirrors surrounded her as a relentless reminder of her humanly existence in a world that clearly did not welcome humans. What kind of twisted torture was this? Why, then, did her dreams bring her here if she were a threat to it?

"I brought you a change of clothes. They are Lulu's, but you look about the same size," a voice said gently above her. Eyes still closed, she hadn't heard anyone enter the cell. She popped up instinctively.

Blaze stood there, a vibrant silver-white dress draped over his arm. She stared at him, startled, not only by his presence but by the strange softness in his demeanor. He held the dress out for her to take with a genuine smile.

Piper took the dress slowly. She hated how fragile she felt under his eyes, like an older brother judging her.

"Are you sad?" Blaze asked softly.

She looked at him, taken aback. "No."

"You're not very good at hiding it. I can see you in the mirrors. Every angle," he accused, and her eyes fell to the dress now draped over her arm. It was stunning. More beautiful than anything she had ever touched before.

"You think I don't know that?" she retorted, heat rising to her cheeks.

"Are you scared to face them?" he asked.

"Sometimes." She knew what he meant—her reflection in the mirrors.

"Why?"

"I mean, don't we all? What if I no longer like what I see…or worse… What if I look and don't recognize myself?" she admitted, the truth slipping out before she could catch it.

She expected judgment, maybe indifference. Blaze just listened.

"You put me in this cell," she went on. "You surrounded me with nothing but my image. You and Colik took me as a prisoner."

"You're right," he said at once, not dodging it. She blinked in surprise.

"The ability to only see yourself—your inability to hide from yourself—is perhaps what you need, Piper," he continued, his tone kind. "A chance to confront who you truly are. Besides, don't all humans enjoy gazing at their own reflection?" He smiled, making a joke. She didn't return the gesture.

"I don't feel like other humans."

"How so?"

"I don't view the world in black and white. I see it in greys…in infinite what ifs. I don't just think *what is*…I think of what could be."

Something changed in Blaze's expression. A softness, maybe even slight admiration.

"A true Dreamer if you ask me." He gave a heavy sigh. "You won't be in the Willows much longer. We've prepared safeguards. The Citadel was never meant to host a human. This Steele—the boy you mentioned— and the Silver Child in the Room of Lockes." Another heavy sigh, "Piper, I need you to know that none of that is normal. You understand that?"

She shook her head. So, he knew about all of that too. Blaze sighed for a third time, folding his arms.

"No," he said, more to himself than to her. "You wouldn't. No one has explained this world to you properly." She said nothing. He studied her a moment, then added, "You are different. I believe that now, but know that being *different* does come with unique challenges."

Piper met his gaze, still uncertain what to say.

"I know what you think of Colik," Blaze said, his tone even. "He's a brother to me, so I understand his ways better than most." His mouth pulled into a sly smile, though Piper didn't return it. "He smooth-talked you into coming here, and perhaps without a realistic cause. Patryk sensed something stirring, and Colik acted before he consulted me. He thought it was right."

Blaze exhaled, the smile fading as his eyes dropped to the folds of her own outfit. "I need you to know, the Royalds don't find joy in containing humans. That isn't why we were chosen. That isn't our designed roles."

His gaze lingered, steady and unflinching. "All we're trying to do is hold back the chaos. We keep it from breaking through faster than it already has."

A tense silence lingered. It was the quietest Piper had been since coming to this world.

"If I'm to trust you, Piper," Blaze said quietly, lifting his eyes to hers, "then I will be truthful in telling you that something is stirring chaos here. If it is not you, then help me understand. Why are you here? Not just how—but *why you*. What do you want from all this? What do you stand to gain?"

Piper hesitated for a breath.

"I want to *stay*," she said, the words surprising even her with how true they felt. "Because when I'm here…I don't feel like I'm broken. I don't feel like I'm wrong or lost or forgotten. I feel like maybe—maybe this world has been dreaming *me*, too."

She looked at him fully, no hesitation in her voice. It wasn't because of all the impossible things she had done here, but from the gut feeling that grew heavier the longer she stayed.

"I don't know why I can dream into the Reverie. I don't know why it feels like it's reaching for me as much as I'm reaching for it. I do know this: in my world, no one's waiting for me. I'm just another girl no one claimed. But here?" She swallowed. "Here, even the impossible pays attention to me. Here, I feel like I *matter*. Even if I don't know how or why yet. Even if it is not in the best way, at least I am in being noticed."

His eyes, with those stormy, shifting greys, watched her in

silence. She could tell he wasn't just hearing her but *feeling* every word.

"I'm not trying to gain power or glory or anything else you're afraid of," she affirmed. "I just want to belong somewhere. For the first time in my life… I think I may have found it. Isn't that all anyone wants? To belong?" The latter question was rhetorical, but Blaze's eyebrow rose.

A longer silence fell between them.

"I believe you," Blaze said at last. "I don't know why the Dreamworld is calling to you, but from what you've told me, I believe it is too."

Her throat tightened. She hadn't expected him to say that. To *understand* her. The anger she thought she was supposed to feel—for him locking her in this room, for that Boygle—began to dissolve. Maybe none of it had gone the right way, but in this moment, she had to go with what felt true.

Blaze shifted slightly and took a small step back sheepishly, like he wasn't sure how much space she wanted. Or needed.

"We've prepared an assortment," Blaze shared, though there was an awkward edge stranding through it. "I believe you could use a glass of petaled wine. After all this."

Piper blinked. Surprised, again.

His smile came slowly, subtle but real. "A peace offering, maybe. I don't want you to feel like a prisoner."

She opened her mouth to correct him, but he beat her to it.

"Yes, I know. I *made* you one," he stated, sighing as he ran a hand through his hair. So that was where Colik must have gotten it. "When I said '*contained*,' I meant that I was trying to keep you safe, but that's not how it felt. I know that now."

He shook his head once, like he was annoyed with himself, then looked at her more firmly. "You'll have new arrangements momentarily. Better ones. I promise."

He gave her a small bow of the head, solemn and sincere, like sealing a vow between equals.

She should've still been furious. Part of her wanted to be and yet, something about the way he spoke—open, unguarded, like an older brother trying to fix what he'd messed up—softened her.

He believed her. He was undoing what he'd done.

Piper nodded, choosing to believe him. "Thank you."

Blaze held her gaze another moment, then turned to leave, but not before glancing once at her reflection in the mirror, a flicker of something crossing his face.

"That gold-plated brace is what I meant by *being contained*. It will keep you in this world, for the moment, but it will *also* keep others from tying to you," He acknowledged, as if he couldn't leave without telling her the truth. Without proving to her that he meant what he said.

Then Blaze left, the soft echo of his footsteps fading, and the door to her cell left open.

Piper didn't move. Not to flee. Not to chase him. Not even to step through the door that had, just moments ago, felt like a cage. Instead, she turned back to a mirror. She stared at her reflection, her fingers brushing the cool glass, testing whether the girl staring back was still her. When she smiled, it wasn't armor. It wasn't defiance.

It was soft, honest, and real.

CHAPTER TWENTY-ONE
THE VANIS ROOM

"Come with me," Colik's voice cut through the silence, slicing straight through Piper's daze.

She flinched. Of course, it was him. Why did it have to be him? Just when she finally had a moment to breathe. To think. To calm down.

She had just slipped into the silver-grey dress Blaze left her. It clung softly to her shape, still folded at the chest as she tried, and failed, to reach the zipper behind her.

He appeared at the entrance of her cell, shirtless and silent. His eyes raked over her like he hadn't meant to look at all but couldn't stop himself.

Even though it took everything in her not to look him up and down, she still stiffened as the rage bubbled back up. Rage she had tried to drown when he let that Boygle drag her down here. Rage from the way he stayed silent while the other two Royalds questioned her, while he watched like she was something to be assessed instead of someone he should have defended.

With it, the memory of the Broken Woods surfaced again. The sharp scent of smoke, the pulse of heat between them, and the way the world had gone utterly silent right before he almost kissed her again after she revished.

Standing this close, the air carried a similar charge. It was restless and unfinished. His gaze dropped to her mouth for half a heartbeat before snapping back up, his jaw tightening like he was holding something back.

Her pulse betrayed her, quick and uneven. For one dizzy instant, she thought he might close the distance again. He didn't move from the doorway. She didn't move either.

"They couldn't have sent anyone else?" she finally broke, shaking her head at the confusing thoughts fighting against her rapidly beating heart.

He said nothing but took a slow step inside. Then another. His expression was unreadable, except for the subtle tension in his jaw when she turned to face him.

"Don't look at me like that," she bit out, cheeks flushing. "You don't get to look at me like that."

Still, he didn't stop.

"You changed," he said, voice low, like he didn't mean to speak but couldn't hold it in. "The dress—"

"I can't get the back," she snapped. "Not that it's your business. Just zip me up." He raised an eyebrow at her. "Please."

Colik hesitated, like he was fighting the urge to say something that might crack both wide open. Then he stepped closer to her. When he reached her, he didn't speak. He just moved behind her, like when he'd helped her leave the Ollopa train. His presence at her back was heat, breath, and remembrance.

"Hold still."

She wanted to whirl on him. *Don't tell me what to do.* But she didn't, because she needed the stupid zipper.

His fingers brushed the base of her spine. It was rough, warm, and maddeningly gentle. The zipper climbed slowly, each inch dragging fabric tighter against her back. Every moment felt more intimate than it had any right to. They both held their breath.

At the top, he paused. "You look—" he tried again.

"Please don't," she cut in. She stepped away before she could second guess herself, fists clenched at her sides. "Say whatever it is you came to say," she forced out. "Then leave. I don't need your help dressing just so I can be angry in a prettier outfit."

He sighed. "I came to get you out of the Willows."

Her jaw clenched.

Great. So now he was *rescuing* her.

"I didn't mean to hurt Dray," she said suddenly. "In the Room of Lockes. I didn't know what I was doing."

Colik went rigid. "Stop."

"I just thought—"

"You did break something, but it doesn't matter now."

A lie.

She heard it. Felt it.

"Doesn't it?" she whispered.

He paced—one step, another—as if strangled by words he couldn't let out. "You keep doing that," he muttered.

"Doing what?"

"Making me question everything." His laugh was soft and broken at the edges. "Royalds, knights…we're supposed to have it together. We're taught not to flinch or waver. Then you show up and I can't—" He cut himself off, jaw clenching. "You unravel me."

Her heart slammed painfully.

"I don't mean to."

"Don't say things like that," his voice cracked. "Don't make this harder."

"Why? Because you might feel something for me?"

"Because I'm trying not to." The blow landed clean and deep. "You're not supposed to be here," he went on, softer.

"Not in the Reverie and not…" He tapped a finger to his temple. "In here."

"Then stop looking at me like you want to forget everything else but me," she breathed.

"I am trying," he growled. "*Fuck*, Piper, I am trying."

He stepped back a fraction, but enough to make her anger spike.

"You're so hot and cold," she snapped. "What do you want from me?"

"Nothing."

Another lie.

The air between them stretched thin, like the swar during *Kryvo i Kross*.

"Let's go," he said. "Before I do something I regret."

She opened her mouth and then saw them. Deep, long and violet scars ripped from bone along his back.

"Where are you taking me?" she whispered.

"See? This is what I mean."

"What?"

"You don't trust me," he said, voice rough, cracking like something old and brittle. "You still don't believe this world is real enough for the truth."

"That's not fair—"

"No," he cut in sharply, shaking his head. His eyes glinted with something sharper than anger. Hurt. "What's not fair is that every time I give you something honest, you look at me like I'm tricking you. Like I'm pulling shadows over your eyes."

She opened her mouth, but nothing came out. His words hit too close. Too clean.

"That," he said, devastatingly soft, "is why this will never work. Why it is not supposed to work. Not…whatever you think is happening here."

Her breath fractured. She hadn't even realized she'd

hoped he'd say *us* until he shattered the possibility with that single word. *Not.*

"You think duty is noble," Colik said finally. "It's not. It's a curse that ends with a human dying." He swallowed, jaw tight. "You're afraid I'll betray you, but I betrayed myself long before you."

Something twisted violently inside her. A slow, terrible understanding clawed its way up her throat. He hadn't come here to save her. He had come to place her somewhere safe. Somewhere contained. Out of sight of the wrong Dreamers. Out of reach of questions, she wasn't supposed to ask. Out of danger not for her sake, but for the political balance she didn't even understand she could disrupt.

She wasn't a person in his eyes. She was a risk. A piece he needed kept on the right square of a chessboard she couldn't even see.

Her voice cracked as she whispered, "You used me."

"What?"

"You brought me here to keep the Royalds from panicking. To hide me. To shut me up."

His face tightened, proving her right in the one way that mattered.

"I trusted you," she hissed.

"I didn't ask you to."

The wound went bone deep. "Oh, go to hell."

"You shared everything with them," he snapped. "You didn't trust me either."

"You weren't saying anything!"

"You didn't give me a chance!"

They stood inches apart, furious and breaking. Then, without warning, he reached out, gently brushing a loose strand of her hair behind her ear. The touch was so soft it made her freeze completely.

"When I become someone you shouldn't trust," he murmured, "you will know."

She swallowed hard. The touch made her feel sick, his words cutting her heart strings.

"Again," he said, voice flat. "Let's go, before this gets worse."

"Fine," she muttered. "Just don't expect me to obey you like some lost little girl."

"You said you were always lost," he shot back. "That's not my fault."

"Gods, you're such a—"

"Monster?" he said dryly over his shoulder. "You already tried that insult."

As they walked, the tension didn't ease. In fact, it coiled tighter, every step feeling like a dare for Piper not to explode.

The marble beneath her feet gleamed too clean, too sharp, throwing her echo back at her like mockery. He never looked back, striding forward, certain she would follow. When a hallway flickered with shadow at their side, the question slipped out before she could stop it.

"What's that way?"

"Just more mirrored cells," he muttered.

Liar.

They reached a hallway carved with horn-shaped arches, each one etched with constellations brought into form. Piper slowed, breath catching, because she knew these stories. She had spent hours in the Dublin Library and Archive tracing the inked star-paths of ancient myths, learning which gods had been hurled into the sky for their triumphs or punishments, and which mortals had been carved into the heavens for their courage, their grief, or the tragedies they could not outrun.

She knew about Hercules bending beneath his labors, Orion hunting what he could never catch, Callisto fleeing as a bear before being lifted into the stars, and Perseus and Andromeda frozen in a rescue that rewrote the sky. She had memorized them all, never imagining she would one day walk beneath their carved, dreaming silhouettes.

"I know these," she said quietly, more to herself than to him, though her voice carried a strange blend of wonder and certainty.

Colik glanced at her, clearly not expecting the words. "You do?"

She moved to the first door, lifting her gaze to the silver figure carved there. "Orion, the hunter," she murmured, studying the tension in the drawn bow, the constellation lines etched with a glow that felt warm. "He always stands ready. Never lowers his aim. It reminds me of Blaze."

Colik's expression shifted at the accuracy of it, something flickering in his eyes that looked strangely like respect.

Piper drifted toward the next door, unable to stop herself from reaching out to brush her fingertips along the glowing point carved into its center. "Polaris," she breathed. "The North Star. The only star that never moves, no matter how the sky turns. The one everything else circles." Her gaze softened, thinking of Lulu's cool stillness and the way she drew the room's attention without ever demanding it. "Fitting."

She felt Colik's attention sharpen on her, his interest suddenly more focused, as though he was trying to see her through a different lens.

"And this one," he said slowly, guiding her toward the third door, "do you know what it is too?"

Piper didn't even need to lean in. The shape was unmistakable. "Sirius," she whispered. "The Dog Star. The brightest light in the entire sky."

The carved hound looked poised, caught between loyalty and danger, its body shaped with a sharpness that hinted at devotion and violence in a single breath.

Piper stared at it longer than she meant to, feeling the air tighten when she realized what it symbolized.

Colik.

He stood just beside her, silent and waiting, as though her response mattered more than he wanted her to know.

"So," he asked with quiet curiosity, "what do you think about this one?"

Pipers didn't know how to say what she really meant. *This one* was a puppy dog following the orders of the hunter.

"I can guess," she answered softly, eyes still on Sirius.

"And?" he pressed, leaning closer.

She swallowed hard. "It doesn't matter," she said finally, choosing the safest lie she had.

For a moment he looked startled, as if he had braced for a blow she refused to give. Something in his posture softened, but it softened the way something fragile does, like it might shatter if she touched it.

Before he could speak again, she stepped past him toward the final door.

This one bore no constellation. No hunter, no guide, no loyal hound. Only a hollow circle scorched into the wood, an outline where a star should have been, empty and incomplete.

Piper stared at it as a faint shiver ghosted down her spine. "Where is the constellation on this door?" she asked.

Colik's gaze remained on the unmarked circle. "There isn't one."

"Why not?"

His jaw tightened, as though the truth tasted heavier than he wanted it to. "Because its star has not chosen a shape yet." He opened the door. "Go ahead."

"Why don't you go in first?"

He stayed exactly where he was, rooted to the spot as if engaged in some silent, stubborn stand-off that he refused to break first. It was comical, the way he held his ground, chin lifted just enough to pretend the moment wasn't ridiculous.

Puppy dog.

With a breath that trembled between irritation and amusement, Piper let out a slow, frustrated exhale, then gathered her skirts and stepped past him into the room. All the frustration simmered at the new sight.

Starlight spilled like silver water across stone that floated above an endless ocean of clouds. Four marble columns, carved with silver lace at their crowns, framed a canopy draped in gauze-thin veils that calmly swayed. At the center rested a bed layered in pale sheets that shimmered faintly with candles circling the pillars, their flames trembling against the soft currents of air whispering through the arches.

Behind her, Colik's breath hitched, so quiet she almost missed it. When she glanced back over her shoulder, he was still standing in the exact same place, but something in his expression had changed. His posture had stiffened a little, as if her stepping away first had knocked him off balance.

His gaze followed her with an intensity she pretended not to feel, lingering on the tiny almost-smile she hadn't meant to let slip. He looked at her as if he could sense she was hiding a thought from him.

He took one single step forward, then stopped, as though afraid that following too quickly would reveal too much. For a heartbeat, Piper could have sworn he looked… disappointed, but only for a heartbeat.

"Right," he muttered under his breath, as if arguing with himself, "fine."

His eyes stayed on her for a moment longer than they should have, softening despite his best attempt to harden them.

Piper tore her eyes back to the room, uncertain if she was inside a room at all or standing at the edge of the constellation cloud. Beyond the columns, a row of mountains rose in the distance, their translucent peaks piercing through the blanket of clouds. This was not the plain cot at Olympus House, nor the narrow space she had always been confined to. This was half sanctuary, half illusion. A place that shouldn't exist yet wrapped itself around her like it had been calling for her all along. In the corner, a harp played itself, its notes hollow and soft as lullabies.

"This is…" she breathed, lost for words.

"…a dream," Colik finished. "This Vanis room is for you."

Her throat tightened, and she blinked at him, heart unsteady. "You weren't keeping me prisoner?" She knew what Blaze had said, but she needed to hear it from him.

"The Willows was always temporary," he said. "We just needed a moment to control ourselves, too."

"You mean you all needed time to decide what to do with me."

He didn't argue. "Believe what you want," he said.

She stepped forward, the clouded floor glowing under her bare feet. "What do you want to do with me?"

Something in him stilled, like she'd struck the one nerve he wasn't prepared to guard.

"Piper…" For a heartbeat—two—he softened. His shoulders dropped. His gaze flicked to her mouth, then her eyes. He even took a half-step toward her, hand lifting as if he meant to brush a strand of hair behind her ear again.

Then he broke. He blinked, shutters slamming down behind his eyes, sealing whatever had almost escaped. "You don't need that answer," he said, suddenly cold. "Not in this moment."

The words felt like a slap. Worse than everything Blaze had said. Worse than Olympus House whispers. Because this wound was personal. Shaped exactly like her.

Silence settled between them, not empty but full, crowded with everything they weren't saying.

I'll meet you at the refectory," Colik said at last, his tone suddenly smooth again. "I think you'll enjoy petaled wine. Might take the edge off, *Pipes*."

Her heart flinched at that nickname again.

"The *what*?" she managed, her voice embarrassingly small.

Hot. Cold. Hot again.

He switched temperatures like it was some kind of sport.

"A place for communal dining," he replied, and to her irritation, he laughed. The sound curled around her, warm and taunting, like he knew exactly what it did to her. "Relax. You'll live."

There it was again, that crooked half-smile, the infuriating charm that made him look both boyish and dangerous at once. An angelic face wrapped around something sharper. Something she should have run from.

She wanted to roll her eyes. She wanted to punch him. She wanted him to look at her again. Morry had warned her about boys like this, boys who ran hot until you melted and cold until you shattered. He just never warned her she'd find one who wasn't even *human*. A beautiful monster disguised in starlight. A wolf wrapped in the shape of a dream.

Her heartbeat betrayed her.

Colik said nothing else. He didn't even look back. He just walked out, letting her glare hit the back of his coat like it meant nothing, like it hadn't cost her something just to hold his gaze.

The door closed too quickly.

She spun after him— "Colik, wait! I don't know where the refectory is—"

Her fingers brushed the door just as voices drifted from the other side. His voice was low and strained.

"She asked again," Colik said, his footsteps stopping not far from the door. Someone had been coming their way.

She heard Blaze's voice as he answered, but Piper couldn't hear him. The room swallowed his voice.

Colik's came through, too clear: "She can't know what she is to the Dreamers." There was a pause. Then a breath. "She can't know what she is to me."

Piper went still. Blaze's voice drifted into silence, his footsteps already retreating, but that final sentence didn't follow him. It clung to her like breath on her neck.

She can't know what she is to me.

Not what. *She.*

She wished she didn't hear it. She wished it didn't matter.

It did.

Piper stepped back from the door, stomach twisting sharply. She didn't know if it was the dress, the room, or the way his voice had broken, but she knew one thing: What lingered between them wasn't over. Not even close.

Not after the Dray incident. Not after what just happened between them, and not after what she just heard.

It was a storm trapped in a bottle, waiting for the right moment to shatter. When it did, she knew it would hurt in all the places she had never been taught to protect.

CHAPTER TWENTY-TWO
THE PETALED WINE

Piper walked beside Patryk, the soft swish of her gown echoing through the quiet hallway as they made their way to dine with the Royalds.

She stood draped in silver-white, the gown skimming her frame perfectly. The asymmetrical neckline swept across one shoulder and fell in clean, unbroken lines, catching every stray shimmer of light. With each step, the fabric moved in a slow, liquid ripple. It was the way she would have always hoped to feel in a dress growing up reading about beautiful princesses and their gowns in castles. Like she belonged to something greater than herself. Not as a prisoner. Not as an orphan, but as someone chosen. As someone *becoming*.

Patryk's grip on her arm was steady but gentle, like he was guiding her out of some unspoken concern, maybe, or quiet respect. His hold loosened as they neared the grand ivory doors, veined in ancient bone.

Patryk, too, had dressed for the occasion. A lilac robe, light as vapor, draped over one shoulder catching the torchlight with a silken sheen. Beneath it, a golden chastity harness wrapped around his waist, climbing his torso until it cinched into a corset-like frame across his chest. It looked childlike in design, maybe even a bit absurd, yet it gleamed with a brilliance so rich, it could have been forged by King Midas himself.

For some reason, she was super nervous. "Patryk...You said you are a Harold to the Royalds?"

He looked at her, surprised by the question, then gave a small smile. "Yes."

"What does that *make* you? Are you a demigod?" She wasn't sure if she were truly asking or just trying to distract herself.

"We are above demigods."

"Above?"

Patryk nodded solemnly. "The gods rule from above, but Dreamers are their instruments. Fallen angels. We are above the demigods. Above mortals. They are the bridge between dreams and mortal law."

She looked at him, confused.

"The Royalds *preserve*." He looked her up and down, then back into her eyes. "You, Piper, in that dress, look like you belong among the Royalds."

She didn't know what to say to that.

The doors opened, and the vast refectory stole her breath. Marble pillars stretched skyward, their veins threaded with silver that shimmered in the glow of floating lanterns. A long, crystalline table ran the length of the chamber, its surface gleaming with silver goblets filled to the brim. At the far end, Blaze sat in quiet command, cradling a glass of deep red as though it were fire made liquid.

"Go on," Patryk murmured with a nudge. "He's waiting for you."

Piper stepped forward hesitantly, trying not to trip on the hem of her dress. She caught Blaze's gaze which softened the moment he saw her.

He stood.

"You look..." his words faltered, looking momentarily

unsure. Then he found his voice. "You look radiant. Sit, please."

Patryk guided her swiftly to the seat catty corner to Blaze. As she slid into place, careful not to crush the drape of her dress, she felt Blaze's gaze still on her, steady and unreadable, long before he lowered himself into his own chair.

Patryk reached for her goblet and filled it with a clear, sparkling liquid. Then he added a single soft pink petal to the surface. It floated for a breath before unfurling, blooming open in slow motion. Color bled outward like a secret spreading through water, tinting the drink a delicate, luminous rose.

"I hope you enjoy petaled wine," Blaze offered, his voice smooth. "It's from Dionysus himself. A gift to the Reverie. A little intoxicating, and a little divine," he said with a slight wink.

Piper lifted the silver goblet and took a cautious sip. The flavor was floral, rich, and dizzying. Almost instantly, a faint tingle swept through her, starting in her fingertips, and climbing the back of her neck. Her muscles tightened with an odd feeling she wasn't sure how to explain. It made her chest ache to speak or confess. To say something real. The urge was small, fragile even, but it pulsed beneath her ribs, her body already knowing the truth she hadn't decided to tell.

She swallowed hard, unsure if the heat rising in her chest came from the wine…or from him.

"A toast," Blaze said, lifting his glass with smooth cere-mony. "To new arrivals, and new beginnings. I would wait for the others, but their affections seem a bit…inconsistent." His mouth twitched. "Especially a certain someone who alternates between glaring at you and hovering like you're a new star in the constellation cloud."

Her stomach flipped. *Colik.* Of course he meant Colik.

Blaze tapped his glass lightly to hers. "Dreamers can be terribly dramatic."

The crystal sang with a soft chime.

His voice shifted when he leaned closer, the warmth in his tone turning deliberate. "I've spoken with other guilds," Blaze murmured. "It seems that you are more important than you think…" He paused, letting the meaning settle. "You are not simply an unusual visitor. You are a shift."

Her pulse stuttered.

"A shift?" she whispered.

Blaze's gaze held hers steadily. "Some here do not yet understand that your presence changes the balance, but I do. I intend to keep you safe from those who might forget your value."

Value.

The word rang through her like a struck bell. The ghostly creatures in the Elphiates had said the same word. A warning, spoken twice now in two different corners of the Dreamworld. Was this the same warning again? Or was it something worse—

The doors to the refectory opened again, pulling her thoughts to a halt.

Colik and Lulu stepped inside, the room seeming to shift around them, and Blaze lifted his glass in greeting.

Piper took another sip of her petaled wine, trying to look unbothered.

It didn't work.

The moment her gaze landed on Colik, her heartbeat surged and heat rushed up her neck. Her face burned, bright and obvious, like her body had betrayed her before her mind even caught up. She hated how instantaneous it was. How automatic. How helpless.

She couldn't stop it if she tried. She did want to try.

Stupid heart. Stupid girl.

"Glad you two could join us. There's much to discuss," Blaze announced, calmly.

"Well, it looks like you can at least *look the part* after all,"

Lulu sneered, eyeing Piper up and down, then flipping her hair, turning her attention to Patryk. A silent cue between them, he rose quickly, pulling out her chair for her directly across from Piper. She sat down with a prideful grin, and Patryk scurried off.

She wore a stunning seafoam-green gown cinched with gold lace riding past her collarbone and around her neck like a regal choker, its shades nearly mirroring Blaze's tunic. There was a peacock stitched on the front and down to the train, its feathers laced with golden eyes looking in all directions. The dress was intentional, demanding attention.

Colik slipped into the seat beside Piper, his arm brushing hers again, like he expected her to lean into him the way she had before.

This time she forced herself still, cold as ice. Her body could betray her on the inside all it wanted, but that didn't mean she couldn't command the outside. Control was a choice, and she clung to it with both hands best she could.

Colik's head turned, his brows tightening.

Piper didn't look at him. Didn't acknowledge him. Didn't even glance. She kept her eyes forward, on Blaze, on the gleaming table, on anything that wasn't Colik.

Lulu noticed first.

She gave Piper a slow, appraising smile, but it quickly faltered when Piper didn't return it. Lulu's eyes cut to Colik, a spark of irritation turning sharp.

"Oh," Lulu murmured, voice carrying in the refectory. "It continues."

Colik shot her a warning look. "Lulu—"

She raised her hands as if warding off a bug. "What? I'm just observing. Some of us have patterns, Colik."

Piper said nothing. She took another sip of her petaled wine. The petal at the bottom glowed faintly, blooming again as if feeding off her pulse. Her nerves were settling with each sip. Was that why they kept telling her she would like petaled wine?

Lulu leaned an elbow on the table; her chin perched on her knuckles as if this were all mildly entertaining. "Honestly, I thought we'd moved past the whole boy-girl crush melodrama." Her gaze drifted pointedly to Colik, then slid back to Piper with slow precision. "If you two are about to spiral into…whatever this is again, should we excuse ourselves? Or do you perform better with an audience?"

Piper's red cheeks went white.

Colik glared. "Lulu, I swear—"

Blaze's eyes sharpened, flicking between them with a strange interest.

"You don't have to worry," Piper said quietly, though the words rang like iron. "There's nothing between us to spiral *anymore*."

That was bold.

Patryk moved around the table at that moment, placing silverware beside each of them with ceremonial care. He refilled their goblets one by one, the clear pour catching the light from the multicolored rose-bush arrangements clustered at the table's center.

His eyes kept flicking up. Quiet. Watchful. Uneasy.

Patryk's hand paused mid-pour, the wine trembling at the lip of the bottle as he caught the tension sparking between them. He said nothing, but the silence around his movements spoke for him.

Colik's breath hitched, and she heard it. "Jealous?" He barked. "How about we talk about your obsession with h—"

"Enough," Blaze said, though his tone carried amusement. Catty corner to him, Lulu gave a deep sigh, as if relieved.

"Fine by me," Piper broke, the words coming out unexpected. She pressed her palms against the folds of the gown, trying to ground herself, but the truth of what she felt kept breaking through anyway. It was quiet, trembling, and becoming impossible to contain.

Silence settled like dust. Patryk scurried away.

Then Lulu laughed, bright and disbelieving. "Well, well. She *can* bite."

Colik swallowed, staring at Piper like she'd become an entirely new creature.

"So, what *all* is there to discuss?" Lulu's voice danced with false delight. She sipped from her glass, her eyes flicking past Piper, save for one lingering look, up and down, which ended in thin-lipped distaste. Piper was starting to know that look well.

"We must talk about the Constellation Ball," Blaze stated, the lightness in his face giving way to something more formal.

Colik's brow arched. Lulu tensed but said nothing.

Before anyone could object, Patryk returned, arms full of lavish platters: jeweled fruits, shimmering meats, wheels of strange cheeses, and delicate greens. The spread was fit for twenty, not five.

Piper's stomach gave a quiet growl at the sight. The food looked too beautiful to touch, like a still-life painting of a banquet come to life. She blinked. Was this even real?

"Please, eat," Blaze said, gesturing gently toward the spread. None of the Royalds moved. Not toward the food, anyway.

In this perfect world, was hunger ornamental?

Piper hesitated for a moment before hunger won her over. She reached for a slice of translucent meat and a ribbon of marbled cheese, pairing it with warm bread dipped in golden-green oil. The taste was earthy, decadent and heavenly. She hadn't realized how much she missed the human act of eating a meal with people around. She took another bite, and another—

A hand settled gently on hers.

"There will be plenty more," Colik said softly, his eyes not quite judging, but close. Piper stiffened. Her cheeks flushed, the weight of old habits from Olympus House creeping up her spine. She nodded sheepishly, retreating into herself.

They were all watching her. Blaze's gaze was curious, Lulu's expression curled in disfavor, and even Patryk looked faintly surprised.

Lulu finally plucked an olive from the platter and popped it into her mouth, turning sharply to Blaze. "Do you really think having the Constellation Ball is wise, given the circumstances?" she asked, her tone laced with venom. Piper knew exactly what she meant. "To show off a *human* and risk the Citadel, with all the Dreamers gathering? Risky, don't you think?" She drew out the word *human* like a curse word.

Blaze sipped his petaled wine and nodded toward Colik. "I think this is the moment when you come clean about what *you* deem worthy to no longer hide. You know Patryk will just find out. What risk comes from having the Constellation Ball with a human among us?" Blaze asked with an accusatory tone.

There was a long silence where Colik gulped down the rest of his petaled wine. Patryk quickly poured him another.

Piper was scared to take another sip. The first few gulps were still working through her, stirring fast beneath her skin. The burn lingered at the back of her throat, seeping into her chest, her stomach and fingertips. It wasn't just warmth, but pressure, like something inside her was being loosened. Her hand trembled with the dizzying urge to spill it all: her true feelings, the secrets she'd buried, the things she'd never dare to say.

Especially the ones about Colik. *Oh*, and Lulu.

"We encountered a few complications," Colik admitted, his voice tight. "A Polaris in the Broken Woods. The Scirges have grown bolder. And the Shades..." He paused, then glanced toward Piper, looking defeated. "The Shades are stirring. They asked for *her* dreams."

He carefully nodded toward Piper.

Blaze straightened at once, fire simmering behind his smoky eyes. "You let her be around them?" he snapped. "Did she give them any?" He spoke to Colik like Piper wasn't sitting right there. He looked furious.

Colik's jaw clenched. "It wasn't like that."

Blaze abruptly stood up, the chair screeching back. That took a turn.

"You *know* the Reverie Laws, Colik! R-Law Two states that dust must not be traded between the waking and dreams, but giving? Giving might be worse. We don't even know how that affects them! How it will affect *her*."

A knot formed in Piper's throat.

"I didn't tell her to," Colik growled. "She did it herself. To save a boy Shade."

"Again—you *let* her?" Blaze's voice echoed through the refectory, sharp enough to make even Patryk flinch. "You let a human risk becoming a conduit for a Shade? Do you have any idea what that could mean?"

"Colik said not to," Piper chimed in, surprised that she was defending him. "The boy was losing dreams. I had to do something to help him. It was my choice."

"While merely breaking a law," Blaze said coldly.

The tension thickened. Then Colik, perhaps realizing the walls were closing in, turned on Lulu. "What about the Polaris?" he said, voice too calm. "You must have sent it into Broken Woods. Why? You didn't say a word."

Lulu froze, her petaled wine halfway to her lips.

Blaze's attention jerked toward her, eyes narrowing. "Is that true?"

Lulu didn't answer at first. Her fingers tightened around the goblet. "I was going to tell you."

"When?" Blaze snapped. "After it raises questions to humans wandering the Reverie to *every* guild?"

"I was *handling* it."

"Like you handled the last *situation*?" he barked.

"Don't turn this on me," Lulu hissed.

"You're all so concerned with your own secrets and wrongful acts that you've forgotten what we're supposed to be," Blaze said, his fury spilling across the room like a wildfire.

Patryk, now seated, reached slowly for the rose bouquet in the center of the table. He plucked a single blush-pink petal and dropped it into Lulu's goblet. A gentle pour of crystal water followed, and the petal dissolved, blossoming into sparkling rose-colored wine.

Blaze looked between them—Colik seething and Lulu stung—then raised his chin.

"Enough. We need to remind every guild what we stand for before this entire Dreamworld tears itself apart from the inside."

He shook his head, a cold resolve setting into his voice. "You've left me no choice *but* to hold the Constellation Ball. We need the Dreamers to gather, the Fatales to watch, and the gods to continue to keep their distance. The Reverie must see us in balance, even if it's just for show."

Piper watched with nervous fascination, taking another sip of the petaled wine. As the petaled wine pulsed in her veins, she realized she had never felt so out of place. The dizziness it carried was courage in disguise.

The invisible weight of her presence twisted the air. She wasn't just being ignored. She was being measured. Still, she found herself smiling absurdly from that strange, floral bravery unfurling in her chest. For once, she didn't mind their scrutiny. Not fully. Because if they were measuring her, that meant she mattered. At least a little.

"What are you smiling at?" Lulu snapped. Her eyes cut across the table like daggers.

Piper startled. She hadn't realized she was still smiling.

"I'm talking about *you*, if that wasn't clear," Lulu spat.

Piper's smile fell. In place of an answer, she took yet another, bold gulp of the petaled wine. It burned down her throat, reminding her of the graveyard when Morry urged her to take another sip of the wine he had. In this moment, the warmth didn't stop at boldness. Beneath the sweetness, anger bloomed—hot and cold all at once—coiling through her veins like it had been waiting for permission. The petaled wine no longer comforted but clarified, stripping away fear until all that was left was a strange, reckless defiance.

She knew, deep down, that wasn't a good thing. Not for someone like her. For an orphan, feeling too much had never been safe. It meant you'd draw attention. It meant you'd be noticed, and being noticed had never ended well.

Lulu's attitude distracted both Colik and Blaze. Colik relaxed in his seat and Blaze finally sat back down.

"Lulu," Colik said smoothly, "I think Piper's quite aware you've been talking about her. You haven't exactly been discreet."

He smirked, then glanced at Piper with a sly, guilty smile. She nearly choked on her own spit. Colik defending her in front of the Royalds? That was new. Dangerous, maybe, but new.

Blaze leaned forward. "Piper, do you think we should hold the Constellation Ball?"

The room stilled.

"You're asking *me*?" she questioned, her voice sharp but low.

"Of course. If we go forward with it, your presence will be its center. The entire Reverie will see you. Are you ready for that?"

Colik shook his head aggressively. "You want her to *join us*? To expose her among the Royalds? I thought she would stay in her room, not be the star of the Royalds show!"

"Has she not already been exposed?" Blaze shot back. "Your little *adventure* was hardly subtle."

His eyes shifted to Piper. "What do *you* want?"

Her lips parted, but no sound came. For a moment, she wanted to cry. Whatever this petaled wine was doing to her, it was doing *a lot* of it.

Blaze's voice dropped to a whisper. "Do you want to stay in your Vanis room or stand by our side at the Constellation Ball?"

She met his eyes.

"Yes."

A beat of silence.

"You want to stay *in this world*?"

Not even a question. "Yes."

Blaze smiled, and with all the calm authority of a king sealing fate, proclaimed, "It is settled. The Constellation Ball will commence."

No one argued, but the tension was thick enough to taste in the petaled wine.

Piper, balanced uneasily between suspicion, desire, and whatever strange fate had taken notice of her, knew she was no longer a guest. She was—like Blaze had said—a shift in the Dreamworld itself.

She took another mouthful of food, hoping it would quiet the rising heat inside her, but it didn't. The feeling kept growing, becoming more restless and uncontainable.

Colik's hands moved with infuriating calm. One hand slowly grabbed her wrist, while the other slid her goblet out of reach without a word.

Of course he had to be nice now. Of course, Colik chose the one kind gesture that made her want to scream. He had maddening conflicting composures—close when she needed distance, distant when she wanted to get close.

Her pulse spiked. She could feel every heartbeat echoing in her throat, hot and loud. For one ridiculous moment, she thought about hiding some of the food in her napkin for later. With every eye at the table trained on her, she forced her hand still under Coliks touch. She couldn't afford to look that desperate. Not here. Not in front of them.

"Are you done yet?" Lulu probed her, her eyebrow raised. She glanced down at her plate, feeling her own body tense in ways she was not proud of.

"I was raised always to finish my whole plate," Piper replied cooly. Maybe she had too much petaled wine. That was one lesson she had taken to heart at Olympus House. A rule so simple it had once felt like survival. As the words left her mouth, something else surged up behind them. An explosion rose in her chest, a pressure rising too fast for her to contain. Pride, anger, or grief, she couldn't tell which. Only that it terrified her to think what might come out next if Lulu kept pushing her.

What had this petaled wine done to her?

Lulu's expression was unreadable. Blaze's lips curved into a faint smirk. Piper's pulse was thrumming too loud, her breath becoming too shallow. Her own voice might betray her before she could stop it.

"You're eating like you've never had a real meal in your life." Lulu's voice dripped with disdain. It was as if she was trying to push Piper's buttons. It was working.

"Lulu," Colik snapped, his tone sharp and protective.

"What? You know it's true. Where did you find this *human*, Colik? A girl on the streets with no parents?" Lulu went on, undeterred.

Piper's stomach dropped like a stone. Her face went pale, the weight of it all hitting harder than the petaled wine. For a moment, she thought she might be sick, until the nausea sharpened into the one thing she had been holding down since the first sip.

Anger.

For some reason, Lulu had it out for her from the first look, and Piper was done pretending she didn't care. Whatever game Lulu was playing, Piper wasn't going to keep losing by staying quiet.

"You're right. I don't have parents," Piper spoke up without thinking, her face heating with anger and embarrassment, her body trembling with emotion. She pushed the plate away and stood up suddenly. Turning to Colik, she demanded, "What did you say to them about me?" Her eyes filled with tears.

"I haven't said one thing about you to her… You barely told me anything about you, so how would—"

She cut him off with an aggressive wave, frustration boiling over. "Quit lying to me!"

Lulu laughed under her breath, her fork clinking softly against her plate. "Oh, spare us the pity party. If you can't handle a little honesty, maybe you want to rethink your choice of staying here."

"No," Piper bit, her voice shaky but firm. "What you call honesty, I call cruelty. You sit here surrounded by your *kind*, your power, and your privilege, and you act like it's your role to cut down anyone who doesn't fit your making."

Lulu's smile tightened. "Careful, human."

"Piper, maybe you had too much—" Patryk said, his face tightening, his eyes moving to her goblet now in front of Colik. He looked embarrassed, blaming himself.

"You're just a mean girl hiding behind your god-like lineage," Piper fired back.

Colik leaned back in his chair, amused. "This just became interesting."

Blaze sat in complete silence.

Piper feature's hardened as she looked at Lulu. "You're right. I've never had a meal like this. I'm from an orphanage, a place for those with no parents. You have a family here who won't abandon you, but I won't sit here and let you mock me, my upbringing, and most of all, my eating habits."

"Please excuse me," she said tightly, glancing over at Blaze. "Thank you for the meal." The words came out steady, but her pulse thundered beneath them as she turned and stormed out. She dared someone to stop her.

F that.

CHAPTER TWENTY-THREE
THE CREATURE'S LOYALTY

Piper surrendered to sleepers' rest at last, her body giving in where her will refused to. The gold brace did its work, pinning her to stillness, and anchoring her somewhere she could not name. She did not wake in Dublin or in Olympus House.

It was not like dreaming. It was not even like forgetting. It was a canvas scrubbed clean, a place without shape or sound or memory. No visions rose. No nightmares clawed. No whispers of gods or dust threaded through her. For a while—she couldn't tell how long—she was simply gone, erased from herself.

Then, as suddenly as a breath drawn in, she was back.

When her eyes opened again, time had betrayed her. It made no sense here, no ticking or measure, only the strange pull of one moment sliding into the next, just as Colik had warned her. In that quiet shift, the exhaustion in her bones had vanished. She felt refreshed and whole again, though she couldn't remember ever feeling anything else. That was the strangest part of all.

Was this what it felt like for a human not to dream?

Steam curled from the bath, catching in the candlelight and drifting upward toward the vaulted arches. Piper eased into the water, the marble edge cool beneath her palms, grounding her in a place that was anything but ordinary.

The water glowed faintly, lit from within, its surface glistening. Beyond the open arches, stars from the constellation cloud reflected in the ripples that spread around her shoulders as she sank deeper into the warmth.

She tilted her head back against the marble. Droplets slid down her throat and collarbone, tracing silver paths along her skin. For a long, uncounted moment, she just breathed. The warmth wrapped around her like a second body, weightless and forgiving, so unlike the thin blankets and rattling radiators of Olympus House. Every knot of worry loosened, as though the water were drawing burdens straight out of her bones and into its glowing depths.

For once, there was no train, no Royalds, and no boys who looked like fallen stars and talked like they knew her better than she did herself.

Just…quiet.

At last, Piper shifted and rose to climb out, water sliding from her skin in streams. She reached blindly for her towel, expecting soft cloth against her fingers.

Her hand closed on empty air.

She frowned, patting along the marble. Nothing.

A small prickle ran down her spine. She turned too quickly, causing her foot to slide on the slick stone. The floor rushed up to meet her, and she landed with a soft, breath-kicking thud.

Heat shot up her neck out of embarrassment, and she

curled her knees toward her chest, instinctively folding in on herself.

Her gaze swept the room, the air turning thick and white. She searched for any sign that someone might be there, when something flickered above her.

Piper squinted, finding her towel drift lazily near the ceiling, bobbing like some smug, weightless ghost.

"What the...?"

She scrambled upright, wincing as marble bit at her knees, and jumped, snatching at the towel. On the second try, her fingers closed around the edge. The second she touched it, the cloth dropped heavily into her hands, as if whatever invisible thread had been holding it decided she'd passed some ridiculous test.

Clutching the towel tight around herself, Piper turned toward the source of the mischief.

A tiny creature hovered in front of her. It was no larger than the span of her two hands pressed together, its body cloaked in midnight-colored fur. Delicate dragon-like wings beat in a soft, rapid blur behind it, and a single curved horn jutted from its forehead.

Sapphire eyes studied her.

"Oh," she breathed, half in awe, half laughing under her breath. "You are so cute!"

She extended a cautious hand toward it, and the creature hissed softly, but it wasn't quite a threat. It tapped her finger with a clawed paw, sharp but careful, then darted backward, hovering just out of reach again. Its tail curled in an elegant S, as though it was drawing some invisible sign between them.

"I see you've met a catdrag," came a voice from the doorway.

She spun, tightening the grip on the towel around her.

Blaze lounged against the frame, one shoulder pressed to the carved stone, his gaze politely angled at the floor instead of her. The corner of his mouth tweaked as if he found the entire situation mildly entertaining and was trying not to show it.

"Didn't anyone ever teach you to knock?" she muttered.

"I did," he said lightly. "The door didn't answer."

The catdrag hissed again, wings flaring. It shifted in front of her, placing its tiny body between Piper and Blaze as if it understood the word door and took personal offense on her behalf. A faint ring of blue flickered in its throat, then vanished when it decided Blaze wasn't an immediate threat.

Blaze lifted both hands. "Not here to burn anyone, little one."

"Catdrag?" Piper repeated, eyes never leaving the creature. "That's an actual name of a creature?"

"In the Reverie, yes," Blaze said. "In the waking world, it would be simply a fun mythical creature."

She smiled.

The catdrag tilted its head as if listening. Its gaze moved from Blaze back to Piper, lingering a beat too long at the inside of her wrist. A warmth pulsed there, small but sure.

Piper rubbed at the spot without thinking. "Why is it staring at me like that?"

"It isn't," Blaze said, but his voice had turned softer, cautious. "It's...remembering."

Her chest tightened. "Remembering what?"

"Hard to say," he replied, which meant he knew more than he was going to admit. "Catdrags don't care much for Royalds or Harolds or R-Laws. They're older than all that. They remember strands, not titles."

Strands.

The catdrag drifted closer, ignoring Blaze entirely. It sniffed at her wrist, then at the faint mark near her palm, its breath warm and tinged with something like smoke and cold metal. When its nose brushed her skin, a ghost of pressure tugged inside her chest.

She sucked in a breath.

The creature's eyes widened, pupils slitting further. It gave the smallest, satisfied purr, then circled once around her shoulders, leaving a trail of warmth in its wake, before perching on the marble edge behind her like it had always belonged there.

"I didn't do anything," Piper said quietly.

"Exactly," Blaze murmured. He sounded unsettled by that. "I will let you get dressed. I'll wait outside the door. Try not to let *it* burn the place down."

He stepped away, the door shutting with a soft click.

Piper stayed still for a moment, heartbeat loud in her ears. The catdrag blinked slowly, then turned its head toward the stars beyond the archway, as if checking some invisible clock written in the constellations.

"Do you live here?" she asked it, feeling ridiculous that she was talking to a cat-like creature. At least it couldn't talk back or argue.

It flicked its tail, then hopped down to the floor with surprising grace, padding toward where her clothes lay neatly folded. One paw landed deliberately on the hem of the dress, pinning it like it was staking a claim. When she moved closer, it lifted its paw, allowing her to pick the fabric up, as though granting permission.

"That's…not creepy at all," she muttered, but something in her chest unknotted. For the first time since stepping foot in this world, the presence at her side wasn't a god or a dreamer or a law. It was just a creature who decided to hang out with her.

Piper gave it a genuine smile.

Once she was changed, she opened the door for Blaze. He stepped into the room, his tone shifting from before. "Piper, I came here to say something else."

She raised a brow. "Not just to introduce me to flying pets?"

He ignored the jab. "I want to apologize," Blaze said.

Piper stared at him, surprised. Of all the Royalds, she thought him the least likely to have to apologize.

"I want to apologize for the Royalds' behavior," he repeated, his tone sincere.

Piper flushed, not at his words, but at how his eyes lingered on her, steady and unguarded, even as he tried to make amends.

"*You* didn't do anything wrong." She wanted to add *this time* but refrained.

"I am the First Royald," Blaze said quietly. "Their actions are mine to answer for. They were out of control—especially Lulu—and I'm sorry you had to bear it." His gaze didn't waver, even as she shifted beneath it.

He hesitated, searching her face. "The petaled wine," he said after a pause, "it heightens emotion. I thought it might help you feel calmer, not angrier." His voice softened. "For someone who's had to hold everything in for so long, that must have felt *different*. Overwhelming, maybe."

Piper blinked, caught off guard. There was no pity in his tone, only an understanding that made her feel uneasy. Embarrassed.

"You've carried pain for a long time, haven't you? I didn't mean to stir it. I meant to give you a moment of peace."

She wanted to say no—to deny it and remind him that she didn't need his sympathy—but the words wouldn't form. Her chest ached with something rawer than anger, something dangerously close to relief.

"It's fine," she managed. "I'm used to it."

Blaze's expression said he didn't believe her. And if she were honest, Piper wasn't sure she believed herself either.

"Well, thank you," she murmured shyly. Colik would never admit he was sorry. His ego would never allow it. Yet here was Blaze, doing it for him. Lulu...she couldn't even fathom an apology coming from her mouth.

He nodded and began pacing around her room like he

had never seen it before. A pause settled between them like a weight. Piper's mind churned with questions and doubts, and then a flicker of understanding. Blaze wasn't just a guardian or any Royald. *No*, he was someone caught in a web of rules and secrets far larger than her or him.

"I sense there's something you're not telling me... *about me*," she asked cautiously, her words flowing before her mind thought through them thoroughly. To her surprise, Blaze snickered lightly.

"The real question, Piper, is, what are you not telling me?" His words struck her like a jolt. She wondered what he could mean. "I know about Hazel too." Of course he did. Lulu had already mentioned her.

"Hazel and Steele trying to tie to me... Is that why you put me in the Willows?" Piper asked.

Blaze took a few steps back, heading to the door before he answered. "If I am to be honest with you, yes. That is why I made sure you had the brace even against your will. More to keep *them* from getting you, not keeping you from leaving here."

"Why care if I stay?"

He didn't answer. Instead, she watched as he made his way back to the door and put his hand on the silver knob.

They stood in silence for a beat, broken by the distant flutter of wings as the catdrag reappeared and settled lazily on the edge of her vanity.

Blaze nodded toward it. "She won't leave you alone, it seems. How intriguing."

Piper looked at the catdrag, who was peering behind a silver beam, her eyes on Piper, wide and excited.

"Why—?" She let out slowly.

Blaze didn't answer her question.

"I want you to explore the Citadel. All of it. Don't just stay locked away in this room. It seems you've been confined to too many cages already."

Piper looked at him, startled. "You're giving me permission?"

"I'm *insisting*," Blaze said firmly. "You're not a prisoner here. If you just happen to stumble across the *Greycene*..." He paused and winked at her as he opened the door and took one step out. "If it is meant to be, you may even run into the creature that keeps me grounded here as well." His voice turned distant and personal all at once.

"Creature? Like the catdrag?"

Blaze didn't elaborate but gave a final glance to the catdrag, who was now curled like a sleeping shadow on the vanity. "Keep your eyes open," he shared. "Not everything here wants you hurt. Some of it might even want you *healed*."

Then he left, quietly this time.

Piper stared at the closed door, letting his words settle in her chest like something fragile and warm. For once, she felt heard. Seen. Not dismissed or managed or pushed aside. Blaze's voice still lingered in her mind. She wanted to believe him, even if every instinct told her she shouldn't trust so easily again. Like she had with Colik

It was irrational. Maybe even foolish, but something deeply human whispered that she should listen. She hoped, desperately, that at least one of the Royals didn't hate her. That maybe, finally, someone here wasn't waiting for her to fail.

That small, flickering hope was enough to make the Dreamworld feel exciting again.

That, and the little catdrag swooping around her ankles, its tiny wings fluttering in delighted circles as if celebrating her mood before she even understood it herself.

After another meal where Lulu barely spared her a civil word, and Colik kept looking at her like she'd stepped into the room wearing a different face, Blaze's gentle questions about her life back in the waking world felt like the only steady ground she had. So, when conversation lulled and no one took notice of her, Piper took a breath, rose, and slipped away to find the place Blaze had called the Greycene. Wherever that was.

He had said one thing about it: *"If it's meant to be, you may even run into the creature that keeps me grounded here as well."* She didn't know what to make of that, but the catdrag had been shadowing her since the moment it found her, as if it knew something she didn't. Its quiet companionship grounded her almost as much as Blaze's words.

Piper slipped into the corridor like a ghost escaping a story she wasn't sure she belonged in. The door to the refectory eased shut behind her, muffling the hush of voices, the clink of silver, Lulu's soft disdain, and the weight of Colik's eyes, as though he kept discovering her for the first time and wasn't entirely sure he liked the feeling.

The light changed as she walked. The torches flickered in shades of grey blue instead of silver. The marble floor beneath her bare feet grew cooler and almost wet while the walls stretched higher, narrowing into soft arches carved with patterns she couldn't name.

She followed that dim path by instinct, half guided by the faint pull in her chest, half by the memory of Blaze's voice saying the word *Greycene* like it was somewhere important, somewhere meant for her.

The deeper she went, the quieter the Citadel became. No footsteps. No doors. Only her breath and the faint whisper of something—*wind? voices?* —sliding along the edges of the wings.

The catdrag padded beside her in loose, confident arcs, wings fluttering now and then as if sensing a shift she couldn't see. It didn't seem worried. That alone helped.

"Do you know where we're going?" she whispered.

The creature whined once, smug and certain, then darted ahead a few steps, tail curling toward an archway at the very end of the hall.

Piper's pulse quickened.

That arch was different. Lighter. Older. The carvings around it glowed faintly, each symbol rippling like water disturbed by unseen fingers.

She swallowed.

"Okay," she breathed. "Why not."

She stepped through.

The room opened before her like a secret remembered. She stepped through a gentle arch of twisted branches, and everything fell still. Greenery everywhere. The walls were covered with vines, wings, and constellations caught mid-motion in the slanted light. A breeze drifted in, carrying the scent of rain-soaked earth, sunlit petals, and something richer she couldn't name. The air also changed, suddenly feeling quieter. More awake.

Piper stopped. She didn't *know* how she had found it, but she knew *this* was the Greycene. The walls breathed with various shades of living green and gentle grey washing over carved stone, veined with vines that climbed and coiled in lazy loops. Some floated midair, their roots glowing softly like nerve endings. Others dangled from above, dripping with blossoms she didn't recognize.

She wandered farther in, drawn without thinking. A tree stood at the center of the garden, its trunk pale as bone-white ash. It was a tree from the Broken Woods.

Piper reached out and brushed her fingers across the bark. It pulsed faintly under her touch, as though greeting her. Or recognizing her.

The catdrag perched on a nearby column, watching her with bright, expectant eyes.

She turned in a slow circle, taking in the entirety of the

Greycene. Everything shined, not with magic, but with presence. The leaves didn't simply hang but listened. The light didn't merely fall. It chose exactly where to land.

"Human, I feel your dust," a small voice chimed from above.

Piper looked up, spotting delicate, golden-winged creatures fluttering between the branches. Their wings shimmered like morning light caught on snow, moving lightly as thought rather than motion. One hovered closer than the others.

"Who are you?" she whispered.

Silently, Piper extended her hand, the gesture instinctive, unsure if she deserved even this much attention. The tiny creature circled once, then landed gently on her wrist. Her gold-dusted wings folded as she settled her weight.

"I am a Dawn. My name is Ellery. I've felt you much, Piper."

"You know my—" Piper began, then stopped. Somehow, *everyone* knew she was here.

"What is your purpose here in the Greycene?" Ellery asked, her voice like a soft melody smoothing out the air.

"To understand if or how I belong in this Dreamworld," Piper whispered, the weight of the words sinking like a stone into her chest.

The catdrag pressed against her calf, as though anchoring her, as though it knew this was the question beneath every question.

Ellery tilted her head and closed her eyes. Gold shimmer floated between them.

"That should be quite easy to understand, given your position with the Royals," she murmured.

"I don't understand what you mean."

"You have a tie...hope...trust...and..." Ellery paused, her delicate face drawing tight. "Something I cannot yet define. That is unusual, but I will not speak in guesses. False senses are dangerous things."

"Oh." Piper's heart sank. That wasn't the clarity she'd hoped for. That wasn't clarity at all. The catdrag chirped in soft sympathy.

"You should know," she continued gently, "all creatures here are bound to something greater. Not controlled but anchored. Blaze is bound to us, the Dawns. We keep him aligned with light and truth. When his fire burns too hot, we soften the edges, so he remembers who he was. Who he is."

Ellery fluttered a wing, and every vine and canopy in the Greycene shivered in response, as though the entire garden breathed with her.

"Polaris is tied to Lulu. A guiding creature. Cold and steady. It gives her clarity in the illusion and the laws. Helps her hold this Dreamworld together even when everything else pulls toward chaos."

"And Colik?" Piper asked cautiously.

Ellery's wings trembled. "Colik is tied to the creature of nature. The atmospheric beast—Dray—belongs to him. Or rather, belonged to him. Dray grounds him in movement, in change. His beast is older than the Glass Mountains and wilder than most Dreamers dare to become."

Piper swallowed hard. "Then why did Dray save me?"

Ellery studied her for a long moment before answering. "Because you're not just a human, Piper. You are something uniquely written. Unanchored and dangerous, yes...but your purpose is large."

The catdrag flew around Piper, its wings brushing her cheek in a reassuring flutter.

Ellery's gaze flicked to it.

"This creature," she added softly, "shouldn't have made itself known to you. Catdrags choose no one. Not even a Dreamer. Not since the Silver Age. Yet it follows you like you are a truth it remembers. That alone should tell you how deeply this world feels you."

A chill rolled down Piper's spine.

Ellery turned its gaze back to Piper. "I know what the Bronze Gink spoke of Piper Knell," she whispered.

"Why me?" Her voice shook, the only question she could grasp in the moment.

"Dray did not save you instead of Colik," Ellery said. "Dray saved you *for* him. Because even chaos has place in design. You carry dust, but not just any dust. The Dreamworld, though it fears your kind, also needs the change you will bring."

"My kind?"

Ellery did not answer. Like Royald, like Dawn.

She tried again. "Is that why Blaze changed his mind about me?"

Ellery nodded, brushing a trail of golden dust across Piper's lips. Her voice lowered to a private hush. "Dust comes from the purest depths of mother nature. Dreamers come from the making of stars. The Royalds are aged stars anchored to the lucents gifted by gods. Humans are born of both. That is why your dreams frighten gods. Why this world bends around you without even meaning to."

Piper understood less than half of what the Dawn had said, but she couldn't force a single question past the tightness in her throat.

"Creatures in this world follow what they recognize," Ellery murmured. "Or what they are told to recognize."

She watched Ellery glance again toward the catdrag, now circling her in slow, protective loops.

Ellery leaned closer and gave a small bow. A shimmer of gold drifted from her wings and dissolved into Piper's wrist. Instantly, a wave of peace flooded through her. Everything that had been churning inside—the fear, the doubt, and the ache—quieted.

Ellery rose to eye level, wings gentle and steady. "Hold on to this peace, Piper. You will need it. When the dream board shifts again, do not let them decide what piece you are. Remember, not every pawn stays a pawn."

The Dawn twirled once, then flickered upward into the dome of silver vines and starlit branches. The catdrag gave a delighted shake mid-air, mimicking Ellery's graceful spin, before darting off into the Greenery's hanging branches.

With a sly smile, Piper closed her eyes and breathed in the peace she'd been gifted, knowing it wouldn't last. For now, she held on to it…for as long as it was *humanly* possible.

CHAPTER TWENTY-FOUR
THE SUMMONING

P iper *still* couldn't have explained time here if her life depended on it. Colik had called it frequency, each pulse creating the next, but to Piper it was colored moments bleeding into each other until the whole scene blurred. Patryk said that was the point. She wasn't meant to understand it. None of them were.

Sometimes she caught the Blood Moon dimming, a slow heartbeat in the constellation cloud, though more often she missed it entirely. When pushing to understand how the Blood Moon worked, Patryk scratched diagrams into the clay ground in the turret outside, trying to give shape to its orbit, but the lines tangled, collapsing into confusing jargon. In the end, she stopped asking, and he stopped explaining.

The Citadel was a whole other beast to figure out. Its wings were vast and winding, lined with starlit windows, with rooms appearing and vanishing at will. One moment, Piper entered a wing of towering, gilded mirrors, their frames writhing with carved vines and extravagant flourishes. The next, she stepped into a sanctuary where the ceiling dissolved into the constellation sky, the stars rippling across pools at her feet, glowing orbs pulsing in step with her heart. The whole place throbbed with life. Even clouds drifted around her ankles as she walked. She felt lighter here. The clouds carried a gentler gravity, and yet where she still felt hungry and tired, no one else did.

I am a human and they are not.

Meals in the Citadel felt strange when taken alone. Piper sat at one of the endless tables, nibbling at glasslike fruits that cracked sweetly between her teeth, tearing bits of warm bread, and dipping her spoon into bowls that looked like spun clouds and sugar. The food was delicious, better than any meal she had ever had in her twenty years in the waking world.

Patryk entered quietly, his shadow stretching across the long, gleaming table before he spoke.

"Can I join you?" he asked her.

Piper's fork paused mid-air. She had eaten a few meals alone, and she did not like it, not even a little. Solitude was something unfamiliar to her. Even in Olympus House there was never a moment of true quiet, not with twenty other children crowded into the food hall built for half that number, elbows knocking against each other, voices rising in a constant, chaotic stream, and chairs scraping across the floor like restless creatures. The memory rose so vividly she could almost hear it, Aisling arguing with Callum over whose bread roll was bigger, Ciara asking to braid Piper's hair, and Penelope at the head of the table insisting they use their napkins even when half the children were too busy giggling to pay attention.

She swallowed quickly and wiped her mouth, the ache of homesickness catching her off-guard as she stiffened at Patryk's question.

"Why am I the only one eating at all?" she asked, her voice thinner than she meant it to be. "I have seen the others lifting glasses and moving forks but never swallowing. It feels like they are pretending."

She almost added that back home, even when she did not

want to eat, Penelope would give her that soft, steady look that was never angry but always concerned, and she would force herself to take a bite so the younger children would not copy her. Here, in this place where everyone mimicked the idea of meals instead of sharing them, the chair beside her felt too empty, the table stretched too far, and the silence pressed in more heavily than she could bear.

Patryk hesitated, and she caught the flicker in his eyes before he sat across from her. "There used to be more Dreamers here," he said at last. "The wings were fuller and noisier, but the gods decided it was better to scatter us. Better to keep the Guilds of Dreamers apart, each to their own corner of the Reverie. Alone, we are easier to control. Together..." He let the thought hang, unfinished, though she heard the truth in it. *Together, they might be as powerful as the gods.*

"And the food?" Piper pressed.

That drew the faintest smile from him. "Brownies," he said. "Little creatures who slip in and out of corners faster than shadows. They make all this. Keep this place spotless." He gestured toward the table, then the surrounding grounds. "You won't often see them as they don't care to be noticed. They are mischievous. Tireless. You give them stones to gnaw at, and they serve with pride. They're the reason the meals never end."

Brownies, Piper repeated in her head. *And stones?* She wondered if they were the same creatures she saw in the Forgotten Land.

Piper glanced at the feast spread before her, suddenly seeing the dishes in a new light. It was strange to be fed by unseen hands in a place where no one else acted hungry at all.

"Dreamers don't eat to survive," he said finally. "We don't need it. Not like you do."

He leaned back in his chair, eyes lifting to the stars shifting above them. The dome opened to the constellation cloud. Most rooms here did.

"The only thing we consume is petaled wine," he added. "Not for sustenance but for the sensation. It softens the edges. We drink it to feel something."

Piper tried to imagine living without meals, without hunger gnawing within her. It felt distant and impossible, like imagining a world without weather, but it made sense in a place like this—where dreams shaped reality and desire outweighed need. When she asked Patryk if it was born or bred, he said it came with transition. Whatever *that* meant.

Despite Patryk being around, for what Piper could only assume was to keep an eye on her, the Royalds had grown quieter altogether.

Colik, whenever he joined them for meals, never spoke to her. He muttered low, broken phrases back and forth with Blaze, the words distorted and slipping into the air like fragments she could never quite catch. Patryk had told her it was Dreamtongue. The Scirges had mentioned it before as well, a dialect she could not understand and probably never would.

Piper caught a few human scraps—*looking…hidden…lost*— but strung together they meant nothing. His gaze never lingered on the food or the table, always drifting elsewhere, as though sitting there was only keeping him from more important matters. She knew he was searching for something, but whatever it was, he gave nothing away. Blaze, though he made small talk when present, felt strangely distant too, which stung more than she cared to admit. Lulu, meanwhile, remained unseen.

When Piper finally asked again, Patryk murmured, "She's handling the Polaris," as if that explained everything. Piper remembered what Ellery had said about the creatures, how they were loyal to Lulu, but that still didn't answer how many Blood Moon rotations could have passed since she last saw her.

It also made her wonder more about how much time had slipped away in her waking world. Then again, when she asked Blaze, because Patryk and Colik made no sense, he said it depended on the *frequency of moments*. Some pulses stretched long, lasting what felt like weeks here, but who knew how long that was in the waking world. Other pulses snapped short, compressing whole Blood Moon rotations into the space of a single heartbeat.

"The distance between the Dreamworld's moons and Earth's moon", he explained once, "was measured not in miles but in lightyears of rhythm. The Blood Moon's rotations never align, never sang on the same beat. *Time* here was not steady, but fractured beats, sometimes rushing, sometimes stalling." That too was no help.

Still, Patryk lingered. He'd taken to finding her in odd places—the overlook near the turret, or the coral reef that pressed up against the front walls of the Citadel. From above, the turret looked carved for combat: circles etched into the stone where Dreamers might once have sparred, deep gouges in the earth where swars had been driven like stakes, and beams crossing high above like a jungle gym the Scirges would have claimed as their own.

It was easy to imagine the place alive. To hear shouts, laughter, and the clash of training drills echoing off the pillars. It stood hollow, only the outlines of some remembrance remaining.

The reef, by contrast, was its opposite. It unfurled in dazzling layers of color, coral rising in arcs and spirals like frozen fireworks beneath the water. Small fish glimmered between the branches, and the sway of the current gave the whole reef a rhythm as steady as breathing. Yet there was something mysterious about it, too. Its beauty felt too perfect, and too complete.

Still, Patryk never stayed long, never said much, and when he would find her, his eyes always looked as though he was on the edge of revealing something. Or waiting for something within her to surface.

One morning, or evening—it was impossible to tell moment to moment—Patryk appeared again. There was no warning, not even his usual lively, flamboyant aura. He simply grabbed her arm as she wandered through a room that appeared to be full of stone Greek statues and pulled her along the wing without explanation.

"Where are we going?"

"The throne room."

The ivory doors loomed ahead, groaning open without being touched. The scent of metal and dust curled around them.

Patryk looked back at her, a rare seriousness settling over him.

"They're waiting."

Piper stepped into the throne room, and her eyes caught on Lulu immediately, who was draped in a deep crimson gown that poured across the floor like molten silk. The cut was daring, elegant, every line designed to command attention, and the leather belt at her waist gleamed with a dark, earthy sheen. It was regal yet untamed.

What struck Piper most, though, was the way Lulu's hair shimmered a new color, the shade burning the same fierce red as her gown. Sometimes it was white, and once an ashy grey, but always it betrayed her emotions, even when her face remained unreadable. Yet, no matter the colors of her hair, Lulu's eyes stayed the same: autumn. Forever autumn. As if some truth about her couldn't be disguised, like leaves caught mid-fall. They looked familiar, but she couldn't think of from where, given they were moving around the room like blades, calculating and hunting, as though whoever came in after Piper was already a piece to be sacrificed.

Colik stood just behind her, withdrawn but impossible to ignore, shoulders locked, bracing against chains only he seemed to feel. His arms crossed tight across his chest, and his expression was unreadable, a shadow half-formed with the light.

Blaze stood beneath the central throne, the room belonging to him. His spine was a pillar, his jaw was carved in iron, and the air above his head bent unnaturally toward him, like the stars themselves were being commanded to obey.

Patryk was already at Lulu's side, his stillness razor-sharp, and his eyes gleaming with the kind of patience that could unmake a man. He looked not at Piper but through the chamber.

The doors groaned shut behind Piper, and the echo rolled through the throne room, a verdict she hadn't yet heard but already felt. Her chest tightened as she stepped forward, the weight of the Royalds eyes pressing against her with each stride.

Having reached Colik's side, a breeze curled through the throne room. It was unnatural and cold, like air was being drawn out. The stars overhead twitched again behind Blaze, their light flickering sharply across his face, carving him into something harder. Conflict was written all over his face, and Piper quickly found out why.

The Shades came.

Eight of them—no, nine, though the ninth didn't bother to hide the arrogance in the way he strolled in, as if he were arriving fashionably late to a party rather than slipping into a chamber weighed down by judgment. They drifted through the side doors like smoke dragged across stone, fluid but slowed by a hollow ache, their limbs barely tethered to their bodies as hunger hollowed them into something unrecognizable. Their onyx eyes scanned the chamber with a feverish gleam... all except the ninth Shade, whose eyes glinted with a cool, unbothered emerald, as if the Dreamworld had not earned the courtesy of his full attention.

Then the Shades saw Piper.

A ripple of recognition tore through their ranks, a violent, shuddering wave that made several collapses to their knees without hesitation. One gasped, the sound jagged enough to shear the silence in two. Another lurched forward, skeletal fingers twitching like strings pulled by an unseen puppeteer.

One Shade didn't kneel. He didn't even blink. He tilted his head and let his gaze trail over Piper with a cold assessment that felt both like a warning and baiting.

Piper's heart jolted, recognizing him instantly.

It *was* the emerald eyed Shade from the Plastrof. He looked even more dangerous, like he had returned wearing mockery as armor.

"Explain your presence," Blaze said, his voice quiet and absolute, the kind of command that usually split obedience from defiance.

The eight Shades dropped lower, trembling, their breaths ragged and broken. The emerald-eyed Shade clicked his tongue, so disrespectfully casual that Blaze's jaw tightened by a fraction.

As if sensing the tension radiating off her, Colik flicked a glance between Piper and the Shade. He did not look pleased to find the emerald-eyed Shade still watching her, his gaze fixed and unblinking. Those eyes hadn't left her since he entered. Piper curled her fingers into a fist, trying to stop the heat rising in her cheeks.

The woman Shade—the one whose child Piper had given dreams to—lifted her head with shaking reverence, grief chiseled into her features.

"We have seen the dreams of humans falter," she whispered, voice splintering. "While our own dreams have withered—" Her eyes latched onto Piper, and the other seven convulsed with hungry longing, yearning carved into every hollowed angle of their frames.

"What is it you are asking?" Lulu cut in. Her voice stayed steady, but her eyes widened with genuine worry.

The woman Shade bowed her head toward the Royald. "We need dreams strands if we are to continue letting human nightmares pass through us. Without a strong tie, we cannot fulfil our role…and live."

Blaze said nothing. His gaze swept the room, his body tense as though he expected more Shades to burst in through the walls like a Trojan horse.

Another Shade stepped forward, older, eyes fogged but still sharp with fear. "As a Guild of Dreamers, how are we to shape, soften, or intensify nightmares if the balance between our dust and theirs is thinning? We are losing the knowledge of the boundary, the line that tells nightmares from dream."

"Where is this—" Blaze began, but the emerald-eyed Shade cut through his words like a blade. "*She* shouldn't be standing by your side," he said, voice smooth but laced with disdain. "Unless you are ready to watch her get torn apart."

The way he said it, felt like a hand sliding a knife between Blaze's ribs. The emerald-eyed Shade turned back to Piper, the room tightening around the space between them. "Come with me."

Blaze stepped forward, jaw ticking. "You don't get to choose where she stands. Or who she goes with."

The emerald-eyed Shade's grin widened, slow and cold. "You do?"

Colik stiffened. Lulu's head snapped toward the Shade. Patryk's breath hitched.

Blaze, on the other hand, advanced with that strange mixture of burning and freezing that only Royalds were capable of wielding without destroying themselves.

"You didn't crawl here out of desire," Blaze said, his voice slicing clean. "You were summoned."

He pointed at the kneeling Shades.

"You," he added, turning on the emerald-eyed Shade, "you weren't invited."

The meaning under his voice was unmistakable. He knew exactly who this Shade was, and he did not like it. Piper's eyes darted from Blaze to the Shades, trying to track the shifting tension in every voice.

The emerald-eyed Shade pressed a hand to his chest, eyes widening in a dramatic mimicry of offense. "Not invited? Gods, Blaze, I am crushed." He paused, then let a slow, wicked smile unfurl. "Oh wait. I'm not."

He strolled a step closer, eyebrow lifting with a razor's edge of mockery.

"I *crave* showing up where I'm not wanted. Being near those who have no idea what I am capable of." His gaze flicked to Piper, and she felt her stomach drop. *No*, she forgot how to breath.

Blaze's eyes darkened. "Name your leader. Who is controlling the Shades?"

The Shade met the Royald's features and laughed. Actually laughed.

"Oh, Blaze," he drawled, so casual it was as if in passing. "If I told you that, I'm afraid you'd do something stupid. Or worse. You'd do something predictable."

A few Shades whimpered. Colik's breath caught. Lulu went rigid.

Blaze stepped closer, heat rippling off him, cracks spidering across the marble under his boots.

"You will answer me."

The emerald-eyed Shade tilted his head again, as if studying a misbehaving pet. "Will I? That sounds terribly inconvenient for me. I hate being inconvenienced."

The room tensed.

"You're toying with me," Blaze said quietly.

"Oh, absolutely," the Shade said, smile spreading, "but not for the reason you think."

The emerald-eyed Shade's gaze slid again to her, holding for a single heartbeat longer than necessary, a silent message carved beneath the sarcasm.

Don't make me come save you again.

Piper felt a prickle run across her skin, a strange tug low in her stomach. She swallowed, unsure why the air suddenly felt charged.

"We don't know the name of the one who guides us," the youngest looking Shade spoke up, her voice trembling. She couldn't be older than Piper and yet the way her face was so caved in, made Pipers heart ache. "He—he claims to be one of us. He shows us dreams... flickers..."

Blaze inhaled sharply, the air splitting around him.

"You are given dreams?" he said. "By him?"

The emerald-eyed Shade's grin sharpened. "She didn't say that, but I will keep taking your guesses."

Blaze's temperature dropped so fast the candlelight's flickered across the throne room. "I will ask again. Who *controls* you?"

"Who says anyone over here controls *me?*" the emerald-eyed Shade purred.

Blaze snapped. "If any Shade asks for a human's dreams again," he said, "I will revish the Plastrof until it forgets the meaning of sleep. Trade dust, and I'll summon the Fatales and let your strand undo itself thread by thread until the Dreamers of Nightmares are nothing but a rumor that even nightmares refuse to recall."

Even the emerald-eyed Shade went still at that, the corner of his jaw tightening.

Then, as if correcting himself, he turned to Piper, stepping forward with predatory confidence. His voice dropped to a low, cold whisper. "You will choose me...when you are ready."

Piper froze, her eyes locking on his emerald ones. She

couldn't make herself look away. Something in his stare pressed against her ribs, familiar but unsettling. Colik stiffened beside her, then shifted in front of her, his arm outstretched as if the Shade might tear her from them.

Blaze's voice cracked through the air. "Step away from her!"

The emerald-eyed Shade did not flinch. "As you call." He stepped back with a taunting grace, and a heavy darkness rippled through the room. It moved like a living thing, swallowing the light. Piper choked on black dust that scraped down her throat. Arms shot out toward her, some strong, some clawed, as if holding her down to make sure she had not vanished into the dark with them.

Blaze ignited, scorching the air with gold-black sparks that tore through the cloud swirling around them. The darkness shattered apart.

The Shades were gone.

Colik and Lulu both had their hands on her, gripping her as if she might dissolve next.

Piper managed a weak smile toward them, though something in her chest tugged sharply, as if something inside her had been pulled tight when the emerald-eyed Shade retreated.

All three Royald's stared at her, Patryk too, waiting for answers she did not want to give. They had no idea she had already met him, and she hadn't prepared herself to speak the truth of that yet.

"Piper?" Blaze's voice came softly from behind the door of her Vanis room.

She moved toward it but stopped short. Her hand hovered near the handle, trembling with a strange caution she couldn't quite name. The emerald-eyed Shade's voice slipped back into her mind—*Come with me*. A plea. A warning. A temptation. She still didn't know which.

Suddenly, she wasn't sure who she trusted in this world anymore. Everything moved like a fever dream, truth bending and reshaping itself around her. Even the tension with the Royald's had changed, twisting into something she couldn't read, couldn't name, and couldn't truly get herself to trust.

She finally pulled the door open, only enough to see him.

Blaze stood there, poised yet uncertain, the faint glow of the corridor light tracing his suit in gold. He looked perfectly regal. Of course he did, but the sight didn't settle well with her. Not after the Shades. Not after what he'd said to the Royalds. Not after realizing that even the things that shone brightest here carried shadows of their own.

His perfection—his status—didn't calm her the same way anymore. Not when the world around her kept shifting beneath her feet. Not when trust had begun to feel like a trick of a dream. "All of this apologizing is going to make me look weak," he said gently, reading the reluctance in her eyes. She didn't laugh, but still, something made her step aside to let him in. He entered slowly, careful with his movements, like he was trying not to startle her. The door clicked shut behind him, and for a moment, neither of them spoke.

She didn't move closer. Neither did he. The light of the room caught on his grey ash eyes, and for a moment, she could see the kind of man someone else might trust again, but she wasn't someone else. Not anymore.

"I can leave if you'd rather," he offered, voice low, as if guilty. "I get that after everything, you might not want to see me."

"No," she said quietly. "Just… I don't know how to feel, alright? Can I feel that way?"

He nodded, looking away. "Of course."

A pause. Then he took a careful step toward the high arched pillars, his hands clasped behind his back.

"I just want to apologize again," he said, more serious this time. "For my own behavior. For how I treated the Shades. Especially the one with emerald eyes. The one who took quite a notice to you."

That made Piper's heart skip a beat. Or two.

"You were... intense."

"I was," he admitted, a flash of shame in his tone. "I needed to be. Not just because I'm Royald, but because you were in the middle of it. I didn't know why they begged you. I am not sure why *he* pressed so hard for you to come with him."

"Begged me?"

He turned, meeting her eyes with something vulnerable beneath the surface. "Yes. They should not have even felt the *right* to ask you for your dreams in the Plastrof." His tone grew tense. "That concerns me more than it should have. You don't realize how rare that is. What that could mean. They should not feel the courage to ask for more of you. Or any of you, ever." Blaze looked nervous.

She didn't respond. Not yet. Her guard was still up, and he noticed.

"I'm not here to control you, Piper," he spoke again. "I can see that you are hesitant about me again," he added. "What you saw prior to that *was* me. I'd like to earn that trust back if I still can."

That made her chest ache, but she didn't let him see it.

"I see how important trust is to you. To humans. How hard it is to regain once broken. I see it with you and Colik."

Piper said nothing. She couldn't. She didn't know what to say.

He turned to face her again, looking graver. "Dreamers—*even* Shades—don't ask for human dust. Not unless they're desperate. Not unless they're being manipulated or called to do so. Or worse, lusting after a control they don't even know they have."

Blaze looked her up and down. "You know him—that Shade—I can tell."

Piper swallowed hard. "I met him once. I do not *know* him."

"Hmm," Blaze said, as if contemplating her words. His eyes moved up and down her again.

"So, which is it?" She quickly asked.

"That's what I'm trying to find out," he admitted. "Like I said, it concerns me, Piper. I've seen creatures twisted by hunger, by obsession. When I saw the way they looked at you —*what he asked you for as if it was nothing*—I had to react, but I regret how I handled it. You didn't deserve to be caught in that. Or even see it. I shouldn't have asked Patryk to bring you in there. I was just hoping for that..." His voice faltered, but she was too nervous to ask him to finish that sentence.

She looked at him carefully. His tone wasn't defensive. Just tired and drained.

"I'm not saying I trust their answers," Blaze went on, "but I *do* trust my instincts. Something about you...it changed them. Stirred the one Shade in an unusual way."

She nodded, trying to understand, but said nothing. They stood quietly for a moment, letting the room silently express feelings neither wanted to share out loud. She could tell he was uncomfortable that she was uncomfortable.

"Can I show you something?" he asked suddenly, his voice softer than before, the edge of a formal Royald command replaced by something real again.

Piper tilted her head slightly, unsure. "Show me what?"

"My lucent," he replied, the word hanging in the air. "My Dreamers' power. The one I'm not supposed to use. Not around you. Not around anyone."

She blinked. "Your lucent?" Ellery had said that word, but Piper had no idea what that had meant.

Blaze nodded once, stepping closer. "Every Royald has one. A gift from the Gods of Dreams, given to us when we were chosen. We were instructed not to use them. We're meant to be ornaments. Beautiful, distant and powerful when it suits the gods' story."

Piper's chest tightened at the word. Ornaments. She thought of the garden at Olympus House on Christmas tree day, when they were each allowed to pick a single rose to press among the Christmas tree. The petals looked fragile against the needles, lovely but already wilting, placed there not for use but for show. She remembered how the children would argue over colors—red, white, and yellow—each trying to believe their choice meant something.

Hearing Blaze, she wondered if that's all the Royalds were to the gods. Roses pinned to someone else's tree. Beautiful, but doomed to wither. Everyone had a story. It didn't mean you knew it, and Piper, sure as hell, didn't know Blaze's story.

"Then why are you showing me?"

"Because you should know the truth," he said simply. "Because I think if we stopped pretending, we might become the things we were meant to be. Not just dream-polished dolls guarding a world, but protectors of *worlds*. Maybe even allies."

Piper swallowed hard. "Why me?"

"Because you're the first real thing to come here in ages," he said without hesitation. "You're not just part of a dream. You're interrupting a Dreamworld."

"Give me your wrist," Blaze said, his voice low and steady. "The one without the brace."

She hesitated, then slowly extended her arm, palm up. His hand closed around her wrist, thumb pressing where her pulse stammered. A strand of red light, like the string of a swar's handle, unfurled between them.

Then he lifted his hand. From her skin, a flame rose, red, coiled, and alive. It pulsed with her heartbeat, and shapes began to emerge. Wisps of light gathered and hardened into outlines—faces she knew, and voices that did not belong here. A kiss pressed into the air, a Shade's warning hand, a white-eyed outline of a boy whispering for her help.

Blaze's eyes glowed faintly as he watched them. "This is my lucent," he said, voice low but unshaken. "A gift traced from Morpheus himself. He forms human dreams from dust, and I form human memories in their dreams. I repeat what has already been formed, and in this case, a memory remembered." The shadowed forms flickered, circling her like smoke-bound echoes, undeniable and damning. "The same gift, only bent toward the gods law instead of endless wonder."

Piper remained silent, but Blaze pulled his hand away from her wrist.

"I don't imagine," Blaze went on. "I reveal. What has been hidden in you, I can recall into shape."

Her wrist throbbed despite him letting go.

"Only when I touch," he added more quietly, his gaze fixed on hers. "Only when I open what Morpheus once gave me."

The red strand flared, then shattered into sparks. The visions dissolved, but their weight lingered. The air in the chamber tightened, and Piper's chest locked as she realized what Blaze had done. Her memories were no longer hers. He had just exposed them right before her eyes.

He didn't speak right away, but his eyes were still glowing faintly, a white trace around the iris.

"I see them," he said at last. "The breaks." Then he inhaled sharply, his glance uneasy.

"The Reverie, or R-Laws," Blaze said, voice tightening. "They have been broken."

Piper froze. *They...* as in more than one?

For a heartbeat, Blaze's eyes flickered. Piper saw the way his gaze shifted, sharp with realization, as though he had connected something deeper. His lips parted to speak, but then he stopped.

The silence stretched between them. Whatever truth he had found, he locked it back behind his teeth, leaving Piper with nothing but the weight of the unsaid.

Then Blaze's gaze shifted, but Piper couldn't read it. Perhaps reluctance. Perhaps reverence.

"Steele broke a R-Law," Blaze said, his voice edged with something between anger and grief. "When he touched your dust to send you back here. That kind of crossing—taking or giving dust between worlds—it leaves scars. Scars that never truly fade. Most Dreamers don't survive even one bishoping."

His eyes fixed on her, distressed and accusatory. "You've endured it twice."

Piper's lips parted. "Patryk mentioned that."

"So, then you know it is the transference of dust," Blaze said. It was a statement not a question. "It's what we've warned all along. Humans shouldn't be able to pass the REM. Their dust is too fragile to transfer into this world. The dust here is heavier and older. When they collide, they tear at each other. That act is bishoping. One dust forced inside another."

Piper wondered if Himyla knew of this word: *bishoping*. That must have been what her friend had done as well.

Blaze shook his head slowly, like he wished the truth wasn't his to say. "Steele knew exactly what he was doing. He used you, Piper. Used you to draw closer to the Reverie and left you carrying the scars of it." He looked her up and down, expecting to see physical scars.

The silence after stretched heavy, thick with the weight of whatever he had just refused to say.

What was he keeping from her?

Blaze stepped back. The lucents glow was gone, but its echoes still pulsed between them, full of law and memory and warning.

Blaze looked shaken. "The Reverie should have rejected

you. Any Dreamer would have been pushed out." His breath stuttered as he stepped back, as if distance might steady him. "Instead…something held you here."

He stared at her as though seeing her for the first time.

"You're not a guest here, Piper," he said quietly. "Someone, or something, is shielding you. Because by the Oneiroi Laws, you should have been erased the moment you crossed."

Piper's stomach dropped. "Oneiroi laws? I thought it was the Reverie laws."

Blaze went still. Even the room stopped breathing.

"The Reverie Laws are surface rules," he said at last. "Child's rules." He shook his head. "Those laws guide behavior. They keep order." His voice lowered. "The Oneiroi Laws decide existence."

A cold pulse swept the room.

"They are older than the Reverie. Older than the gods who wrote the R-Laws. The Oneiroi Laws govern dream dust itself. They decide what may survive the crossing between worlds." His gaze dragged over her face, searching for something she did not know how to offer. "You broke one simply by being here. O-Law Zero states that dreams dust severs what does not belong. You should have been severed the moment you stepped foot in the Reverie."

Piper's throat tightened.

"Wh—why wasn't I?"

Blaze did not answer but looked more afraid.

"I need to hide what I saw," he muttered. His hand trembled as he dragged it across his mouth. "Before the Solari senses this. If they do, Piper… they will not hesitate. They will uphold the old law."

In the heavy silence that followed, she felt—for the first time—what it meant to be something the Dreamworld should have erased.

Piper's brows furrowed. "What do you mean, *hide* it?"

"The Fatales don't need the lucent to detect a Reverie law

broken," Blaze said, already moving, his hands skimming the air. "They *feel* them. It's how they enforce the dream laws. They'll see your strand the moment you bishop again or touch a Royalds lucent apart from mine." His words came fast, low and tight. "I can shield it for some moments, but they will start to wonder. Come here." His latter words were a strong demand that Piper wasn't used to hearing from him, only Colik. Still, Piper listened.

Blaze spun a golden circle around her with his fingers and a strange warmth pressed gently against her skin. It sank deeper, like a ceiling of movement in her veins, before he stopped. The way he was looking at her was as if all the secrecy was falling on him and he was struggling to find the words to tell her. It was not a good look. It was fearful, if anything.

"You have no idea what you're in the middle of, do you?"

Piper shook her head slowly. "I'm trying to understand."

Blaze looked at her like it hurt to say what came next. "Understand what? Ask what it is you've been holding back from asking."

She thought about it. What *did* she want to know? One word kept coming to mind. "What *is* the Fray?"

He hesitated, then sat at the edge of her clouded bed uninvited, as if explaining it demanded grounding.

"The Fray is older than the Reverie. Older than the gods. It's not a place, but a force. A living mechanism that weaves the dreams of mortals into the pattern of the world. Every strand of stardust, every nightmare and hope, all of it flows through the Fray." Blaze sighed heavily. "Like the Fates with life. The Fray wields human fate in their dreams."

Silence thickened between them. Then Blaze added softly, as if ashamed, "You can still leave, if you choose. I will take that brace off you if you so choose." He looked down at her brace, then met her gaze again. He looked sincere. "That is the one thing they have not taken, your will. If you stay, you need to know this…"

He didn't stand up, but his voice dropped to something raw. "I am truly not sure how the Reverie will survive with what is bound to happen. What you are about to become."

Something flickered behind his eyes, a truth he shouldn't know, a truth he didn't want to speak.

Piper's breath caught.

He must know an inevitable outcome others did not.

Blaze swallowed hard. "Piper… earlier, with the Shades, especially the emerald-eyed one, I owe you an apology."

Her head lifted.

He exhaled shakily. "I treated them like they were beneath me. Like they couldn't feel. Like they were only nightmares meant to obey the Royalds, but when you let me use my lucent, it showed me things I have questioned my entire existence, and suddenly everything made sense."

The confession shook him. A faint stunned smile touched his lips, with more awe than happiness.

"I can't tell you everything that came from what I saw," he murmured, his gaze pulling away as if the remembrance was too much to meet her gaze. "I understand it. I thank you for showing it to me."

He looked up again, surprised at himself. "The lucent can be good, if it is used correctly. I always doubted it, thought it deceived more than it ever revealed. You proved me wrong."

Piper blinked at him, a warmth rising in her chest that she didn't know how to name. "If it can be good," she said slowly, "then why don't the Royalds use it that way? Why does it feel like all of you are fighting the good just to pretend you're the bad? Why act like the answer is somewhere else when it's right here, in what you already hold?"

Blaze let out a hollow breath, part laugh and part defeat. "The Royalds believe they are good. The gods do not always agree."

His gaze lingered on her longer than it should have, tracing her face with something like recognition, too gentle to be suspicion and too reverent to be coincidence.

"Maybe you," he said quietly, "might be the one who turns them around."

A chill rippled up her spine. "Why would I do that?"

There was a beat, a flicker, the smallest shift of his mouth, as if he had spoken the truth and then smothered it before it could escape.

"Because," Blaze said, stepping close again, his voice lowering, "some things in this world only answer to you." He smiled but didn't elaborate. He didn't need to. The truth was there in the way he looked at her, in the way he had gone pale at the sight of the lucent, in the way he stood. "Let me show you one more thing," Blaze said. "Another form of my lucent. *My* frequency of memories. Where all my memories echo at once."

He didn't even let her say no, as he locked eyes with her. "Do not blink."

She held his gaze, watching his irises darken—his usual grey swirling into a cosmic black, ringed with silver like twin eclipses.

"Watch my remembrance—" he whispered.

Shadows coiled around them, rising from the ground in thin wisps, and the air shifted. It wasn't cold. It was weightless, completely engulfing everything around them.

The walls of Piper's chamber shimmered and stretched, the air thickening with the scent of earth and green leaves. The marble floor softened beneath her feet, turning to soil, rich and dark. Vines crept along the walls, unfurling slowly until they became thick curtains of leaves, filtering dappled sunlight through unseen canopies.

She was looking *upon* the memory—an aerial view.

Around her, towering trees with white ash bark and needle-like leaves rose from the soil. Ferns curled at their bases, and vines of the Lavyrinthos climbed the trunks, shimmering faintly with light.

She heard Blaze's voice, before she saw him. "The Greycene," he whispered to himself, then she watched as he moved to a slender tree and placed his palm on its trunk. His expression softened.

A glimmer darted through the vines, and from the greenery emerged a tiny figure, radiant in golden ivy and wings of maize light.

"Don't forget the smallest creatures," she chimed, her voice like wind kissing wind.

Blaze's eyes lit with something unguarded. "How could I forget the Dawns?"

The Dawn floated to his wrist and bowed her head. "Blaze, my loyal friend."

"Ellery," he greeted with a wide smile.

"What brings you to me?" she asked.

"I need clarity," Blaze admitted, his voice low. "Peace... and answers."

"Ah." Ellery's wings shimmered. "The human girl."

Blaze shrugged, his moves innocent and childlike while Ellery hovered higher, studying him. "You were chosen to carry a burden others would break under. Do you still not understand why I gave my loyalty to you?"

Blaze looked down. "Some moments, I question it."

"You were not the strongest," she said gently. "Not the kindest. You were the one who listened even when silence was easier. You are loyal, Blaze. You do not dwell to control, but to the balance. That is why I am loyal to you."

He breathed deeply, as if her words stitched a wound he hadn't realized was open.

"I've kept your trust," Blaze said. "Though I can feel it fraying. As is the Fray itself."

Ellery nodded. "The Bronze Gink spoke of Morpheus' Promise. Colik and Piper, both heard it." Blaze's eyes widened, his hands turned to fists. "Prepare, dear Blaze... The Dreamer will be exposed. If a new age commences...dust will go to war."

Blaze stilled. "This short of a cycle?"

"Fate doesn't wait for readiness, even within dreams. The Dreamworld is moving. So must you."

"How do I prepare?" Confusion filled his bones—confusion and an uncertainty he hadn't felt in many moments.

"Observe and prepare those around you," Ellery said, her glow dimming slightly. "You have grown used to trust, but now some watch your title with envy. The role of Royald can be a lure for those who do not know it's true meaning."

Blaze's jaw clenched. "You think someone would try to take our title. My title?"

"I think someone already is," she said quietly. "Be careful how you wear the crown, Blaze. Especially in front of Dreamers who've tasted control but never earned it."

A chill passed through him.

"And the girl," he said, the question surfacing before he could stop it. "Colik used the sandtie to keep her here. To stop her from fading between worlds. He said he had no choice, but—"

Ellery's wings stilled. It was the closest thing to gravity she ever showed.

"A sandtie between a Dreamer and a human should unmake them both," Blaze pressed. "One dust consuming the other. That is the law. That is what always happens."

"Yes," Ellery said carefully. "That is what always happens."

The distinction hung between them, quiet and sharp as a blade not yet drawn.

"She didn't unravel," Blaze said.

"No."

"Why?"

Ellery was quiet for a long moment, her golden wings folding and unfolding like a thought being turned over. "When two strands are incompatible, the weaker one dissolves. That is the nature of dust. It does not share, it surrenders." She drifted closer to him, voice dropping. "But when two strands recognize each other... they do not consume. They remember."

Blaze went still. "Recognize."

"Her dust did not fight his," Ellery said. "It knew him. And his knew her. The sandtie held because it was not forcing two foreign things together." A pause. "It was rejoining what had already been split."

The Greycene breathed around them, leaves trembling without wind.

"That isn't possible," Blaze said, though his voice carried no conviction. "Silver strands were severed. Sealed away. There are none left that could—"

"And yet," Ellery interrupted gently, "she did not dissolve."

The silence that followed was the kind that rearranged things.

"And...Colik is not a part of the Silver Age," Blaze said, his eyes widening as the realization hit him.

More silence followed, when finally, he exhaled slowly, staring at nothing as he asked, "Does Colik know what this all means?"

Ellery's expression was not quite sorrow and not quite relief. "He felt the sandtie's effect. Whether he has allowed himself to understand it—or question it—is another matter entirely." Her glow brightened briefly, as if punctuating the thought. "Colik has always been better at holding truths at arm's length than facing them directly."

Blaze let out a short, humorless breath. "That much hasn't changed."

Ellery's wings flicked once, scattering dust. "Trust, but not blindly. Not anymore. And remember, Piper is not your sole responsibility. She is another's reflection that must awaken on its own."

"I—" Blaze didn't know what else to say. There was so much to decipher there that he would need to reflect on. Process, and like Ellery said—prepare for.

"Let her walk the Citadel. Let her feel it. If she's meant to find what anchors her to this world, she will," Ellery continued, but not in the way Blaze had hoped.

"The creature?"

She smiled. "Yes. If the strand is true, they will find each other. The Greycene favors those who carry contradiction. You, Blaze, are nothing if not contradiction wrapped in honor."

He bowed his head in gratitude, words failing him again.

With a final flicker of golden light, Ellery vanished into the canopy.

The remembrance faded, and as their connection gradually dissolved, it left a lingering coolness, making Piper's body shiver from head to toe.

Blaze broke their gaze, and in an instant, they were back in her Vanis room. He blinked, and Piper blinked with him, the silver haze retreating from his irises until only the usual smoky grey remained.

"What did Ellery mean by—by *all* of it? What—why show me that?" she tried to get out, her voice unsteady.

Blaze didn't answer immediately, as if contemplating his response. It was a heavy question that surely would result in a heavy response. She didn't understand what the Dawn meant by reflection, awakening or Colik's sandtie to her not causing any true harm. She didn't know when this moment occurred —how soon after they came to the Citadel.

When he did speak, his voice was low, not tense, but quiet and certain.

"I wanted you to see *me*."

Piper stared at him. That was *not* the response she expected. Or hoped for.

He held out his hand, not toward her, but palm-up, open and steady. It wasn't summoning but offering.

"My frequency isn't like Hazel's. Or Steele's. It's short. Passed down from Silver Children who didn't vanish but adapted. I wasn't born in the Age of Gods. I came after. Was born *because* of it. I can't reach back through ages. I can't call down echoes from the beginning of the gods' worlds."

He looked down at his hand, as though the truth shimmered just beneath the skin.

"I can only feel what still lingers in the various moments. Emotions left behind. Moments sharp enough to hold their shape for a few frequency events, maybe. That's all."

She watched the faintest ripple of light flicker in his fingers, then fade.

"Hazel sees history," he said. "Steele sees consequence. But me? I only see *now* and can reveal recent moments."

A silence settled between them, that was not necessarily cold but most certainly unsure.

"Trust doesn't come easy in this world either," Blaze said, his voice roughened by memory. "Ellery gives me truth and peace. Something she gave you too, from what I've heard."

He looked at her— really looked—his expression was unguarded. He let his hand fall slowly to his side.

"With all I've shown you…it is yours to choose," he said quietly, stalking off. "Whether you choose to trust me again or fear me."

Piper had no words. Though she wanted to ask again what it all meant, she knew he wouldn't tell her. That was the pattern she had learned by now—the gods moved the pieces and the Royalds held the board, and neither told the human standing in the middle of it what game was actually being played.

Blaze was kinder than most and that only made the withholding worse.

With the hollow thrum of her heartbeat and the bitter taste of it on her tongue, she silently watched him walk out.

CHAPTER TWENTY-FIVE
THE TRUE COLIK

"What are you doing?"

The voice snapped through the steam. Piper jolted upright, nearly slipping on the smooth edge of the soaking basin. She hadn't heard the divider shift, hadn't sensed Colik until he was suddenly there, a silhouette carved clean through the fog.

So much for privacy. Apparently, that was optional in the Reverie.

She yelped and snatched the nearest towel, wrapping it around herself in a frantic, dripping twist. "I was in a bath!"

Colik leaned against the archway as if it belonged to him, his gaze angled elsewhere yet still annoyingly confident, and entirely unbothered by her panic or lack of clothes.

To the gods, what a bath it was.

This one was even better than the last. The water was warm in the way only the Reverie could manage. It was soothing and sauna-thick, steeped in lavender oil and crushed pink petals that floated like soft confessions across the surface. Steam curled in slow halos around her shoulders. Candlelight flickered from stone alcoves, painting molten gold along the walls.

The basin's marble edge was smooth beneath her fingers,

cool where her skin wasn't submerged. She didn't know how long she had been in it, only that she'd sunk into the warmth the way one might return to a memory they'd forgotten they needed.

Baths were becoming her favorite part of this world.

Silent. Soft. Safe.

Moments where she wasn't alone the way she had been at Olympus House—forgotten and surrounded by noise yet hollow inside—but alone in a way that felt chosen. Held. Almost whole.

Even in this bath, her mind betrayed her.

A shiver slid down her spine, uninvited. The emerald-eyed Shade flickered across her thoughts. The way he'd said, *come with me*, low and certain, like a promise he expected her to keep.

The way his look said, *don't make me come save you again*, in a tone that curled somewhere between warning and something she absolutely was not ready to name.

Heat rose beneath her skin, confusing and unwelcome.

Why was she thinking about him here?

"I knocked," Colik said, breaking through her *almost* pleasant thoughts.

She glared, knowing he was lying.

He lingered in the doorway, his gaze dragging over her in a slow and deliberate sweep, studying her with an intensity that suggested he was weighing something dangerous and unresolved inside himself. His eyes traveled from the dripping ends of her hair to the curve of her knees drawn beneath the towel, and for a fleeting, breathless moment, the warmth that bloomed in her chest rose with an alarming certainty that had nothing at all to do with embarrassment.

It was not anger she felt. It was heat, and the kind that had been creeping into her thoughts with unnerving frequency since she arrived in this world, threading itself into moments she should not be thinking about and stirring feelings she did not know how to control.

Everything here was designed to twist her, to take her by surprise and unmake the things she had always believed she understood about herself. It was making her question everything she thought she knew: every choice she made, every instinct she relied on, every feeling she trusted, every boy she thought she could neatly categorize, and most of all, every kiss or desire she had convinced herself she was too sensible or too guarded or too unwanted to ever let in.

Her pulse stumbled as memory rose through her like a tide she could not hold back.

The Broken Woods. His breath warm against hers. The single suspended moment before the woods burst into flame around her, a moment caught between danger and something far more reckless that neither of them had dared acknowledge.

Wrapped in steam and candlelight, with her heart thrumming in her throat and every thought tangling with unwelcome heat, Piper found she did not trust herself, her body, or the aching pull in her chest that was determined to betray her.

She forced her face blank, hiding the memory as quickly as it rose, burying it beneath irritation. "You did not knock. I don't have *that* bad of hearing," she said flatly, turning away before he could see the color rising to her cheeks. She pulled the towel tighter across her chest.

She felt his gaze follow her anyway, heavy and knowing, as if he'd caught the thought she was trying not to have.

"I'm here to take you somewhere. It's important." His voice was clipped, but a flicker of hesitation slid beneath it, like even *he* knew he had intervened in something personal. I've heard that before. Piper rolled her eyes.

"Well, give me a few *moments* so I'm not dripping wet in front of the entire Reverie," she bit out.

"I'll be waiting," he said shortly.

She muttered curses under her breath and slammed the divider shut between the bath and her dressing alcove. Behind her, the steam still curled softly in the air.

As she reached for a second towel and tried to shake the chill, he'd brought in with him, she couldn't stop thinking about how rare it was to feel cleansed, not just on her skin, but in her *bones*.

Piper dried off quickly, rubbing the towel down her arms, over her collarbone, then twisting it around her hair. The air was cooler, but the scent of lavender clung to her skin. For a moment, she lingered in its warmth, letting the chill of the stone floor seep only halfway into her bones before dressing in silence.

The dress laid out for her was nothing like the ones back at Olympus House—no worn knits or patched sleeves. The gown that Colik must have moved from her bed to over the divider was something conjured from a dream.

She slipped into it slowly, first drawing the long folds over her shoulders, then fastening the chains that draped delicately across her arms. The bodice hugged her form in a silver-blue silk, cinched with silver clasps at her waist, the jewels threaded like constellations. Lace drifted down her arms, while the long train of the dress spilled to the ground in more white feathers.

When she turned, she caught her reflection in the mirror. Her skin wasn't pale with cold. Her cheeks were pink from the heat, and her collarbone was kissed with lavender oil. Her damp hair had curled into loose waves around her face. She didn't look like a girl who lived in the background of other people's stories or the girl from Olympus House anymore. It took a few meals with the Royalds and a few baths in the basin, but she looked like someone who belonged here.

For a moment, she looked like a Dreamer.

That realization—that terrifying flicker of *maybe this all could be true*—unsettled her more than Colik barging in uninvited. She turned away before the thought could settle.

Colik was still standing outside the divider when she emerged, arms crossed, his jaw set in that unreadable way he did when trying too hard not to look interested. Or guilty. His eyes flicked briefly from her face to her dress, then back to her face—and stayed there.

"Ready?" he asked, but his voice didn't carry its usual edge.

She moved past him, slow and deliberate. "Is this the part where I ask if you're going to try to kill me?"

Colik's smile faltered as he fell in step with her. "If I wanted to kill you, Piper, I wouldn't be so afraid to touch you."

That silenced her.

Instead of leading her down a familiar wing, his hand brushed against her arm, guiding her toward a side passage she hadn't noticed before. The air shifted as they entered it. Much cooler and carrying the scent of stone and something faintly wild, the corridor opened into a wing unlike any Piper had seen—a waterfall.

It spilled down the cliffside in a white cascade, while mist swept through the open arches in silver veils, clinging to her skin. Piper stopped, breath catching in her throat. She hadn't even known the Citadel sat upon such a cliff. It always looked to be floating along a wave of clouds.

Colik lingered beside her, though he did not look at the falls. "We are only allowed in this wing for the Constellation Ball," he said softly, his voice drowning out by the waters roar. "It's easy to forget what all the Citadel hides."

The marble beneath them gleamed like polished ice, streaked with veins of gold that caught the slight crimson glow of the Blood Moon beyond the arches.

She reached for the railing, fingers brushing wet stone, eyes wide as they walked. Clusters of black roses spilled over it. Is that—

Piper held in a gasp. She wanted to grab one—to follow

through with her deal with Colik—but with how he was eyeing her, grabbing a black rose was out of the question.

Her fingers grazed the roses, and Colik moved with her, his stride unhurried, though whatever weight he carried made the space between them tense. Lanterns high on the archways burned with pale white fire, the light striking his sharp features and, for a fleeting moment, softening them.

At last, the path curved, revealing two immense doors. Twin serpents coiled up their edges, masked in ivy, moss, and decadent greenery. It looked like the entrance to the Greycene.

"Where are we?"

"The Orph Ballroom." Colik's voice carried a quiet intimacy that made her stomach tighten as he pressed his hand against the door.

Piper's eyes lingered on the snakes. Their carved heads rose from the shadows. Emerald eyes fixed in an unblinking stare that followed her no matter how she turned. She wondered if those eyes could come alive and shape themselves into some kind of monster waiting to strike.

A chill slipped through her. She thought of the emerald-eyed Shade. Then another memory rushed in. The dream she told Morry with snakes curling around her arms. Their bodies tightening. Eyes like mirrors that watched her from every angle. Eyes that never let her go.

For a heartbeat she went still. It felt too familiar, as if she had been here before with the same green eyes waiting for her to look back.

A flicker of fear gripped her. Were her dreams warnings? Or were they moments yet to come, bleeding ahead of themselves until she was forced to live them twice—once asleep and once awake?

Colik pushed the door open, and Piper slipped past the serpents, their stares burning at her back.

Inside, she stopped, breath caught in her throat. She

thought she could no longer be surprised by anything this world offered her, and yet the grandeur of the room left her stunned.

It was all gold. Light poured down in streams from above, striking the gilded floor so it gleamed like glass, threaded with veins of gold that curved into intricate patterns. All around, sheer draperies cascaded from the ceiling, falling in endless waves that shimmered as though spun from sun rays.

It was the orbs that caught her breath. Dozens—*no*, hundreds—of white spheres hovered in the air, glimmering faintly as they floated between the folds of the fabric. They swayed with the current of unseen air, glowing like new moons adrift in an ocean of crimson-white light.

A shiver ran through her. For a moment, it looked like what the Room of Lockes might have once looked before it became a prison for the Silver Children. It was achingly beautiful, but the beauty felt edged with what Blaze had called remembrance—with something lost. As if the room itself remembered what dreams had been before the gods had bound an entire age in cages.

"Familiar?"

Colik studied her. She nodded.

"It is the only room in the Citadel that is gilded," he said. "Both the ages-old Elphiates Citadel and the Reverie Citadel were granted a single chamber, built as a remembrance of the world before the Silver Age—a time when everything was still gilded and awake. It stood as their way of honoring what once was."

He looked around the glowing walls. "The Elphiates was not always like what you saw. Once, every part of the Dreamworld had color and shine and life. These rooms were meant to remind us of that, so the ages would never be forgotten."

Colik moved a step ahead, his presence steady, but Piper could not stop herself from pausing in the doorway, staring upward as though she might catch one of the orbs falling into her hands.

With the snake dream still haunting her, Piper looked at the cruel echo hidden in such beauty. Could grief and beauty be the same thing?

The sparkling white drapes spilled down the walls, concealing windows, or something she could not see. Along the edges, great arches curved upward like the trunks of gold-plated trees, their branches shielding the dome from the constellation sky above. Through the curtains of fabric, the Blood Moon's light seeped in, staining the gilded glow with a reddish hue.

"This is where the Constellation Ball will be held," Colik said, his voice quieter. "I thought you'd like to see it before all the chaos."

Piper nodded, caught off guard by the gentleness in his gesture. There was something in his eyes, as if he were at war with himself. As if he were unsure of what to say, how close he should stand, or what his next move ought to be. The look he gave her was torn between restraint and impulse.

"What is the purpose of the Constellation Ball, really?"

For a long moment, he said nothing, the orbs hanging low, glowing like pale apples suspended in a dream. At last, he exhaled. "The Constellation Ball isn't only a celebration. It is remembrance. It honors the dreamers freed from the gods' control. Not all were so fortunate."

She knew he meant the Silver Children. "Is that why you didn't want me near Ha—the Silver Child?"

His gaze lifted toward the glowing spheres. "The Silver Children were punished because they were too wild and uncontrollable. They wanted to be like the gods themselves. Zeus ended the ages where gods and humans could live as one and bound the humans who once lived immortally in their dreams away."

Piper's chest tightened. "Punished…for daring to be more than what they were? What did the Shades mean by *balance*."

He shook his head, disappointment softening the edges of his eyes.

"The Shades are the closest thing we have left to the Silver Children. Yes, the Scirges carry their bloodline, but the Shades… they are what the Silver Ones would have become."

Piper felt the words settle in her chest like a stone dropped into deep water.

Nature versus nurture—she knew that battle too well. An orphan born from someone who hadn't wanted her, raised in a world that hadn't quite wanted her either. She had always felt like a mistake stitched into the wrong life.

Here the rules felt different. Maybe a world she wasn't born into could still choose her. Maybe the Reverie, strange, dangerous and full of dreams and chaos, could nurture what the waking world had never cared to see. Maybe belonging didn't start with blood at all.

He leaned in, his voice dropping to a warning, "The Shades see human fears. Think about it—to know a human, why ask them what they dream if you know what they fear?"

She was speechless. He was right. She would be more scared for him, or anyone to know what she feared over what she dreamed.

When she met his eyes again, she saw the flicker of something unguarded, an intensity that felt dangerously close to longing. At once it shifted, shuttered, leaving only the sharp mask again.

His steps grew restless, his presence charged, as though he wasn't sure whether he wanted to keep her close or push her away.

"One more thing, then I'll leave you be," he added, lifting a finger to silence any protest. She gave another small nod, a smile tugging at her lips despite herself.

Colik guided her across the room until they arrived at a

grand piano, its polished ebony surface glistening in the dappled light. Perched atop the keys was a majestic owl, its feathers shimmering with various colors of black, grey and steel silver. Its eyes were an orb of red and orange. It was like Piper was looking into the sun.

He nodded at the owl, and with a graceful flourish of its wings, the owl began to play, its talons gliding over the keys with an otherworldly finesse.

"It is called *One to One Night.* A song of Nyx." Colik whispered as the first notes shimmered through the air. He acted completely normal about an owl playing a piano. "A dark lullaby and older than creation."

Before she could question it, he stepped to her side. The nearness of him tightened her chest, and he extended a hand. "Dance with me."

Piper's eyes shot to his. Her first instinct was to pull back. Part of her still feared making the same mistakes, falling into the same gravity that drew her toward him. Yet something in his face stopped her. His eyes held a conflict she could feel more than see, as if two halves of him were fighting for the right to speak. There was desperation in the small, hopeful curve of his smile, like a plea he was too proud to voice.

She didn't know if she should trust him. Maybe she was foolish to even try. She hoped she could learn again, and maybe the first step was choosing to believe him for one breath longer.

Slowly, she placed her hand in his.

He drew her into the heart of the ballroom. His palm was warm, steadying her even as the melody trembled through the air in minor keys filled with longing. As they moved, the room awakened. The owl's fiery eyes closed as it played, its feathers shifting shades of grey. Each note hovered before them like droplets of starlight, bright for a heartbeat, then fading into the dark between them.

Colik bent closer, his voice a breath at her ear. "There is

something you should know. At the Constellation Ball, there is a Reverie Law. A Dreamer must end the night with the one they are most bound to."

Piper blinked up at him, pulse quickening. "End the nig—"

"The last dance," He interrupted, as if catching on to what he said. What she thought he meant. "If an R-Law is broken," he murmured, tightening his hold as the music continued, "anyone in the Dreamworld can call upon Solari. She is the Severer of Dream Strands. Her distaff can cut the tether of a Dreamer, or of you. A single strike, and you would become dreamless."

"Dreamless…" Like what Blaze threatened the Shades with. "What does it mean to be—"

Colik spun her, his hand at her waist warm enough to steady her when her steps wanted to falter. She wasn't a good dancer. She knew it in the uneven catch of her feet and the small hesitations she could not hide. Yet he moved with such certainty that he almost hid her mistakes, guiding her just enough to make her believe she was gliding.

Almost.

Because he kept slipping out of reach. One moment he pulled her close, his palm firm at her back, the heat of him sinking into her skin. The next, he eased away, forcing her to follow, making her chase the space he created. It felt like a game he didn't realize he was playing. A quiet push and pull that left her breath short and her heart uncertain.

Cat and mouse. Near then far. Warm then cold. A dance that wanted to be intimate but refused to settle into comfort.

The world blurred around them. The orbs. The owl's low song. The blood-red glow that bled through the drapes. What filled her instead was him. His breath at her hair. His heartbeat under her hand. The way his fingers tightened for a single moment as if he couldn't help it. As if something in him cracked before he pushed her away again.

The feeling with him was always like this. Intense. Pulling. Never simple.

Part of her wanted to fall into it again, wanted to let herself be foolish enough to hope she could trust him the way she once had. She knew how stories like this ended. Princesses who fell too hard always paid the highest price. They always had, but dancing with a prince did not make her a princess, if he did not choose her.

Still, the invisible pull between them wound tighter. She felt it coil under her ribs, binding her to him in a way she did not choose and could not break. Maybe it was the sandtie. Maybe it was the kiss in the Broken Woods. Maybe it was something older that neither of them had words for yet.

His eyes found hers, raw with something he fought to hide. Piper did not pull away. "We almost broke a law already," she whispered, remembering the Shades, remembering the danger, feeling the truth settle between them like a held breath neither dared release.

"With the kiss…if I hadn't stopped myself." His voice hardened, but the edge was brittle, a shield against what flickered in his eyes. "We cannot risk it again," he said, lower, as though the walls themselves might overhear. "Do you understand?"

Piper gave an unsteady nod. Her eyes moved away from his, over his shoulder, and to the owl. The owl's sun-lit eyes closed momentarily as it pressed the keys carefully, each claw striking a note with surprising grace. Its melody wandered like a meandering river, carried by a haunting flute-like tone, the owl's head tilting rhythmically as it played.

Her eyes moved back to his. "So, I have to dance with you because I am tied to you?" she wondered out loud. "Because of the sandtie? Because of the kiss in the Broken Woods?"

He drew her closer, his composure slipping for a heartbeat, like he wanted more than the dance. More than the R-Laws would permit. The mask slid back into place.

His steps grew strained, restless, as though he no longer trusted himself in her orbit.

"No," Colik said, his voice steady. "Because *I am* bound to you."

He didn't clarify what the *no* referred to—whether he was denying the sandtie, the kiss, or both—and Piper was too shaken to ask.

The owl struck one final sound like the chime of a distant bell. Sparkles of golden-blueish light filtered through the beams above, casting a warm and radiant glow around them. In that rare moment, everything stood still. As the last notes of the melody faded, all that remained was the lingering echo of the enchanting lullaby of Nyx.

In that fragile space between the last note and the stillness that bound them, Piper wondered if she was dancing with a fallen angel, or with the boy still fighting not to let her fall.

"There's one last thing I want to show you," Colik said, with a short smile, and backed away from her. Piper raised an eyebrow. "I thought this was the last surprise."

"It is, I am just not done showing you it."

He gave a shrug, then led her toward the sparkling drapes cascading along the ballroom wall. With one motion, he drew them aside, revealing floor-to-ceiling windows and a door framed in golden metal.

"*This,*" Colik said, stepping aside for her to get the full view, "is the best part."

Beyond lay the open Dreamworld, its sky unfurling in a constellation cloud that looked more like the raw fabric of the heavens than weather. Piper had seen constellations drifting through the Citadel's grounds, but here they floated higher, suspended among the clouds, as though the stars had descended just enough to breathe on her.

This was the feeling she loved above all. The one that made her believe this truly was a world stitched from dreams. The air was not sharp enough to make her shiver, but crisp, alive and the breath of a world in motion. It was endless, lucid, and impossibly clear. Each star shimmered as though scattered dust played chase with starlight, their light and particles woven into the Blood Moon's orbit. A rush of cool, unsympathetic air swept past them as he pushed the door open. It reminded her of Dublin, of stepping outside when the first frost lingered over the city, hinting that summer was ending and autumn was just beginning.

"Can you give me something about the weather or seasons here?" Piper whispered, feeling his warmth as he stood beside her, close—too close. His presence pressed against hers as he braced his arms on either side of her waist against the rail. The gesture startled her. It was gentle, human-like. The stillness of it shuddered.

"Seasons change, Piper. In the beginning, Demeter shaped only two: spring and autumn. Then Hades took Persephone to the Underworld, and Demeter's grief created winter in the mortal world. Here, in the Dreamworld, that balance broke. Winter became the only season we have. Humans kept four, but the Reverie did not. Time thinned, then stopped, and with it the shifting of colors and life. What you see among the constellation clouds will stay exactly as it is. Unless chaos rises…unless darkness takes everything whole."

Piper said nothing. The words settled in her like falling snow, soft but heavy. Time standing still. A world caught in winter. She understood it too well. She knew the silence winter carried, the way everything held its breath, frozen between moments.

It stirred something buried deep inside her, something she never named. The meaning of white. The stillness in a window she once looked out of, watching the world from behind cold glass.

A small shiver ran through her. She felt paused between who she was and who she was meant to become, waiting for something inside her to finally thaw.

He leaned on the railing, eyes lifting to the sky. "Beautiful," he breathed.

Piper nodded, unsure whether he meant the heavens or something else. When she glanced at him, she caught him looking at her instead. Her breath snagged, and she turned quickly back to the constellation cloud.

"The Blood Moon," she whispered. "Why is it red?"

"Because it is bleeding," he said, his voice hoarser than it had just been. "Because the line between remembrance and dreaming is thin here. The Blood Moon is what protects Dreamers from the things we try to forget."

"Forget what?"

His gaze never left hers. "That nothing in the Reverie is real. Not dreams. Not loyalty. Not love."

"Colik…"

The space between them collapsed, and for a moment their lips hovered a breath apart. The very thing she had been waiting for since the Broken Woods, ignited. Colik leaned in, his forehead brushing hers, their mouths so close she could feel the shape of his next breath.

For a heartbeat, it felt inevitable. For a heartbeat, she thought he might choose her.

Then he froze.

A shudder went through him, and he tore himself back as if burned, eyes wide with something like horror at what he had almost done. His shoulders locked, his jaw snapped tight, and the look that overtook him was the storm Piper had feared. The one she had spoken of without realizing he'd been listening.

"You don't understand," he said, voice low and cracking. "You think this"—he gestured between them— "is some story. Some fairy tale where the beast becomes the prince because you believe hard enough. Because of one kiss."

Piper flinched.

He didn't stop. "Duty comes before love here. Always.

CAROLINE LEE

Gods lust. They hunger. They take, but they do not love." His multi-colored eyes hardened. "And the Dreamers they formed aren't any different. We were shaped from their flaws, not their mercy."

Her chest ached. "Colik, I—"

"No." He stepped back from her, voice rising. "You think I'm choosing you? You think this is real? I nearly kissed you out of instinct, not want. Duty pulls stronger than desire in the Reverie. Even when it feels like both."

The words shattered something inside her.

"I let you think it meant more," he said, softer. Crueler. "That was my mistake."

"So, it was nothing?" She couldn't believe what she was hearing. And then again, she could. He wasn't a real Royald. He was a child dressed up as one.

"It was never meant to be anything," he said. "This isn't a love story. Not for you. Not for me."

She shook her head, desperate. "The way you looked at me…the way you've been acting—"

"That was necessity. Dust answers dust. When my beast chose you, I used your tie. That is all."

"Dray…" she whispered. "I told you I didn't know—"

"You didn't ask." His voice cracked into a snarl. "You broke its loyalty to me without thinking! When Dray left me, when my creature stopped responding, do you know what that did? It split my dust. It hollowed me." He stepped close enough that she felt the heat of his anger. "It undid me, Piper."

Tears pressed behind her eyes. "I didn't mean—"

"That is the curse of humans here. You never know. You just act and hope the dream bends for you." His tone sliced the air. "You walked into our world and started pulling at every strand you touched. You—*human*— are the chaos we all feared."

Her breath trembled. "You said you tied me to keep me from disappearing."

"Yes," he said, voice suddenly flat. "I should have let you go."

She stumbled back, gripping the railing.

"I saved you," he went on, quieter. "Not because of you, but because someone had to maintain balance. Someone had to handle the stray human strand. Finding you was duty, Piper. Nothing else."

The Blood Moon glowed like a wound above them. She couldn't move back any further, but she felt the air tighten around them, suffocating her.

"Then why did it feel real?"

He looked at her for a long, unforgiving moment. "Because dreams don't lie," he said. "They will let you lie to yourself."

"Colik..." she whispered, shaking. "You're saying this because you're afraid of how you feel."

"No." His eyes closed once, slowly, like he was choosing cruelty over weakness. "I'm waking you up."

He turned toward the door. "Enjoy the stars while you still believe in them. They're prettier that way."

Then he left her, boots striking stone with a cold, final rhythm. The gold-plated door to the ballroom shut behind him with a dull, deliberate thud.

Piper remained frozen on the balcony, the Blood Moon pulsing overhead like a bleeding heart.

How could a dream twist into a nightmare in a blink of an eye?

CHAPTER TWENTY-SIX
THE FRAY

Piper left the Orph Ballroom like someone waking from a too-long nightmare, only to find herself in another. Her thoughts chased themselves in fast, sharp circles.

Colik was a monster. A true beast of a Dreamer.

Her chest tightened with each breath, lungs constricting like she'd swallowed smoke. Her hands wouldn't stop shaking. That wasn't just fury. It was hurt.

She'd barely held herself together as she slipped out, her breath shallow, legs moving on instinct. The Citadel's marble wings stretched before her like a labyrinth with hollowed walls, arching ceilings, and cold silence.

She didn't know where she was going, only that she had to keep moving. She had to put space between herself and the truth of what Colik had just said. Her footsteps echoed too loudly against the floor, a sharp tap-tap-tap that bounced off the stone walls and returned distorted, as if someone else were walking beside her, but no one was. She was alone.

So alone.

The tears came.

She stumbled down a stairwell she didn't remember,

deeper into some quiet wing lined with closed doors and flickering chandeliers. The white light blurred as she blinked and blinked again, but it couldn't stop the ache in her throat. How many damn wings were there?

She wanted to go home.

The thought came fast. It was uninvited but real. She wanted her old room at Olympus House, Penelope's hard but caring gaze and Morry's smile. She wanted chipped mugs, rain tapping the windows, and the ache of being ordinary.

She wanted anything but this. Because this Dreamworld was all a lie. It didn't want her. It never had, and the boy who made her believe she could find a place in it had just wished she'd never come at all.

That was the part she didn't know how to swallow. Colik was never supposed to matter. Not like this. Yet here she was, shaking in some endless wing in a dream castle not meant for her, unraveling alone.

Because of *a boy*. A stupid, shattered, infuriating boy who felt too much so he chose to walk away. Pretending to have never cared.

Piper passed beneath the towering stained-glass windows, each one burning with its own inner light, as if the memories trapped within them refused to dim.

The first window glowed gold, where a king sat upon a throne of wheat and starlight while small figures—probably humans— moved around him. A halo of sun-shards circled his hcad.

The next shimmered silver, pale as a newborn moon. Children made of light stood at the edge of a vast room, threads spilling from their fingers. A dark goddess hovered behind them, her shadow curling around them.

The third window blazed in bronze and ember tones, depicting an age of war. Warriors clashed in a burning field, spears rising toward a sky split with lightning. At the center, a lone figure—someone who reminded her of Colik, though she couldn't say why—drove a blade through a giant of smoke.

She slowed at the fourth, bound in deep amethyst and iron blue. A warrior lifted the severed head of a serpent-witch, another walked a labyrinth of bone, and a musician reached for his love across a curtain of glass, their fingertips forever an inch apart.

The last window flickered in blackened crystal. A void swallowed the constellations as gods dragged their wounded children away from the collapsing sky. A crowned figure stood at the edge of the abyss, something that looked like power blazing through a storm of shadows.

Their eyes glittered as if turning to watch her pass.

She dropped her gaze and quickened her pace.

Corner after corner bled into one another, the glasswork slowly peeling away. The wing grew narrower, the ceilings sank lower with every turn, and the chandeliers overhead went from radiant blue flames to a dimming sickly blue, casting shadows that trembled and lengthened along the walls.

The marble underfoot dulled, then darkened, until it transformed completely to a black stone veined with red. The air dropped to a chill, and then—whispers.

They came not as voices, but as strands of sound, as if someone had plucked a harp made of string and silence. Each note brushed against her skin, pulling at her memories like strands unraveling in the dark.

The wall of the Citadel split open, revealing a staircase that grew out of the cliffside itself. Its railings tangled with ivy and ghostly lights that winked and vanished. The sound of rushing water rumbled nearby, though the waterfall itself was nowhere to be seen. She had slipped behind it, into the hidden hollow of its roar.

Piper suddenly realized that this was no ordinary part of the Citadel. Her limbs moved without asking, and she placed a foot on the first step, then the next, climbing upward through a tower that didn't seem like it should exist.

At the top, a single door waited, thick in ivory, cold to the touch. The door opened without resistance, and Piper stepped through before she could change her mind.

What lay beyond the door was nothing she expected. From above, enormous spheres of woven lattice hung, exhaling sparks that drifted down like stardust, vanishing the moment they brushed the ground. Everywhere here was the same but different. If that made sense at all.

It wasn't just light. Strands—thin, and glimmering—wove themselves across the chamber, stretching from column to column, drifting through the air, suspended as if time itself had frozen mid-motion. Some strands pulsed faintly with colors of crimson, gold, and silver. Others frayed at the ends, threatening to unravel. It looked like a ball of yarn magically flung across a room, and the loose strands were seared into the vibrating ground.

Was that the frequency Patrick talked about?

She stepped forward, the floor beneath her gleaming like polished ruby, catching the glow of every trembling strand.

Then, a single red strand slipped from the tangle above and drifted down before her face. Something deep in her bones screamed at her not to touch it, with the same primal warning that whispers *don't press the red button*. Her hand rose anyway, quivering, compelled by a need she couldn't name. Her fingertip brushed the strand.

At once, the chamber dissolved.

Before her eyes shimmered a vision, clear as sunlight on glass:

Ciara and Deeno crouched on the cracked sidewalk outside the rust-stained gates of Olympus House. Chalk dust covered their hands, and the pavement was a messy masterpiece of pink stars, yellow circles and something that might've been a blue dragon if you used your imagination.

"It's Piper," Ciara announced proudly, tapping the chest of two chalk figures with white hair. "And the Silver Girl from her dream. They are going to have a fight, and Piper is going to explode the sky with stars."

Deeno snorted. "Stars are yellow, Ciara. Not pink." He dragged a stick of black chalk across the concrete, sketching a crooked, shaded figure beside the two with white hair.

"What's that supposed to be?" Ciara asked, smudging one of his lines with her sleeve.

"The monster that stands at the end of my bed at night," Deeno said dramatically. "Doesn't ever move though, just watches." He colored two big red eyes over the black chalk. "Piper is gonna save me. She saves everyone here, obviously."

Ciara rolled her eyes. "Right, because she totally left to fight monsters in the dark. She is too light for that. She will light up the sky!"

She began dotting little chalk stars around one of the girl's head. "She will win the fight."

Piper's throat tightened. She wanted to laugh—they were ridiculous —but their words landed heavier than they should have. It wasn't that they didn't just believe her stories, but they acted like they knew she was gone.

She stared at the shadow Deeno had drawn. Something about the crooked arms and bent head with red eyes made her lean closer, uneasy curiosity prickling her skin.

It hit her.

A sharp stitch ripped through her side, sudden and brutal, as if the chalk figure had reached out and stabbed her with its own outline. She gasped, clutching her ribs. The pain laced deeper, binding her to what she'd just seen, like the drawing itself remembered—

The vision shattered. The children vanished. Only the glowing red strand remained, quivering in her hand, before it frayed and dissolved into ash.

Half-grateful and half-terrified of what she had just seen, Piper trembled at the sudden chain reaction she had set loose. It felt like watching a long, fragile line of dominos fall, each one tipping the next faster than she could breathe.

Strand and strand fell, until a statue crashed down, massive and towering, its stone skin split by streaks of burning light that bled through the fractures of red strands. It looked like a god, every muscle carved with the weight of his burden as it held something on its shoulders: a circular vault, its surface etched with runed veins that pulsed of molten gold. The vault turned slowly in his grasp, its surface shifting as though it were not made of moments pressed into shape.

The seams were sealed with amber wax, and a red strand coiled around it like a thorned serpent guarding its own skin. A golden spiral looped at the top, and in the center of the lid, a single bronze eye lay closed, yet still watching.

The statue's gaze was steady and unyielding, daring her forward, like an unspoken welcome.

This was no vault meant to be opened.

Piper didn't lift the lid. Instead, her fingers traced the looped letters carved into its surface. The symbols shivered beneath her touch, glowing faintly, as she read the age-old encryption:

"Break the seal and the Silver awakens.
Loose the strand and the ages fall.
Open the Vault and the gods unmake themselves."

As the last syllable left her lips, the chamber trembled, and *she* appeared. Her form was silver and not quite solid, her edges unraveled and reknitted with every breath. A strand, blood-red and glowing, looped from her wrist, disappearing into the mirrored-laced walls like it was tied to something far, far away.

It was the Silver Girl. The *Silver Child*— Hazel.

Piper stood frozen, every part of her bracing for something she couldn't name. She didn't understand. Hazel was supposed to be locked away, unreachable. Sealed in the Room of Lockes.

Yet, she was here. Not just a flicker or echo.

But here.

"We did it!" Hazel breathed, her voice trembling with something that was part wonder and part madness. Her silver eyes devoured Piper's face, wide with manic joy, like she expected Piper to smile back and rejoice.

As if this had been a prize for them both.

"I—" Piper's throat choked into silence. Hazel began to clap, her hands jerking with unnatural rhythm, the strand shackled to her wrist shuddering with every flicker of movement.

It was then that Piper understood—Hazel didn't expect to be freed from the Room of Lockes. She wanted Piper, here. Why?

"You helped me get inside the Fray," Hazel said, her voice more thought than sound, threaded into Piper's very mind. Piper looked around. *This* was the Fray…

Oh, shit.

"You can finish it. Please. Open Pandora's Vault. Cut my strand. End the gods' chains on us. Free me. I can free all the Silver Children."

Piper staggered back a step. "No… I can't. You tricked me."

Hazel's head snapped, her silver hair sparking, her form flickering like a faulty star about to collapse.

"No," she hissed, though the sound came wrapped in a

smile. "Not tricking. *Guiding.* I had to touch you first. That was the beginning. This—" she gestured toward the vault glowing and pulsing between them, its surface leaking strands like smoke from a burning cage— "this is the end. This is how the Silver Age rises again. How humans take back their dreams. Not borrowed. Not broken. Immortal."

Piper's breath stuttered. Her head shook violently. "I don't even know what this is. *Pandora's Vault?* Like the myth?"

Deep inside, she did know. She felt it in her ribs, in the phantom stitch in her side, and in the scars of every dream she had walked through. Everything in the Reverie bled from the myths—the Fray, the gods and the Royalds. Even the petaled wine she had swallowed. Of course, the gods would lock the Silver Children in something that could only be undone by human hands.

Horror filled her features, and her chest tightened.

What had she done?

Hazel's form shimmered, translucent, and she leaned close though her body never moved.

"You *do* know. You feel it. That strand you're afraid to touch belongs to you. Pandora's Vault?" Her smile fractured into a soft rage. "That is the real cage. Our punishment was not in the Room of Lockes, but the separation of what ties us to this world. You have the power to undo it. You were always meant to."

Piper's eyes flicked to Pandora's Vault. Its surface shook. "No." Her voice cracked. "This isn't about you. This isn't about the gods. All this time...you've been using me."

Hazel's expression shifted from surprise to sorrow, then to something cruel. "Isn't that what they did to me?" she asked softly. "The gods used me, then sealed me away and called it mercy. This world abandoned me, but you—" She pointed, her arm trembling as a pulse of silver surged through the floor beneath her feet. "You could have opened it."

Piper's heart pounded. "This isn't just about freeing *you*. If this is Pandora's Vault, what else is inside?"

Hazel's voice snapped, brittle and sharp. "You think not opening it is saving me?" Her eyes flashed. "You're damning us both."

Snap. A strand behind her cracked like lightning.

Hazel flinched, her body flickering violently. Piper saw Hazel fraying, her form barely tying to the Fray's reality.

Pain twisted in Hazels eyes, like a child about to throw a temper tantrum. "No matter," she hissed. "I still have the sandtie."

Piper's stomach lurched.

Hazel's smile sharpened with a terrible calm.

"If you won't do it on your own…" She lifted her hand, and from her fingers unraveled a red strand, thin as breath, but sharp as a blade. Piper froze as it flickered in the air and then *latched* to her, hooking into her wrist, her ribs, and her throat. She gasped, clutching at her side, but the string only multiplied, weaving around her body in quick, deft strokes, binding her like a puppet caught on invisible wires.

Piper tried to pull away, but her limbs betrayed her, jerking forward under Hazel's control. Her own hands lifted against her will, trembling but unyielding.

"No," Piper rasped. "Stop—stop this!"

Hazel's silver eyes blazed. "You were meant to open it. If your will hesitates, then your body will obey."

The strings tightened, pulling Piper step by step toward Pandora's Vault. It wasn't painful, but lack of control held a pain of its own. Her fingers stretched toward the lid. The symbols etched on its surface glowed brighter with every inch, pulsing in rhythm with her heart, each beat screaming against her.

Hazel's voice wrapped around her like silk and chains all at once.

"Open it, Piper. Free us. Free me. Let the Silver Children dream again."

Her soul clawed against it. Her body didn't listen.

Hazel wove faster, the strands binding Piper's fingers around the seal, guiding her hand to the red cord coiled at its center. The vault's symbols flared white as her skin made contact, but nothing happened. The wax held. The seal held. The vault recognized the touch and found it wanting.

Hazel felt it too. A flicker of frustration crossed her silver features.

"Not touch," she murmured, almost to herself. Then her eyes sharpened. "Blood."

Before Piper could pull back, Hazel's strand coiled tight around her finger and *bit*—a precise, cold sting, so quick she gasped more from shock than pain. A single bead of red welled up at the tip of her finger. Silver and mortal both. The scar on her thumb pulsed in recognition, as though it had been waiting for exactly this.

"No—" Piper choked.

Hazel pressed her hand down.

The moment blood touched the seal, the vault *knew* her.

The aged wax did not melt. It *withdrew*, pulling back from the blood like something alive and afraid, the symbols blazing so bright Piper had to turn her face away. The red cord unraveled on its own, strand by strand, as though the vault itself was opening in answer to what it recognized in her veins rather than anything Hazel had forced.

That was worse. Far worse.

"No!" Piper screamed, but it was already done.

Pandora's Vault sighed open, and the chamber erupted. A wind burst from the pedestal, hot and electric.

The walls rattled. Hundreds of strands tore free in a furious storm, flaring outward like lashes of lightning. With them came visions—dreamed memories:

A mother set her child adrift on a river and watched him vanish.

A firefighter died in the flames trying to save a family.
A boy cried alone on a doorstep in the rain.
Two lovers' hands fell away at the same moment.
A man stared at a book, chasing a message he'd never solve.

Each dream cracked Piper open from the inside, their weight pressing against her ribs. These weren't hers, but the collective longings, fears, and hopes of humankind, loosened into the air like wild stars.

Hazel laced.

Piper stumbled toward the Silver Child, her hand lifted high, a swar now in her grip—*where had it come from?* — glinting with molten metal. Her other hand forcefully grabbed the red strand tied to Hazel's wrist.

One snip. That's all it would take.

Hazel watched her, eyes wide and bright with hope despite controlling Piper against her will. "Please," she whispered tenderly. "Please. I've been in the Room of Lockes too long. I don't want to *forget* who I am."

Piper's grip tightened, tears flooding her eyes. Just as she raised the blade—

BANG.

A slam echoed through the chamber, thunderous, like a new dream breaking open. Fog spilled from the corners, soft and gold tinged.

From it stepped Lulu.

Only, it wasn't quite her. She shimmered like an illusion. For a breath, she looked like Penelope. Then like Colik. Then, suddenly, like Zeus himself, making Hazel stumble back, her grip on Piper's hand breaking.

Lulu's face kept shifting, flickering through illusions Piper couldn't name, each one sharper, and uncanny. Yet beneath them all, the steady glow of Lulu's presence remained. It was constant, watching, and terribly awake.

"Lulu…" Piper whispered, not sure if she was really seeing the Royald or the vision she wore.

Lulu smiled faintly, a dream pressed into a mouth. "Illusions aren't lies, Piper. They're truths wearing different shapes."

She raised a finger, and the chamber unraveled into a field of poppies beneath a midnight sun. Then into a wing of endless doors, all whispering. Then into a shoreline where the stars bent low, murmuring secrets into the tide. Reality buckled repeatedly, fractal and weightless.

Hazel reeled, her silver, translucent form glitching and trembling. "Stop it! You're twisting the strand—"

"No," Lulu said sternly. "I'm showing it a world without you."

Lulu opened her palm, and the illusions closed in, like sleep. Hazel's body flickered, unraveling into silver strands. Her scream bent sideways, warping into silence, until her form collapsed altogether.

Free at last, Piper dropped to her knees, gasping, tears streaking her face. Her hands shook as though she still wielded a swar, though no blade was there.

Lulu waited until the last flicker of Hazel was gone before stepping from fog. Her eyes were no longer shifting but steady autumn daggers.

"Piper...whatever tie the Silver Child had to you...it's more than strange." Her voice lowered, reluctant. "It is not normal."

Why did every keep telling her that but in a dumb cryptic way?

She knelt beside Piper with a kind of tired gentleness, her hand steadying Piper's trembling shoulder.

"I had to wait," she said softer. "Hazel's hold on you was too strong. If I'd come a moment before, she would've used me against you. I needed her distracted."

Piper's lips parted, but no words came. She clutched at her side, still feeling the phantom sting of Hazel's puppetry.

Lulu's gaze lingered on Pandora's Vault, still humming with faint strands.

"The Fray isn't a machine, Piper. It's a presence. A place where dreamers are born, not of flesh, but of strand. The gods wove fates here, for dreams themselves."

Piper's breath hitched. "Hazel... She said I could free her."

"Yes," Lulu whispered, sorrow glinting in her autumn eyes. "She didn't only want to free herself. She wanted to unseal Pandora's Vault. To spill out the unwrought dreams. The ones never anchored into human lives. She believed if they were freed, humans could live forever in the Reverie, dreaming immortally, never waking as they did in the Silver Age."

Piper staggered back, her face pale. "I—"

"You didn't know," Lulu interrupted gently. "Hazel tied herself to you in the Room of Lockes. She used you as a tether, waiting for the moment you were weak enough to stumble into the Fray."

Silence pressed between them. Piper stared at her hands as though they were guilty, traitors of her own body. Lulu reached out, covering them with her own.

Weak. Was that all she was ever going to be?

"Weak enough?" Piper whispered.

Lulu's gaze softened, but her words were steady. Piper had never seen this side of her before. *I didn't know she was capable of a motherly side. One that* cared *for her. Or at least protected her.*

"You are still human, Piper, no matter how much you try to be something else. Humans, when their emotions become too heavy, always reach for what feels familiar. The Fray is that place. It's where dreams themselves are born, where they braid into human dust. To someone like you, it will always call when you feel lost."

There was another stretch of silence.

Finally, Piper stood slowly, unsteady on her legs. "I didn't mean to," she whispered, voice breaking.

"I know," Lulu said, rising beside her.

There was a long silence. Piper waited, half hoping Lulu would keep talking, and half fearing what else she might say. Lulu stared out at the floating red strands, her expression unreadable.

When she still didn't speak, Piper's voice broke the quiet. "Why did you save me?"

"Do you want the truth?" Lulu asked. Her voice thinned, and Piper felt the slightest urge to step back. She shook her head anyway, even though she was terrified to hear it.

"Besides my role to guard the Fray," Lulu said slowly, "I was trying to correct a mistake I made once before."

"Mistake?" Piper whispered.

Lulu's expression shifted, the warmth draining from her eyes until a deep, unreadable darkness remained. "Don't think this is the end of it, Piper. Hazel wasn't the only one who saw something in you. The Fray saw it first. It reached for you. It recognized you." Her breath trembled. "What the Fray recognizes... it does not let go of."

Piper's pulse stuttered.

Piper's knees buckled, but she stayed standing. "Then why am I still here? Why didn't she win?"

"Because I came when I did. Because of what Phantasos gave me."

Piper blinked, swallowing. "Phantasos...the God of Illusions?"

Lulu nodded. "He was the gentlest of the Oneiroi, but also the most dangerous for humans. Like I said, illusions aren't lies, Piper... They are truths turned inside out. He could weave entire realities from strands, not to trick, but to teach. His gift was not destruction, but perspective. He could make someone forget themselves in a dream or remember what they had been trying to deny."

"That is a lot of power."

Lulu lifted her wrist, shaking the gold brace. "The gods contain all of us in some form." A shimmer of silver fog curled between her fingers before dissolving.

"That is my lucent. I can bend what's around us, bend what someone sees, even bend what they believe. Not forever, but long enough to unmake their hold. I bend illusions to protect dreams, and mask truth so it can survive. When I folded the chamber, when I wove the poppies and the doors and the shoreline, I wasn't just distracting Hazel. I was reminding the Fray of a truth without her. I showed it a dream where she had no place."

Piper's breath came fast and uneven, her chest rising in shallow bursts. "You erased her?"

So, it was that easy.

"I wove her out," Lulu said quietly. "She was made from aged strands, Piper, and strand listens to illusion. I didn't kill her. I reminded the dream to forget her. That is why Hazel's tie broke. That's why I was able to close Pandora's Vault. This is what I was born to guard—unfinished human dreams."

Her gaze lingered on the vault, its surface still humming faintly. "I don't think she's gone for all ages. Hazel was clever and stubborn. She might find her way back. If she does…"

Lulu stopped and shook her head. Then her eyes locked onto Piper's, whose were wide-eyed with concern and confusion. "You must be wondering how she reached you here at all. How something locked in the Room of Lockes found its way into the heart of the Citadel."

Piper said nothing, but her expression answered.

"Hazel was a Fatale before Zeus caged her," Lulu said. "The Cloner. The Fatales are not bound by walls the way other Dreamers are. Their nature is to travel the strands and move where the strands of dreams lead them. A cage holds their body. It does not hold what they are." She paused. "The moment you touched her in the Room of Lockes, you gave her a strand to follow. A tie, however faint, is a road to a Fatale. She couldn't leave the cage physically, but she could project along the thread you unknowingly gave her. Just long enough, just far enough, to reach you here when you were most unguarded." Lulu's voice hardened, as she lifted her wrist again. "These braces don't work in here, as power and law are untethered in the Fray. It is why I was able to use my lucent to its full extent and why Hazel was able to haunt you like this. Cages hold the body. A tie sets the rest of them free."

Piper went cold. That was why Colik told her not to touch Hazel or her cage.

"You can tell no one this happened. Not Blaze. Not Colik. Not anyone in your human world."

Piper's brows furrowed. "Why? They deserve to know what's inside that vault…what Hazel tried to—"

"No," Lulu cut her off. "If you speak it, even whisper it, the gods will hear. They are tied into every name, every story and every foretelling. To reveal what happened here is to call them down upon you. You have survived this, but I promise you a human would never survive the wrath of the gods."

Piper could hear the humming of the strands above, and her heart beating like a drum.

"When Hazel forced you to open Pandora's Vault, the unwrought strands scattered. My lucent wove illusions over them, folding them back into ash before they could take shape. Hopefully they were contained in the Fray, burned to ash. But if even one escaped?" Lulu shook her head. "It will seek a body. A dream given flesh, and that is worse than the Fatales if the gods were to find out."

Piper swallowed hard, but Lulu wasn't finished. Her voice softened, though the weight of it pressed heavier than before.

"The Fatales clone, measure and sever," Lulu continued, her tone firm. "The gods? They devour. They will not allow a mortal—or even a Dreamer—to touch what they locked away.

They would rather unmake you, one human, than let humans and gods truly live as one again."

Piper trembled, her lips parting but no words rising.

Lulu straightened, the silver-tinged fog still curling faintly around her as she turned toward the door. Her steps were quiet and deliberate. Then, just before she vanished, she glanced back over her shoulder.

"Bury this. Bury it so deep even your dreams can't find it. Because if you speak of it, if the gods hear, what you faced in the Fray will feel like mercy."

For a heartbeat, Piper thought to call after her. To beg her not to leave. To ask how she was supposed to carry this alone.

Her throat stayed locked as Lulu vanished, leaving only the faint pulse of the resealed Pandora's Vault and the unbearable weight of a secret Piper dared not speak.

Did Lulu not know that humans were the worst secret keepers?

CHAPTER TWENTY-SEVEN
THE DRESS OF WINGS

Piper couldn't tell how long the Citadel had been quiet for. Perhaps a single rotation of the Blood Moon, though time here was slippery and meaningless. That was the point, apparently to live inside the frequency of moments rather than measure life in memories and schedules. She was still learning how to handle that.

The Greycene was gone, as if it had never existed. Lulu had vanished too, again. Blaze lingered at a distance, his gaze kind but with some recognition she couldn't unravel, but of course, he offered no explanation. Even Patryk, who usually haunted her like a shadow, hadn't appeared outside her Vanis room.

Loneliness pressed in. At this point, she would have even welcomed Colik's company, if only to have someone to speak to. Ever since she stumbled in the Fray, she hadn't dared stray far from her Vanis room or the throne room. The rest of the Citadel felt wrong. Like a mirror she couldn't see herself in anymore. Wings looped back on themselves. Staircases led to nowhere. Doors she *knew* had been there before now stared at her as blank stone. It was like the Citadel was playing hide and seek with her and winning.

Piper sat on the edge of her bed in the Vanis room, knees tucked to her chest, trying to convince herself she still had control of something. *Anything.*

Then she heard the rustle of claws on polished stone. The catdrag flew from behind a beam above, its body shimmering in the dim light, scales rippling with midnight and sapphire, feline eyes glowing. It moved without sound, but its presence filled the room. She hadn't seen the catdrag since the Greycene.

It landed with a soft thump on the edge of the bed, purring low and deep, like it was forming a fireball in its throat, but choosing not to release it. Piper stiffened, instinct prickling, but didn't move.

"Hey," she whispered, her voice small. Unsure whether to smile or flinch. "You again."

The creature tilted its head, studying her with an unreadable expression. Then it stepped forward and gently nudged her hand with its whiskered snout. She didn't expect how warm it was. How deliberate. How knowing.

It circled once, slow and silent, then pressed its weight against her side, wings folding tight to shield her from something unseen.

That's when it happened. The panic in her chest—the dread that had gripped her since the Fray—loosened. Her breath softened, her shoulders lowered, and a strange, impossible warmth seeped into her bones. It reminded her of the Greycene, of Ellery's touch, like someone had reached into her thoughts and turned the noise down to a whisper.

The catdrag didn't speak, but it didn't have to. Its comfort was both a presence and unknown promise. She didn't know how she knew all of this, she just *felt* it.

Piper closed her eyes, just for a moment. And for the first time since the Fray, she felt safe again.

Then the catdrag suddenly drew back, ears twitching

toward the door. It raised its tiny snout and exhaled in warning.

A cloud of *blue fire* hissed from its throat, arcing through the air in a perfect crescent. Suspending like a veil between Piper and the door, the flame formed a jagged arc that blazed with a protective intent.

Piper didn't scream. She barely even flinched as she knew it wasn't meant for her.

"Piper!" Patryk's voice cut through the haze. He was already halfway into the room, hand on the hilt at his side. His eyes darted from the blue flame to the catdrag, then Piper behind it, and froze mid-step.

The creature didn't move. It simply blinked once, its tail curling around Piper possessively, its purring resuming. The flame between them pulsed gently.

Patryk raised both hands slowly, wariness flickering across her face. "I am not here to hurt her," he said carefully.

The catdrag didn't retreat, but stayed curled at Piper's side, its slit-pupil eyes tracking Patryk with measured calm.

His jaw dropped slightly in awe. His brow lifted, something having clicked into place. "That's...*unexpected*," he murmured. "And pleasantly surprising."

Piper blinked. "What is?"

The catdrag turned its luminous eyes to Piper. For a moment, it was like they were studying each other, reading each other in a language that only they could decipher. Piper gave the smallest nod, instinctively.

The catdrag responded at once. The blue flame it had conjured moments ago flickered, curled on itself, and vanished in a single shimmer. The barrier was gone, but the creature stared.

Patryk stepped forward cautiously, but his gaze never left her. "It seems a catdrag *chose* you."

"Chosen me?" Piper asked. "What does that even mean? Like an atmospheric beast?"

He shook his head slowly. "Atmospherics are *bred* for companionship. Tied to its loyalty to one, but catdrags?" He let out a short breath. "A catdrag doesn't choose loyalty. It seems it has become loyal to you."

"How—"

Patryk chuckled, answering her question before she could fully ask it. "Because it protected you from me. They don't protect anyone but themselves. They are selfish little creatures, and yet, you were able to prove a selfish loyalty to it."

He looked at her with new weight behind his eyes. "You do know what that means, don't you?"

Piper's voice came out smaller than she expected. "Honestly, no."

"It means you can't *just* be a human. It means what we all suspected all along has truth to it." He said it like a revelation. "Blaze has Ellery. Colik *had* Dray."—*so he knew?* — "Lulu's Polaris follows her. These creatures don't bind to mortals. They bond to Dreamers. To forces tied to the Reverie itself. It's how a Dreamer finds permanence in this world."

Piper's heart thudded.

Patryk's smile grew, laced with something boyish and bright.

"This changes everything!" He turned, practically giddy, pacing toward the edge of the room. "The Royalds are going to be so excited when they hear. Well, Blaze anyway, though I know he had his suspicions…" Patryk went on, so pleased. "They have been treating you like an anomaly. An accident." He laughed under his breath. "You're not just a human who wandered in."

I knew it!

He faced her again, eyes lighting up like someone seeing stars for the first time. "You're something the Fray marked. Something it might've been waiting for."

Something the Fray marked? Piper's stomach tightened.

The words echoed louder in her head than Patryk had said them.

As a Harold, Patryk always acted like he knew more than he let on. Like he had been born with secrets etched behind his eyes, but Piper had kept her promise. She hadn't spoken of what happened in the Fray. Not to him. Not to the catdrag. Not even to herself out loud.

Her gaze flicked to Patryk, studying him. Did he know?

Before she could read his expression, he looked away too quickly. He turned instead and gestured to the soft dress draped over the vanity chair in the corner, its fabric shimmering.

When did that get there?

"Come, Piper," Patryk said lightly, already striding toward the vanity where the dress lay waiting. "We have the Constellation Ball to prepare for. It commences momentarily."

His voice dropped into a whisper as he passed the catdrag, giving it a respectful nod. "You're not walking in as an outsider. You're walking in chosen."

The catdrag still didn't move. It blinked slowly, still curled at Piper's side, its warmth a quiet anchor that Piper didn't know she needed until now.

Piper glanced down at it, heart still unsure, but steadier. The creature's gaze met hers, calm and young.

She exhaled softly. "What should I call you then, little friend?"

The catdrag purred, the sound deep and steady. Piper's fingers hovered above the catdrag's velvet-scaled head. Its eyes, a kaleidoscope of sapphire and silver, blinked once, then twice, both slow and knowing.

"Hmm," she murmured, brow furrowed. "You don't look like a Whisper or a Flicker… and you're not wild like a Spark."

She trailed off, thinking aloud, the way she used to name the stray cats in the alley behind Olympus House. Only this was no alley cat. This was a cat-like creature with a dragon's wings and soul. It had, for who knows what reason, chosen her.

The catdrag tilted its head slightly, waiting. The shimmer of its scales caught the light in patterns that looked like writing.

Then, suddenly, Piper felt it—not a word, but a pulse in her bones, a vibration she had felt before, echoing like some half-remembered truth.

Not a name she had chosen. A name she only saw.

"Pollux," she whispered. The syllable slipped past her lips as though it had been waiting in her marrow. She remembered that name in her studies about constellations.

The catdrag's head lifted, ears pricking forward. Its wings trembled with a restless, shivering energy.

"Pollux," Patryk repeated slowly. "Old Vescarpse…from the myth of the Twin Lights. Cantor's companion star. It means twin ember."

Piper looked down at her companion. Pollux blinked slowly, its luminous eyes catching starlight that wasn't there. It leaned into Piper with the gentle weight of trust, its scaled head pressing against Piper's ribs like a heartbeat outside her own.

Piper didn't smile, but her shoulders dropped, like the Fray had both tested her and rewarded her…for not willingly giving into Hazel's demand.

"Come now, Piper! I still need to get ready myself." Patryk pressed, pulling out items from the drawers of the vanity that Piper had never realized were drawers.

Piper rose, causing Pollux to quickly fly off, and walked over to Patryk. She looked at the dress. Her eyes widened, her mouth slightly gaping open. It was even more beautiful than the last dress she wore, if that was even possible.

"Isn't it stunning? It is a privilege to wear a dress like that."

"Like what?"

"Oh…" Patryk looked confused by her confused look. "I think it is best if *he* tells you. Sit. Time to doll you up!" He sputtered, genuine excitement in his voice.

He? Patryk had already carefully moved the dress to the bed and motioned for her to sit down.

The rose vanity was stunning, exuding elegance and charm. Its frame was crafted from rich, dark mahogany, beautifully contrasting with the delicate pink roses that laced its surface. Penelope would have died for this rose covered vanity.

Once seated, Piper noticed all the brushes lying out on the marble top. The myriad colors of powder before her looked more suited for artwork than makeup, a skill she knew she lacked in both. She had never worn makeup before, and the confusion in her eyes, gave it away.

Patryk chuckled. "Grounded white lead from the Greycene's garden." He was standing behind her, a slight smirk on his lips, looking at her through the reflection. His hand went to pull back her hair, then he stopped.

"May I?"

"Of course," she replied.

Patryk turned Piper's chair towards him and began to select a brush and powder palette. She closed her eyes, bracing herself for what was to come.

"You see, I may know about beauty on the outside…" Patryk began, his voice soft and soothing as he delicately applied makeup to her eyelids. "I do think you *know* beauty. Your beauty seems deep…deep down on the inside." He gave a small laugh.

"How do you mean?" she asked, feeling the cold, liquid paste spread across her cheeks. He didn't answer her question. "The Greeks used white lead for their faces, but we use it for the shine around the eyes. Fresh berries are for the lips. Lingonberry, wolfberry, or white mulberry?" he inquired, his hands moving with practiced precision.

"I trust your judgment," Piper said, her eyes still closed, having no idea the difference in the options he gave her.

"A white mulberry, pressed with malachite, would show best for this occasion," he shared, delight sparking in his words.

She opened her eyes slightly, to find herself mere inches from Patryk's face. Up close, he had a layer of glitter and makeup on, too.

"What is my role at the Constellation Ball?" she asked, hoping getting information from the Harold would be easier than prying answers from the Royalds. *If any*, she wanted to add but didn't. They were always arguing, always hiding pieces of the truth. Patryk, at least, had never given her reason to fear asking.

He didn't answer.

She waited, hesitated, then tried again. "How am I supposed to 'be' in all this? Everyone keeps telling me about roles and duties. What if I don't want the one they're trying to force on me? How am I supposed to learn it without losing a part of me that I didn't know there was to lose?"

Patryk paused, stilling the brush he held. Then he finally spoke, his tone softening into something older, wiser, and brotherly.

"In stories of gods and their children, there is a pattern," he said. "They adapt. They discover who they are before they let the heavens decide it for them. Some learned their lineage and chose to carry it. Others fought back against fate even when their bodies could not. Power is rarely the thing that saves them. It is who they decide to become with or without it."

Piper's breath stilled. "So, you think I can choose?"

"I think," he said, resuming his careful strokes, "that you already are. You survived your world believing you were weak, but weakness is only a story someone else taught you. Here, you learn a new one. You learn your lineage, your strength, and your place. You do not let anyone—god or Royald—decide it for you."

Her throat tightened.

Patryk stepped back just slightly, approving his work even though her eyes were still closed. "The Constellation Ball does not assign roles, Piper. It reveals what you already carry, but the choice to live it or change it. That is yours."

Piper had no words. She simply looked up at Patryk, a quiet respect softening her features, and let a small, grateful smile form. She hoped he saw it. She hoped he understood what it meant.

"Keep your eyes closed until I am done!" He called out. She widened her smile and followed his command. "Ooh, I am going to add mesdemet for your eyes and kohl for the lining," he said, sidetracked.

"I do not know what any of that is," she admitted, allowing him to change the subject.

"Mesdemet is a mix of copper and ore for your eyelids, and kohl, perhaps a form of coal from your world, is used to line your eyes," he explained.

"Sounds like art."

"Is makeup not art in some way? And a face a canvas?"

His words hung in the air, and she was unsure how to respond. The idea of her face as a canvas felt absurd, especially compared to the beauty surrounding her, like Lulu, and even the woman Shade, though hers was a darker, more dangerous kind of beauty.

Eyes still closed, there were a few more light, deliberate touches on her face. Brush bristles like the sweep of a feather, a cool fingertip at her cheekbone, and the faint tickle of powder drifting down her face. There was a rhythm to it. He was patient but sure. Patryk was painting something far more important than skin.

Somewhere in the silence, his voice returned, softer now.

"Where I come from, it is said that a true artist doesn't just paint what is there, but what the subject might become."

She tilted her head slightly but didn't open her eyes. "Where is that?"

"A place far from here," he replied, his voice tinged with a distant warmth, "where the mountains are so high they scrape the clouds, and the night sky is never empty. In those skies, winged stallions carry dreams safely across the dark. In our legends, it is the steed of heroes, much like Pegasus was to Hercules in your world's myth's. Loyal. Tireless. Bound not to the rider's glory, but to their purpose."

Her lips parted, yet no words found their way out. She didn't know whether to laugh at the strange comparison or hold it close like a secret. Even as the thought settled, something tugged at the edges of her mind, like a story once told to her before, though she could not, for the life of her, recall where or when.

Finally, she sensed him step back. "Take a look and let me know what you think."

Nervously, she opened her eyes again and gasped at her reflection.

"Patryk! This is... I look like a—"

"Goddess?" he suggested. "Perhaps even a Royald?"

"Yes..." she breathed.

"A human's complexion is already flawless. I did what was necessary to make you stand out even more," he remarked, pride flickering in his eyes like the glint of starlight on a restless wing.

"Now, I must see that the Brownies have completed the final touches in the Orph Ballroom. They tend to mesmerize over the gold more than set it up for proper show. Do you need anything else from me?" Piper shook her head, but he still bowed in reply.

"I will never *need* anything from you, Patryk..." She informed him gently. He looked at her, surprised. "I may ask something of you, but please know, I want us to be friends," she went on, surprised at herself for being so forward. Patryk stared hard, contemplating what she was saying, but then he shook his head again, as if the words clicked.

"A friend with a Harold? Are you sure?" he asked, a hint of skepticism lacing his voice.

"Positive," Piper said genuinely.

Patryk smiled wide, his white teeth blinding, but then something in his expression faltered. Piper saw a flicker in his eyes, like he wanted to say something he'd been holding back. She held her breath. Maybe he didn't want to be her friend.

"Well..." he started, then paused. His fingers toyed with the edge of his laced robe, the glitter on his knuckles catching the light. "Before I go, may I offer one little... Harold suggestion?"

Piper blinked. "Please."

Patryk leaned in, dropping his voice as if the Vanis Room itself might listen. "At the Constellation Ball, when you stand before the dais...the thrones. Look at them closely. Think about the Ages they come from. What each Royald represents."

He hesitated again, then smiled, softer this time, something tender threading through the sparkles. "My new Dreamer friend... think about what that might say about *you*."

The words left a strange warmth in her chest.

Patryk winked, the hesitance gone as quickly as it had appeared. "Well. I will see you at the Ball... *friend*." He pranced off, jewels chiming faintly as he vanished through the doorway.

Piper watched him disappear, his footsteps already fading into the soft hush of the Citadel corridors. The Vanis Room settled again, and she turned slowly back to the vanity mirror, her hands brushing the frame like it might vanish if she looked too quickly.

For a long moment, she just stared.

The girl in the glass looked like her but also didn't. She barely recognized herself, because this reflection wasn't someone she'd ever been allowed to imagine.

She had always scoffed at girls who spent time painting their faces, layering powders and pigments like a clown. She'd said it was fake, performative, and a way to mask what was already there. If she was honest—deep down, achingly honest—it had only ever been jealousy. She hadn't had the luxury. Not the money. Not the skill. Not the permission to see herself as someone worth beautifying.

What Patryk had done wasn't an act of disguise. It wasn't a mask. It was a delicate unveiling of the person she might have been all along, if someone had simply bothered to look. Or help her see.

Her green eyes shimmered with a smoky depth, a quiet edge that didn't erase her intensity but refined it. Her lips wore a tone she'd never dared to try, soft but certain, a kind of muted boldness that matched the fire she so often buried. Her cheeks, warm with a natural flush, looked less like something to hide and more like a secret she was finally allowed to keep.

She smiled again, wider this time, her eyes crinkling at the corners with something like wonder.

Maybe, for once, she didn't have to apologize for the parts of herself that felt too much. Maybe now, she could wear them like parts she was proud of showing.

Just when she thought she couldn't possibly feel more radiant, more powerful, more wholly herself... She put the dress on.

The moment the gown touched her skin, she gasped. The fabric flowed around her in pale steel blue cascades that caught even the faintest light. The cut was delicate, bare backed, with strands of diamonds and fine beading draped across her shoulders like constellations strung together.

Unlike the other gowns made of silk and lace, this one was feathered in all the places that mattered. Soft trails of them spread across her bust and down the train of her backside, woven seamlessly into the silk so that each movement looked like wings unfurling. At the hem, the feathers grew longer and more untamed, brushing against the ground in whispering arcs.

When she walked, the feathers stirred in ripples. Her hand came up to rest gently over her cheeks, where the warmth of Patryk's careful touch still lingered. With that warmth, a confidence stirred. Not the desperate kind of confidence that tried to prove itself, but a quiet certainty born from survival. From standing tall when the ground kept breaking beneath her.

Her thoughts, uninvited but persistent, turned back to the Fray. To Hazel's cruel manipulation. To the moment the Pandora's Vault had opened.

When she thought about it, it had to have been a test, because why else would the Broken Woods have chosen her? Or the catdrag? Even the Fray, wild and unrelenting, had marked her, perhaps even twice.

What if this world wasn't unraveling beneath her feet, but unfolding its edges to let her in?

She did a slow spin, the wings of her dress brushing against her arms like a benediction.

Piper closed her eyes and inhaled deeply, the kind of breath that filled every hollow space in her lungs and soul.

"I'm not just surviving," she whispered to her reflection, her voice firm, steady. "I'm becoming who I was meant to be."

She turned again, the fabric trailing behind her like ripples—

"Fuck the dream in me." Colik's voice floated in from behind her.

Piper froze mid-spin, startled. She turned slowly, half-expected mockery on his face, but what she saw was admiration. Or maybe she just wanted to believe that's what it was.

"I beg your pardon!" she barked.

Her stomach twisted. She folded her arms quickly, guarding herself from his gaze. There was an awkward moment where neither of them spoke.

"Patryk said it was a privilege to wear a dress like this," she finally said, too fast, too sharp. The words tumbled out to mask the flutter in her chest. "Don't tell me—"

"You're my guest," Colik said quietly. "So, you wear my wings."

There was more silence. It was thick and charged. Then Piper tilted her chin slightly. "Lovely."

Colik hesitated. "Ignore what I said earlier—"

"Don't try to redeem yourself," she snapped, her voice cutting through whatever apology he was about to make. Just when she thought she might enjoy this ball, he had to go and remind her who he really was.

He raised an eyebrow. "So, you don't like my feathers on that dress?"

Her cheeks heated up but she held her ground. "Just because it came from you doesn't mean I'm going to bow to you, *Royald*."

"That's not what I meant," he said too quickly.

She didn't respond. Instead, she gave one last, deliberate spin, the hem of her dress brushing her legs. Then, without a word, she walked toward the doorway, chin high.

"What do you mean *your* feathers?" she asked, echoing his earlier words now that they unsettled her more than she cared to admit.

Colik's expression remained unreadable. "That dress was made from *my* wings. Ripped off my back."

She blinked. "From your back?"

"Yes. You wouldn't understand," he replied with a crooked smile, evasive as ever. Something flickered behind his eyes. Something he wasn't saying.

Piper reached for the front of her chest, running her fingers lightly over the feathers stitched into the fabric. They were soft. Real. Regal. She shivered at the thought that what he said was true.

"You really gave those up?"

"I didn't say I gave them," he said, voice low. "Only that you're wearing them."

"So stubborn," she muttered, half to herself.

"Say again?" Colik's eyes narrowed.

"Nothing."

He smirked. "I could say the same about you."

His voice had softened. He stepped back, hand on the door, posture just formal enough to make her feel like she was being presented.

She found herself scanning him up and down, and as much as she hated to admit it, Colik looked ever like a Royald.

He wore a sleek black coat stitched with sky-blue strand that caught the light like frozen lightning. It was elegant and sharp, just like him. The embroidery traced the seams with quiet precision, matching the exact hue of his multi-colored eyes. Beneath the coat, a silver-collared shirt gleamed faintly, fastened with dark buttons like drops of ink. Across his back, subtle feathered patterns hinted at the wings he'd lost. He looked haunted, and untouchable.

Piper was very thankful for the pink blush on her cheeks to hide the heat rising in them.

He nodded toward the corridor. "So, are you ready?"

Piper inhaled deeply, hoping the answer might be somewhere in the air. "As ready as I'll ever be."

He motioned her through the door, her footsteps light but her mind heavy. The dress shimmered. The Citadel ahead glowed faintly with starlight. Somewhere, music played.

She was dressed like a goddess, standing beside a Royald. She finally *looked* like she belonged, but next to him, every step forward felt more like a performance than a truth.

Colik's voice stopped her before she turned the corner.

"Oh, and Piper…"

She paused, turning halfway, bracing for another insult. "Yes?"

His eyes met hers, steady and unreadable.

"For now…just pretend."

She blinked. "Pretend what?"

"That you belong here."

Piper studied him, her expression carved into something unreadable, before she gave a single nod. It was sharp, deliberate, and far from certain.

"Yeah," she murmured to herself. "Because we look so perfect."

Colik's answer came low, a rasp that was nearly swallowed by the silence. "The perfect lie."

She heard him, her final thought striking like a knife: *What if the lie becomes real?*

CHAPTER TWENTY-EIGHT
THE CONSTELLATION BALL

What Patryk and the Brownies had done to the Orph Ballroom was impossible to miss. Gold did not just decorate the room but saturated it. The pillars gleamed with deliberate streaks, as though an artist had brushed molten sunlight into every crease. The floor had been stitched with gilded veins the ran through the ballroom like many rivers of blaze.

Sparkles had been dusted across every surface, and at the precise center of the room, an enormous chandelier hung with diamonds trembling in its frame.

Beneath the external splendor, Piper *felt* the fault lines. The chandelier's glow flickered as though one breath away from smashing to the ground and when the music rose, she caught a single off-keynote, sharp as a crack in a mirror, before it was drowned back into harmony.

Colik walked ahead and Piper did her best to follow with a happy face. It was this that made her repeat the word *pretend*. It was him still being cold but acting as if it were an honor to wear his wings, that made her heart feel hollow and her smile forced. The Broken Woods really had broken them. That still hurt.

Around her, the air suddenly shifted, and from the corners of the vaults above, shapes began to descend. They looked like ghosts woven from light, drifting downward in slow, weightless spirals. Their bodies were nothing more than cascades of stars, each one flickering into the illusion of dancers. They swept across the ballroom floor as though remembering steps from ages long gone, twirling in pairs and bowing in silence.

Piper's breath caught, but Colik leaned in. "Stellar phantoms." His voice was low and even, as if respecting their presence. "They are spirits of the constellations who are summoned to dance and entertain. Do not fear them. They are only light, not beings."

They rose and fell in weightless rhythm, some stepping briefly on the floor with a spark before lifting again, as though gravity itself had forgotten them. Their presence was a celestial current that swept Piper along, making her feel as though she too might dissolve into the dream of ghostly light.

As they crossed the center floor, one phantom peeled away from the drifting cluster. Its star-stitched form glided toward her, its outline sharpening, focusing solely on Piper. Cold starlight gathered at its edges, and when it reached her, it bowed.

Its head dipped to her, and cold light washed over Piper's skin, a shiver racing up her spine. The phantom rose, its form lingering with a strange, expectant tilt, as if waiting for her to acknowledge a role she didn't know she'd inherited.

Colik stiffened beside her. Then he sharply grabbed her hand and pulled her away from the stellar phantom. Piper's pulse hammered, each step away from the phantom reminding her she was not a goddess or a Royald, but a human girl in borrowed feathers.

Pretend, Colik had told her. Pretend she belonged. Pretend she was not the lie at the center of this perfect scene.

"We must hurry, before they arrive."

They? Ah, they. The Guilds of Dreamers.

Piper's heart raced, both with excitement and nerves. She wasn't sure what to expect out of this event, but something in the air told her it was not going to be anything she could have even dreamed of expecting.

As they walked toward the far end of the ballroom, directly across from the doors they had entered, Piper saw the dais of the Royalds. To think the throne room had remarkable thrones. They were nothing like these. Like Patryk had told her, these thrones were not just decorations, but embodiments of the very Ages from which the Royalds themselves had risen.

Blaze sat on a throne with vines of gilded flame curling up its sides as though the Gold Age itself breathed through the metal. It glowed warm and relentless, a sun caught in ivy.

Beside him, Lulu's throne was forged from fractured silver plates and cracked mirror shards. Shining with dazzling white light that caught every light in the room like an illusion, it was a throne made from the splinters of the Silver Age, beautifully broken.

Colik's empty seat smoldered with a steady, molten glow, its bronze edges burnished and scarred. The throne looked hammered, tempered, and the very image of what Piper would think of the Bronze Age.

She had briefly read about the gods ages when she came back to her waking world. That was three, so that made the fourth throne—

Beside the three Royalds, and carved more recently than the others, sat a throne of black iron. Its surface gleamed dark as a starless sky, edges sharpened like forged resolve. Nothing adorned it. No jewels. No vines. No shine. Only the brutal honesty of the Iron Age.

Piper pushed her shoulders back, willing her legs to keep moving, and stepped up to the dais after Colik.

Blaze rose first as she neared, his robe shimmering in white and gold, the fabric alive as if the ivy from his throne had rooted in him. She understood more than ever why Ellery would have chosen him to be loyal to. He had an earthy, old soul presence. His smile was slow, deliberate, but his eyes were pinning her in place.

"Welcome to the Constellation Ball," he said, putting out a hand to help her up the last few steps.

Piper took it, her cheeks warming at his touch. She wanted to look away, but his gaze was like gravity, those grey corneas like a sliver of a moon, that pulled at her chest.

Then Lulu leaned forward. The crack in her stone-carved throne caught the light like a scar, and her fiery-red gown coiled at her feet.

"So," Lulu murmured, studying Piper with a smile that never reached her eyes, "The human arrives at last."

Piper instinctively shifted closer to Blaze, the warmth of his presence steadier than she would have liked. Lulu noticed, of course, and her smirk sharpened, curling like her dress in satisfaction.

Piper forced her lips into a polite curve, though her chest trembled. She let go of Blaze's hand and moved to the black iron throne next to Colik.

Pretend, she repeated in her head. Pretend you belong. Pretend you are not afraid. She hated how Colik had gotten into her head. Just when she thought maybe she could belong here...

Blaze's eyes lingered on her, unreadable, but clearly noticing the conflict in her eyes. There was something else in his stare too. He was searching, as if he knew something she didn't. As if the sight of her confirmed a truth he wasn't ready to speak aloud.

"You wear Colik's wings well, Piper," he said finally, low enough that only those on the dais could hear. "Almost as if they were yours too."

The words sank into her skin like a secret accusation. She felt her pulse spike, her hands curling as she took her seat. She prayed the chandelier wouldn't shatter before her heart did.

Colik sat at the bronze throne next to her, and as if on cue, Patryk glided to the nearest set of drapes lining the ballroom walls. He wrapped both hands around a thick golden rope that shimmered like a sunlit bell pull, and gave it a firm, ceremonial tug. The sound was soft, yet it carried through the room like a summoning.

The drapes began to rise.

From their vantage point on the dais, Piper could suddenly see every angle of the ballroom, every hidden corner unveiled. Only now did she understand what those drapes had concealed when Colik first brought her here.

The sparkling drapes completely parted with a soft rush of air, unveiling a grand, spiraling arena of glittering stone, tiered in perfect concentric rings like a celestial echo of the Roman Colosseum. Each level sparkled, gilded patterns sweeping across the tiers with scenes of Greek gods and goddesses etched directly into the stone itself. A goddess with her spear raised. A god crowned in rays of fire. Another with his wings unfurled.

Tall, ornate columns ringed the structure, supporting elegant archways draped in flowing strands of ivy. Small white blossoms dotted the greenery, glowing faintly like clustered stars.

The air felt charged and expectant.

These must be for the Guild of Dreamers, but—

"Where are the Dreamers?" Piper whispered. Colik's mouth curled into something between amusement and impatience.

"They were waiting for us to arrive." He gave a sly smile. "Watch."

The towering ivory doors Patryk stood beside—doors Piper hadn't even realized were doors—groaned open. Tall and sharp in his lavender sash, Patryk lifted his chin and spoke, his voice effortlessly carrying across the ballroom.

"Royalds." He bowed briefly toward the dais, though his eyes lingered on Piper. "Allow me to seat our guests."

Beside him, the first guild glided in. They had white hoods, silk masks, and eyes like slitted lanterns. Piper gasped softly. "The Routs…"

Colik leaned close, his voice brushing her ear. "Dreamers of chase. You've seen them before."

They moved in pairs, each step identical to the last, as though puppets on one string. When Patryk gestured, they filed to the far-back tier, their movements eerily synchronized. The moment they sat, the silence deepened.

The doors opened again, and a cool breeze swept in with the next guild.

"The Cryos," Colik whispered. The Cryos moved like water frozen mid-wave, their garments flowing in shades of white and pale blue. Shocks of white hair framed their dark faces, and their eyes glimmered a stunning ocean blue. Even their footsteps echoed like ice cracking on a lake. "Dreamers of loss. They reside in the Untold Brine."

Patryk led them to the opposite side of the amphitheater, where they sat in hushed whispers, each turning their gaze upward toward the open dome swirling into the cosmic constellation cloud.

Then came heat, and another Guild of Dreamers arrived in a flood of shadow and flame. With slender bodies adorned with draped silks and glimmering jewelry, their steps rang with chains tipped in small black orbs. As they moved, they conjured fiery rings of blue with ash-dark centers, spinning them poetically in the air. The smell of ash followed them.

"The Vixens and the Dreamers of intimacy."

"Intimacy?"

"Don't tell me I have to explain what that means?" Colik said, chuckling at the heat rising in Piper's face. She pressed her palms on the cold iron of her seat, hoping it would stop the heat rising in her.

"You wish—" she forced out.

Patryk steered them to their seats in the lower tiers, nearer the center, where their flames could be admired by all. Their laughter drifted, low and suggestive, bouncing against the sparkling stone arches.

Lulu rolled her eyes. "Typical."

Piper held back a laugh, wanting to make fun of her so bad, but refrained.

The doors opened again, and childish chaos arrived.

The Scirges poured in like animals having escaped their cages. They tumbled, whooped, and hollered down the aisles, leaping two steps at a time, earthly dust trailing behind. There were more of them than any other guild so far, their energy filling every void in the room.

"They'll never sit still," Blaze muttered under his breath.

Patryk wrangled them, guiding them to an entire swath of stone seats along the middle tier.

Then the doors opened again, and a hush fell as another Guild of Dreamers entered, clad in tight violet jewels and leathers, their eyes burning sharply, like they could see straight through skin into bone marrow. Piper quickly looked away.

"The Emers," Colik explained, though softer. "Dreamers of exposure. They make mockery of dignity and great protectors."

Patryk guided them to a high arc of seats, where they sat rigid, like guards posted to watch the room. Their presence felt heavy and intense.

"How many are there?"

"Seven in total."

A gust of dusty wind tore through the ballroom, sharp enough to lift the edges of Piper's gown and almost punch the air from her lungs. Her stomach lurched as the chandelier trembled overhead, scattering trembling shards of light across the floor.

Matching the decadence of the Orph Ballroom, the next

Guild of Dreamers had double wings that unfurled into sheets of pure gold, each feather catching the starlight and throwing it back in dazzling sparks. Their tight gilded bodysuits clung like a second skin, molding them into living statues of light. Masks shaped like sleek bird beaks hid their faces entirely, erasing all trace of gender or expression. Piper couldn't tell if any were male or female, only that they were magnificent, unsettling, and the epitome of otherworldly.

To think the Scirges were true fantastical beings.

"Cabras. The dreamers of flying," Colik whispered, his tone carrying a tension she didn't miss. "They don't attend lightly."

Patryk led them to the uppermost tier, where they perched more than sat, their gilded wings folding like sun storms pressed into order. Piper counted silently.

"That is only six guilds," Piper commented, remembering the darkest ones, the Shades. There was a tug in her stomach at the thought of the emerald-eyed Shade. Why did his eyes burn into her mind every time she thought of Dreamers of nightmares?

Colik gave a coy shrug. "The Shades, but given what happened in the throne room with Blaze, I would be more than surprised if…" His voice trailed off as the doors opened for a final time. The Shades entered, and there was a clear sense of desperation about them. They were dressed entirely in black, except for their wrists, which had the same gold brace as the Royals. As Piper. No other Dreamer had the gold brace. Only the Shades and the Royals.

"Spoke too soon," Colik said, his voice growing tense, mirroring the change in the room's atmosphere.

"The gold braces on the Shades… They have the same ones as us?" Piper spoke. She looked around Colik toward Blaze, but his eyes were stone cold on the Shades. He must not have expected them to come either.

Colik looked down at his gold brace, then at Piper's. "They are called connectors."

Piper frowned. "Connectors?"

"Yes," he said, voice low as Patryk guided them through the shifting ballroom. "Because everything here is connected. Dreamers, Royalds, Shades. All of us are tied to the REM, to the Citadel, and to the frequency that keeps this world stable."

His eyes flicked toward the higher tiers where Shades lingered in shadows. "The Shades are the most dangerous beings in the Reverie. The Royalds..." He tapped his own brace once. "We are the most powerful."

He leaned slightly closer, his tone flattening into something edged. "So of course the gods impose extra perimeters. Boundaries. Containment. They need the Shades restrained. They need the Royalds monitored."

Piper's breath caught. "Even the Royalds?"

"Especially us," Colik said.

Patryk led them to their seats near the center. Dreamers glanced at them, then quickly looked away as if even meeting their eyes might invite something too dangerous, or too uncontrolled to endure.

By the time they were seated, the ballroom was full, every tier alive with flickering light and movement. Each guild in its circle, all aligned like constellations. Above, the stars themselves pulsed in rhythm with the gathering, as though the cosmos had joined the audience.

Patryk hurried to the dais and swept into a bow so elegant it made the diamonds on his sleeves cascade with light. "Royalds, the guilds are seated. The Constellation Ball commences."

The words struck the ballroom like a spark and the room came alive.

Music burst from the hidden alcoves, with harps swelling like sunrise, drums beating like distant thunder, and strings weaving through the air like threads of dream dust. The floor rippled with light as various Guilds of Dreamers rose and made their way to the center floor.

From the shadows near the pillars, Brownies emerged in flurries of motion. Their tiny, iridescent wings fluttered like jeweled insects. They zipped through the air carrying gold goblets overflowing with sparkling water that glimmered like bottled galaxies. Others carried bouquets of roses, each petal glowing faintly, pouring their petals into crystal basins to create petaled wine that twinkled pink, white and red.

The music climbed higher. More Dreamers spiraled across the marble.

The ballroom became a universe in motion.

Finally, Blaze moved, his golden ivy throne burning behind him as he descended the dais. Behind him, Piper caught sight of the grey-black owl with sun-light eyes settling before the grand piano, its talons striking the keys with melodic grace, drawing from them a song so hauntingly beautiful it tied the ballroom together.

He stopped before Lulu and extended a hand.

"Lulu, will you grant me the grand owl's first dance?"

With a seductive grin, she rose, slow as a statue stirred awake, and placed her hand in his. The two of them stepped into the center of the ballroom, the music swelling like an unseen tide around them. The Dreamers stepped back, respecting the move of the two Royalds.

Piper drew in a breath she didn't mean to. Beside her, Colik did not move. His expression was impenetrable, but his gaze tracked them with a tightness that spoke of more than curiosity.

"Do they have to dance first because of that one Law too?" Piper whispered. Blaze and Lulu looked carved from the synonymous force of fire and illusion, their bodies moving in strange accord with each step across the floor.

Colik leaned close enough for her to catch the low scrape

of his voice. "Not all dances are with whom you are most bound to."

Wasn't Lulu bound to Blaze?

Though the ballroom spun with starlight and the grand owl's song, she couldn't shake the feeling that something was cracking with every graceful step they took.

Still, Piper's eyes were glued to Lulu. She was breathtaking. The dress was born for her body, every step pulling flames across the floor. The gown, woven in red-feathered light, unfurled with her movement. When she turned, layered trails of fire rippled outward, red and gold igniting in the candlelight. Her sleeves trailed in burning wings, the skirt blazing open in molten orange that bled into black, like lava cooling on stone. Dancing, Lulu looked untouchable, like an empress of fire, illusion, and the brightest star in a night's sky.

Blaze on the other hand, was dressed in white. Not the color of purity, but the kind that burns. It was blinding. The fabric caught the firelight of the ballroom like snow laced with flame, every seam traced with gold stitching. He always wore dark colors, so the white looked strange on him. Off. As if this moment had dressed him in something that didn't belong. Something meant for a moment that only he had planned for.

"Are those Blaze's wings?" Piper whispered to Colik, who also looked somewhat transfixed.

"No," he said quietly. "Those are hers."

"She has her own wings too?" Piper breathed, though she realized how dumb that must have sounded. *Of course she did.* She was a Royald, with a lucent from the God of Dreams.

"Yes, she is an original Dreamer," Colik said, voice steady but distant.

"Hers don't look like yours. Why?" Piper pressed, wanting to understand. *Needing* to understand.

"She wears phoenix wings."

Piper held back an annoyed gasp. Not fair. *Of course she did.*

"And yours? What feathers do I wear?" Piper asked, trying to meet his eyes.

"A swan," Colik said with a half-smile. Piper glanced down, doubting the comparison.

"Do you have something against swans?"

"No," she answered, gaze lingering on him. "Not at all."

Their shared glance held a quiet tension, like two players aware of the stakes, wary of giving too much away. He was doing a much better job of pretending than she was.

She tore her eyes from Colik and back to the center of the ballroom. Blaze and Lulu's dance flowed like a story told in fire and golden light, each step a silent conversation.

"Colik, Piper—good to see you both again." A voice came from the side of the dais, and Piper turned, surprised but relieved to see the familiar figure. Cyril's bright eyes scanned them both, his smile sincere but slightly sharper than usual.

"The Polaris has been nowhere to be seen," he said, lowering his voice slightly. "We thank you for that."

Colik dipped his head. "Anything for a fellow guild."

Cyril looked between them, his gaze resting a beat longer on Piper. "You've made an impression, Piper. Not just on the Scirges." He leaned in slightly. "You've stirred the other guilds here. Even the Cabras came down from the Glass Mountains to watch *you*. That is rare."

She blinked, stunned, and Cyril chuckled gently. "You're not just surviving here anymore, it seems. You're starting to find your place." Then, with a final glance at Colik, and something like approval in his eyes, Cyril gave a casual wave and slipped back into the dream-thick crowd, leaving behind a silence that buzzed between them.

Colik didn't say a word, but Piper could feel it. The tension rose between them again, as neither of them were ready to admit how deeply the truth of Cyril's words had struck.

"It's my turn," Colik said suddenly, standing with quiet determination.

"For what?"

He extended his hand, mirroring Blaze's earlier gesture for Lulu. Piper hesitated under his steady gaze, feeling small and uncertain.

Pretend that you belong. Colik's words played in her head yet again.

The Orph Ballroom spun around them in dreamlike shimmer and hushed wonder. She caught a glimpse of herself in the dais floor's reflection.

Her eyes fell back on Colik, who dressed every bit like a Royald, but was so childish that to her, practically *defied* what it meant to be a Royald. Some Dreamers looked their way, some curious and some judging. It was Lulu's effortless grace on the dance floor that unsettled her most. Piper could never move like that. She couldn't even fake that. It was one thing to dance with him alone, but in front of a crowd…

Hell no.

Colik leaned in, his breath grazing her cheek. "If you take my hand, you can't let go."

"Oh yeah?" she muttered, tension slipping into sarcasm. "If I do?"

"Then you'll stop choosing me. I told you that in this moment, that is everything."

Her mouth parted slightly. "*Gods.* Why does that sound like a bad line from a soap opera?"

Colik blinked. "I honestly don't know what you are talking about," he admitted. "Since when are your choices a joke?"

Just like that, she took his hand. As they rose together, the unspoken tension between them pulsed, impossible to define. Piper couldn't tell if it was real or just another side effect of the Broken Woods.

The music shifted and turned into a slower, stranger melody that bled through the walls of the ballroom as Colik guided her toward the center, where the Dreamers whispered in hushed awe. His formal coat was woven in deep dark blue that drank in the shadows and trimmed in bronze and veins of gold that were too bright for him. He looked regal and immaculate, every detail belonging to royalty, as though the gods themselves had stitched him into this world.

When Piper lifted her gaze, it was his eyes that unsettled her most. His multi-colored eyes that once brought her excitement, now made him look untouchable, and too noble.

He led her into a turn, her thoughts going back to the Ollopa train: the glass floor rushing with sky beneath her feet, the way she'd fallen forward, the door yawning open, and Colik's hand seizing her waist to pull her back from falling out. She remembered, too, his voice after as he told her she could jump, stay forever, or let him push her. That memory clung to her now like a bruise. No finery, no brilliance, not even illusion of royalty could scrub that away.

"You know I am not a good dancer," she admitted shyly.

"You're just stiff," he said. "Just listen to me."

He spun her gently. She stumbled but righted herself, his hands steadying her. Too steady. Every step with him in this ballroom felt like standing at the edge of that train door, waiting for the moment his hand would steady her, or let her fall.

"I'm going to place my hand on your lower back," he whispered.

"Okay."

He hadn't asked the first time they danced, but then again, he hadn't yet said all those things he did. The words that broke her. That broke any part of them that could have been.

The touch jolted through her like cold steel. It was the same sensation she'd felt standing on the Ollopa's platform, the rails humming beneath her feet, the endless drop gaping when the door opened.

"Follow me and please, for all the gods, *relax*."

She tried, to the Greek gods she tried, but his palm pressed into her spine and his other brushed her palm without closing, and she knew he would never let her forget how close danger lived inside him.

"Do you like it when my fingers graze you like that?" he asked, the smirk not playful but sharp. A predator testing her. Piper's heart raced and body tensed at his words.

No.

"Yes."

Her heartbeat drowned the music. Their movements weren't Blaze and Lulu's elegant spectacle, but sharper, and more perilous. Like the Ollopa train, their dance was beautiful in design, but built for humans to run, with the hope that they would fall.

"This song—" she started, but the words broke in her throat.

"Twirl," he commanded. She obeyed, skirts spiraling, until he pulled her back in, too close and aligned. She hated how natural it felt, as if danger belonged against her skin.

"This song," he said, voice low, "is called *The Melodic Ora Eli.* Composed by the Muses in Dreamtongue. It means the Melody of Dream Borns."

"So, gods *really* are real?" she asked, breathless. It just came out, but she realized instantly how stupid it sounded. At least in the Reverie.

Colik met her gaze. "After all this, you still doubt?" The way he looked at her was part surprised and part relieved.

Piper shook her head, trying not to let him get inside her head. "Where I come from, gods are myths. Stories. It's hard to believe, that's all…not that I don't believe anymore."

"Yet you ask?" His smile was the same one he'd worn in the Broken Woods, when he said to trust her. After he kissed her. "Curiosity kills more than dreams, *Pipes.* Some dreamers never make it off that train. Some are persuaded to fall." His hand pressed deeper into her back, and her breath hitched.

She had nothing to say, so they danced in silence, his hand guiding her across the floor the same way he had steered the atmospheric beast in the game of *Kryvo i Kross*. He knew exactly what he was doing, every step precise, every turn intentional, yet it felt less like a dance for two and more like a quiet act of winning.

Around them, some Dreamers continued their sweeping arcs of starlit movement, while others simply watched. Piper fixed her gaze on his shoulder, forcing herself not to meet the eyes she imagined staring from every tier. Her cheeks were already hot enough without the added pressure of a crowd witnessing whatever this was between them.

"You're a curious one," Colik finally said.

"Sorry?"

The grand owl's melody darkened. Colik's hand hovered an inch from her cheek, then returned to her waist. She knew that he knew what damage he could do if he closed that distance.

"Don't ever stop being curious," he murmured, lowering his chin until it nearly touched her hair. His eyes dropped to her lips, then snapped back to her gaze. The war inside him was plain, but whichever side won, Piper knew she would never be safe with him.

"I don't plan on it," she whispered, biting her lip.

"That's very unhuman of you."

"How so?"

"I thought humans were selfish, not inquisitive."

"I told you," she said softly, "I'm not like most humans."

"No," he breathed. "You definitely are not."

Their eyes locked. His hand hovered near hers again. His face lowered to meet hers—

A throat cleared behind her, loud and deliberate. "Can we cut in?" Blaze and Lulu stood there. Colik released Piper instantly, stepping back without a word.

"May I have this next dance?" Blaze asked, hand extended

toward her, his voice carrying easily over the hush between songs.

Piper hesitated, her pulse skipping, then gave a small nod. Before she could second-guess it, Lulu's smirk cut the air, as she claimed Colik's arm and spun him into the crowd. The two of them vanished into the swirl of dancers, leaving Blaze's hand waiting, steady and certain.

Piper took his hand, and he drew her into the rhythm with practiced ease. Around them, the Dreamers spilled back onto the floor, their movements rippling outward as the midnight-blue owl bent over the grand piano again. Scirges twisted and turned along the floor in uneven bursts, while Cryos glided with movements so measured they felt carved from ice. Mist shimmered briefly where their feet touched, vanishing before it could settle.

The Shades themselves stood apart, their presence less a dance than a haunting. Their hunger vibrated in the stillness, and the Emers surrounded them with quiet poise. They did not move to the rhythm so much as listen to it, watching the Shades with an intensity that made Piper's skin prickle.

"I know I'm not as thrilling as my brother," Blaze cut through her thoughts, a faint curve to his mouth. "Still, I can dance. A Royald must know at least that much."

His tone was light, but the steadiness of his hand unsettled her, as though Blaze had been carrying the weight of this dance for far longer than this moment.

"This color suits you," he murmured, eyes lowering to her gown. "Almost as if it was made for you. A steel-silver among a room stemmed from gold."

Piper nodded, unable to find words. The sincerity in him made her restless, made her want to answer truths she didn't even know yet.

"Colik said these were his wings," she whispered, brushing the fabric. "Why does it matter so much that I wear them?"

Blaze's smile was thin, fleeting. "Already asking about him.

I was hoping to keep your attention for one whole song." Her blush warmed the air between them, but he leaned closer before it could ease.

"You've been searching for your place here," he said, his voice falling into something quieter, something that felt less like conversation and more like revelation. "Your place isn't one of ours. It's what stirs when you enter a room. It's what bends when you choose to stay."

She blinked up at him. "You're saying I don't belong?"

"I'm saying you belong more than any of us." He twirled her gently, his hand tightening for a moment, anchoring her to the words. "That is what terrifies every Dreamer. That is why every Guild of Dreamer came."

Her chest constricted. "You?"

Blaze's smile didn't reach his eyes. "Especially me."

The constellations above wavered. Piper glanced toward the tiered stone seats, and high among the carvings sat the emerald-eyed Shade. Piper's heart skipped three quick beats.

He wasn't dancing. He wasn't moving. He was watching her. His cloak shifted, revealing a hollow flicker of a face before the darkness swallowed it again.

"You want answers," Blaze continued, his grip loosening, testing whether she'd stay. "Just know that answers are dangerous. They bind as much as they free. Still—" His gaze flicked toward the grand owl, its talons pressing harder into the keys, the music quickening. "Something is coming. Something none of us can dance our way around."

Her throat tightened. "What do you mean?"

"If the frequency of moments holds true, it will be sooner than I think." His jaw set, voice dropping to a whisper. "Know this, Piper. You were not brought here by accident. Whatever cracks you've seen in this world...they open for you."

The words thrummed through her, heavy with both warning and promise.

Just then, Colik broke from the crowd, stepping beside

them. His gaze was tearing into hers, silently reminding her of what he said about dancing the final dance with him.

What if she didn't want to be bound to him?

"Ready?" Colik asked, his voice low, and his heat undeniable. Blaze waited for Piper to make a move.

She hesitated, then turned toward Blaze. "I think I'd like one more dance with him."

Colik's jaw flexed. "You know what this means."

His eyes were on Blaze when he said this, but Blaze's smile was faint, shadowed by something Piper couldn't name. "She chose. You will have your final dance."

Shaking his head, Colik stepped back, the ice in his gaze never leaving Blaze. Blaze returned the look with quiet resolution, and Piper swore she saw guilt beneath it.

When Blaze pulled her close again, his hands carried more tension. He led her easily, his hand steady at her waist, but the steadiness felt borrowed.

"You carry questions," he said, his eyes drifting past her shoulder to the other Dreamers. "The right answers come when you ask the right questions."

Piper studied him, suddenly wondering if the ballroom's brilliance wasn't hiding her weakness, but his.

"Holding this Constellation Ball isn't just about me," she murmured, surprising herself. "Is it?"

Blaze exhaled softly, but he did not answer her. Instead, his gaze flicked toward the grand owl on the piano keys, wings half-spread as though using its whole body. The melody curled through the room like a dark lullaby, soft enough to be ignored, but old enough to be dangerous.

"This is the Song of Erebus," Blaze murmured. "Called *Hymn to Ora*." Blaze's hand tightened slightly at her waist, then he leaned in, his voice a whisper between the notes:

"In the thi 'lora where ora drowns slow,
Nyx walks saeth paths only darkness knows.

> In ola, all kross will blend—
> For every ora-eli soul must fall before it can
>   mend."

She had no idea what most of the words meant, recognizing only Nyx and *kross*, the Goddess of Night and the word for *fate* in Dreamtongue. Yet the lyrics settled in her chest like cold ash.

Blaze didn't smile. He didn't need to. "That," he said, "is the part the gods never knew happened."

They danced in silence, then Blaze's smile curved faintly, touched by sorrow.

"It appears that everything here is about you and Colik." He twirled her, and when he drew her back, his grip softened, not in tenderness, but in release. "You burn, Piper," he said, voice pitched so low it felt stolen from the music. "So does Colik, though I can't see what binds you two. Whatever it is, it lies beyond even my age."

Amidst a small dip, where Blaze's lips were so close to Piper's ear that it sent shivers down her bare back, he whispered, "Protect the Citadel at all costs. Protect Colik at all costs. Or it will be the cost of you."

CHAPTER TWENTY-NINE
THE BLACK STAR

A s Blaze lifted her from the dip, Piper felt the Shades watching. Their hollow eyes followed every move, and every turn, the weight of their stares pressing against her ribs until it hurt.

"Ignore them," Blaze murmured, gaze steady on hers again, as if he didn't just give her a tremendously cryptic and nerve-wracking warning. "They don't decide where you belong."

Her throat tightened. "Why me?"

"Because where I said that the Dreamworld bends for you," he said simply, understanding what she was asking, "Colik bends with it too."

She swallowed hard. "I—I don't understand. I thought whatever was between us in the Broken Woods was... gone. Broken." She finally admitted out loud what she had felt for days, or moments. She wasn't sure how many frequencies of moments it had been.

"Ask Lulu about being broken." Blaze hesitated, his smile faint. "She would know more about the Broken Woods fate than anyone."

A chill rippled down her spine. She wanted to press him, to demand what he meant, but Blaze smiled.

"Lulu knows you belong too," he continued, voice warmer, feeling like a shield. "She won't show you, not in the way you want anyway—her lucent won't let her—but she's already fighting harder than anyone to keep you safe. Trust her, even when it terrifies you."

"She does terrify me."

"Good." His wink was brittle, fleeting. "That means she's doing what only she can do."

Piper let out a small, nervous laugh. Relief, though brief, loosened her chest. That had to be partly true. Lulu saved her. Blaze's shoulders eased at the sound, though his eyes darkened.

"You're allowed to laugh," he said. "Even here."

She glanced down at their steps. "It's just... I've never belonged to something worth staying for."

"You do now. You're not a guest anymore." He twirled her once more, pulling her close with careful ease. "If you choose to stay, I'll stand beside you for as long as I can."

Her heart stumbled at his phrasing. "If I go?"

"I'll remember you." His voice didn't waver. "Always."

Why did that sound like a goodbye?

The music thinned, slowing toward its end. Blaze's eyes dropped down to her wrist. His hand brushed the brace, pausing at the latch. "Again, I could release it."

Piper caught his hand before he could. "No," she said softly. "Not yet."

Pride flickered across his face then dulled with something heavier. "There's one more thing," he paused. "About Colik."

She tensed in his grasp. He was a good dancer. Formal yet soft. Softer than Colik at least. "I know. He hates me." Blaze gave a short laugh, as if needing the humor. "Whether he says it or not, he's already chosen. Long before you, he chose duty before everything. Even love."

Her chest ached.

"Knights don't get to love, Piper," Blaze said, his voice dimming with the song. "They get to bleed." He hesitated, eyes lingering on hers. "He has played hot and cold with you —yes, we all have noticed—because he knows no other way to be. Colik is a Royald, yes, but he also is young. Childish. Still growing into the role this world formed for him."

A large knot formed in Piper's stomach.

The final chord fell into silence. Blaze let go of her hand, his smile soft but marked with sorrow. Around them the dancing Dreamers blurred, but his focus never left her.

He bent in a low bow; his words so faint she felt them more than heard them. "Don't look around. When it begins… if I give you a command—even with my eyes—do it. No hesitation."

Her breath caught. "Blaze—"

"Don't move your lips. Just remember what I said." His lips barely moved. "Now smile and promise me with a nod."

Piper forced a closed lip smile, dipping her chin.

Blaze rose slowly, and his shoulders dropped with subtle intention. He did not speak or meet her eyes again, but simply turned, and began walking back toward the dais, his white cloak catching the diamonds light of the chandelier above. He moved with the tenseness of someone carrying out something already decided.

For a beat, Piper didn't follow. She waited, half-expecting him to glance back. To offer her a hand, a signal, or anything, but nothing came.

She stepped forward to follow him or at least tried to. It was so gradual she didn't notice the Dreamers beginning to conjoin, drifting across the marble in fluid, soundless steps. One turned. Then another. Then three more. Soon they were no longer scattered dancers but part of something larger, their movements folding into one another until a circle began to take shape at the center of the floor.

They didn't surround her all at once. It was subtler than that, and more elegant, like a tide returning to shore, quiet, but inevitable. They wove themselves into the rhythm of the room with deceptive grace, some spinning, dancing with the stellar phantoms, the Scirges chasing them. Each motion seemed innocent on its own, but together, it became a current she couldn't push against.

She moved left, but a Dreamer swayed into her path.

She turned right, and a Dreamer stopped in her path. But unlike the Shades or Scirges messing with the Stellar Phantoms, the other Dreamers hesitated to get too close to her.

The music hadn't changed, but the air had grown heavier. Piper turned again, trying to catch sight of the dais.

Blaze was already seated, his eyes sharp on hers. She couldn't read his expression, but she knew, without knowing, that this wasn't abandonment, but placement. He had left her precisely where he wanted her to be.

"THE   RING   OF   DUST   AND   ASHES COMMENCES."

The proclamation came from nowhere, rolling through the Orph Ballroom with the force of thunder. From the dais, Patryk stepped forward. His lavender cloak unfurled behind him as he lifted one hand, gathering every breath into a single held moment. The Dreamers obeyed, falling still.

"We gather," he intoned, voice carrying with calm ceremony, "beneath the Dreamers' Belt, where memory, dust, and dreams converge."

Piper couldn't look away. Patryk stood tall, spine straight as a blade, his silver collar catching every flicker of constellation light. He looked impossibly proud, his eyes glowing, like this was a moment he had rehearsed a thousand times, and it was stage time.

"The Constellation Ball is no mere celebration," he continued. "It is a union of stars, of ages, and of Reverie law. The Dreamers' Belt holds the waking and the dream in balance. It was woven from the first breath of dust the gods bestowed, but it cannot endure alone. It requires three. Humans believe in one world because the gods wove that belief into them."

He let the silence stretch, gaze sweeping over the gathered Guilds of Dreamers.

"The Royalds—guardians of dust and dream, bearers of the lucents of the Gods of Dreams—are chosen not to just rule, but to anchor the Dreamers Belt. Without their bond, without the unity of the guilds beneath them..." His voice darkened. "The Dreamer Belt frays. And with it, so does the Reverie."

Stillness spread across the floor. Cryos with frost lining their lashes. Vixens masked in fiery brilliance. Cabras robed in feathers that whispered like golden hour. Emers gleaming like carved amethyst. Scirges poised in childish salute. The Shades unmoving, though their shadows were restless.

Patryk turned back to the dais, voice rising. "Behold the Royalds."

He motioned to the right. "Our queen: Lulu, Royald of phantoms, illusions and dream-echoes."

Lulu stepped forward, crimson silk trailing like spilled petaled wine. Her face was a forced calm, and her hands curled faintly.

Patryk gestured left. "Our king: Blaze, Royald of the golden crown. Of Reverie Law and truth."

Blaze advanced, every step echoing like a judgment. His white robe shimmered with threads of gold, while his eyes were shadowed with the weight of something he refused to voice.

Patryk hesitated before centering himself. "Colik stands as knight, sworn to the swar of sleep. To where monsters kneel and shadows stir."

Colik moved forward slowly, his chest rising too quickly, each movement strained with the effort of concealment.

Piper's eyes caught on the swar camouflaged at his hilt, its outline flickering faintly.

The Royalds stood veiled in gold, silver, and bronze. Patryk lifted his hand once more. "The Dreamers bow."

One by one, the Guilds lowered in respect. The Cabras coiled low, feathers whispering. The Vixens swept into deep curtsies, red silk cutting sharp through the air. The Routs bowed their silver hooded heads. The Cryos moved in flawless unison. The Scirges dropped to one knee with practiced, mocking elegance. Even the Emers bent stiffly, their purple crystalline forms gleaming in obedience.

The Shades did not bow. Did not even kneel. Instead, they remained still, shadows restless but unmoved.

A tense note sliced through the silence. Blaze's jaw twitched, his gaze flickering once toward them. Yet he did nothing. He gave no command, nor issued a rebuke. He faced forward, the fracture in his silence more dangerous than words. Lulu stiffened beside him while Colik's fists clenched, ready for war.

"Continue." Blaze's voice cut through, low and storm thick.

Patryk inclined his head, then raised his eyes to the constellations. "Let the stars bow in return."

The ballroom floor ignited, a spiral of icy flame unfurling like the petals of some ancient, frozen bloom. Blue fire licked outward in curling arcs until a radiant ring rose around Piper, casting fractured sapphire light beneath her feet.

Through the flames, seven Vixens glided forward, their bodies traced in molten gold and crushed starlight. They moved with liquid grace, bending the air to their will.

Above them, the constellations bent, then broke into a slow swirl. Stardust rained in perfect order, like a celestial coronation. Colors of the stones and crystals poured from the sky: sapphire, amethyst, onyx, bronze, opal, peridot, and crimson.

Piper's gaze caught on one Vixen who lingered as she passed, her ember-bright eyes locking with Piper's. She winked, a knowing spark hidden within the grandeur, as though the spectacle itself were not for the Royalds at all, but for her.

Gasps rose from every corner of the golden walls as heads tilted back, jewels and dresses catching the stars in a thousand flickers. Music slowed, strings drawing out a trembling note as though the very sound wished to bow alongside them.

Piper had thought the Constellation Ball was just a name. Here, she saw the truth.

The constellations literally bowed to those in the Orph Ballroom.

Leo, the lion of night, dipped it's great, burning head, three long arcs of tail stars coiling behind it. Cassiopeia, once frozen on her celestial throne, tipped forward in an elegant arch. Cygnus, the swan, folded its wings mid-flight, while Andromeda slipped free from her chains of fate. Aquila, the eagle, hovered in a bowed arc, talons tucked in.

Then came Orion.

The hunter lowered his belt of starlight and sheathed his sword, the bright scatter of his shoulders and knees drawing in. At his side were Canis Major and Canis Minor. The dogs circled Orion's feet, their heads lifted, their bodies poised between guard and companion.

Then Orion's bowed head shifted, not toward the Royalds, not toward the gathered Dreamers, but toward Piper. Just enough that the hunter's shadowed gaze found her where she stood in the crowd.

The Great Bear, Ursa Major, twisted away from its eternal circle around the North Star and stretched across the constellation cloud, its shadow sweeping across the ballroom floor, pausing over Piper as though laying down a mantle of protection. Ursa Minor, the cub, followed close, while Polaris's steady glow shifted to fix on her alone.

Around her, other Dreamers whispered at the display, but Piper couldn't look away. A strange warmth strung through her chest. This was more than beauty. It felt like recognition.

The sky exhaled, each constellation bending low, in gratitude of the Dreamers' Belt, whose strength bound the worlds together. Around her, she heard the whispers of the Dreamers.

"Dust to dream."

"Mortal to God."

"Soul to star."

For a heartbeat, the Orph Ballroom moved in perfect unison. In the next, a ripple tore through the constellation cloud. It was sudden, sharp, and unmistakably wrong.

One of the Vixens dropped to her knees, hands carving frantic spirals in the air. The others followed, caught in her panic, repeating the motion like a contagion. The stars above stuttered, and the rain of light faltered. The constellations spasmed, twisting mid-formation. Symbols turned on themselves. Harmony collapsed into distortion.

The Blood Moon suddenly appeared, bleeding through the sky in warning. And then the constellations shattered completely and a black star formed.

It was not a hole and not a sun, but something far worse. A sucking wound in the sky. Light collapsed inward, tearing like fabric ripped from its seams. The constellations shuddered as they were dragged toward it, their crystal-bright stars pulled from their places and devoured one by one.

The dancing Vixens vanished in a swirl of perfumed dust and trailing silk. Cryos forms evaporated into mist. One remained, statuesque, eyes wide with something like awe. Some Emers vanished in flickers of violet light, while others hovered near the Shades, their hands twitching with indecision. The Routs tightened their hoods and slipped away in silent ranks, but one broke formation, rooted in place. The Scirges bolted in quick bursts, darting toward the ivory doors. Cyril and another Scirge who Piper recognized but never met, stayed behind, most likely curiosity gluing them in place. The Cabras rose into the air, metallic wings blazing, sweeping through the arcs of the pillars. Two broke away and perched on a beam high above the ballroom, their eyes locked on the dais, as if waiting for something more.

Yet, all the Shades remained exactly where they were. Still as statues, rooted to the floor. Some leaned forward, shoulders straining like they were trying to flee, but something held them.

Piper's bones chilled as the stars above screamed. She knew she should get to the dais, but she wasn't sure how to maneuver through the mad crowd of scurrying Dreamers.

Then, lightly and unexpectedly, someone grabbed her hand. Piper spun, ready to tear free, but the breath snagged in her throat the moment she saw him.

The emerald-eyed Shade.

He stood far too close, as he murmured, "Do not move." He felt dark, dangerous, and oddly calm. The words weren't a threat. They weren't even a warning. They were low, controlled, and utterly impossible to resist. Piper obeyed without question.

The black star pulsed outward, continuously swallowing light like a living void. Another crack split the air, low and thunderous, as though the Dreamworld itself had been struck by a god's hammer. Each heartbeat throbbed against Piper's ears. Then the star unraveled around her, its shadow twisting into a hurricane of black ash. A tunnel carved through darkness, aiming solely at her.

Blaze took notice before anyone else. He stepped forward with his hands lifted, a conduit for Morpheus' lucent, and the air itself recoiled around him, bending and twisting, whispering warnings she could not hear.

Gold flame surged along his arms, licking over skin and bone with its own free will. It flickered and danced like candlelight, soft at the edges but sharp at its core, burning with a clarity that felt too vivid to belong to any normal man.

The laurel crown above his head erupted. The bay leaves shimmered like molten smoke, writhing and restless. For a breath—so faint Piper might have imagined it—the smoky spiral jerked, as though caught by an invisible tug.

Blaze's veins bulged along his arms, molten gold beneath the skin. His eyes had changed, grey corneas glowing hot ash, like the smoke of a fire that devoured worlds. There was pure fire in his eyes.

"In the name of the First Dreamer," Blaze's voice tore through the Orph Ballroom. "Be still!"

The black star above the Citadel twisted open, ragged and writhing, tendrils of darkness lashing directly at Piper.

"Dreamfire," the Shade breathed at her side. "Relax."

Suddenly the black star froze, halted mid-collapse, caught in invisible strands of dreamfire laced with dark clouded lining flowing from Blaze's raised hands. The room shivered as if reality itself had been jerked on a leash. The constellations groaned, bending and warping, until a dome of shimmering, lucid energy started to seal the black star out.

Yet a sudden look on Blaze's face said that the dreamfire didn't behave like it normally did. Blaze's head turned slightly, his gaze sliding past Piper's shoulder. To the Shade standing behind her.

The Dreamers stood frozen, suspended between awe and terror. Even the Shades stammered, their shadows twitching, unsure how to hold their shape. Except the emerald eyed Shade behind Piper. He stood still, silent, but with a calm that clashed with the rest of the fear spreading in the ballroom.

Blaze lowered his arm by a few degrees, the gilded dream-fire curling back to his wrist, flickering like embers fighting death, but the power did not leave. It lingered with a heat that made the very air ache, and a rhythm pounded against Piper's chest as though the flame itself carried a heartbeat.

Piper watched his jaw lock, his eyes lifting again, yet his attention snapped once more, fleetingly, toward the Shade behind her.

The dreamfire released, and a sweep of dusty darkness rushed through the ballroom, so quick and subtle that the Dreamers who had lingered never even looked up, but Piper was watching. She saw it curl around her like a thin veil of ash, gathering at the edges of Blaze's fire and pushing it upward, higher, and harder. The dreamfire flared with sudden strength, burning brighter than it had before, as though the darkness itself had fed it.

For a breath, the ash-lined surge lit the room with fierce clarity, the flames rising just enough to force the black star back into nothingness. The dome was fully sealed.

The music stilled and the constellations above held their breath.

Every flicker and twisted surge of that flame was tied to Blaze. Powerful, and a mad, violent, beautiful kind of protection. What Piper wanted to know was who—*or what*—had created the dusty darkness.

From the way Blaze's stare fell on her, he was wondering that too.

CHAPTER THIRTY
THE SHADES INTERLUDE

D ozens of Shades still lined the floor, silent and still, their obsidian eyes trained not on the Royalds at the dais, nor on the black star that had just tried to engulf the entire constellation cloud, but on *her*. The black star added emphasis to Piper's inconvenient position.

It was not curiosity in their eyes, but something *seen*. Their attention pinned her in place, vultures recognizing the new scent of a weak animal.

She was that weak animal. A *human*.

Their movements were quiet, deliberate, and unnervingly coordinated. Like a net tightening around her, they wove across the floor with every breath she dared to take. The circle narrowed, seamless and inevitable, as though the layout conspired to draw her in.

Ahead, the Royalds stood frozen and too far out of reach. The Dreamers who had chosen not to dance on the floor remained seated at their stone perches, their gazes fixed and unblinking. From their vantage, the room no longer resembled a ballroom meant for celebration, but an amphitheater staged for spectacle, with Piper at its unwilling center.

Why did Blaze leave me here?

"Take my hand." His voice was low, sharpened with both promise and threat. Piper startled, breath snagging as she faced him, remembering the emerald-eyed Shade from the Plastrof at her side. The Shade leaned closer, darkness clinging to his features like an accessory. "Let me show you how to really dance."

Her stomach dropped, the deepness and confidence in the tone of his words pulling at parts of Piper that she didn't know existed.

Stop it.

She could not forget that he was one of them. Before she could argue, he lifted his other hand. In it, was a single black flower, with petals darker than ink yet shimmering faintly as if lit from within. A flower she instinctively knew was not meant for mortals. A flower she knew that Steele had asked her for. How would he have known? Or was it mere coincidence?

"For you," he whispered.

Piper froze, unsure whether this was a gesture of danger or devotion. Or both. The Shade didn't wait for her to decide. With a slow, deliberate tenderness, he reached up, sliding his fingers through her hair. His touch was careful, brushing back a loose strand near her temple. The petals glinted as they neared her face, catching on the faint glitter Patryk had dusted into her hair in the Vanis Room.

He tucked the black flower behind her ear, the stem pressing warm against her skin.

"What is that?"

He was quiet for a moment, his emerald eyes dropping to the petals resting against her temple. "In this world, the black flower means death," he said. "It grows only in forgotten places. Where things go when the Dreamworld is finished with them." Something shifted in his expression, brief and unguarded. "We give it to what is already lost." His voice dropped lower, almost to himself. "I have never given one to something living." His gaze moved over her face with a slow, unsettling reverence, as though she were something he had no category for. "You are the most alive thing I have seen in this world. And that terrifies everything here far more than death ever could."

Her breath trembled. Unmoved by her faltering glance, his hand extended, a gesture that was less invitation than possession. Her chest tightened, not with the kind of fear that spurred escape, but with the kind that hindered her, rooting her where she stood, forcing her to feel every deafening beat of her heart as her eyes moved to the dais.

Sensing him, Blaze's gaze was on her, his expression unreadable but his ever-so-subtle nod unmistakable. It was the silent command, or plea, that she promised to listen to.

It said: *Dance with him.*

Keeping her promise, but feeling like a lamb in the lion's den, she placed her hand in the emerald-eyed Shade's. His fingers closed around hers, refreshingly cold and sure. Then he spun her into motion, swift and seamless, his body folding into hers with a presence too sharp and practiced being anything but calculated. One arm swept behind her waist like a guardrail, the other lifted their joined hands, locking their bodies in rhythm.

His hold was too tight to be safe, and yet too careful to be cruel. There was no music, only the exposed hush of the ballroom, and the fault lines Piper had subtly sensed from the moment she walked in. Still, he moved her across the floor, no music needed, the Dreamworld shifting with them in quiet elegance and borrowed grace.

The Shades began to shift around them, quiet and cautious, stepping out of the way without ever truly retreating. They formed a loose ring on the dance floor, circling like wolves too intrigued to pounce. Their eyes still followed Piper, with hunger and obsessive curiosity.

She could feel them breathing her in, her presence among them disturbing something sacred or forbidden.

The other Dreamers who had stayed behind were noticing too. Their gazes flicked between her and her dance partner. Between the delicate way the Shade moved with her, and the unsettling way the others orbited her like moons caught in some new gravity, she wasn't sure what was about to happen to her.

Could she trust a Shade?

Piper's eyes had been anywhere but on the Shades face. The panic in her was rising fast, bubbling beneath her skin, clawing for a way out. She needed a distraction, something to break the spiraling thoughts. She'd been trying to not step on his feet either.

So, she did the one thing she hadn't dared. She looked up at *him*, and her breath instantly caught.

He was already watching her, *only her*, and not on the scene unfolding around them. Among the circling Shades and the sealed dome above by Blaze's dreamfire, his eyes stayed locked on her like he'd never seen anything else worth looking at.

She remembered the green in them from the Plastrof. She told herself it was just the water, that the emerald hue must've been a trick of light, given he was a Dreamer of nightmares. Now, with nothing between them but air and candlelight, she saw the truth. They were green, and not just any green, but a perfectly, unnervingly, vivid emerald. Like they'd been carved from gem light and set there to see through her.

"Do you always dance like this with strangers?" Piper whispered, breathless from more than just the steps. She needed a distraction from her first attempt at a distraction.

He leaned in, and his lips brushed close to her ear, the tone in his voice like thunder rumbling in the distance. "Only when I want to watch the light in their eyes," he crooned. "You, *Oneiroikos*...you burn too bright for your kind."

"Oneir—"

He spun her fast—too fast—forcing her words to drop and focus, to move, and surrender to the dance. His fingers pressed against her bare spine, guiding her toward the narrow pocket of safety between the still lingering Shades. A shiver ran up her spine from where he touched her skin.

"You don't have to enjoy this too much," he growled softly. "Don't stop moving. They're testing you. They want your dust."

A Shade leaned forward, his fingers twitching for her. The emerald-eyed Shade moved sharply, cutting their path with a turn that brought Piper flush against his chest. She could feel his heartbeat, fast and slow at the same time, if that was even possible. He pulled her left, spun her right, then stepped out of the reaching arms of another Shade who had crept in too close.

"They're drawn to you," he said through clenched teeth, his breath brushing her neck. "I see why." He inhaled her scent, making her heart skip a beat. "You smell like the beginning and end of a dream. They want what I have in my arms."

Her heart skipped another beat as she caught sight of one cloaked Shade whispering into another's hollow ear. Her skin crawled and she turned back to her dance partner.

"I didn't mean to draw them," she breathed.

He laughed, dark and quiet. "You don't draw them. You *wake* their craving."

With every pass, their steps cut between Shades like wind through ash. One figure reached out with elongated fingers, grazing the hem of Piper's dress. She flinched. Her dance partner pulled her into a spin so sharp she lost her footing, but he caught her, their bodies colliding again in a rush of heat and breath. Her fear.

He turned her into a dip, angling her away from another Shade's grasp, his palm bracing her back like a wall.

"They can't take your dreams," he whispered. "Unless you give it to them again. They will try if they get hold of you. It is what we do." Was that what he—

Another Shade suddenly leaned in too far, breaking her thoughts. In a blur, the emerald eyed Shade reached out with the hand on her back, caught the Shade's wrist midair, and twisted it away without breaking rhythm. A flicker of green fire leaped through his eyes.

He pulled her into back him, his voice brushing her ear again as he spoke. "You're truly something, Piper," he murmured, low and intoxicating. "I've never seen one so desired. Lucky me that I get to be this close."

The words slid into her like a forbidden secret. One she had no right to want but suddenly craved. Another shiver trembled down her spine, betraying her even as every instinct warned her, she should pull away.

He was a Shade. A Dreamer of nightmare.

She found herself moving with him, no longer resisting, but following, caught in the strange rhythm that bound them. The Shade's touch had changed. It was less urgent, and more certain, his hand guiding hers, having learned the shape of her steps. While she learned his.

"We are about there."

There? Her thoughts stuttered. Where was *there?*

Around them, the ballroom had become a maze of wanting, Shades and Dreamers alike straining forward, either to see what was going to happen, or contemplating a move themselves. Every step now felt deliberate, and unpredictable.

Finally, the circle broke, and they slipped through the last row of lingering Shades. The floor opened wide before them again, their dance stopping naturally in front of the dais.

Oh, there. Of course. He was leading her to safety. Again—*A Shade. A Dreamer of nightmare.*

All three Royald's gaze burned on them. Blaze looked relieved, Lulu was unreadable, and Colik's jaw was clenched. Piper swore she saw a smirk cross Patryk's face, but it fell before she could be sure.

"What did you do?" Colik said, his voice a low rasp, thick with dread. "That was against the—"

Blaze put a hand up to stop him. "Enough," he said, his voice firm, controlled, but carrying the weight of the command that silenced the ballroom again.

The Shade's hand slipped from Piper's with a quiet grace, clearly not ready to let go.

She turned instinctively to him, one last look, but he was already stepping back, vanishing into the fold of Shades.

Lulu's voice cut through the space. "Well, that was rather counterproductive." Her eyes shifted from Piper to Blaze. "You left her out there like bait," she hissed, every syllable sharp with accusation.

Piper's stomach twisted. *No*, he wouldn't have—

"I know." Blaze's response shattered Piper's plea.

Another hush fell across the ballroom. Then, laughter. Not from the dais, but among the Shades, who began to part once more.

Tall and cloaked, a man stepped out from the Shades. He moved like royalty, but Piper knew he didn't belong. His robe looked human made, gloves covered his hands, and his face showed skin too pale and eyes too calculated. The way he moved was deliberate and confident, but not fluid like any Dreamer.

Piper's eyes snapped from the mysterious man to the Royals. It was clear they didn't know who he was either. They knew what he wasn't. He was like Piper.

Now *him* she recognized. He had to be a human. He had the same human crave in his eyes to belong that she did.

His arrival wasn't loud. It was worse. It felt inevitable. Then the Shades *knelt*. All toward the mysterious man, except the emerald-eyed Shade.

Lulu gasped. Colik held his breath. Blaze no longer looked relieved but paled. The Shade who had danced with her remained upright behind the mysterious man, eyes turned just slightly toward the dais. He did not move, nor kneel. His eyes bored into Piper's.

Her breath faltered. Her hand twitched at her side, skin still haunted by his touch. The cloaked man's presence opened a flooded gate. What had been a silent unity among the Shades became a storm of voices:

"She is a human too."

"A human among the Royalds?"

"Not even a Dreamer—"

"Not in the Outwards…"

"What makes her different?"

It was like when she first met the Scirges, but the aura was off. It was entirely wrong, and as if the Royalds felt it too, they reacted instantly.

Blaze stepped between Piper and the Shades, and Colik, already at her side, had his hand on the hilt of his hidden swar. Lulu lined the other side. The other Dreamers—those who hadn't fled—stayed distant observers in what was some standoff.

Piper's eyes tore from the restless Shades and caught Cyril watching her, his fear sharp and meant for her alone. Her pulse hammered, but she forced herself to turn back to the cloaked figure at the center.

Without a word, the man lifted his hand. Instantly, the Shades stilled, their whispers collapsing back into silence at his command. Then his voice cut through the thickening air, sharp enough to split the hush in two.

"Well," he said, "that was quite the performance."

He stepped forward, slow and unhurried, eyes gleaming.

"Who are you?" Blaze asked, his voice a quiet growl.

The man laughed. "As shows go, I'd say this one had flair. The dance, the stars, the lucent flaring to seal the ceiling…" He tilted his head, a smirk ghosting his lips. "You wanted me out of the darkness? Well. Here I am."

Blaze didn't move, but the strain showed.

"What do you want?" he asked through gritted teeth.

The man sighed, as though the question bored him. He paced slowly up to the dais, eyes sweeping over each Royald in turn.

"I don't want chaos," he said, almost gently. "I want what once was." He stopped directly in front of Blaze. "I want to stand where you stand. As Royald."

Stunned silence rippled through the Citadel. Even the Shades flinched.

Colik shifted instinctively, placing himself half in front of Piper, knuckles white around his unseen weapon.

Lulu's voice cut sharp. "How did you get past the Boygles? The Polaris patrols every entry. Nothing walks through those doors uninvited."

"I didn't come through the doors." He said it simply. "I have my own guard. A shadowed one."

The silence that followed was a different kind entirely. Blaze's expression drained of everything except recognition. Lulu went rigid. Colik took a slow step back, the color leaving his face in a way Piper had never seen—not anger, not grief, but something terrifyingly close to fear. None of them explained it. None of them needed to.

Blaze barked a short, humorless laugh. "You're mad. How do you have a Shado—"

"Mad?" the man interrupted, grinning. "Or merely resourceful. Once, humans could dream like gods. There was no wall between waking and immortal wonder. The gods, and now Dreamers, choose order over greatness. Fear over truth." His voice carried the same heat as Hazel's had. The same conviction. The same wound beneath it.

Lulu's eyes sharpened. "A human. The Polaris... it was tracking *your* dust."

The man tsked. "I am partly human," the man said. "I am something older. I am a Mimic."

The word fell like a stone. The Shades stirred, some brittle with laughter, others bowing low, the name pulling obedience from them whether they offered it willingly or not.

Himyla's voice echoed in Piper's mind. *The friend who vanished. Dust turning to ash until nothing human remained.*

"You are the chaos spreading."

The Mimic's gaze slid to her as though he'd caught the memory mid-flight. His smile sharpened.

"Shades are fragments born from nightmares," he said. "Mimics are the whole dream devouring itself. Mortals who crossed too far, whose will hollowed, whose dreams twisted them into hunger. We are what happens when the R-Laws break and break again."

Blaze stepped forward. "Whatever you are, you are not welcome here."

"Welcome?" His smile was all teeth and shadow. "No. This is merely a Shades' interlude." He spread his hands toward the gathered guilds above. "The Royalds condemned the Golden Age. Silenced the Silver Age. Yet they have allowed her—" his gaze swept to Piper, "—a human—to walk this world as if she belongs. Take dust. Break strands. Open gates." His voice turned to ice. "If you refuse to grant me what she has been given freely, I will summon the Fatale."

Colik snapped. "Why us? The gods ended those ages. We only protect what came after."

"Because this is the closest to the gods I will get. And because she is not merely human," the Mimic said. "Not anymore. Possibly not ever."

Piper's pulse stumbled.

Something shifted in Blaze's face—a tightening around the eyes, a breath held too long. He didn't speak. But Lulu noticed. Patryk noticed. Colik noticed.

The emerald-eyed Shade stepped to the Mimic's side, his features taut. "She has blood of silver in her," he rasped.

The room went silent.

Blaze closed his eyes once, slowly. It was the resignation of a man acknowledging a truth he had been circling for too long.

"Silver blood. Silver dust. A silver strand woven into flesh," the Mimic continued. "Mortals bred to be gods, tossed into the human world. Only those with the blood of silver have the right to cross into this one, as gifted by Zeus himself. It is written in the *Book of Godspells*. The day the Silver Children were severed, some strand slipped loose. Released by someone who should never have had that power."

Hazel. Piper saw her remembrance again without meaning to.

"Only dream dust in the waking world—a tether, a touch, a spark—can wake what was left sleeping in her," he continued. "The beginning of a becoming."

"Steele," Piper breathed.

Lulu's eyes shot to Blaze. "That is why Pandora's Vault woke for her. I thought it was chance—"

"It was blood," Blaze said quietly. He hadn't known about the Vault until this moment but was trying to not look shocked. Or angry. She could see it in the way his jaw set, the way his composure held by sheer force of will.

"No," Colik breathed. "That's impossible."

"Is it?" Blaze turned to him. "How did she tie to Hazel? To Steele? But not entirely to you? The sandtie held, but it still broke. Silver strands tie to one another soundly. Blood recognizes blood."

Colik went pale.

"For decades I was nothing but dust trying to form," the Mimic said. "When she opened the Vault, my strand loosened. My body formed. Her hand—her blood—broke the seal." He let the words settle. "The Fatales will come for the source of the fracture. Which leads back to her. Unless I give them something else to attend to first. A broken law perhaps?"

"That's the real reason," Colik said, his voice low and

hard. "Not justice. To redirect Solari onto Piper while you buy yourself a passage here."

The Mimic didn't deny it.

Lulu's breath fractured. "Her dust… her eyes… the scar… gods, she is—"

"A child born of silver," the Mimic finished, bowing his head slightly toward Piper.

The Shades rustled like wind through bone.

Piper couldn't breathe. Her hand. Her choices. Her blood. Every thread pulled back to her. Colik was right. She was the growing chaos. Her and the Mimic—two humans in the Dreamworld.

Her gaze found the emerald-eyed Shade across the room, and the look that passed between them needed no translation.

What have you gotten yourself into now?

CHAPTER THIRTY-ONE
THE REVERIE LAWS

N o body moved. Not Piper. Not the Dreamers watching from the tiers above. Not the Royals.

The Mimic lifted his hands and what followed was older than sound. It was a language that had no business in a human throat, each syllable tearing the air apart as it left him, opening something in the space between one breath and the next that had no name in any tongue Piper knew. The chandelier above them shuddered, its diamond veins trembling like a struck bell that could not stop ringing. Dust rose from the floor in thin, twitching threads, climbed a few inches, and fell apart into ash.

The Shades felt it before anyone else did. Their bodies shivered, silhouettes fracturing and snapping back together in rapid, ecstatic pulses, the way a flame responds to a wind it has been waiting for.

"He's speaking Dreamtongue," Patryk rasped, the painted colors on his cheeks drained away until his face looked skeletal. "The dialect of the Fatales. No human should know it." His lips parted, trembling. "The Fatales will feel it. They must."

The dome of starlight above them pulsed, and then a

single silver tear slid free. It hung in the air, gleaming, before drifting downward. The moment it fell, the floor shook, its roots answering a call.

"Do not say a word. Got it?" Lulu hissed, her words razor-sharp.

Piper nodded, though her pulse thundered so hard she felt it might break her ribs. She didn't understand until the tear began to change.

It stretched as it fell, thinning, widening, then spilling itself apart like liquid glass. Silver threads pulled from its center, unraveling into a sheet of light that spread across the Orph Ballroom.

Darkness fled, and from the curtain of radiance stepped a figure. She was shaped like the tear that birthed her. Every motion was fluid, impossible, and clearly dangerous. Terror clung to her features, but beauty burned through it. Even the light bent, curving toward her.

Colik's voice broke the silence. "Solari," he breathed, "the Severer of the Fray."

The being moved like a celestial spirit, her body quite literally made of liquid starlight. Two iridescent eyes gazed out, vacant yet omniscient. Around her right wrist, a red string spiraled upward, pulsing like a vein. Like Hazel's wrist, and yet this string was redder. Sharper. Controlled.

As Solari glided to the center, the Royalds straightened. Their faces turned to stone masks. She raised her hand, and the humming broke into silence.

"You summon me," she said, not to the man, not to the gods, but to the Royalds.

The Mimic slanted his head beside her. "A Royald has broken R-Law One. Dust has been traded between waking and dream."

Solari tilted her head ever so slightly. Her voice, when it came, was jagged with authority. "Who holds the dust?"

All eyes turned to Piper. The Shades leaned forward, while

the Dreamers in the surrounding tiers of seats narrowed their gazes. Lulu reached for her but didn't touch. Colik coiled. Blaze stood still, his stillness more restraint than surrender.

"I am…" Piper began, but her throat closed.

Solari slid forward, the floor folding beneath her steps, and with a single lifted hand she shattered the remaining illusion of silver tear.

"I am not here for R-Laws," she declared, her voice slicing through the ballroom like a cold blade. "Those are childish games. Rules for Royald theatrics. The Reverie is older than your ballroom dances. The Oneiroi Laws sit above them, forged for matters far greater than petty balances of dust."

The room stilled. Even the Shades halted.

Solari's eyes found Piper. "I am here," she said, "because the Silver Strands have begun to unravel. Pandora's Vault is no longer sealed. The Dreamworld is remembering what it was meant to forget."

Piper's lungs burned, splitting under the weight of the words before she even understood them.

Blaze's voice cracked like thunder, stepping forward with desperate ferocity. "If a Law is broken, then it is I who broke it."

"Incorrect." Solari didn't even turn her head. "The Oneiroi Laws," she continued, "were crafted to prevent what you allowed. To keep the Silver Strands asleep. To ensure she" —her gaze stayed on Piper— "never found her way back into the Reverie."

Piper turned her gaze to Blaze, but he was in clear shock. This was not good.

Solari lifted her hand. "The Mark is not of Severance," she said, her voice deepening with something older than time. "It is of Summoning. This is not a Dreamer's fate. This is the fate of Silver."

A tremor cracked the floor.

Blaze let out a breath, while Colik's entire body stiffened, shock carved deep into his face. Lulu gasped, her eyes widening with a dawning horror.

Whispers rose from the Dreamers, overlapping and sharp, the Orph Ballroom filling with the frantic hum of fear. Red light—thin as an invisible string—shot from Solari's hand and seared itself into the golden veined floor below.

The mark that flared there was both hook and thread, spiraling vertically, unfinished, and pulsing.

"The symbol…" Lulu's voice broke to a hush. "…of the Fatales."

Then the mark writhed. The ground trembled, split open, and widened into a wound through which something vast clawed its way upward. A shriek spilled through the room as a creature emerged. It looked part phoenix and part pterodactyl, with molten wings veined in black-red fire, and talons gleaming like blades capable of cutting through stone.

Chains bound it, burning with silver fire, dragging the beast into obedience. Behind those bindings stood Solari, her presence bending the beast's molten form to its knees.

The mysterious man stepped back from Solari, a smile curving his lips, but fear flickering behind his eyes when the creature rose its beak.

Then he turned to the Shade with emerald eyes.

Blaze noticed, but just as he was about to try and stop him, the Mimic touched the Shade's cheek with two fingers, murmuring something too soft to hear.

The Shade's green eyes blew out like candles. His skin cracked. His outline dissolved. Darkness swallowed the Mimic whole as he reverted into black dust, nothing more than a nightmare collapsing inward.

"Coward!" Blaze cried out, but stayed rooted, every line of him tense, as though braced for judgement. Lulu met his eyes, seeing something she recognized but couldn't yet explain.

More Dreamers panicked. Some bolted through the

draped pillars, others froze, and a few stared because something in the Reverie itself demanded witness.

The creature screeched behind Solari, floor buckling, beak yawning open to reveal a spinning core of dust that hummed with the power to unmake.

"My Anchor," Solari commanded, voice ringing with the force of the Oneiroi. "To sever the Silver Strand."

Patryk stepped back, shoulders sinking. He did not look shocked seeing the Anchor but would not interfere.

Piper wanted to scream, to pass out, or to pinch herself. She swallowed hard, having never seen anything like it. It made her skin crawl.

The Anchor lowered its molten wings toward her.

Colik stepped toward the beast, shoulders squared, his hand pulling free his swar. The thin, pencil-needle weapon beamed as it caught the light from the orbs above, a red string tethering its hilt to his wrist like blood made bond. Blaze mirrored his approach, his fists clenched, and fire burning behind his eyes.

The Anchor shifted, its head snapping between them, dust churning in its jaw like a dragon ready to unleash fire. It rose from the floor, and a breath of fragile motes streamed from its mouth, swirling in the air like a chemical reaction. She felt them—the grit of human dust, the silken pull of Royald dust, and the electric tingling of stardust—all tangled from the moments unraveling.

Then the Anchor turned on them, drawn not to the Royald brothers, but to Piper.

"No—" Colik's voice cracked, but it was too late.

The beast shrieked again, its chains lashing out and snapping around Piper's arms, her waist, and her throat. She gasped, the air torn from her lungs as the metal bit into her, the Anchor binding her without hesitation.

Solari leaned back, watching from a distance, her features untouched by pity, conflict, or interest.

Lulu grabbed at the chains around Piper, but the moment she touched them, they seared her skin. She cried out and pulled back, eyes wide with horror.

Colik lunged forward without a moment's thought. His swar flashed like silver fire, slicing across the Anchor's chest. The beast screamed. Piper screamed. Agony tore through her shoulder, the same cut appearing on her flesh, hidden beneath the cruel chains. Panic swelled in her chest.

Blaze roared, his fury breaking loose. Dreamfire burst around his fist, hot as a star, and he drove it into the Anchor's chest. Piper's body arched, white-hot fire searing across her ribs. She screamed, her throat raw, the sound ripping through the air. For a heartbeat, she thought she wasn't even in her own body anymore, but in the beasts.

Was it tying its pain to her?

The Anchor howled with her, its voice tangling with hers until she couldn't tell which one belonged to her lungs. Her body collapsed by Lulu's side, shaking and convulsing. Fire and metal collided into her skin, thrashing inside her like they wanted to tear her apart from within. She clawed at the chains, desperate for air, but they only sank deeper.

Please—get them off—please, I can't breathe—

Patryk's gasp cut through the noise. The chains weren't just binding her body. They were digging inside her like thorns. The hot and merciless pain laced into her veins, curling through bone and breath. The weight of it made her want to sob, but she couldn't. She could only choke.

Her vision blurred as the Anchor's eyes burned hotter, molten and endless, alive like the fire in her lungs.

It's severing me, Piper thought through cringed teeth, terror clawing through her as darkness pressed at the edge of her sight. *From the inside out.*

Colik slashed at the beast's wing and Piper's arm flung behind her. The chains tightened and Piper screamed again.

Patryk's voice broke through the chaos from behind them

all. "Stop!" He cried out. "It has *anchored* itself to Piper!" His eyes were wide with terror. Lulu looked paralyzed.

"Fuck!" Colik cursed. Blaze staggered back, his eyes whipping to Piper. They had both been so focused on the creature that they didn't see what state she had been in. His face fell, with shame and ache. Colik looked angry, like a knight ready for battle. It was a look she had never seen on him before.

Around them, the few Dreamers left reacted too. A murmur rippled through the Scirges', the fall-born Dreamers shifting uncomfortably as Piper's screams echoed. The Cabras turned away, the sight of dust unraveling, as if too damning to watch. From the Emers tiered seats, sharp laughter died into nothing, their cruel smirks dissolving into wide, unsettling eyes.

"Every wound you give, it gives to her!" Patryk explained in panic.

The Anchor thrashed, chains tightening, feeding on Piper's desperation. Her whole-body shook. Her screams cut through the stone, and the beast screamed too. Its pain was Piper's pain.

Lulu jolted, and as if in fight mode, turned to Solari. "Stop! You're killing her!" Her voice cracked raw. Colik's hands shook on his swar, rage and helplessness carved into his face.

"It's not just her body, but her dust. It's taking everything she is," Blaze whispered in revelation.

Solari's gaze did not waver. "Dust and flesh are never parted clean. One dies first, for the other to separate." Her voice was as cold as the void.

Piper sagged against the chains as dust unspooled in the Anchor's molten lungs.

"Ahhhh!" She yelled as the beast slashed its hurt wing, flapping it aggressively to keep it hovering in the air.

This was worse than Hazel's puppetry, worse than any shame or pain she'd known. She saw defeat hollowing Blaze's eyes, Colik's rage, and Lulu's helplessness mirrored in the hard set of her mouth. Spots blurred her vision.

Stay conscious.

Lulu dropped beside her instantly, hands shaking. "Piper—Piper, look at me—look at me."

Her lucent burst open in a flare of lit illusion, a bending of pain and nerve and sense. She pressed it to Piper's sternum.

Suddenly, her agony blurred.

Not vanished—illusion was a mirage—but muddled, softening at the edges, as if Lulu had lifted a veil and slipped something gentler between Piper and the pain. The fire dimmed to embers. The suffocation eased, the burning settling to pulses.

Lulu's illusion curled under Piper's skin, cooling the raw edges of her nerves, and weaving false sensations.

"It's alright," Lulu whispered fiercely, even though nothing was alright. "I've got you. Just breathe."

Piper gasped as the worst of the pain flickered like a mirage, replaced by a distant echo of waterfall mist, trembling rose petals, and cold morning dew—the illusions Lulu forced into her senses. Each breath became survivable. Barely.

"I have her! Attack it now!" Lulu screamed at Colik and Blaze.

The brothers nodded, and the fight raged before Piper's eyes.

Colik struck again, his swar a flash of red meteors, slicing through the chains. Sparks erupted, metal screaming, but the links regenerated instantly, slithering like living serpents around Piper's body.

"Die you bastard!" Colik bellowed, voice cracking, attacking with wild, furious precision.

This time the Anchor lunged at him. Blaze intercepted, fire bursting into a spiraling whip that lashed around the creature's throat. The beast thrashed violently, dragging both

Royalds across the stone as they held on, refusing to let it reach Piper.

"Patryk!" Blaze roared across the chaos. "Now! Get the Boygles! Send them after the Mimic—go!"

Patryk didn't hesitate. He bolted toward the far pillars, voice rising in sharp Dreamer command, summoning every Boygle in the Citadel with trembling urgency.

The Shades shifted, startled by the sudden call. Some bolted, but not all of them. Piper's vision was so blurry she had no idea if the emerald-eyed Shade had stayed or fled.

Screw him. He helped the Mimic flee, leaving her—

She screamed as a flame hit the Anchor in the back, causing Piper to jolt forward, her back blaring with heat. The world flickered in waves of pain and illusion.

She clung to Lulu's lucent like a lifeline. Every time the Anchor screamed, her bones rattled. Every time Blaze hit it, heat ripped across her ribs. Every time Colik cut it, she felt skin split somewhere on her body.

Lulu's illusion swirled harder, fighting to overpower the beast's relentless pull.

"Stay with me," Lulu whispered, brushing hair from Piper's face. "Hold on. Please." Her voice cracked. Because even her lucent couldn't stop the chains from crawling deeper, threading themselves into Piper's dust, pulling at something deep and fragile, but only holding back some pain.

Blaze and Colik were fighting like they were made of fury itself, but Solari's beast was winning.

Dust around them screamed. The ballroom floor groaned. The chains squeezed until Piper's vision blurred with static, the only thing keeping her from losing complete consciousness being Lulu's trembling hand pressing illusion after illusion into the cracking shell of her mind. The chains still scorched her skin like a third-degree burn. Lulu looked weaker.

Everything narrowed to one cold fact: there was only one way to stop it. "Just let it take me. I don't belong here anyway.

End this," Piper croaked through the chains restricting air flow.

The beast wasn't finished. It writhed, glowing with terrible light, and lunged for Colik again.

Lulu screamed as more chains lashed out, slamming into Coliks chest with the weight of a mountain. The sound of impact cracked through the room as he was hurled across the floor, his body crashing into a golden pillar. The stone split with a sickening crack.

Blaze jolted, but Lulu's scream cut through him. "Colik!"

Piper's breath caught in her throat as she stared. His body lay crumpled against the broken stone, blood sliding into the cracks of the floor. It mixed well with the golden marks laced into the ground.

The creature screeched, and the sound rose with Piper's pain until they were one again.

Around them, the Dreamers flinched. Their faces turned pale in the fractured starlight, pride falling into horror. Some covered their mouths while others gripped the stone of their seats until their knuckles turned white. No one moved. No one dared. Patryk had returned, but hid along the walls, alongside the Dreamers. This was the Royald's battle to fight.

The Anchor slashed around, celebrating, and with it so did Piper. Slash after slash covered her body only to dissolve as if a dying nightmare to only form again. Colik laid across the center floor, heaving, trying to pull himself up, the pain and storm in his chest plain across his face.

Blaze manically looked from Colik to Piper then to the crowd of Shades. He was looking for someone. Through tears, Piper's eyes followed his and met the half-shrouded Shade again who saved her from the Plastrof. His emerald-green eyes were harsh but sorrowful. His head moved in the faintest shake, subtle but certain, and she caught the message clear as breath:

Live.

She wasn't sure if it was toward Blaze or her, but at that word, something shifted.

Darkness on the floor stirred—barely a ripple—and rose up her legs, coiling around her spine in a slow, silent climb. It didn't numb the pain. It redirected it. Lulu's illusion flickered beside her, softening the air around Piper, blurring the edges of the world so the burns on her skin faded, but because the agony was no longer in her skin.

It slammed into her mind instead.

A pressure burst behind her eyes, sharp and blinding, as if someone pried her thoughts apart with cold fingers. Nightmares she had outrun for years crawled through the cracks, skittering, whispering, and dragging their claws across the softest parts of her.

Voices she hated. Memories she feared. Demons she knew too well. The ones that always told her she was nothing. The ones that curled into her skull like rot.

She felt them alive, writhing, and painfully familiar inside her mind: the ache of being unwanted, the sting of being forgotten, and the quiet certainty that no one had ever chosen her first.

What was worse? Physical pain or the mental agony of the worst parts of her past?

Then Blaze moved before the beast could strike again. His lucent flared, his dreamfire igniting so violently it rattled the very air around him. With a roar, he slammed his fists to the floor, and a wall of dreamfire erupted. It stretched between them and the Anchor, blazing like a shield, but Blaze's whole body shook with the effort of keeping it standing.

The chains struck against the flames, sparks exploding with every hit, and Piper could feel the wall trembling under the blows. Heat pressed against her skin, searing, but she didn't hurt—not physically or mentally anymore—and she quickly understood why.

Blaze was burning himself out to protect them from the

Anchor. Sweat poured down his brow, his teeth clenched tight as his arms trembled. The dreamfire pulsed in tune with his ragged breaths, thinning each time the Anchor slammed against it. Still, he held.

Live, the word repeated in her mind.

"Blaze—" she gasped, her eyes moving from the Shade to Blaze. His features twisted in anguish, the weight of everything pressing down on him. His stillness cracked.

"My lucent!" Blaze interrupted, his eyes meeting hers, but grey's ever so bright. "It's the only thing strong enough to stop this…"

Piper blinked through pain. Lulu's face went white.

"You have to take it," Blaze said, his voice cracking. "It'll burn the chains anchored in you. I can't be here when it happens. I can't stand between you and it."

Lulu's gaze snapped to Piper, her voice trembling. "You—? That would mean—"

Both fell silent as the Anchor roared, its spiraling mouth of dust and Blaze's lucent ripping the air apart. The chains snapped forward, hammering the wall of dreamfire, each strike sending shockwaves through the chamber.

The shield blazed high, Blaze's lucent holding, but every impact shook his entire body. Sparks exploded across the gleaming floor, flames bending inward as if the beast's will alone could smother them. Piper could tell the wall wasn't unbreakable. It was Blaze's strength, his lucent, and his very life holding it in place. But it wouldn't last for long.

The Anchor shrieked again, its mouth gaping wider, spewing a torrent of dust that struck the flames. The shield wavered, thinning, the fire line retreating inch by inch as Blaze's knees buckled.

Still, he refused to fall. His hands pressed against the air, his voice a hoarse growl as his eyes stayed hard on Piper. "You can't stop this without taking my lucent, Piper."

"Yes, I can!" She begged, not knowing what he meant but

knowing there had to be something else besides what he was saying. "We'll find another way. Colik will—"

Blaze's gaze shifted to Colik, who was struggling to stand, his multi-colored eyes locked on Blaze in disbelief.

"The gods feared dust would learn to dream again," Blaze grumbled. "So, they bound it to one name. One promise."

Piper's chest clenched, a surge of pain following that made her gasp.

"Morpheus' Promise—you can't Blaze—" Lulu choked out.

Above, Solari looked resolute. It appeared she, too, would not intervene.

"Morpheus swore the Dreamer would be protected even if it damned the rest of us."

The words struck like a stone dropped in water, rippling outward. He wasn't looking at Piper when he said it…

Both hers and Lulu's gaze turned toward Colik. He stumbled forward, his face raw with confusion, eyes searching as though Blaze had spoken in a tongue, he himself couldn't understand.

"Blaze—what are you talking about?" His voice cracked, edged with desperation.

Blaze gave a faint, broken smile, sorrow darkening his eyes. One hand held the Anchor at bay, its molten chains thrashing against the swirl of fire wall made from flame-dust he'd conjured. It was an eye in the heart of a hurricane. The searing heat bit into her skin, every nerve becoming aflame again as he weakened, yet she forced herself to focus on Blaze's words. She *needed* to hear them.

"You will know soon enough…" Blaze said, then caught Piper's wrist with his open hand—the one without the gold brace—and pressed his palm hard against it. His lucent flared off his skin, burning white-hot, then poured into her in a flood of heat that stole her breath.

Piper stumbled back as fire tore through her veins. It wasn't just heat, but weight, like a storm of suns pushing into her body. Her knees buckled. "Blaze!" she screamed. "Stop—you're killing yourself!"

He didn't let go. The shield of dreamfire still blazed before them, walling the Anchor back, but now it flickered, thinning, as Blaze's strength split. With every pulse, he grew weaker, his skin paling, dust slipping from him in golden waves. Piper felt herself growing stronger in his place, the dreamfire he gave her burning brighter with each breath she stole from him. It was burning the anchored metal inside her skin.

Then the chains on her suddenly broke, and the tight, anchored feeling in her released, causing her to gasp for breath. The Anchor roared too, but this time Piper did not mimic it. Her tie to the beast was severed.

"Protect him, Piper," Blaze rasped, voice rough with strain. "Colik is the only promise the gods ever kept. Don't let him fade. Keep him lit."

Her heart broke. Tears blurred her eyes as she tried to wrench her wrist free, but his grip was iron. "No—stop—please!" Her voice cracked. "Don't do this!"

"Blaze!" Lulu cried out.

Colik staggered forward, his pain forgotten, rage and terror flooding his face. "Blaze! Don't you fucking dare!"

Blaze's other hand shot out, and a wall of fire burst forth, wrapping around him and Piper like a burning cage, sealing Lulu and Colik out. The flames climbed higher, screaming against the wind, their light blinding, and their heat unrelenting.

From the outside, it looked like protection, like Blaze was just shielding her, but inside the wall of fire, the truth rushed through her bones. He wasn't saving her. He was saying goodbye.

Was that Blaze's plan all along?

"Blaze!" Colik roared, slamming his fists against the fire wall. His voice shook, desperate, tearing from his chest. "Don't you leave me!"

Blaze turned, his storm-colored eyes filled with something achingly human. He looked at Colik as if this had always been the end. "I need you to let me die, Colik. *One for one.*"

"What the—!" Colik's voice cracked like shattering glass. His whole body shook as he beat against the fire. "You bastard —you manipulative bastard!"

Blaze gave a broken laugh, ragged and breathless. For a moment, it sounded like the old him. He managed a smile, thin but bright. "You must stay bright, *brother.*"

The last of his lucent ripped from him in a flood, surging straight into Piper. It sucked into her chest, bottomless and terrifying, filling her until she thought she might burst. It too wrapped like the chains around her heart, her lungs, her bones, every part of her, searing her alive from the inside out. This time it didn't burn with pain, but with a strength that Piper had never known.

Blaze staggered. The fire-cage flickered, and the great shield before the Anchor cracked and fell.

The Anchor roared, its spiraling mouth wide, dust and light twisting like a storm. Then it struck, and a ball of searing dust-fire burst from its mouth and slammed into Blaze full-on. His body arched back, the sound of bones breaking sharp as thunder. Dust exploded from him in a violent flare, gold and grey, flooding the room. For one final moment, he was light itself, his figure blazing, brighter than any star Piper had ever seen.

"No!" Lulu screamed.

"Blaze!" Piper's scream tore her throat raw. She reached through the exploding dust flares, but her fingers met only heat and air.

Colik's roar joined hers, fury and grief ripping from his lungs.

Blaze was gone.

His body shattered. Ash scattered across the ground like sparks, glowing for a heartbeat before dimming into nothing. Where he had stood, there was only silence, and a hollow in the air where his dreamfire had been.

Piper clutched her chest where his lucent still burned inside her, too heavy, too bright, and *way too* much. Tears streamed down her face, blinding her as her scream broke into sobs. Her ribs were going to split with the weight of what he had left in her.

Colik stood frozen, fists trembling, his eyes wide and wild with a grief that was too large for one body to hold. His lips parted, but no words came, only the echo of Blaze's sigh of resolution still burning in the smoke.

The Anchor shrieked in victory, its chains rattling like war drums, but the chamber didn't feel triumphant. Even the Dreamers shrank back, their pale faces stricken, their pride crumbling to ash.

That's when Solari moved.

She glided back to the center floor, her stride as graceful as it was merciless. Silver strands spun from her fingertips, and with a single deliberate motion, the Anchor's bindings unraveled. Not ripped, not broken, but undone, as though the creature had never been written into the ballroom at all.

Its screech died in its throat. Chains fell silent at its feet. The beast convulsed once, then dissolved into a cold bloom of red-ashy smoke.

"Interesting," Solari said, her voice quiet but echoing, as if spoken through a cavern of old law. Her gaze swept across the Royalds, resolute. "What we have is the reshaping of a role. A strand given purpose anew."

A shiver moved through the chamber. Solari lowered her hand, and for one breath her eyes fixed on Piper with warning, and—*was that pain?*

Then before Piper could breathe, Solari's fingers curled

around the red string at her wrist. She gave it a single, deliberate tug, and her form dissolved into a ripple of law and ghostly shadow, fading from the ballroom as if the Dreamworld itself had swallowed her command.

CHAPTER THIRTY-TWO
THE NEW ROYALD

An eerie silence fell across the Orph Ballroom. Not a whisper. Not a breath.

Colik dropped to his knees beside the ashes, his swar clattering to the floor. His hands sank into the dust, streaked with black blood. His face crumpled, raw and undone.

He curled his fingers around the only thing left—Blaze's golden laurel crown. The moment his skin touched it, it flared white-hot. Smoke hissed up, blistering his hand. He recoiled with a strangled breath.

That was when the Shades moved, drifting from the stone seats in unison, silent as falling dust. Their shadows elongated, stretching toward the center of the ballroom.

Then a black seam opened in the air where their silhouettes touched, rippling like a curtain of midnight pulled loose from its frame. It deepened into a hole, the same as the black star but on a smaller scale, swallowing the golden veined floor beneath, drinking in everything it touched with a strange, quiet hunger.

Every Shade stepped into it, dissolving without sound, until only one remained. The emerald-eyed Shade. He hesitated at the edge of the void, the darkness tugging at his feet, yet he resisted long enough to lift his gaze. His eyes—green and impossibly bright for what he was—locked onto Piper.

For one impossible breath, the room stilled. No gods. No Royalds. No Laws. Only those eyes, seeing too much.

Softly, he whispered, "don't come looking for us."

The words brushed her mind like a hand stroking a flame, then he stepped backward into the void. The darkness swallowed him whole, folding closed with the faintest shiver, as though it had never existed, leaving cold air and the stinging echo of the warning.

Only then did Piper realize the few Dreamers who had lingered for the spectacle had fled as well. They had not stayed to watch a Royald die. Or perhaps they had sensed it and were not brave enough.

Standing back up, Colik's shoulders rose and fell with each breath, too loud in the hush, and too jagged to steady. The ballroom felt colder, emptied of its light.

"You weren't supposed to give in," Colik whispered, staring at the ashes. They didn't answer. Blaze was gone.

Lulu did nothing but stare at the ashes, as if sheer will alone could pull Blaze's form back together. Patryk's eyes locked on the crown, waiting, expecting it to move, to shine, to do *something.* Anything.

Piper turned slowly, her face pale, her eyes shimmering with unshed tears. And just like that, her knees buckled. She collapsed onto the ballroom floor, her palms scraping through Blaze's remains. The ash clung to her skin, hot and searing, because it wasn't only ash. His lucent burned inside her, pulsing in her chest like a second heartbeat, filling her lungs until every breath came ragged and sharp. Her body shook with the weight of it.

She pressed her hands to the floor, choking on sobs. "Blaze…"

The laurel crown glimmered faintly where it lay, close

enough for her to touch, but she couldn't lift her hand. Not yet. Not while her chest still burned with his sacrifice.

Tears blurred her vision. Her chest was iron. Her throat, ash. All she felt was fire—*his fire*—inside her bones. It was a painful reminder that she hoped she would not have to live with forever.

Colik stared at her, pale and stricken, every breath shaking him apart. Then, standing up, his gaze turned back to the ashes, his lips barely forming words. "I didn't know," he whispered hoarsely. "To the gods—I didn't know."

Piper's gaze tore to him, sharp and wet. "Then why would Blaze say—"

"I don't know!" Colik's voice broke. He dragged a hand through his hair, stepping back like the ground beneath him was unsteady. "Shade whispers, Blaze's cryptic words...none of this makes sense."

Piper saw the flicker of dread in his multi-colored eyes. The truth he didn't want to face.

Then he bent. Not just grieving, not shattering as he had with Dray, but folding into a darker place—one he had either buried deep or never known was there.

Ash drifted through the air, catching on Piper's skin, stinging her eyes, sinking into her chest and lungs. She gasped in recognition, and Lulu's eyes shot to hers.

In the fire to the past.

The words of Morpheus' Promise, spoken by the Bronze Gink, seared through her mind, louder than the rising lucent coiling around every vein in Piper's body.

"Colik..." Piper said, standing up. It came out as hardly a whisper. "I didn't—"

"Don't." His voice snapped like a whip, making her flinch. "Don't speak. Don't *dare*."

His eyes, raw with loss, burned with hatred and betrayal. "He protected you," he snarled. "You make him do this?"

"I didn't want this," she said, her voice cracking. "He made that choice—"

"No!" Colik roared. "He died because of *you!*"

She backed up a step.

"He protected you!" Colik shouted. "He believed in you. Now he's—" His voice caught. He looked away, but it was too late. The fury poured through the cracks.

Piper's lips parted, but no sound came. Her whole body trembled. Lulu shook her head slowly.

Colik forced his gaze back to the ashes. To what was left of the only brother he had. His hand was shaking.

"He trusted you," he spat. "Now he's *dust.*"

"I—" Piper began, but her voice failed.

Lulu bent down to pick up the crown lying on top of the ashes, but it burned her as it did Colik.

"What the—"

Patryk gasped, and Colik's eyes shot over to him. "What is the meaning of this?" Patryk shook his head; the words lost to him. His eyes widened and moved toward Piper. Lulu's gaze followed, catching on.

"Piper, grab the crown," Lulu stammered.

Piper blinked at her, stunned. "Me…"

"Just pick up the damn laurel," Colik bellowed, stepping back in an abrupt, desperate motion that made it clear he didn't trust himself near it. Or her.

She looked from Colik to Lulu, then to Patryk, who gave her a slow, reverent nod. With breath trembling, Piper approached the crown. She reached out, half expecting it to burn her the way it had seared Colik and Lulu.

Instead, it welcomed her, just as Blaze's lucent had.

Silence fell over the ballroom.

Then, Colik gasped, sharp as a blade leaving its sheath. Lulu's hand flew to her mouth. Patryk's eyes widened with something like shock mixed with amazement.

"It appears she is one of us." Patryk's voice was barely louder than breath.

Her fingers brushed the gilded metal and its surface rippled, not like polished steel or molten fire but like a reflection disturbed by a memory older than her world. The reflection deepened, and there he was.

Morpheus.

Black feathers framing a mantle of living night. Eyes of void flecked with distant stars. Not in the room, but inside the crown itself, watching her.

His voice thundered through her bones, not through the air. "A new world will not rise in wonder, but in darkness. The find..." His gaze struck the spiral scar on her thumb like a verdict. "Is she."

The chamber trembled. Dust swirled around her feet like a gathering storm. The laurel crown flared white-hot again, then lifted itself, descending onto her head with the quiet finality of fate.

Then a figure formed from dust and starlight. He was tall, robed in midnight blue, with constellations stitched into his garments. Feathers draped his shoulders like wings dipped in night.

"Morpheus," Patryk breathed, bowing without conscious thought. Piper was speechless. *No*, thunderstruck. *No*, in disbelief.

A real god?

"My roots began this," Morpheus intoned, dream-dust curling around his palms. "I broke the law in secret, and the gods have never forgiven me."

His gaze passed over Lulu first. She stiffened as though he had placed a hand upon the deepest part of her memory.

"Humankind ever is the flame that endures in emptiness. Birr and smeddum."

Dust showered from his fingers like the embers of a dying star. Lulu's breath hitched.

Morpheus turned to Piper. "The transfiguration. A dream carried across worlds. The one the gods feared would return."

Piper's knees nearly buckled under the weight of his words.

Then Morpheus' gaze slid past her to Colik, the shift in the God of Dreams' expression unmistakable. "And you," Morpheus said, voice resonating through the marrow of every Dreamer present, "you felt it from the beginning and chose to say nothing."

Colik went still. Lulu's head snapped toward him in shock. Patryk froze, lips parted. Piper stared at him, the laurel crown burning against her temples.

Morpheus stepped forward, black feathers stirring like storm clouds behind him. "On the Ollopa train, you felt her presence the moment she stepped on board. Not recognition. Not certainty. Something older than both. The pull of dust that knows its origin. Like called to like, and you felt it before you had words for it."

Dust lifted around Colik's feet like a rising tide.

"You told yourself it was instinct. That it meant nothing. That humans sometimes carry stronger dust than others." Morpheus' voice was not cruel, but it was exact. "Then you used the sandtie to keep her from fading between worlds and she came back whole. Unraveled by nothing. Consequence touching her not at all."

A pause.

"You have performed a sandtie before, Colik. You know what it does to a human."

Colik's jaw tightened but said nothing.

"She should have dissolved," Morpheus said simply. "Or you should have. That is the law of incompatible dust. Instead, nothing happened. Because her dust did not resist yours. It remembered yours." His gaze did not waver. "That was the moment your instinct became knowledge, and you said nothing."

Something cold twisted inside Piper. "Colik…" Her voice barely escaped. "Is that true?"

Colik's breath was ragged, his mismatched eyes wide with a truth Piper had never seen laid bare in him before. He didn't answer, but Morpheus did.

"Then the Bronze Gink spoke the full Promise aloud," Morpheus continued, quieter now, which made it worse. "Whatever doubt remained within you was gone. You heard every word. You stood beside her and felt your own dust shift in answer to it, and still you said nothing. Still you brought her to the Citadel framed as a liability. A problem to be contained." His voice dropped. "Not as what you already knew she was."

Colik flinched as though struck.

"You protected her only so far as she fit your own want. I chose you but hesitate that I chose well."

Piper's breath stung her lungs. "You knew," she whispered, her voice breaking. "After the sandtie. After the Bronze Gink. You knew."

"I wasn't certain—" Colik started. "Then Dray saved us— you—"

"You were certain enough to hide it," Morpheus interrupted.

Colik's hands curled into fists, the fight going out of him all at once. "I was trying to protect her."

"No." Morpheus sounded disappointed in the way only someone with ages of patience could. "You were trying to protect yourself from what it meant if you were right."

"You wanted to be right so that you had the advantage to —to what?" Piper spat out.

The ground slipped beneath her. Every moment of trust she had extended to him rearranged itself into something she didn't want to look at directly.

Lulu shook her head, her eyes hard on Colik. "To take Blaze's spot as *the* Royald—no longer a knight."

"No! That is not true."

Colik met Pipers eyes, and she understood the shape of it. Not a single lie, but a slow accumulation of silences. A feeling on the train he'd dismissed. A sandtie that proved too much and went unreported. A prophecy spoken aloud in the Broken Woods that he had absorbed and buried. Each one a choice. Each one made without her.

"You knew," she said again, softer this time. Not a question. Not an accusation. Just the truth of it, settling. "I begged to know and you knew."

Morpheus turned to Piper, his tone final. "You cannot stay. The god's eyes will turn to you, and their fear is louder than their wisdom."

A gate unfolded behind him, its dream stone blocks glowing with age-old light. It looked so familiar to her. Piper squinted past him, and he let out a deep breath. Like he had unleashed a part of her that had been hidden in her mind or memories, she recognized it from a far-off dream.

She knew it was the Gate of Horn.

Piper took a half step back while Colik took a half step forward. Morpheus lifted a hand to stop him. "She must return," the god said.

Colik's eyes stayed locked on Piper. Raw. Panicked. Guilty.

The ballroom hung in stunned silence, the air trembling with the echo of Morpheus' revelation. Piper stood frozen beneath the burning weight of Blaze's crown, her breath thinning, and her pulse thundering.

Colik took another faltering step toward her, but Lulu moved faster. She caught his wrist, fingers digging in just enough to make him stop. Her autumn eyes glittered with fury and something like heartbreak, though she hid it beneath a perfectly composed face.

"You fool," Lulu breathed. "She will never forgive you for this." Colik went rigid. "You lost her." Lulu's words were venom sweet and quiet. "She hasn't even left yet."

Piper ignored both. She didn't care that Lulu was scorning Colik, or that Colik felt any guilt at all. He lied to her, and there is no doubt that Lulu had known something about it too. She stole a quick glance at Patryk, who refused to meet her eyes. So, apparently, did he.

She turned her back to all of them, her body shaking, and the lucent within her settling. It was like her own internal anger was easing the blaze inside her, or she had more control of it than she did when she was revishing.

Regardless, Morpheus' words still rang through her bones, but the meaning refused to settle. She felt as though she were standing at the edge of two worlds at once, both collapsing beneath her feet.

"I... I don't understand," she whispered to the God of Dreams, trembling, her fingers curling helplessly at her sides. The Gate of Horn flickered behind him. She was inches from his touch, from the familiar feeling of him, like he had been in her dreams before.

Morpheus' expression softened, though it wasn't comfort she saw. It was something aged and weary. Like regret. "You will," he breathed.

Dust bent toward him, the ballroom dimming as if it tried to hide what was coming. Then his hand lifted, and red poppy seeds glimmered in his palm like sleeping embers.

"Wait—Morpheus—don't—" Piper recognized the small seeds from the Elphiates, when she held her breath. From the Lavyrinthos, when they almost made her fall asleep.

"It is protection," he said softly, "and mercy."

He came close enough that she felt the warm breath of a god at her cheek. His shadow curled around her like a veil pulled over the truth.

"For now," he whispered, "sleep."

He blew. The seeds struck her skin like embers, bright and searing, and Piper staggered as the world spun into ribbons of dissolving starlight.

She would have fallen if Morpheus hadn't caught her, lowering her gently, his fingers brushing a strand of hair from her temple. His touch did something inside her, something she couldn't name, and an old echo stirring awake in her dust. Again, a memory flickered against her mind: the outline of a window rimmed in white light, a shadow lurking just behind her shoulder, and a red strand tugging at her wrist long before she ever knew what it meant.

The sensation shuddered through her, as if something she had forgotten had been waiting for this very moment to rise.

Patryk stepped forward, voice steady through the storm. "The third Royald."

As Piper's consciousness slipped, she felt Morpheus' voice inside her mind rather than in her ears, a secret sound-woven truth meant for her and her alone. Just like the Silver Child in the Room of Lockes.

"Not the Royald they expect."

Darkness curled at the edges of her vision.

"Not star, nor harmony, nor crown."

The dream cracked like glass, but Morpheus continued to whisper into the pieces. *"Of the forbidden kind,"* he whispered, the pieces drifting around her like silver dust. *"The Royald the gods swore never to name again."*

A sudden and sharp pull yanked at the core of Piper's being. She wanted to gasp, to deny it, or ask what she was meant to become, but the dream closed over her like a rising black tide, dragging her downward before her voice could surface, before her lungs could beg for air, and before the Royald with multi-colored eyes could reach for her.

Complete silence fell into the black tide, her eyes and ears shutting off the Dreamworld though not by her own choice. Within the darkness of her mind, her body stilling into a forced sleep, a red strand tightened at her wrist, and a faint whisper of the God of Dreams forced her to answer to a name she had never known was hers.

"Royald of the Elphiates."

For a heartbeat, Piper couldn't move. Her body was locked, as if refusing to let her act on a dream. Then a sharp crack split the air. Steele tapped his distaff the moment it brushed her, and the jolt ripped her free. The dust claiming her body as whole again. The world sucking her back here.

"Well, well. Unlike the other human, you managed to come back to the waking world." He smirked, glancing at the clock on her nightstand. "Five hours and fifty-five minutes. Not bad."

"Other hum—" Piper's eyes flashed to the window. It was dawn.

He looked even worse than the last time she had seen him. The hollows beneath his eyes had deepened, and his hand around the distaff was trembling. Not from cold but from effort.

In that moment, he looked like a Shade.

"Steele." Her eyes narrowed on him. "What is happening to you?"

His jaw tightened. "Every moment I exist here without the book, the more this world is in danger." His head tilted slightly, a ghost of the smirk returning. "I warned you before. There will be consequences between this world and the Dreamworld, with nothing holding either side in place."

Piper stared at him. "You're saying both worlds—"

"Bleed into each other. Yes." He said it plainly, as though the scale of it bored him. "Dreams walking freely in the waking world. Waking world bleeding into the Reverie. Every law the gods ever wrote to keep them separate, undone. The Fatales will not negotiate with that kind of fracture. They will sever everything connected to it." His unseeing eyes found her with unnerving precision. "Including you."

The silence between them was full of everything she didn't want to be true.

"The Book of Godspells," he continued, "is the only thing that will reveal *my* way back to the Dreamworld. It was written for exactly this—for Silver Children who crossed where they shouldn't. It contains the law older than the gods' laws. The one that governs the crossing itself." A pause. "Without it, I am a hole in the fabric of two worlds, getting wider by the day."

Piper looked at the lines on his skin. The frost that never melted. The breath that never clouded.

"How long do you have?" she asked quietly.

He smiled, but it didn't reach anything. "Not as long as I did yesterday."

Steele's gaze dropped to the dark petals tucked behind her ear. "Now," he said, the weight of everything settling back behind a devious smirk, "about that black flower."

THANK YOU FOR READING!

I hope that you enjoyed reading *The Dreamer* as much as I enjoyed writing it. If you have a moment, please hop online and consider posting a review! As an indie author, I depend heavily on word of mouth and the feedback and support of readers like you.

Thank you!

ACKNOWLEDGMENTS

To my friends who read the earliest versions (HA! I'm so sorry), my BETA readers Josie and Jacqui for their thoughtful feedback, and my ARC readers Kara and Gabby—you are all such incredible people for helping me shape the best version of this book. I truly cannot thank you enough!

To Blake, for the constant encouragement during those late nights and long weekends of writing, and for the beautiful website (www.carolineleebooks.com)! Your motivation—and pressure (in the best way)—is the reason I felt confident enough to get this book out into the world at all.

To Mrs. Gebhardt, my 8th-grade teacher, who encouraged me to read my story Rags to Riches in front of the entire class and showed me that I could write something people wanted to hear. To my parents who gave me a life that otherwise might not have turned out quite so fortunate and blessed.

To everyone else in my life who patiently (or not so patiently) listened to me ramble about this story for years, wondering if I'd ever bring it into existence.

Thank you, thank you, thank you!

To my readers, from start to finish: you are why I write. I hope this story finds you when you need it most. If you know my past at all, you know that I wrote the first draft—of thirty different drafts—when I needed it most. Piper is a girl who is lost and slowly, but surely, finding the confidence and voice that was within her all along—rising, piece by piece, into her own constellation. We all have different stories, and grow up in different ways, with some paths easier than others.

To myself—I DID IT! Years of writing, planning, editing, and redrafting... but I. did. it. I couldn't be prouder for sticking through and creating a story that I not only love but connect to on such a deep, personal level. Remember, your dreams were different, but so were your nightmares.

Thank you all again! Our shared love for fantasy, Greek mythology, romance (you just wait), and the sheer joy of story-telling is why this book exists.

To Katie (@kjaspersendesigns) for the amazing book cover design, and for bringing my poorly drawn sketch of a map to life!

Finally, I thank my editor, Tabitha (@tabs.edits), for the in-depth developmental edits, copy line editing and proofreading.

Dream on, readers. The Reverie sees you.
Where book one may end, a far older story begins.

www.ingramcontent.com/pod-product-compliance
Lightning Source LLC
Chambersburg PA
CBHW022016050726
47499CB00004BA/1021